A Soldier of India

A Soldier of India is set in that traumatic period for the British Raj in India, the Mutiny. Jhansi, then a small state recently annexed by the British, is dominated by the enigmatic, forceful personality of the Rani, a young, embittered widow. When mutiny breaks out in the cantonment in June, 1857, culminating in a massacre that the British were never to forget or forgive, how much—if at all—is the Rani involved with the mutinous sepoys? Into this bloody tragedy are drawn Martin Lalor, an officer of an Irish regiment who is not unaffected by current political and economic troubles in Ireland, and Alicia Wentworth, a young Englishwoman visiting India for the first time with her father, a Director of the East India Company. *A Soldier of India* graphically and movingly depicts the fears, hardships, bloodshed, loves and hatreds of those historic days when British mastery of the fabulous Indian sub-continent trembled and wavered on the brink of disaster, and how the lives of the three central characters, consequently, were scarred irrevocably.

By the same author
The Last Crusader

TOM GIBSON

A Soldier
of India

ST. MARTIN'S PRESS
NEW YORK

ROBERT HALE LIMITED
LONDON

© *Tom Gibson 1982*
First published in Great Britain 1982

ISBN 0 7091 9686 5

Robert Hale Limited
Clerkenwell House
Clerkenwell Green
London EC1R 0HT

First published in the United States of America 1982
For information, write: St. Martin's Press,
175 Fifth Avenue, New York, NY10010

Library of Congress Catalog Card Number: 81–52952
ISBN–0–312–74245–2

Photoset by
Kelly Typesetting Limited
Bradford-on-Avon, Wiltshire
Printed in Great Britain by
St. Edmundsbury Press
Bury St. Edmunds, Suffolk
Bound by Weatherby Woolnough

Contents

Glossary

URDU/HINDI

ayah	housemaid
bagh	garden
bania	Hindu shopkeeper, usually a moneylender also
bashars	huts used as offices, stores or barrack-rooms
bhisti	water carrier
burra	big, large
chai	tea
chaprassi	official messenger
chatti	earthen gourd to hold cool water
chowkidar	watchman
chota	small
daffadar	cavalry sergeant
dak bungalow	Government rest house on a country route
dhooli	covered cart
inshallah	if God wills it
jeldi	quickly
killadar	commander of a fort
kote	lock-up, eg, arms kote for the safe custody of weapons
kukri	Gurkha knife
kutcherry	landowner's revenue offices
lakh	one hundred thousand
lungi	sarong-type garment
maidan	open area, common land
nawab	Muslim prince
pani	water
pargana	a large number of villages grouped administratively for revenue purposes
pugri	turban or thick head or hat band
raja	Hindu prince
rani	Hindu princess

rissaldar,	
rissaldar-major	native officers of cavalry
sadhu	Hindu holy man, mystic
sepoy	infantry soldier
sowar	cavalry trooper
sudhra	untouchable
syce	groom, horse handler
thakur	petty nobleman, landed gentry
thana	police station; administratively, several villages under the jurisdiction of a particular police station
tunda	cold
taikhana	underground room for coolness in the hot weather
tek hey	I am all right
tulwar	sword
Walayatis	foreigners, eg, Afghans, Pathans
zail	a grouping of villages for revenue purposes but lesser than a pargana

BRITISH ARMY

AA&QMG	Assistant Adjutant and Quarter Master General, a senior staff officer who deals with personnel and logistics
ADC	Aide-de-camp, a personal staff officer to a General Officer
ADMS	Assistant Director of Medical Services
Adjutant	A commanding officer's staff officer
AQ	A broad Staff term covering personnel matters and all aspects of logistics
Brigade Major (BM)	A brigade commander's senior staff officer
BC	battery commander (of artillery)
CRA	Commander Royal Artillery, the senior artillery officer in a formation
CRE	Commander Royal Engineers, the senior engineer officer in a formation
NCO	non-commissioned officer, eg, corporal, sergeant
RAMC	Royal Army Medical Corps

BOOK ONE
JHANSI

1

The Coming Storm

As much as Martin Lalor loved India, there were times when he hated her. Four o'clock on a June afternoon, when he lay bathed in perspiration on his bed after awaking from a deep sleep that the oppressive heat had induced, was such an occasion. The stale taste in his mouth and the slow, torpid reaction of his mind irritated him intensely. He remained prostrate, hot and uncomfortable, gazing at the ceiling of the bungalow. The slatted windows, closed to give some semblance of cool darkness, had only succeeded in denying the entry of any air. Slivers of bright sunlight intruded into the room from a side window unprotected by the verandah.

Some slight movement from him must have alerted the punkah boy, dozing with the dedication of his calling in the adjoining room. Above him, the canvas sail of the punkah began to flap again as it creaked to and fro on its weary cycle. He resignedly watched the punkah and its slowly jerking cord that disappeared through a hole high in the wall. The slight relief that it gave by stirring the stifling air somehow seemed to symbolise to him India and the British, though why, in his haziness, he was not sure. Perhaps it was the little punkah wallah, a small half-naked brown boy of about twelve years, now wondering fearfully whether the sahib had detected his slumbering and was angry. Possibly it was because, as a British officer, he realised how utterly dependent the British were on the Indians, even on an illiterate lad as the punkah wallah, subsisting on a few annas a day.

Not that he was British, he reminded himself. But he had taken the Queen's salt and despite strains on that loyalty, with the news from Ireland in recent times and even from Australia where his cousin, Peter Lalor, had led the Eureka Stockade affair against the goldfields authorites at Ballarat, Victoria, three years ago, he had remained true. He had two wounds, from Ferozeshah 1845 and Sevastopol 1854, to prove this. Whatever his secret thoughts and aspirations for the Irish nation were, his conscience was clear.

He sat up and swung his legs over the side of the bed, tightening up the lungi about his waist. Even this slight movement brought fresh outpourings of sweat that glistened wetly on him and soon trickled down his bare chest and legs. As he mopped himself with a towel, he was forced to smile. The punkah now began to beat agitatedly.

His depression lightened further when his eye caught the calendar on the table by his bed as he reached to pour a tumbler of water from the earthen chatti on the floor. His youngest sister, Cecilia, had sent it out from Ireland for last Christmas but such were the vagaries of the mails for India that he had received it only two months ago. Still, he accepted philosophically, it had arrived nicely in time for Easter. The calendar was in the form of numeral cards giving the date and month that were set in a metal outline of Ireland standing on a base of Irish granite. When Ireland was turned over, the date of the next day fell down. He had often pondered wryly that Peter Lalor, below the equator, would have appreciated this total orbital movement of Ireland. The date now stood, as he looked at it, drinking the cool water appreciatively, at 1 June. 1857 in India was now well into its searing summer heat. The monsoonal rains, to cool down and succour Central India and the Punjab, were still a month or so away.

He stood up and walked through the sitting room of the guest bungalow to the verandah. The starkly clear light made him blink momentarily but the fresh air, though warm, was a relief. He avoided the trellised, closed-in ends and sat in a cane chair, staring across the parched, brown maidan towards the sepoy lines of the cantonment. A faint breeze was stirring, kicking up small whirlpools of dust on the baked earth of the parade ground. In the distance, a bugle sounded faintly. The sowars of the 14th Irregular Cavalry, the gunners of the native artillery battery and the sepoys of the 12th Bengal Native Infantry would now be turning out for the afternoon parade. Frederick Dunlop and his subalterns, Matthews and Taylor, and Campbell of the cavalry, would soon be riding over to join them.

He was sitting there for several minutes, brooding over the latest news from Delhi, when Amin, his Kashmiri Mussulman bearer, appeared with a tray of tea and biscuits. The stocky brown man with pleasant bland features and sweeping black moustache set off by the rakish, upturned flair of his pugri, placed the tray down on the wicker table by Lalor with some deliberation.

"Tell me, Amin, what have you heard today?" Lalor poured the tea into the cup and reached for the milk and sugar.

"Bad news again, sahib. The people here keep saying that the Government has caused ground bones to be mixed with the flour sold in the market and now that two regiments of sepoys have been blown away from the guns at Calcutta."

"It is all lies, Amin. You know that".

"Yes, sahib. I know that. But that is what the people say."

Lalor nodded and Amin departed as silently as he came. Moodily, Lalor drank his tea.

It seemed now a long time ago but, in fact, only nine weeks had elapsed since he had received a summons in the battalion lines at Bombay to go to the Orderly Room where the Commanding Officer wanted to see him. Grizzled old Harry ffrench-Blake, colonel of the 86th, had fixed his agate blue eyes on him and had said bluntly in his gruff, abrupt way: "Lalor, I've got a rum one here, and all the way from Army Headquarters too. A burra sahib of the Court of Directors of the Company—a Director himself, no less—is out here for the first time. He's for a tour of Central India—Indore, Bhopal, Saugor, Jhansi, Gwalior, Agra and on to Delhi—and he's asked for a Queen's officer to be his Military Assistant. What's his name again? Ah, yes, here we are—Sir Julian Wentworth. He'll have an escort of Company cavalry commanded by a Company officer but no doubt he wants a Queen's officer as his MA to give him impartial advice, not weighted by his own lot, as he goes about. The officer selected has to have a good knowledge of the country and able to speak Urdu or Hindi, preferably both. Well, that's you, Lalor."

"But, Colonel, I've only just returned from the right wing of the Regiment in Aden," he had said mildly. He realised that his words would have no effect at all but he also knew that he was expected to protest.

Harry ffrench-Blake had grinned. "I'm quite aware of that. It just happens that you're the man for the job. Not only have you the right qualifications but you're a bachelor and this simplifies my problem immensely—you could be away six months and I don't want any pining memsahib on my hands. Wentworth has asked for a field officer but Captain Lalor will have to do. If you get on well with himself and help him compile a good report to his fellow Directors sitting in their cosy cubby hole in the City, a word from him to the Governor-General could get you promotion without purchase. So, my boy, I would advise you to take this job with open arms. Anyway, as your colonel, I'm ordering you. Now let's go to the Mess for a drink".

The time soon proved hardly propitious to go touring, escorted by a troop of fifty sowars from the 1st Bombay Cavalry. At Indore they had heard news of the mutiny at Meerut on 10 May and of the march of the mutineers to Delhi. Then came intelligence of the rising of the Company's native regiments at Delhi where, incredibly, no Company European troops were stationed. Now they had reached Jhansi whose garrison was also only native troops.

"Hallo there, Captain Lalor. Are you up and about?"

Lalor came out of his reverie and glanced in the direction of the call. Cornet Adrian Meadows, 1st Bombay Cavalry, came swaggering boyishly along the bungalow path, dressed casually in a light cotton shirt, trousers and sandals. Lalor smiled. He liked the youthful, cheerful Meadows, a fairheaded 20 years old with merry blue eyes and clean-cut features brick-red from days of travelling in the Indian sun.

"I'm up, but I'm not sure I'm about."

"What about coming for a walk, old soldier? If we're to do justice to Dunlop's wine tonight, we should work up a proper thirst."

"What a grand idea. And very good thinking, too. Have some tea while I dress."

When Lalor re-emerged, he was buckling a pistol about his waist. Meadows looked at him anxiously. "I suppose I should have brought mine, too?"

"One weapon between the two of us should be good enough. Not that I'm really expecting any trouble, mind you. I just think that you feel such a fool if there is some strife and you've nothing with you. It's feeling the fool I'm afraid of. I should warn you, though, that I'm a fairly wild shot with a pistol."

They walked away from the bungalows of the officers lines along the edge of the cantonment, passing without comment the charred remains of the two bungalows that had been mysteriously burned down two days ago, just before they arrived. As if to distract their line of thought, Adrian Meadows motioned the avenue of trees, bright with orange-red blossom among dark-green leaves, through which they strolled.

"What's the name of this tree, Martin? It's most attractive when it comes out."

"The krishnachura. Known in English as the firegold tree."

"It was flowering when I disembarked at Bombay last year. I've been in India a whole year now."

Lalor smiled but said nothing. They left the perimeter of the cantonment and walked steadily across the plain eastwards. Though it was now late afternoon, the sun was still hot and soon their shirts were sticking clammily to their backs. About them, the rugged crags surrounding Jhansi plain were bathed in the early evening light. They followed a baked dirt track that wound through the black soil of cultivated fields.

Meadows came out with the thought that was now uppermost on everybody's mind. "Do you think that this trouble at Meerut and Delhi will spread, Martin?"

"I've a terrible feeling it will. There's since been that outbreak at Aligarth on the 20th. After all, it's been going on since March when that episode at Barrackpore occurred. The affair at Meerut could not have been more badly handled—degrading in front of their fellows those eighty-five sowars of the 3rd Bengal Cavalry who refused to take the new cartridge. Now, instead of just having to contend with the tantrums of the Brahmins in the infantry, we've alienated the Muslims who form most of the cavalry. The march to Delhi and the rising there will have great significance to every Indian, Hindu or Muslim, prince or sepoy. I fear that matters can only get worse."

"How could they have made such a mess at Meerut? With a battalion of the 60th, the Carbineers and two batteries of British artillery there!"

"The longer you're in India, the more the sun addles your brain. Look at me."

Meadows laughed. "You're not so slow. Anyhow, Sir Julian seems quite taken with you. He listens to all you have to say."

"He hasn't much choice, has he?"

They crossed the sandy bed of a dry watercourse and climbed the far bank to sit on a log lying by the straggling, gaunt roots of a large banyantree. They faced towards the city and the cantonment three miles outside its walls. The sun was glowing a deep vermilion red, hanging low towards the horizon. Jhansi Fort, on its great rock above the city, dominated the panorama. Lalor found himself staring at it.

Meadows followed his gaze and said curiously: "I wonder how the old boy is going to get on with the Rani tomorrow? You heard Captain Skene say today that she's a fairly formidable woman."

"Well, as I'm sure he's only going to tell her the same bad news she already knows, I should say that it will all be rather short and frosty. I personally think the woman's been hard done by. Sir Julian would have been better advised to avoid her. Still, I admire his sense of duty in facing up to her. With this sepoy trouble, there must be many like her who could be tempted to take advantage of it and stir up as much turmoil as possible against us."

"And Jhansi's no Meerut—there's not one British soldier here, John Company's or Queen's. I wonder if she has agents among the sepoys this very moment?"

"Alexander Skene seems confident that all's well. Remember

his letter Erskine at Indore showed Sir Julian, saying that he had no doubts about the loyalty of the troops here? And he seemed to think a lot of the Rani, too."

Meadows stirred the dust idly with a twig for a few moments, then looked up earnestly at Lalor. 'Well, I'm sure my fellows are loyal to the core. They're my own troop and I've been with them at least nine months since I landed."

Lalor said blandly: "Spoken like a good Company officer devoted to his men. I'm sure that the same was said in the Officers Mess at Barhampore, Barrackpore, Meerut, Delhi and Aligarth the night before their fellows ran wild."

Meadows flushed angrily. "That's a very bad joke, Martin! I take it that it was meant to be a joke?"

"I'm sorry. You're right, a bad joke."

"You really are just another superior and cynical Queen's officer, Martin, behind that Irish blather. All you fellows in Queen's regiments have to worry about is whether your men will get on the drink or mixed up with native women."

"True enough. As a member of an Irish regiment, I readily concede that you're right about the first hazard."

Adrian Meadows's ire gradually subsided but he still stared moodily at the dust patterns that his twig had traced. Lalor slapped a hand on his young friend's shoulder and said apologetically: "I'm sure your fellows are faithful. They look a good lot to me. At least you're Bombay Army and not that bloody temperamental Bengal Army. You've trained them well and no doubt they will follow you gladly in normal times. The only thing I would say, Adrian, is that these are no longer normal times. There are all sorts of factors: that bloody stupid greased cartridge, a shortage of officers in regiments as the best have been taken for political duties, too many bible-banging commanding officers whom the sepoys think with some justification are out to convert them to Christianity, and characters in high places who bear terrible grudges against the English because of Dalhousie's policies. Dalhousie was probably right but I do think that he went at his fences rather quickly. And bear in mind that we broke up the Mahratta Confederacy not all that long ago and this woman here, the Rani, apart from her own grievances, is a Mahratta. There must be many waiting in the wings, praying for the English to fall. And the catalyst could be the sepoys. These people are not fools. For instance, I'm sure they know, just as you and I do, that almost all the Company's artillery is manned by sepoys."

"You keep saying the English," Meadows said testily. "Aren't we all in this together?"

"True again. Meant only in the loose generic sense, Adrian old son. Just as a chap from Lancashire, confronted by a Pathan, Punjabi and Madrassi would lump them altogether as Indians. Let's say what the natives call us, Feringhees. You're right. We Feringhees are all in this thing together."

The sinking sun was now resting on the jagged rim of hills beyond Jhansi city, a diffusing red orb. The light was beginning to soften and fade.

"Adrian, as soon as Sir Julian has seen the Rani, I'm going to advise him strongly that we must turn back and retrace our steps as fast as we can to the nearest British garrison in a safe area, which would be that artillery battery at Mwow. This is not the time to go journeying on to Gwalior and still less to Delhi. Do you agree?"

Meadows nodded soberly. Lalor went on: "I hope that the fact that he has his daughter with him will serve to persuade him. He can be obstinate."

"Alicia's a sweet, beautiful girl," Meadows murmured. "What do you think? We've never really discussed her, have we?"

"What is there to discuss? To be sure, Alicia is a good-looking, likeable lass."

"She's keen on you, Martin, y'know."

Lalor laughed at the spontaneity of the allegation. "The sun is now beginning to get at you, just as it began afflicting me a long time ago. She's more your age than mine. It must be you, the dashing young cavalry commander, who really impresses her."

Meadows shook his head wistfully. "No, I'm afraid not. Though that's what I've been hoping, of course. But I'm discounted as a red-faced pimply boy still wet behind my pink ears."

Lalor had to laugh again. Yet, behind his heartiness, he felt sorry for his young friend. "It's only for my Irish jokes she looks to me—to tide her over our tedious journeys and dull overnight stopping places. Otherwise, I'm an ageing captain of 32, with no money and less prospects, and a bog Irishman to boot. No, Adrian, I'm just light company—if I may flatter myself to that extent. Besides, she's not really my type—a little too English rose-like for my earthy tastes. Give me a violent redhead or a sultry brunette any day! If I were you, I wouldn't despair if you admire the young lady. I've seen the glances she gives you when you're riding at the head of your men. And you come from a county family. Isn't your father the Dean of Norwich?"

Meadows looked at him tensely. He said very formally: "Thank you, old man. I had no idea. I appreciate your encouraging words."

Lalor stood up, smiling. "Come on, we must get back. Not only are we getting very serious but it's also growing late. A burra tunda whisky pani and a hot bath calls."

They re-crossed the dry creekbed to the winding path that led back to the cantonment. As they came around a large bush, two vultures ahead on the dusty track hopped and lumbered into ungainly flight before their big wings, slowly beating, lifted them cumbersomely away into the twilight. Beyond, across the plain, the sun was disappearing with pastel shades of colours shooting across a sky dappled with ruffles of placid cloud. Before them, as they walked on, Jhansi Fort stood darkly in the distance against the dim light of the dying evening.

"More bad news has just come over the telegraph, "Alexander Skene said quietly at the dinner table that night when the servants had cleared away and had left the room. "Mutiny has now broken out at Nasirabad."

"Where is that?" Sir Julian Wentworth asked quickly.

"Rajputana. At least, it's rather a long way away."

"But it could indicate that this business is widespread—and is spreading?"

"It could, sir," Skene admitted, "but at least Central India is still untroubled."

Lalor sat back in his chair and contemplated the scene. Three spirit lamps along the table cast a soft, shadowy light about the dining room where the large punkah overhead barely caused their glass-encased flames to flicker as it swayed slowly over them. The formal dinner, in honour of the Director, at which the men perspired stoically in their high-collared red jackets, was in Captain Frederick Dunlop's bungalow in the cantonment. Captain Alexander Skene, Superintendent of the Jhansi Agency, had his house in the city and it was not considered politic for Wentworth to enter the city gates before he had his audience with the Rani.

At the head of his table, the garrison commander, Captain Frederick Dunlop, 12th Bengal Infantry, presided in a pre-occupied way, for these were worrying times and everybody was prey to his own brooding thoughts. On the right of this big, stolid man with his wispy, balding fair hair and thick moustache, and opposite Lalor, was Alicia Wentworth and even this vivacious young woman had looked subdued and apprehensive when she heard Skene's announcement. Lalor studied her. He had not been completely honest with Adrian Meadows under the banyantree when he had denied being attracted to her. She was an energetic, cheerful outdoor girl, so very different from the many young memsahibs whom he had seen during his years in India. Her fair skin had tanned gently during their days of travel, highlighting her blue eyes and golden-brown hair, well-combed and shaped to the nape of her slender neck. He enjoyed her company very much, as she also had a nice turn of wit, and he thanked the perspicacity of that austere widower, Sir Julian—or her own determination—which had ensured that she had accompanied his visit to India.

At the other end of the table, acting as Dunlop's hostess, was Felicity Skene, trim, brown and mousy, surprisingly like her husband, a spare, wiry, freckled Scot whose serious, thoughtful features showed the gnawing doubts of the present unsettled times. Lalor could see that she was almost sick with fear, for the Skenes had two young daughters with them. At her right hand, opposite her husband, sat Sir Julian Wentworth. The more Lalor saw of this tall, thin, sallow and rather humourless man, the more he liked him. This was a little strange, he had to admit to himself, for Wentworth was the epitome of all the casual English superiority against which his Irish soul revolted. The Director came from a wealthy Midlands manufacturing firm and after an excellent start in life at Winchester and Cambridge, had made an assured entry into the City of London where the progeny of money proceeded to acquire more money and affluence. Yet, as old Harry ffrench-Blake had predicted in his rough way, Wentworth leaned heavily on his advice, listened to his suggestions and acted accordingly. The Director was astute enough to realise his ignorance of the real India and honest enough to recognise it before a subordinate.

The final member of the company, sitting diagonally across from Lalor and between Alicia and Skene, was Captain Francis Gordon, 10th Madras Infantry and Deputy Commissioner of Jhansi, a forceful, enthusiastic character to whom Lalor had taken an instant liking. Adrian Meadows had been invited to dine with the subalterns of the garrison, including the three surveyor lieutenants from the Royal Engineers, Powis, Burgess and Turnbull, at Powis's bungalow. Powis was the only married junior officer, with a wife and small daughter at Jhansi.

"I didn't mention this while the others were here," Skene went on, "I didn't see what good it could do, only make people worry more, and after all, we were meant to have a convivial gathering of our small community to welcome you. We don't see many distinguished visitors at Jhansi, Sir Julian."

A murmur of approval rippled about the table from the Jhansi hosts. Earlier Skene and Dunlop had held a drinks party on the verandah to which all the British and senior Anglo-Indian officials had been invited, even down to non-commissioned ranks, a startling departure from the usual strict caste protocol that the present troubled times had caused. Lalor recalled the strained faces, especially of the women with children in Jhansi. He thought back to the Carshores and Andrews, Collector and Deputy Collector of Customs, who each had four children, Quartermaster-Sergeant and Mrs Newton with two children, Sergeant and Mrs Millard, Royal Engineers, who had three children. It had been a slightly-pathetic assemblage, with all bravely ignoring the insects drawn to the lamps and the all-embracing warmth that enveloped everyone in damp discomfort. Yet he had no doubt that the occasion had inspired value. He saw, as the reception went on, how the morale of everybody, including the women, rose noticeably. And he had to concede that it was the dry, aloof Sir Julian who contributed mostly to this mild upsurge in spirits. The Director, a man of little small talk, had moved conscientiously between each small group, clutching his one glass of sherry, and had listened and spoken sincerely. Perhaps it was the Director's presence, exposing himself and his only child to the same unmentionable fears with which they now lived daily, that restored some cheerfulness to them.

"I must ask the obvious question, Dunlop," Wentworth now said to the garrison commander, his features set, his pale blue eyes searching and direct. "How do you view your troops standing up to all this rumour of disorder elsewhere about them?"

Dunlop leaned forward on the table, his florid features flushed. It was almost as if he had been yearning for somebody, particularly the Director, to ask him that question. "I am utterly convinced that my men are loyal, sir. Both the sowars and the sepoys have accepted the new cartridge with no trouble at all. I know that my officers think the same way as I do."

Wentworth returned his attention to Skene. "At Indore Erskine showed me your last letter. You were quite positive that you weren't worried about the situation here. Is that still your considered assessment? I know we've discussed this before but I got a rather disturbing feel from the good people you invited along to meet this evening."

Skene hesitated. He tugged at his sandy moustache reflectively and toyed with his empty wine glass before he looked up at the Director.

"Yes, sir, it is. Dunlop is in close touch with the sepoys every day and I accept his advice fully. This is also my overall appreciation of the general scene here at Jhansi."

"Meaning the Rani also?"

"Yes, I do. I have great confidence in her. You'll be aware that recently I gave her permission to raise a small force to protect her and her property. These are mercenaries from outside, mainly

Rohilla Afghans and some Pathans, and only a hundred or so.''

"Skene, you gave me an excellent briefing this morning—which will be more than useful when I pay my call on her tomorrow—but I must ask your honest opinion on a fundamental issue regarding her and this whole crisis that the Company and British presence in India now find ourselves in. You clearly made the point to me that she is an embittered woman because we disallowed her claim for her adopted son to succeed as Raja, even though she paid considerable money to appeal to us in London, and it doesn't take much imagination to realise this. The logical process of thought from that fact is that she would hardly be human—or, at least, not a Mahratta princess—if she didn't try to make capital out of our present difficulties with the Bengal Army.''

"Sir, I have no doubts about her whatsoever. I believe she is straight with us and that all she cares about is what she calls 'my Jhansi'. She isn't interested in this charade at Delhi where the mutineers have set up moth-eaten old Shah Bahadur, the last Mughal, as their figurehead—much against the old chap's will, I would suspect.''

"But she was brought up in the court of the Peshwa we deposed and exiled to Bithur after we broke up the Mahratta Confederacy in '17. She must speculate what could be in it for her if events continue to go badly for us.''

Skene answered almost defiantly. "All I will say, sir, is the one clear thing she has been concerned about was to get a fair decision on the inheritance of Jhansi—and I'm sure that is what still entirely occupies her mind. I personally don't believe she got that—a fair decision I mean—and neither does Erskine, and Malcolm, Erskine's predecessor, who got his knuckles rapped by Calcutta for saying so. If the Company could have been just a little magnanimous—indeed, I would even say, wiser—all of us in this room would certainly feel happier.''

Lalor saw Wentworth stiffen and retreat visibly into his official shell. The Director replied rather icily and formally: "The Court of Directors gave full consideration to the Rani's submission, Captain Skene, and whatever the wisdom or otherwise of that decision, it is irrevocable. It's water under London Bridge which can't flow backwards. We would all do well, in view of our meeting with the Rani tomorrow morning, to bear that salient fact in mind.''

An awkward silence set in after Wentworth's rebuke. Fortunately, Dunlop's bearer appeared with a boy carrying a tray of liqueurs. While the bearer slowly progressed around the table, pouring requested drinks, nobody spoke. Lalor caused more delay by asking for a long whisky pani with ice.

When this arrived and the bearer had departed, Francis Gordon, a tall, dark-haired, usually humorous man about 28 years old, said seriously: "Alexander, I agree with all you say about the Rani, as you well know anyway. If we are concerned about the safety of our small community here—and I of course include Anglo-Indians as well as British—we don't have to worry about her. What we do have to face up to is that it's our sepoys— whether we like to admit it or not—who are the threat. How do we really know that they are exempt from this strange, sinister mood, or frenzy, that seems to be sweeping through our garrisons? I honestly feel that we owe it to the women and children amongst us to take some obvious precautions now. The time has come, in my judgement, to evacuate married quarters in the cantonment, and your house and mine in the city, Alexander, and base ourselves in the Fort until this emergency has blown over."

Dunlop erupted, livid with anger. "Obvious is the word, Gordon! Such a move would only surely indicate that we are frightened, that we expect the worst and that we are now waiting for it to happen. I will say again—I have every trust in the sepoys of my Regiment, and so has Campbell regarding his cavalry. Are we out to destroy this trust? Which is mutual, I might say! You should know this—you're an Army man."

"Frederick," Gordon said patiently, "I assure you I realise that mutual trust between the officers and the sepoys is what keeps our Army going—indeed, any army. But things have gone wrong over the past few months and they're not getting any better. We're an isolated Company garrison, without any European troops. All I am trying to say is that while you and I are paid to take chances, wives and children are not."

These words of Gordon, a bachelor, effectively silenced Dunlop, a married man whose wife and children were in England. The garrison commander stared helplessly into his glass of brandy. Lalor looked across at Alicia whose troubled eyes met him. He drank deeply from his whisky pani. He knew that her father, at his left hand, was listening and watching intently. He was relieved when Alexander Skene spoke in his deliberate, measured Scots way.

"Francis, we've been over this ground before. We all know, as officers, there are good regiments and there are bad ones. What happened at Meerut, Delhi, Aligarth and now Nasirabad are examples of the rotten apples. Probably those units were all badly-administerecd, with a lack of understanding and com- munication between the sepoys and the officers, and from what we know of the Meerut business, that was certainly badly handled by the senior officers of the garrison. I fully agree with what Frederick says. He has faith in his sepoys and I back this. And I heartily disagree with your suggestion of a precipitate retreat into the Fort. Think of the effect that would have on the native mind. What would the trouble-makers—if we have them—stir out of that?"

"Alexander," said Gordon quietly, almost as if he was talking to himself as he looked down at his own brandy on the table, "I am now at the stage when I wonder whether we are concerned too much about the possible effects of this or that on the native mind and not thinking enough about the danger which we may be placing our women and children in by this somewhat luxurious exercise."

Lalor saw that Dunlop was about to explode again with bottled-up emotion. He was also sorry for Skene who had gone pale and tense. Gordon's shaft about endangering women and children had been ill-advised. However, he was not prepared for the question that Alicia Wentworth spoke crisply to him through the unhappy silence that followed Gordon's blunt pronouncement.

"Martin, what do you think should happen here?"

He shifted uncomfortably in his chair, feeling all eyes on him. He took a sip of his whisky and looked across at her. She was charmingly dressed in a royal blue brocaded gown which set off her honey-coloured hair and light brown suntan. Her blue eyes studied him appealingly.

"Alicia, I'm a mere visitor here, like your father. We're here to learn about the local situation, not to pretend to be experts. And we've been in the station a mere thirty hours or so. It's hardly for me to say."

Alexander Skene folded his arms on the table and looked across at him in a hard, penetrating way. "No, Miss Wentworth is right, Lalor. All of us would like to know your feel of our problems—if, indeed, we have one. You're a soldier of some Indian experience and we recognise this."

"I came back from Aden to the headquarters of my Regiment only three months ago and, as you know, we're stationed in Bombay. I'm quite out of touch."

Skene smiled patiently. His brown eyes and drawn freckled face looked very tired. "Lalor, I know I speak for all of us. We're interested in getting your views. If they're rubbish, we Jhansi fellows can always have a laugh."

Lalor looked at the Superintendent of Jhansi Agency, weighing his words quickly in his mind. He decided to speak the hard truth. "I agree wholeheartedly with Gordon. You should now take refuge in the Fort—after this news about Nasirabad—at least for the families."

A gasp went about the table. For a terrible moment, Lalor thought that Felicity Skene was going to break down. She stared at her husband wordlessly, looking drained and distraught. He again felt sorry for Skene whose lips pursed with strain. The Superintendent leaned back in his chair, looked directly at him and said coldly: "But on the intelligence I have at present, my decision must be otherwise."

"But what about the intelligence you don't have—which in sum may be greater and rather more disturbing?"

"I am not fey or clairvoyant, Lalor. I can only read the facts as they are known to me."

"True. And I'm not saying that if I was in your position, where you see all sides and have the ultimate responsibility, I wouldn't have made the same decision. However, what I do wonder is whether you are being too swayed by your trust in the Rani? Now don't get me wrong. You're perfectly entitled to trust her—and are doubtlessly right—but just how much influence or assistance could she exert on our behalf, assuming there is a conspiracy? You've given her authority to recruit a hundred or so ruffians. What use are those fellows, armed with matchlocks, against the sepoys if they rise? She would be almost as much at their mercy as we would."

"But what if she was in league with the sepoys if they are disaffected, Martin," Alicia asked quickly, "instigating them and perhaps even their secret leader? This would surely protect her."

"That could be so. Except we all appear confident that the Rani is reliable. The uncertainty—and the power—lies with the sepoys."

"You're entering into my responsibility and judgement there, Lalor." Frederick Dunlop said stiffly.

"I know that, and I speak with all temerity. Obviously, I'm quite ignorant of local conditions. You must be the sole assessor of the loyalty and dependability of your own troops. It just strikes me that there is a powerful and insidious undercurrent about our native garrisons, particularly now that Delhi is in rebel hands. I feel that this virus is spreading and what guarantee have we that Jhansi is going to be immune? That's the real reason why I support Gordon and say that it might would be a wise and simple precaution to house the families in the Fort until our whole position in India stabilises—which it won't while Delhi is held by the mutineers."

Francis Gordon was about to speak impassionedly but Sir

Julian Wentworth held up an arresting hand and said to Felicity Skene: "Perhaps we might withdraw to the verandah, my dear, and take our coffee there? It's becoming warm in here and, also, possibly we're over-heating through our own fault."

With a scraping of chairs, the dinner party, less the two women, drifted out to the spacious verandah. Lalor inhaled the sultry air that closed in like a moist blanket and persuaded himself that it was marginally cooler than inside. He leaned against a verandah post, gripping his half-full whisky glass, and looked at the dark outline of the sepoy lines across the maidan under a full moon.

A match flared by him and Gordon stood there, lighting a cheroot.

"The Director got his analogies wrong," said the Deputy Commissioner lightly. "Water can flow backwards under London Bridge. The Thames, as far as I'm aware, is tidal."

"I think he meant that the Court of Directors' unfavourable ruling was set in stone like the foundations of London Bridge."

"Thank God, you spoke some sense in there. We're right, y'know."

"Perhaps we are. But, of course, it's easy to give advice without responsibility."

Gordon was suddenly called away by Skene, who was talking to Sir Julian and Dunlop, and Lalor was left alone with his thoughts. He was sipping the remains of his whisky minutes later when he caught a subtle whiff of perfume. He was delighted to find that Alicia had come silently on him from inside the bungalow.

"This has become a very downcast party," she said drily.

He laughed and said easily: "Not with you here, it isn't."

She smiled. "I expect you say that to all damsels beleaguered in garrisons that are about to break out into mutiny?"

"I do, indeed. But for you, my dear, I mean that sincerely."

The smile faded from her and she looked up at him deeply. She broke the tension by saying softly: "I hope that Captain Gordon and you are wrong, Martin."

"No more than Gordon and I hope, too, I promise you."

"Why doesn't Captain Skene take the precaution of the Fort for the families? It would reassure the women so much."

"He's concerned not to show any sign that could be taken as mistrust of the sepoys. This in itself could provoke trouble which otherwise might remain dormant. Or even be taken as weakness and fear. I'm afraid Company officers pride themselves on knowing what they call the native mind, as you heard at the table."

Felicity Skene came out to the verandah and joined them. Alicia deftly directed the conversation to riding, as the two young Skene daughters, Megan and Katie, had each just been given a pony as a present from their parents. When they had been talking for a short while, Alicia's father came over and said apologetically to Felicity: "My dear, would you excuse me? I still haven't quite got over our recent days on the road and, of course, this heat doesn't help a newchum like me. Also, I have this meeting with the Rani tomorrow morning, so I had better collect a few thoughts and do my homework. Thank you so much for the splendid opportunity you gave me tonight to meet all our worthy people in Jhansi and, again too, for the excellent dinner."

Wentworth said goodnight to all in turn in his grave, courteous way and Alicia left with him for their bungalow nearby, lighted on their way by two bearers with hurricane lamps. Alexander and Felicity Skene, also Francis Gordon, departed in a carriage for the city, escorted by a dozen sowars of the 14th Irregular Cavalry, the very men, Lalor thought wryly, who could murder them in their beds one night soon. He and Dunlop, who good-naturedly had buried his prickliness of the dinner table, sprawled in cane chairs and drank whisky panis until well after midnight, conversing in a desultory, easy way. Despite his bulk, Dunlop was a keen horseman and spoke nostalgically and affectionately of hunting in Ireland, with its green turf, sharp morning mists and sweeping rain showers.

At 1 o'clock Lalor returned to his own bungalow, answering the hoarse salutation of the chowkidar who appeared out of the darkness. As he peeled off his sodden shirt in his bedroom, he wondered about the Director's meeting that morning with the Company's recent litigant, the widowed Rani of Jhansi. He undressed fully and lay down on the bed wrapped in his lungi. Before he blew out the spirit lamp, he turned over Cecilia's calendar and the date dropped down to 2 June 1857.

2

The Rani

The progress of Sir Julian Wentworth, Director of the Honourable

East India Company, to the court of the Rani of Jhansi was as impressive as the Superintendent of the Agency and the Garrison Commander could make it. The whole wing of the 14th Irregular Cavalry, resplendent in their full dress of aquamarine blue pugris, red tunics with yellow facings, and dark blue breeches with a broad yellow stripe, paraded under Lieutenant Peter Campbell to augment the mounted ranks of Adrian Meadows's troop as the escort. The band of the 12th Bengal Infantry, in red tunics with white facings, played the cavalcade from the officers' lines to the main gate of the cantonment where the quarter guard, drawn from the artillery battery in blue tunics with scarlet facings, turned out to present arms, their dark, moustachioed faces staring impassively ahead as the bugler sounded off.

Lalor rode alongside the carriage in which Wentworth and Alexander Skene sat stiffly as the crudely-sprung vehicle bumped and lurched between sunbaked ruts on the dirt road that straggled to the city. Soon they were all sweltering from the heat with the fatalism that was all part of the overdressed Englishman's fortitudinous tolerance of India. The Director wore a grey frock coat and striped trousers, complete with wing collar and a pearl grey tie. His only concession to the local environment was a white sun helmet. From time to time Lalor glanced with some fascination at the wing collar. On any other man, its starched pristine impeccability would have crumpled and dissolved. Both he and Skene, each in tight-collared red tunic, medals, sash and sword, were perspiring freely. Though the hour was only nine o'clock, the morning sun was already fierce.

Lalor adjusted his own sun helmet, its white pugri trailing over his neck, and settled down to enjoy the ride to the city. The road wound through groves of tamarind and mango trees, interspersed with Hindu temples, until they topped a rise. Before them loomed the massive bulk of Jhansi Fort on its great rock base, with the walled city lying clustered about its south-eastern and eastern flanks. The large round towers and huge ramparts of the Fort gave an aura of power and impregnability, borne seemingly with the confidence of centuries.

The leading ranks of the escort threaded their way through the crowds of curious onlookers who had streamed out from the city to stare at them and began disappearing through an entrance in the walls which Lalor heard Skene say to Wentworth was the Datia Gate. Soon the carriage rattled through the narrow gate where a group of heavily-armed guards with wild, straggling beards and roughly-tied pugris—the Rani's Rohilla Afghan mercenaries, Lalor guessed—gave a shambling variety of hand salutes. Inside the city they clattered noisily along narrow streets until they came to a large two-storeyed building coloured a deep yellow ochre. The cavalry turned away into a stables area opposite and the carriage, drawn by its restive, half-trained ponies, lumbered precariously through the archway of the palace entrance, accompanied only by Lalor.

Once through the archway they came into a spacious stone-paved courtyard whose centre had an attractive garden of green grass and flowering shrubs surrounding a fountain. As the carriage lurched to a halt and Lalor dismounted, syces ran forward to hold the horses. Nearby, still and silent like friezes in a Hindu temple, stood a group of ornately-dressed court officials.

When Wentworth, looking curiously impressive with his long, lean frame clad in formal dress, stepped down, a stocky, middle-aged Hindu with a strong face and a greying moustache, dressed in the richly-brocaded green coat and white breeches, came forward and introduced himself as Mazumdar, the Vazir. A bout of handshaking went on, with the Director, followed by Skene and Lalor, meeting the Diwan, the treasurer, the Kotwal, the chief of police, and a cluster of other officials. When this slightly-confused ceremonial was over, the Vazir turned and beckoned Wentworth to a nearby door. The Vazir led the whole party up narrow, steep stone steps into a long, elongated room covered in rich carpets and decorated about its walls with painted wooden panels depicting black buck, peacocks and floral designs. At the far end, masking another door, was a white latticed wooden screen. Facing the screen on the carpeted floor were rows of cushions. Lalor and Skene looked at each other.

Mazumdar invited Wentworth to take the central cushion at the front which the Director did without demur, though Lalor could see that he was clearly puzzled. The Vazir then motioned Skene and Lalor to sit in the front row also and then settled himself at Wentworth's right hand. The court officials trailing in rear sat down on the ranks of cushions behind them. As the Vazir began to engage his distinguished visitor with halting English, a stream of servants padded into the room by the entrance they had used, bearing silver trays laden with tea, glasses of water and sweetmeats.

They drank the tea and chewed the cloying sweetmeats while Mazumdar pressed with some deliberation his conversation with Wentworth, about when the monsoon rains would come, about the crops, about the progress of the Grand Trunk Road advancing slowly from Calcutta to Delhi. Skene and Lalor occasionally broke into Hindi to ease the strain on the Vazir's limited English. The topic of the sepoy mutinies focussed about Delhi was tactfully ignored.

When the tea had been drunk and long cleared away with the remnants of the sweetmeats, they still sat there, incongruously facing the bland anonymity of the purdah screen. Lalor could see that the Director's well-disciplined patience was beginning to wear thin. Even the Vazir's determined, if uninspired, conversation had dried up. Skene was irritated and restive.

"She's never done this to me before—in all our dealings," he whispered agitatedly to Lalor.

"She seems to be making some kind of point."

After several more seemingly interminable minutes, a slight sound came of the double doors of the adjoining room beyond the screen opening. A silver bell tinkled gently. Lalor got a waft of perfume and sniffed appreciatively. He saw the outline of a figure settling down behind the screen.

A feminine voice, soft and melodious but speaking with a steely ring of determination in slow, heavily accented English, came from the other side of the purdah screen.

"Welcome to Jhansi, Sir Julian. I would have liked to have said 'to my Jhansi' but, as you are well aware, this is a matter of some dispute between us."

Wentworth was equal to the occasion. "Thank you, Your Highness, for your welcome and, indeed, for receiving me. I knew that once I had the opportunity to visit India, I could not do this without seeing your beautiful state. I can understand why you love it so much."

The unseen Rani went on to ask Wentworth about his tour and his impressions of India and a conversation of some studied politeness developed between them. What an extraordinary scene, thought Lalor, and really quite humourous. The unfortunate Sir Julian obviously needed all his tact and powers of concentration to talk coherently to a lattice screen. Alexander Skene glared at the screen in baffled frustration. The Rani, in her secluded isolation which also permitted discreet one-way observation as well, had psychologically outflanked the Director and the Superintendent with some finality.

Gradually, the inconsequential exchange petered out and the short direct question for which they had been waiting came to Wentworth from the other side of the screen. "And what have you come all this way to tell me, Sir Julian? I am very pleased that you are delighted with Jhansi but you and I have greater things on our mind than its beauty. What is the news you bear from London?"

"I am directed to inform you, Your Highness," Wentworth said stiffly and formally, "that my fellow members of the Court of

Directors of the East India Company find themselves compelled, however reluctantly and regrettably in your personal circumstances, to uphold the Doctrine of Lapse as propounded by the previous Governor-General, Lord Dalhousie. They cannot recognise the case for the inheritance of your adopted son, Damodar—adopted somewhat hurriedly, we had to observe, at the deathbed of your late husband—and there can be no more appeals against this decision. We heard out your able advocate, John Lang, in London and we pondered and weighed the evidence for a very long time but, ultimately, the verdict went against you. Madam, I must say hardly, and finally, that the door is now completely closed on this matter."

"But Captain Skene and Major Malcolm, his superior at Indore then, both believe in the justice of my case!" The Rani's voice was still low but she was obviously struggling to maintain control of herself. "Why do you ignore men whom you have placed in positions of great trust and responsibility and who know well what is happening about them in India?"

"I take your point wholly, madam. You are rightly referring to estimable officers in whom the Company—and, indeed, the Crown—has utter confidence. But, necessarily, they see only their local situation—"

"But it is the local situation—my local situation—that I am concerned about! Do these men whom you have placed amongst us to ensure good government, law and order—do they mean nothing?" The Rani's interruption was fierce and thick with passion. Lalor and Skene again glanced at each other.

"What I was going on to say," Wentworth answered coolly, "is that the Governor-General's Council at Fort William, Calcutta, whose advice London is bound to treat with considerable weight, see the broad canvas of the whole picture."

A pause set in. The atmosphere in the durbar hall was now charged with emotion. The hidden Rani was becoming heated and this strange impersonalised dialogue between her and the Director could degenerate badly. Lalor's cushion was nearest the open window from which the cries of the street intruded on the silent, tense scene and he stared out over the jumbled rooftops of the city. All it needed now, he thought philosophically, was for the Rani, doubtless a formidable betel-chewing wench, to crash through the purdah screen and leap forward to wield a tulwar down on the Director's thinly-greying skull. As he pondered this possibility, he became conscious of his own back exposed to the court officials sitting in packed ranks behind him.

As if to confirm the sensation of farce that was beginning to grip him, two pied mynas landed abruptly on the broad stone sill of the window and in the perky, cocky manner of their breed, strode about, crying out raucously. He watched them with some fascination. The two birds ceased their calling and strutting and began to preen themselves, their yellow beaks diving into their black and silvery feathers, oblivious of the human bodies sitting gravely waxen and silent inside the room.

The Rani spoke. To Lalor's relief, and probably far more to Wentworth's and Skene's, he thought, she was now contained and cool.

"Sir Julian, I realise what I have to say will have no effect whatsoever. However, let me say at once that I appreciate your frankness and, indeed, your personal honesty in troubling to come to see me. I am sure you did not have to do this. But I must tell you, as a Mahratta woman from a noble house who married into another noble house, my case simply—away from all the dry legal papers and the arguments you listened to in London. My husband, on his deathbed, adopted a boy from another branch of his family as his son, with full Hindu rites and according to the custom of our people, in the presence of the British Agent. You may say that this was done at the last moment, as he was dying, but the proper rituals were gone through. You, the English, have always cleverly consolidated your military conquests in India by respecting and acknowledging the religious beliefs of its various peoples—except, of course, occasionally when it did not suit the policy from Calcutta and this would seem, in my bitter view, what has happened with my Jhansi. Damodar, now my beloved son in all meaning of the word, should be recognised as the rightful ruler, heir to Jhansi. The customs and traditions of our people demand this. My husband, even when he had barely any strength as a dying man, wrote personally to Lord Dalhousie asking for his protection for me and Damodar—that I should rule Jhansi until our son came of age."

A brittle silence again settled over the durbar room. Lalor glanced at Skene who raised his eyebrows expressively. He looked again at the open window near him. The two pied mynas were asleep, heads tucked under a wing and standing on one yellow leg. He wondered if British interests in India were as dormant and precariously balanced as those two birds.

"The Governor-General had to reject your husband's submission," Wentworth said firmly, "because Jhansi had never been an independent entity. Jhansi as a state was created by us British when we defeated the Mahratta Confederacy in 1817. I know these are painful words to you, madam, because you are a Mahratta but these are the hard facts of history. Before '17, Jhansi was a minor province in the territories of your Peshwa of the

Mahrattas, a subedarship, a governor's province."

"You are well-versed in recent history, Sir Julian, especially as dictated by the English. But, I repeat, my case rests entirely on the ancient traditions of religion and history which our people understand. The Governor-General ignored my memorandum on this whole crucial aspect."

"The Governor-General had established a strict policy on these complicated inheritance issues from which he refused to depart."

"Particularly, as I have said before, when this policy was designed to work in favour of English interests."

"He did allow your appeal to the Court of Directors which John Lang, if I may say so again, very ably represented."

"At considerable cost to me! And, perhaps not unforeseen, ultimate failure."

"We tried to be as generous as we could to you, madam. Your adopted heir was allowed the personal estate of your late husband, you were declared not to be subject to British courts, and you personally were granted a pension of sixty thousand rupees a year."

"From which I had to pay my husband's debts! And the Company even took away the revenue of the villages that went to the upkeep of the temple of Mahalalshmi where the ruling family of Jhansi have always worshipped."

Wentworth had clearly had enough. He leaned forward and said tersely: "Madam, I honestly don't think there is any value for either of us to go back over this well-trodden ground. The decision on the inheritance of Jhansi has been taken irrevocably by my fellow Directors and rightly or wrongly—for it was not unanimous—it went against you. Jhansi was annexed in 1854 and there the story must now end."

"Annexed five months after my husband's death! Dalhousie must have had barely time to read his letter!"

"I am willing—indeed anxious," Wentworth went on, in some desperation Lalor thought, "to represent to the Governor-General, and certainly to my colleagues in London also, any areas where you feel you are being unfairly treated—apart from the main issue, of course—and where you think I may be able to help. The question of the revenue for the temple you mentioned might be an instance. As you know, I will be in Jhansi for two more days. I would be pleased to have any brief from your Vazir on any particular subject you care to give me and I will do my best. But, I must reiterate, I can't change the basic overall situation you find yourself in. The annexation of 1854 is immutable."

Silence again developed in all its heaviness in the room. Lalor looked again at the two mynas on the window sill. They still slumbered, heads tucked under a wing, on one leg. The Rani's voice, disembodied behind the screen, quickly returned his attention.

"I don't understand all your big words, Sir Julian, but only a fool would not get their meaning."

Lalor thought that suddenly she sounded very flat. John Company's power had borne down on her, as it had done over the years with many a native ruler. However, he was both relieved and impressed when Wentworth hurried on to say almost apologetically: "I am only empowered to say what I have just said. This is not to say that I do not personally sympathise with the main burden of your case."

Again, quiet and stillness from behind the screen. Lalor found himself staring intently at its bland exterior.

"I think I believe you," the unseen voice eventually said calmly. "Not that it would appear I have much choice. Now, I wonder, if you will believe me?"

It seemed to Lalor that Wentworth became defensive and apprehensive. However, the low, pervasive voice of the Rani allowed him no time to say anything. She went on: "I do not have to tell you, even a newcomer to our country, that the English are now in very serious trouble. The Meerut and Delhi mutineers have acclaimed the old man you called the King of Delhi and kept on a pension, as emperor. Information reaches us that some of your other garrisons in far stations are joining the rebellion also. And these are not just figments of court gossip—every pargana, zail, thana, village throughout northern and central India is now hearing this news. Every peasant in the fields, every labourer in the bazaar, is now looking at you, waiting to see if you are going to fall down in the dust forever. This is India, Sir Julian, and India's ways are subtle. Most of the people are very passive and only wish to tend to their crops or trade their merchandise in peace but they are also knowledgeable victims of periodic waves of aggression by factions that succeed one another. They have seen conquerors come and go."

"Like the Mahrattas?" Wentworth asked sharply.

"Like the Mahrattas," the soft voice from behind the screen agreed. "Like the Mughals, the Persians, the Afghans, the Sikhs and now the English. You are being challenged and are in difficulty, just as all those before you before they crumbled away. You will need all the friends you can muster to prevent your ultimate decline and defeat."

"The English have their many friends deep-rooted already among the people you know so much about, madam. Even I know that. I won't recount all the benefits we have brought about—not only social ones but also practical economic ones such as a fair taxation system and land reform—for I hope you realise these. No, I am sure the greatest gift we have given the common people in both town and countryside is law and order, instead of incessant war, marauding and pillage. I am told that the years since 1830 are called the English Peace.''

''But that peace is well and truly broken now and in the heart of India too, Delhi. You must not put too much reliance on the people, Sir Julian, whether you have their good will or not. They are powerless and what support they can give you will last only as long as you can ensure protection. They will soon change their loyalty to those who are successful in wresting power from you. From what we hear from Delhi, these could be the sepoys of your own Company army.''

''We're facing some temporary disaffection in one or two regiments which, I assure you, will be stamped out rigorously very soon. Our Commander-in-Chief is marching on Delhi now. The Punjab is sending reinforcements to him.''

''You disappoint me, Sir Julian, if you really believe your first statement. Or, even worse, if you expect me to believe it. I know that you must say brave words to me but I only hope, for your sake, that you do not believe them either. This business of the sepoys has widespread effects far beyond what you think that has led peasant soldiers to mutiny.''

''What are you suggesting, madam?''

''That all manners of men are waiting to see the extent of the trouble the English are in. Perhaps not even a stranger to India such as yourself needs me to list who some of these might be—the deposed King Of Oudh from where many of your Brahmin Hindu sepoys in the Bengal Army come from, the Muslims who yearn after the old Mughal glory, the exiled and pensioned-off Peshwa of Poona and his Mahrattas, the Sikhs who you crushed only a few years ago, many a Rajput and Mahratta raja with his eye on possible plunder among the chaos. What my message really is is that your Company, all the English, need every friend you can count on at this time. I, Lakshmi Bao, Rani of Jhansi, am very willing to be one of those friends. You should make use of me.''

Lalor and Skene both looked keenly at Wentworth. He remained staring at the screen, deep in thought for several moments.

''The Company, and therefore the English, have always thought of you as a friend, madam,'' the Director said quietly, ''and I sincerely hope we still can.''

Lalor, trying to be a detached observer of this curious

encounter, was slightly saddened by Wentworth's reaction. The Director had been doing so well in this strange, disembodied dialogue and now he suddenly lapsed into official negativity. He could see that Alexander Skene, staring moodily down at his polished black boots, was disappointed.

Another pause. Then the voice behind the screen spoke, in that same steely, determined tone, Lalor thought, with which they had been greeted. "Thank you, Sir Julian, for our talk which I found most interesting. I hope that you will enjoy the rest of your stay in Jhansi. I will see you again before you depart."

The bell behind the screen tinkled again and the court officials, led by Mazumdar, got silently to their feet. Wentworth, Lalor and Skene rose also. The two pied mynas, startled by the movement, lifted their dishevelled black caps from the dreamland cover of their wings, lowered a second yellow leg to the sill and glared with yellow-ringed eyes inside. With harsh cries of protest, they took wing as curtly as they had arrived.

"I think we are being politely thrown out," Lalor murmured to an unresponsive Skene.

Mazumdar ushered Wentworth courteously across the carpets of the durbar room and the entourage closed deferentially behind Lalor and Skene. As their Army boots crashed down the stone steps leading to the courtyard, Lalor felt that they were beating some kind of retreat.

Under the archway they ceremoniously shook hands with Mazumdar and his officials as they took their leave. While Wentworth and Skene settled themselves into their carriage, Lalor mounted his horse, a big strong chestnut he called Paddy, and rode out to meet Adrian Meadows who was waiting with his troop lined up in the street with Peter Campbell's 14th Cavalry formed up ahead.

"How did it go?" Meadows asked curiously.

"In boxing terms, Adrian, it was a hard, close bout. There were no knockdowns, though I did think the Rani had the Director on the ropes once or twice. I would have thought that the Rani won on points. The Director could have taken the bout in the closing minutes—at least, as far as I'm concerned and I suspect, Alexander Skene, too—but he declined. The Rani laid it on for him, too. It baffles me, but as he said in there, he sees the big picture, we don't. Lad, we're now going to Skene's for a post-mortem. Get word to Peter Campbell to lead us there."

Thirty minutes later, with the exception of Peter Campbell who remained outside on duty with the escort, they were all sitting in the living room of Skene's house inside the city under the slow beat of its punkah. Though it was not yet noon, Wentworth surprised Lalor by asking for a brandy and soda, despite Felicity Skene's offer of tea. Skene and Lalor gratefully asked for a glass of beer, though Adrian Meadows dutifully accepted the tea. Wentworth even made a concession to the heat by taking off his frock coat which allowed the others to remove their red jackets.

"Well, what did you make of all that?" he asked Skene.

The Superintendent of Jhansi Agency was in a state of some puzzlement himself. "I've never seen her use that purdah screen before. When she became a widow, all I can say is that she became a very emancipated one, especially for a well brought-up Hindu woman. None of that degradation of shaving off her hair, of becoming a nonentity and chattel in the dead husband's family, for her. If anything, she seemed to develop her own personality, probably to protect the boy's future, and became very outgoing."

"I realise that we have hurt and humiliated her," said Wentworth slowly, as if he was thinking out aloud. "She was just hitting back in some tortuous, feminine way."

"But she was holding out the olive branch, Sir Julian. I do believe that if we could let her know in some positive form that we trust her and somehow would meet her halfway in some form of alliance, she could be very helpful, not just here but throughout the Mahratta country. And, as she well knows and let us know that she knows, we do need all the allies about us that we can rally."

"Yes, I see all that, despite what I said at the Palace and which she saw through at once. But what I can offer her that is anything of substance? These things take time to arrange, even to clear with Calcutta, let alone London."

"These are extraordinary times, Sir Julian," Lalor said quietly, "and it's perhaps a case of putting your money down now on the right horse or not taking part in the race at all. A telegraph message to Fort William might now find the Governor-General and his Council thinking very much on those lines, too. I see your problem just what to hold out to the woman but if we can solve this, it could do us a lot of good."

"Lalor's right, sir," Skene said warmly. "When I allowed her to raise her own force of guards, a great change for the better came over our relations. The trappings of power, prestige—*izzat* they call it—count for so much here and the Rani's no exception."

"And the *izzat* of the Company is now in peril," said Wentworth, almost wearily. "Yes, I agree with all you both say. These times do need quick and unorthodox remedies. Perhaps my mind has been too legalistic so far. I'll try to think of some concession we can make towards her position, though I'll have to get the Governor-General's agreement. This means it will happen well after we're gone but, I hope, not too late to help you and Dunlop."

Alexander Skene looked across at Lalor, relief showing on his drawn, tired features. He settled back in his chair to enjoy the remains of his beer. Now that he had come to his decision, Wentworth seemed to relax also. He sipped his brandy and soda meditatively and then looked wryly at his companions.

"Do you know, gentlemen, that this morning was the first time I've tried to conduct business with a wooden screen?"

They were still laughing when Felicity Skene came back into the room, looking slightly excited. She said to her husband: "Rao Chaudri has arrived from the Palace."

"Show him in, dear."

They stood up expectantly. Skene said urgently to Wentworth and Lalor: "This chap's Mazumdar's right hand man."

A slim young Mahratta of average height, with good-looking, aquiline dark features and a small trimmed moustache and well-dressed in a white pugri, brocaded brown jacket and white breeches, entered the room. Lalor recognised him as one of the officials who had accompanied them at the audience with Rani.

After saluting them with some ceremony, the visitor said gravely in faultless English: "I am Rao Chaudri, assistant to Mazumdar, Vazir of the Rani. Her Highness commands me to convey to you, Sir Julian, that she would be honoured if you and your daughter, the officers in your party, Captain and Mrs Skene, and the officers of the garrison could come to dinner with her at the Palace tonight. She offers her apologies for the shortness of the notice for this invitation but she has suddenly realised how little time you have in Jhansi before you continue your tour."

Wentworth glanced at Lalor and Skene but quickly returned his attention to Rao Chaudri. "Kindly inform Her Highness that I and my daughter, indeed all of us, would be delighted to take dinner with her tonight. I thank her for her thoughtful kindness."

"Then the Rani will expect you one hour after sunset."

"Will you yourself have some refreshments with us now?"

"Thank you, Sir Julian, but I must get back. There are many arrangements to be made."

Rao Chaudri made a farewell obeisance and left the room as silently as he had appeared. Wentworth waved his companions to sit down again and took up his drink.

"I can guess what your suspicious military instincts are," he said to Skene and Lalor, "but I gave the only answer I could."

Before either could speak, Adrian Meadows ingenuously echoed their thoughts in his enthusiastic way. "But what a wonderful way to snare us all if some dark skullduggery is afoot! All of us trapped in the Palace except for a couple of duty officers in the cantonment."

"But we don't consider the Rani is a potential enemy, Meadows," Skene said with controlled exasperation. "So let us not bandy about words like skullduggery and traps."

As the Director was also staring rather bleakly at the subaltern, Lalor went to the rescue of his young friend. "You're right, Adrian, like a good soldier to look at the worst case but I would think what's behind this sudden invitation is that the Rani is anxious to talk further with Sir Julian and face to face, too, in a more relaxed atmosphere. After all, she's invited ladies and so she can hardly eat her dinner alone behind her purdah screen. You may well find the evening, sir, quite interesting and very good value."

The Director looked at him keenly. "Yes, by jove, she is having second thoughts and anxious to talk further. I wonder what she has in mind? Or is she just eager to try to pump me, to draw me out? Either way, it could be a fascinating dinner, as you say. I'd certainly like to find out her views on what is happening about us, or could happen about us. I'm sure there's little she doesn't know about. It will be, anyway, a matter of great moment to break down the barrier of the purdah screen."

The small gathering in Felicity Skene's living room rose and her visitors from the cantonment took their leave. During the journey back, Adrian Meadows, unabashed by his near-disaster comment on the social occasion that lay ahead of them that evening, rode casually beside Lalor by the Director's rumbling carriage while his be-medalled, splendidly bearded Rissaldar-Major, Sikander Khan, led his troop.

"Well, Martin," he said seriously, "at least we seem to have got a free dinner out of the Rani at the end of the day. But it's just not the dinner, y'know. I've heard so much about this Rani that I'm looking forward to seeing what she's really like. Aren't you?"

3

Dinner at the Palace

When Lalor looked about him in the Palace that evening, he saw all the brilliance and colour of a minor court in India. The bright hues of the women's saris, the ornate dress and flaired pugris of the state officials and Bundela thakurs from the nearby countryside, and the dress uniforms of the British, in their red tunics with different regimental facings and heavily laced with gold braid, tight blue trousers with regimental coloured stripe and booted and spurred, blended into a diverse scene as they stood talking in a spacious, high-ceilinged room. Tables stood heavy with trays of sweetmeats and brass vases of flowers. White-garbed servants moved unobtrusively about with decanters of chased silver, pouring wine or fruit juice.

The Rani had arranged her somewhat impromptu party very well, he thought. But after half an hour she had still not appeared. When the introductions were finally and laboriously over and the Bundela women clustered silently together while their men also grouped to stare stonily at the British, he knew that they needed her badly. At least Jhansi was a Hindu court where the women could appear with their husbands and, for which he was even more grateful, liquor could be served to the Feringhee.

He was struggling to make conversation with the Diwan when he heard Adrian Meadows, who had drifted over to him, say hoarsely in his ear: "Martin, look!"

He turned. He had become conscious of a sudden hush and that the Diwan was staring past him. A woman, dressed simply in a sari of white muslin which clung tightly about a full figure, was shaking hands with Sir Julian and smiling pleasantly as she spoke. A pearl necklace and pearl earrings were her only adornments.

"Here's your sultry brunette," Meadows murmured irreverently.

Wentworth slowly ushered her about the British guests. She nodded to the young officers of the garrison and stopped to talk to Felicity Skene. Gradually she came over to where they stood.

As she shook hands with Alicia Wentworth, her perfume drifted about him. Her features were handsome rather than being softly and femininely beautiful, with a thin-bridged well-shaped nose, full wide mouth and intelligent, discerning dark eyes. Thick black hair, parted in the middle and brushed to a sheen until it gathered in a luxuriant cluster on her neck, set off her smooth brown complexion and contrasted vividly with the white sari. A certain commanding presence radiated from her.

Her conversation with Alicia tailed off and she moved slightly towards him. She gave him a curious guarded half-smile and held out a well-groomed hand.

Sir Julian introduced him as he took her hand. Though her palm was soft, her grip was surprisingly firm.

"Good evening, Captain Lalor," she said in that deliberate, accented English that he had heard from the other side of the purdah screen that morning.

"Good evening, Your Highness."

"I am told you know India very well."

"I've served in India, off and on, since 1844 but I think it would be a brave man—certainly a rash one—who said that he knew India very well."

The Rani laughed. Some warmth came into her appraising eyes. "Well said!" She looked at Wentworth by her side. "Captain Lalor is lost in the infantry, Sir Julian. He should be employed by the Company in the political field. Perhaps we who feel a grievance at your hands would never have been placed in this position."

Lalor saw that the Director was taken back by this unexpected barb. He tried to create a diversion. "But perhaps the time has now come, Rani, when the talking is over and the best men are again needed in the infantry."

The dark eyes regarded him. "Is that what you really think?"

"Rather firmly. And wouldn't you agree?"

Her expression became disarmingly bland. "I don't think that my opinion could be of any use, Captain Lalor. I am just a mere woman, a pensioner of the Company, who has managed to recruit and arm a few rascals to ensure law and order in the streets of the city and protect the peasants in their fields. That is the extent of my military knowledge."

"But I hardly need to tell you that the ways of India, certainly to us Europeans, are mysterious. Bad news travels faster here than in most places."

She still looked at him evenly but he could see that she was nettled. He had pushed her into a corner where she had to make a stance. "Sometimes, in India, Captain Lalor, it is best to hear only what you wish to hear.''

''Meaning there could be more bad news for us?''

She smiled. ''Who are us, Captain Lalor? Me, the pensioned widow? You, the soldier upholding the fat but now very worried Company? The old Mughal, now held half-captive against his will by your former sepoys in Delhi? The simple peasants in the fields, the toiling craftsmen and labourers in the towns and cities?''

Sir Julian Wentworth cleared his throat. The Rani moved away. She swept past Adrian Meadows, waiting dutifully to meet her, and went on to talk to Alexander Skene and Francis Gordon.

''You've upset her,'' Alicia breathed to him. ''Was that really necessary?''

Before he could reply, Adrian Meadows said almost gleefully: ''Well, Martin, she certainly fixed you there.''

''Yes, I think she did.''

Rao Chaudri appeared to present himself with diffidence to Alicia. Lalor appreciated the handsome young Mahratta's intervention though, after several minutes, Chaudri's eyes were still only for her. She, in turn, seemed quite taken with his poise and ease of conversation. Lalor glanced at her secret and devoted admirer, Adrian Meadows. To his amusement he detected in those brick-red features, with their alert blue eyes and sunbleached eyebrows, growing alarm.

An unseen gong boomed softly and the British guests were gathered and shepherded into an adjoining room. They entered another large room with cushions clustered in circles on carpets about a central open space of polished mosaic tiles. Tall, polished brass stands holding oil lamps gave off a scented smell. The Rani led Wentworth to a middle group of cushions by an open window and began disposing her party about her. Rao Chaudri ushered Alicia, Lalor and Meadows towards her and Mazumdar brought Alexander and Felicity Skene and Francis Gordon; Frederick Dunlop had insisted, with some obduracy, on remaining in the cantonment. The Rani gave Lalor a strange, questioning look and abruptly pointed to the cushion at her left side. Adrian Meadows, waiting for no direction, plumped down beside him, for the obvious reason that Alicia was sitting opposite with the attentive Rao Chaudri. Alexander and Felicity Skene sat across from the Rani and Sir Julian and Mazumdar sat at the Director's right hand. Francis Gordon lowered himself on to a cushion between the Vazir and his wife, a dumpy, motherly woman in a brown sari who sat with downcast eyes but Felicity Skene quickly rallied to his support.

When they had settled down, servants padded in with silver

decanters of wine and Lalor and Meadows refilled their goblets thankfully. Lalor was agreeably surprised to see that the Rani took a slim glass of wine and then observed disapprovingly that the Director declined and asked for water instead. The water could do him far more harm than the wine. As if in accord with his diagnosis, a doleful pair of musicians sitting in a far corner began a soulful dirge with sitar and drum.

Throughout the meal the Rani ignored Lalor and confined herself almost entirely to the Director, Skene and Mazumdar. However, he was well-occupied with Alicia, Rao Chaudri and not least, the talkative, irrepressible Meadows who was constrained to notice the Rani's pre-occupation elsewhere and whisper in his ear: "She's still cooling off, old boy." The meal, appetising vegetable soup and a chicken curry not too fiercely hot for newly-arrived British digestions, was excellent and served with faultless organisation. It was all so different from some native courts he had known during his service.

When the dishes had been taken away and they had washed their hands, the Rani spoke to him suddenly. "I am told that you are Irish, Captain Lalor."

"Yes, I am."

"I hear that the Irish are also an oppressed race."

"Also?"

She was looking at him impassively. That blank mask had slipped over her face again and her dark eyes seemed almost uninterested. But he noticed that she kept her voice low and confidential. And she had picked her moment well. On either side of them was animated conversation, even laughter.

"Meaning that you too are oppressed by the English?"

She smiled, slightly bitterly he thought. "Now I do not think that I said that, Captain."

He nodded and fell back on a philosophical vein that came useful to him when he wanted to be obtuse. "Too true. The trouble is that the English language can be a trap to us foreigners—it really all depends where you put your also's and too's."

"Then at least you will admit that you're a foreigner serving with the English—even if you will not say whether your nation is oppressed?"

"Again true. But I do have an advantage. You see, the Irish understand the English whereas the English don't understand the Irish."

"Then it is very possible that we have much in common?"

She spoke with quiet emphasis, her eyes searching into him. He retreated into formality, slightly on guard. "Rani, if we are comparing the disturbed state of the Company's army, I really don't think that the English Crown has any worries about its Irish soldiers, whether those serving in English regiments—of which there are a great proportion—or in the Irish regiments as a whole. That hardly indicates hostility between the two nations."

"Come, Captain Lalor, you know far better than I what men will do for pay. To be fed and clothed, to be given a roof over their head and regular money—what temptation for a poor people. Look at the Company's Army—no shortage of recruits, I am sure."

He remained silent and reached for his wine. As he drank, he felt those dark eyes boring into him. He placed his goblet down and said bluntly: "With respect, Rani, I think you are confusing Queen's regiments with the Company's. Irish regiments are loyal."

"As long as they are not stationed in Ireland? And I am sure that this is well-arranged that they are not—at least, when trouble is in the wind. As we know to our cost here, the English think a long way ahead. They are not fools."

He had to smile. She was clearly no fool, either. But she did not give him even the glimmer of a smile in return. She was serious. He decided to be equally forthright. "Is there going to be trouble here for the English—or even the Scots, Irish and Welsh as well—from the sepoys?"

She did not change expression. "How should I know? I am not in the Army."

"I can't believe," he said gently, "that anything goes on in Jhansi that you are unaware of."

"The Army is closed to me. You seem to forget that my Jhansi has been annexed and the garrison is here to keep us in order. The only communication I have are instructions what I am to do next."

He decided to press on with his probing. They still seemed to be talking in confidence. A loud murmur of conversation was going about them.

"But what if the garrison is disaffected and you are of similar mind?"

"Who said that I am disaffected, Captain Lalor?" she asked sharply but there was no rancour in her voice.

"I withdraw that," he said quickly, "I'm sure it's quite the wrong word. Shall I say that you're unhappy about being under British orders, just as a number of sepoys in Delhi appear to be also?"

"You must not put words into my mouth. You're a soldier and not even seconded to the political administration, certainly not a lawyer. You should know that my long dealings with the Company have given me a suspicious legal twist of mind.''

''I'm sorry,'' he said innocently, ''I've an elder brother, Tom, who's a lawyer in Ireland and I'm beginning to sound like him. What I really meant with my original question was that you must hear through your household what are the rumours sweeping the bazaar. That's all I'm asking.''

She smiled. ''You must never believe all the stories going through the bazaar, Captain Lalor, as then you could become only totally confused. You well know that also.''

Sir Julian Wentworth then spoke to her and she turned away to listen to him. Lalor drank deeply and meditatively from his goblet again. Had she been sounding him out or was he just a convenient, selected target for her to vent some of her bitterness? A certain amount of planning and forethought had gone into whatever it was that she wished to do. She had placed him beside her so that she could talk to him and she had clearly done some investigation into his background. It still could have been all merely fortuitous, he told himself. She had positioned him at her left hand because he was Sir Julian's Military Assistant and she was probably a thorough hostess who found out all about unfamiliar guests.

He became conscious that a silence had surrounded him. He was somewhat surprised and embarrassed to find Alicia staring questioningly at him and Rao Chaudri smiling almost secretively to himself. Adrian Meadows leaned confidentially against him and whispered: ''That was a long chinwag, Martin. What are the state secrets?''

''The Rani is frightened that an Irish regiment may be stationed at Jhansi. I was sympathising with her.''

Meadows laughed heartily and even Alicia smiled but Lalor thought that Rao Chaudri still eyed him speculatively. The young courtier gave him some unease. Was it because his English was so fluent and accentless and that he exuded a rather superior charm? Behind that elegant veneer, did he really hate those whose manners and ways he had so perfected, Lalor wondered.

As he drank more wine, wild, almost violent music burst out. The torpid apathetic pair of players in the corner had been reinforced by another six musicians with both string instruments and drums. To the louder and more emphatic rhythm, ten dancing girls swept into the room and swirled about in the open central space. Their black eyes were heavily ringed with khol, their black hair shone with lacquer and white teeth gleamed between red lips. Flimsy muslin covered oiled, smooth dark skin between silk pantaloons and scanty bodices barely containing their full breasts. Bangles clashed about their bare feet and arms as they danced.

"My word, Martin," Meadows said softly, "what beauties! This is really something."

The music started in a slow, insidious tempo and the nautch girls swayed gracefully to it. Almost imperceptibly, its beat and volume began to increase. The strings became more strident and vibrant and the drums throbbed louder. The dancers, their bodies glistening, seemed drugged as they writhed in unison and responded to the rhythm. After several minutes they swung about and solely faced the Rani's party with their swaying ranks. The music was now even more intense. Lalor, as he looked up at the girls, suddenly realised that they were now all watching him as they danced. Had he imbibed too much wine? He wondered as he reached out and drank more but he had a hard head and he knew it was not that.

The music stopped as abruptly as it had thrust into life and the dancing girls fled with a clash of bangles and a waft of cheap perfume mingled with perspiration. In the silence that followed, the Rani turned to him with a faint smile.

"Captain Lalor, I think you enjoyed the girls. Do tell me which one you liked and she will be yours."

He found himself blushing, for some extraordinary reason. All eyes were on him as her voice had carried in the hushed atmosphere. Had she instructed the dancing girls to keep looking at him? Why was she singling him out?

"Thank you, Your Highness," he found himself saying, "but they are all so beautiful that I couldn't choose between them."

She laughed. He felt irritated. She was clearly enjoying herself.

"But you cannot have the whole lot!"

"Then it must be none. For I cannot hurt the other nine by selecting one."

"I will see that the girls hear what you have said. This will at least comfort everybody except the girl who thought she should have had you—which will be each one of them."

He took a deep breath. Before he could respond, she turned away to a rather bemused Sir Julian Wentworth. Gradually, the conversation about him picked up again. He looked across at Alicia but she avoided him rather obviously to talk to Rao Chaudri.

"Personally, old boy," Adrian Meadows said to him with his usual disarming frankness, "I think the Rani has taken a shine to you. Those nautch girls were never in the race."

To his relief, Meadows' words were lost on those about them.

After they had drunk coffee, the Rani and Sir Julian stood up and whole assembly rose. The British went about to take leave of their Bundela hosts. Lalor thought that Mazumdar, though taciturn and bleak, was an honest, if somewhat unyielding, character. He was not sure about Rao Chaudri but was drawn to his easy charm and intelligence. The Diwan and Kotwal were negative bureaucrats who looked hesitatingly at the Vazir before they spoke.

When his turn came to say goodbye to the Rani, he found her again distant and appraising but her handshake was strong and warm.

"Goodbye, Captain Lalor, I enjoyed your company. I like a man who can laugh at himself. These are rare in India."

"Thank you for your hospitality, Your Highness, which was delightful. I appreciated both the wine and the food, and as you know, also the dancing girls. However, I must warn you that the Irish are a modest race and easily embarrassed."

She laughed and warmth came into her eyes. As quickly, she became serious and withdrew her hand. "I hope we shall meet again," she said simply.

She turned away and he knew that he was dismissed. He moved off after the others who were filtering slowly from the room as their hosts stood patiently back. He heard Skene say: "Let's go back to my house, Sir Julian, and have a wee dram before your ride back to the cantonment."

"Well, gentlemen, that was a pleasant evening. Far better than I ever expected. What did you make of it?"

The Director was slumped in the same chair in Alexander Skene's sitting room that he had occupied that morning, gripping a whisky and soda. Sitting around the room were Lalor, Skene, Gordon and Meadows. Felicity Skene had discreetly taken Alicia away to her bedroom to talk.

"All I make," said Skene in his Scots way, "is that Lalor should be Superintendent here. He seemed to be drawing far more out of the Rani than I have done for a long time."

"Yes, what was that all about?" Wentworth asked curiously.

Lalor answered blandly. He believed in telling the hard truth, however sensitive the question. For some reason, his Irish accent seemed to thicken as he spoke. "She was asking—or telling me, I forget which—if it was not true that the Irish are oppressed by the English."

His Army colleagues burst out laughing. Even the austere Sir Julian permitted himself a chuckle. Lalor looked at his brother officers in some wonderment, though he had fully expected this reaction. They were all his friends, the best type of British officer, and Skene and Gordon were even Scots. Yet how could they be so blind to what was happening in Ireland, especially out in the rural countryside?

The Director quickly became his familiar searching, analytic self again. "Which means that she really considers herself oppressed by us. I'm very taken by that woman, quite impressed. She's intelligent and she knows what she wants. But I do wonder if she's just not too clever and was acting out a part for us tonight?"

"In that case," Skene said, "she was certainly acting out another part this morning. While I wouldn't say she was hostile, I also wouldn't say she was over-cordial. I stand by my original assessment of her—she's honest with us but is very sour over how events, dictated by us, have turned out for her. Wouldn't you agree with that, Gordon?"

"I would—and without hesitation," Francis Gordon said.

"Then I will tell you, gentlemen," the Director said with some gravity, "that, stemming from our discussion at midday, I did inform her tonight that as I am now returning the way I came, I will speak with Henry Mercier at Indore about her whole case and see what we can do between us to re-open it with Calcutta, using the considerable lever of her loyalty to us in these troubled times. This does put quite a different complexion on things. I must say that this seemed to cheer her greatly."

Spontaneous murmurs of approval came from Skene and Gordon. Another round of whiskies was summoned by Skene and the introspective Julian Wentworth looked mildly pleased with himself when he took his replenished glass from the bearer.

"So you've decided not to continue the tour any further, sir?" Skene asked.

"Yes, Lalor has persuaded me that it would be wise—discretion before valour and all that—for us to retrace our steps now, to go no further. I do this with utmost reluctance as I don't like admitting defeat, which of course this turning-back is. But I accept Lalor's advice fully. I realise that if I press on to Gwalior, Agra and finally Delhi, I become another worry and embarrassment to the authorities. Moreover, while I don't mind hazarding my own life—and I appreciate with all humility that you fellow servants of the Company and the Crown have been doing this for many years in the call of duty—I would be risking my only child's life and, frankly, having lost her dear mother only two years ago, this is too much. We will leave Jhansi the day after tomorrow."

"You've made the right decision, Sir Julian," Gordon said bluntly. "Get back to the safety of that Bengal European battery at Mwow as soon as you can."

"I do think that you're over-dramatising the situation, Gordon," Skene said tersely. "All that has been said is what we all know, that there is serious strife in the Delhi area. We have peace, law and order in the Jhansi Agency."

Skene looked angrily down at his glass of whisky. Fortunately, Wentworth was not listening and appeared to be contemplating his own thoughts. Lalor was about to intervene when Adrian Meadows, who had been sitting silently in an armchair in the corner, flushed with wine, suddenly said: "What do you really think of the Rani, sir?"

"Well, I must say I enjoyed this evening immensely. Possibly because she made such a change of face—if that's the right phraseology as I didn't see her face this morning but it didn't seem to be too favourable then—and also I felt that I had something worthwhile to say to her. As I've said, my boy, she's sharp, perceptive, definitely very competent—I'll grant her that."

"And good-looking, too, sir," Meadows said with the solemnity of the half-drunk. "Wouldn't you grant her that also?"

"If you like the exotic, Meadows," Wentworth replied with a slight touch of asperity.

Well, I certainly do, thought Lalor. He remembered her physical nearness and the hint of her perfume. Possibly too exotic for Threadneedle Street but a beauty in the Bombay Presidency and Central India.

The Director stood up. "Gentlemen, the hour is getting late and the escort has been waiting long enough for us. Thank you again, Skene, for your hospitality. I must collect Alicia and say goodbye to your wife."

Later, as Lalor rode through the Orchha Gate beside the carriage carrying Wentworth and Alicia out into the darkened countryside, he thought about the evening. It had been not only curious and intriguing but strangely pleasant, as even the Director had admitted, but he was still not clear in his own mind about some of its nuances. He was, however, certain about one thing. Lakshmi Bao, Rani of Jhansi, was a remarkable woman.

In the cantonment he escorted the Director and Alicia to their bungalow and said goodnight. He then waited, mounted and armed, by the edge of the maidan for Adrian Meadows to return from falling out his troop in their lines and supervising the return of their weapons to the arms kote. Eventually, two riders came cantering towards him through the night and he recognised, as they neared, Rissaldar-Major Sikander Khan with Adrian Meadows. This was a sign of the times, he brooded. Meadows was slightly bibulous but well in control of himself. Sikander Khan was accompanying the subaltern to protect him.

Lalor wished the veteran a cheerful goodnight and saw Meadows to his bungalow where he yielded to the usual temptation of one final drink. They sat out on the darkened verandah tunicless in perspiration-soaked shirts, drinking whisky pani. The conversation developed rather one way as Meadows dwelt at some length on 'how stunning' Alicia had looked that night, allowing himself in passing some fulmination against 'that smooth Hindoo', Rao Chaudri. Somewhat to Lalor's relief, he barely mentioned the Rani and Lalor, only half-listening, pondered about her as he stared out into the still, warm night.

An hour later, when he lay down on his bed in his own bungalow, he found himself still thinking of her.

4

The Dak Bungalow

The morning sun was already hot and Lalor, without glancing at his watch, knew that the time must be at least 9 o'clock. He stood on the road by the officers' bungalows with Joseph Evans, the Anglo-Indian civilian official from the Commissariat Department, looking across the maidan to the cavalry lines. The baggage wagons, drawn by oxen, were lined behind them, laden with trunks, tentage, camp stores and all the impedimenta of a burra sahib's progression through India.

Lalor noticed again that the small host of camp followers who accompanied them—bearers, cooks, drivers, bhistis, tent erectors, sweepers—were still unusually silent.

"Are they glad to be leaving?" he asked Evans casually.

Evans nodded. He was a correct, precise man in his late twenties, good-looking in a serious way with his sallow, clean-shaven face and well-brushed black hair and always impeccably turned-out. He was dressed in a brown lightweight frock coat and brown trousers, white shirt and, even in the summer heat, a black tie knotted with some flourish, with a white sunhelmet squarely placed on his head. Lalor liked him. Though he was difficult to get to know, he was efficient and Lalor had soon realised early in the tour that he understood both British and Indian minds equally well.

"Yes, they are, sir. They are nervous of this place."

"Why?"

Evans' grey eyes regarded him. "You know the reason as well as I do, sir. There is going to be trouble with the sepoys."

Lalor turned away and stared back over the deserted, bare maidan. They were now seeing the first tangible manifestations of that trouble. Their column had been due to leave at 7 o'clock, as the wagons had been almost fully-loaded the night before, but Adrian Meadows and his troop had not appeared. At 7.20 a.m., a shaken Meadows had ridden back to him to say that there was some trouble in the cavalry lines, that the 14th Irregular Cavalry were refusing to parade and this was affecting his men. Dunlop and Campbell were there, talking to the sowars, and he had to get back. After he had galloped off, Lalor reported to a non-committal Sir Julian Wentworth and a silent Alicia and he asked the Director to remain in his bungalow until the situation had settled down. Alexander and Felicity Skene, also Francis Gordon, were with them to say goodbye and he left them drinking tea in a sombre atmosphere. The worst of those few minutes was the stark fear on Felicity Skene's face. Her two young daughters, Megan, aged 9, and Kate, 7, were with her and they had stared wide-eyed at him as he recounted his sobering news.

As he stood there, he wondered if he should also go to the cavalry lines. He decided against it. He was a stranger to the sowars and his duty was to be near the Director. He thought over the events of yesterday, their last twenty-four hours in Jhansi. After a final round of discussions with Skene, Gordon and Dunlop, Wentworth had given a reception that evening in the small Officers' Mess of the cantonment for all British and Anglo-Indian officials and their wives, and, later, a farewell dinner for both the political and military officers of the garrison and their ladies. Some insidious spirit of depression and apprehension had penetrated both gatherings. Perhaps it was the packing-up and loading of the baggage of the Director and his party, with its implication of retreat to a more secure area. Both the drinks party and the dinner had little jollity and several long silences.

Lalor strolled along the column of wagons with the tactful Evans, pausing now and then to try to make a joke with groups of servants who sat, huddled and watchful, on the loaded chests and boxes, waiting to leave. He could see that they were tense. He got little response from his somewhat laboured sallies.

After another half-hour, Meadows came in sight between the barrack hutments, riding at the head of his troop. Relieved, Lalor sent Evans to inform Wentworth and Skene. As Meadows came closer, he saw that Dunlop was with him. The garrison commander's heavy features were grey with strain as he reined in.

"I'm sorry about this, Lalor. It's our fault. Our fellows have got at your lot."

"Don't worry. A couple of hours in our journey won't make much difference."

Dunlop dismounted ponderously. Lalor looked up at his young friend, Meadows. The young subaltern was silent and almost in a state of shock. Sikander Khan, alongside him, was grim-faced. Lalor scanned the ranks of the sowars behind them. He saw a mask of angry truculence over each dark face.

Dunlop spoke softly and urgently. "The 14th have got the bug all right—the one from Delhi, I mean. It's more than that bloody cartridge. As I've said before, they've accepted it and the Enfield rifle without any obvious trouble, though I suppose there was the usual backstage muttering. I'm sure it's this Mughal business at Delhi. They're all Muslims, as y'know. And now they've infected your troop."

"Is there anything we can do?" Lalor said to him. He felt sorry for the big, worried man whose ordered world, against all his steadfast predictions, was now crumbling about him. "We could easily stay on for a few more days to help you steady things down. I'm sure that the Director would readily agree."

Dunlop shook his head. "No, get out of here while the going is good and before your men get fully contaminated. We may depend on it that the sepoys of the 12th are also unreliable. Let me say, however, before you go, that your Rissaldar-Major played a blinder over there. It is not only thanks to him that your fellows eventually paraded but it's on what he said, with his personality,—the way he put it over to all of them—that I'm hoping we can get the 14th normal again. Ironically, it's our Rissaldar-Major, Kala Khan, who's the trouble-maker. I'll have to speak to Skene what we do about him. He should be arrested at once. Then we come to the usual dilemma whether this precipitates more trouble."

Sir Julian and Alicia emerged from their bungalow with the Skenes and Francis Gordon and came over to them. A sad round of farewells, charged with emotion, began. Felicity Skene and Alicia were near to tears when they embraced and both did cry when the Director's daughter stooped to kiss Megan and Kate, standing stiffly frightened and holding their mother's hands but stemming their own tears. After Wentworth, Lalor shook hands with Skene, Gordon and Dunlop. They all smiled grimly and tried to joke wryly. With the upset Felicity Skene, he discarded formality and kissed her on both cheeks. He could feel her slight body trembling under his hands. He bent down and softly kissed the two little girls.

When he moved away to Paddy, his horse, he was not feeling too composed himself. Emotion, as well as drink, was the curse of the Irish, he reflected. Frederick Dunlop came with him and said bitterly: "I intended to give you a troop of the 14th for at least three days but you'll now be far safer without them."

"Yes, I think that we've got enough of our own fellows to watch."

Wentworth, looking strained and even paler, mounted his horse and Lalor helped Alicia into her saddle. In their journeying, both father and daughter preferred to ride, rather than jolt and bump in an unsprung cart over the baked, rutted tracks that purported to be roads.

Lalor then mounted and with his nod to Adrian Meadows ahead, the train of Sir Julian Wentworth, Director of the Honourable East Indian Company, moved off to retrace its path back to Indore by way of Saugor. Slowly, the column advanced to the main gate of the cantonment and Wentworth, Alicia, Lalor and Meadows moved their horses to a flank to wave back finally to the small, pathetic group in the distance outside the officers' lines.

As if to emphasise the deteriorating situation, the guardroom was conspicuously devoid of any quarter guard turning out. The lone sentry had the grace to present arms.

They had been slowly moving for about two hours across the hot, dusty plain and were nearing the banks of the Betwa river. All four of them, Wentworth, Alicia, Lalor and Meadows, were riding together at the head of the column to escape the dust. Little was spoken as Jhansi and its Fort dropped behind them. Lalor felt that some pre-ordained doom was hanging over the small band that they had left behind and he sensed that each one of them considered that they were running away, abandoning their own kith and kin.

He was deep in his own misgivings when Adrian Meadows called to him across the Director and Alicia who rode between them. "Look, Martin!"

He stared through the heat haze in the direction of the subaltern's pointing arm. Ahead, about six hundred yards away on a long ridgeline overlooking the Betwa beyond, was an immobile group of horsemen.

He said nothing until they had gone another hundred yards or so and more by intuitive guess than eyesight, he said to Wentworth: "I believe it's the Rani, sir."

"What the devil does she want?" Wentworth muttered sourly. "To deliver an ultimatum, now that we're seen to be having trouble?"

"I doubt it," Lalor found himself saying without hesitation. "The Betwa is where her territory ends—or at least, where it used to end. She's probably only here to wish you Godspeed and, perhaps more importantly from her point of view, not to forget to remember her to Fort William."

The horsemen began streaming down the slope of the ridge, led by a rider dressed all in white. They came at full gallop down the track to confront them. Lalor halted their own column and they sat in their saddles, watching the cavalcade pounding towards them. The figure in white, though swathed from head to toe and wearing a veil against the dust, was obviously a woman. Behind her came about fifty Rohilla riders, armed with match-locks, lances and big, curved tulwars.

Lalor watched the Rani as she approached with some admir-ation. She came at them headlong and then reined in dramatic-ally, skilfully controlling a wild-eyed brown mare. She lowered her veil, her dark eyes gleaming. What a sense of theatre, he thought.

About and behind her armed retainers drew up with equally-practised horsemanship on their rough, scrubby mounts. He looked at them quickly as she waited for them to subside, jostling in a growing cloud of dust, before she spoke. They were a wild, tough-looking lot who looked as if they would do anything for pay. Their leader seemed to be a big hulking fellow with a henna-tinted uncombed beard and a large broken nose who, festooned with cartridges, sat a big rawboned white horse behind the Rani.

"I come to bid you a final farewell, Sir Julian," she called to the Director, "and Miss Wentworth, too, of course. You are about to leave Jhansi for the territory of the Raja of Orchha. He is no friend of mine, so we must part here."

Wentworth mumbled a few words in formal reply. Lalor looked at him. He appeared worried and pre-occupied. Perhaps he was unwell.

"I am sorry that you are leaving Jhansi so soon," she went on in her deliberate way, "but I am sure that you have made the right decision to return to Indore. Please give my best wishes to Colonel Mercier."

Wentworth cleared his throat. "Rani, you probably hear things quickly. You will know that we have had some trouble in the cantonment this morning with the cavalry. Is this going to get worse?"

"I have told you before, Sir Julian, I have no inner knowledge of what your sepoys intend to do. They certainly do not take me or my servants into their confidence. However, if you have had trouble this morning, I am enough of a realist to suspect that more is coming."

"In that event, I hope that we can rely on you," Wentworth said bluntly.

"Of course you can. But what use am I? I only have these rascals but they too would slit my throat and rob me if I failed to pay them."

Wentworth gave a half-sigh, half-groan, and lapsed into silence. The Rani began chatting easily with Alicia and shook hands with her and an unusually-subdued Adrian Meadows. She nudged her horse over to Lalor and gave him her hand in that firm grip.

"Take good care of Sir Julian and Miss Wentworth, Captain Lalor. And, of course, yourself."

"That I will, Your Highness. And thank you again for your grand hospitality."

He thought those discerning eyes gave him a rather enigmatic look. "I hope you may come back to Jhansi to enjoy it again."

She turned abruptly and held out her hand to Wentworth. "Goodbye, Sir Julian, and a safe and pleasant journey. You may rely on me to do what I can for the British in Jhansi. I hope that I will be seen to be acting in our common interests. That I will remembered for what I try to do and that a proper understanding will be taken of me and my cause."

"You may depend on it," the Director said fervently. "What you do for us, if mutiny does break out here, will not go unforgotten or unrewarded." He paused and a touch of steel came into his voice. "You may also be certain that anything you should do against us will not go unnoticed."

She smiled slightly but Lalor saw that her eyes were not humorous. "Sir Julian, we Mahrattas have cause to know the ruthless streak in the British when their interests are at stake. So, I am sure, do the Sikhs and the Muslim princes. I am what we call in Hindi *ganyi*—a person who weighs up all the factors and follows the course that is likely to win. There is going to be much trouble for the British all over northern and central India but I believe you will be victorious in the end. Why? Because you will still have enough of my countrymen fighting for you to enable you to defeat those hostile to you. In matters of power, we both speak the same language and understand each other. Goodbye, Sir Julian, and I wish you and your party well."

The Rani kicked her horse and rode off, followed by her Rohillas. She glanced briefly and expressionlessly at Lalor before she replaced her veil and moved away. He stared after her as she cantered off in the direction of Jhansi city.

"What an extraordinary woman," Alicia Wentworth murmured, echoing all their thoughts. "I really don't know whether she likes us or not, whether she is on our side or not."

They watched the Rani and her band until they came obscured in their own dustcloud. Meadows waved his troop on and they went on at a comfortable walk, the baggage wagons lumbering behind them.

"I think she unveiled herself then in more ways than one," Wentworth remarked to his daughter, "when she said that she is pragmatic, that she would support the winning side."

"As a sporting man," Lalor said drily, "I'd say that means only that she would shift her bets very easily. She's prepared to say now that she reckons we'll win through in the end, especially as your reviving the Jhansi issue with Colonel Henry Mercier means so much to her. But later, if we continue to have more disasters?"

"I take all that," Wentworth said soberly, "but it's the immediate plight of our friends in Jhansi that concerns me greatly now. If she can do anything to help them over the next few days and weeks, that at least will be something. Do you think I offended her by being so direct with her before she went off?"

"Not at all. She may not have expected to hear your warning but she's no fool, as I think we're all agreed. She would certainly have known that's what we're all thinking."

Slowly they approached the river bank, passing the long ridge where the Rani had waited for them. At the ford, Lalor asked Meadows to stay with him on the home bank while Sikander Khan with half the troop escorted Wentworth and Alicia across the river. He used the pretext that Joseph Evans, riding in rear with his wagons, might have difficulty in getting some of the more heavily-laden over the ford. He really wanted Meadows alone. They sat their horses out of earshot of the sowars, watching the first wagons enter the water.

"Is there any ringleader in your troop who caused this trouble this morning or had they all just been swayed by the 14th?"

Meadows's youthful red features were taut and concerned. "We have a ring-leader alright, Karim."

Lalor knew Karim quite well. He was one of the three daffadars, a big, well-built man with a heavy moustache who was clearly the best soldier and the strongest personality in the troop after Sikander Khan. He had just gone across the river with the half-troop accompanying Wentworth and Alicia.

"I was sorely tempted to place him in close arrest this morning," Meadows went on, "but decided against it. We had enough problems on our hands without inviting more."

"How many of your troop do you think are reliable? Presumably Sikander Khan is as loyal as ever? Dunlop was most appreciative of his efforts this morning.''

"Solid as a rock. Still the splendid fellow he's ever been. The other two daffadars, Nurus Salam and Jahangir, are right behind him. But apart from them, there's probably only half a dozen or so of the youngest sowars who've just joined. They'll obey explicitly anything that Sikander Khan tells them.''

"Good. When we reach the dak bungalow at Madhupur this evening, we'll work out a plan for the worst case. The first thing is to ensure that the cart carrying the reserve ammunition is driven straightaway into the compound before they have time to think about it. We'll keep the ammunition with us in the bungalow.''

Adrian Meadows looked at Lalor gravely. Over the last few hours, his young, enthusiastic features had matured perceptibly. "It doesn't look too good for old Dunlop, Campbell, Taylor and Matthews, does it? You heard what the Rani said. Things are going to get worse before they get better.''

"No, it doesn't. Nor for Skene and Gordon. Or for Felicity Skene and her two little girls and the other families.''

Meadows groaned in despair. "Oh, God, I feel so bloody helpless. We seem to be scuttling out of it all and leaving them to it. But what really humiliates me is that we couldn't really have helped if we'd stayed. My own men are now suspect.''

Joseph Evans was now coming to the riverbank with his rear wagons and Lalor prepared to leave. He said to his young friend lightly: "Cheer up, old son. When I was your age, I lost a whole company of the 86th in Lahore in '46 after Sobraon. I found them all dead drunk two days later but, managed, with the help of the priest and the pipe-major—who was also drunk but could hold his drink with some style—to round them up. My colonel was not pleased. I'm going now to brief Joseph about the ammunition cart. You get over to Sir Julian and Alicia and keep an eye on Karim. I'll rejoin you when all the wagons are across.''

They reached the dak bungalow at Madhupur late that afternoon, hot and tired from the long, slow march along the dusty road that wandered through forest alive with chattering, active groups of monkeys and colourful birds. In the bigger clearings, spotted deer grazed and once, a family of wild pig trotted across the road ahead of the column to disappear into the thickets. The route was almost deserted, except for one large camel train that came plodding towards them with a string of merchants and their guards who had banded together for safety against raiding parties and marauders from the more unscrupulous minor rajas and thakurs through whose territory they passed. At noon they had halted and dismounted to drink tea and eat fruit under the shade of some large tamarind trees. Normally, Lalor would have sent Joseph Evans ahead with a small escort as advance party but he dare not split their party after the morning's incident. Though the great trees of the forest gave some shade as they moved south, the sun burned down scorchingly out of a cloudless blue sky and they were all dehydrated by the searing heat and drenched with perspiration when they arrived at Madhupur.

They had stayed at the dak bungalow, a convenient day's march away, en route to Jhansi. For the uncertain situation they now found themselves in, its lay-out suited Lalor well. The bungalow was big and spacious with six bedrooms and a wide verandah in front and in the small enclosed area of the servants quarters and kitchen in rear was a well. At a radius of eighty yards from the house, a stout stone wall some nine feet high boxed in the grounds which were covered in dry brown grass with one solitary tree at the back. Into this compound, as well as their personal baggage and cook's wagons, was quickly run the ammunition cart, true to their plan, and its precious contents unloaded into the bungalow. Only their personal bearers and the Goan cook were allowed inside the compound. Meadows's cavalry troop and all the other camp followers, with the wagon train, were encamped in the nearby forest.

After tea, brewed with some urgency by the bearers, Sir Julian and Alicia retired to their bedrooms to rest after the journey. Lalor, Meadows and Joseph Evans sat out on the verandah in cane chairs, still drinking their tea. All the wagons for the bungalow had now been driven out empty of the compound gate where a sentry already stood.

"Tonight," Lalor said, "the three of us will stand guard in turn, starting at dusk and ending at first light when we'll stand to. We'll close the gate. The sentry stays outside."

"What about Sikander Khan?" Meadows asked him. "Do you want him in here with us?"

"No, he's far too useful outside with the sowars where he belongs. If there is any agitation, hopefully he might be able to damp it all down. However, we'll have to brief him carefully that if the situation is getting out of hand, he's to fall back on us here, bringing all the loyal men he can muster."

"That could be dangerous, sir," Joseph Evans said in his quiet, precise way. "It could be a trick. Or we could be rushed by the rest at the same time."

"I know. But we've got to trust Sikander Khan explicitly. He's really our only hope. The three of us—four, counting Sir Julian— don't stand a chance by ourselves. We'll need every rifle we can muster. Adrian, you and I had better go and have a chat with Sikander Khan now. The sooner we get the picture straight with him, the better.''

In the woods outside, they picked their way through the trees past sowars busy making camp for the night. Lalor sensed a strange, uneasy atmosphere at once. All the men ignored their presence by busying themselves ostensibly with their bedding rolls, cooking pots, saddles and harness. A sullen controlled hostility from the silent sowars permeated the still forest glade.

They found Sikander Khan talking to one of the daffadars, Nurus Salam, by the animal lines. Both senior NCOs stiffened to attention and saluted as they came on them.

After an exchange of pleasantries, made as jocularly as he could, Lalor said curtly: ''Well, Rissaldar-Major, is all tek hey now or are we to expect further trouble from the men?''

The grey-bearded veteran looked tired and old, as if he was feeling every day on his twenty-five years' service. His fine brown eyes studied Lalor fatalistically. ''It all rests on how this sickness we have got from the 14th Cavalry develops, sahib—whether it goes away or gets worse. There could be a sudden fever tonight or tomorrow. But I hope—and pray—that it will pass away.''

Lalor nodded. ''I agree that the next twenty-four hours are all-important. If the worst does happen, how many men do you think would rally to us.''

Sikander Khan hesitated. ''About nine or ten, sahib, but that includes Nurus Salam here, Jahangir and myself.''

''I understand from Mr Meadows that Daffadar Karim was the instigator of the difficulties this morning. Should we arrest him and put him in chains, or will that just provoke trouble?''

''At this time, Captain sahib, Karim seems to have the ears of the sowars, I do not. It would be wise not to challenge him openly until we get to Saugor.''

Lalor felt sorry for the old soldier. The old bull elephant had been displaced from the leadership of the herd by a younger, stronger bull.

''Meadows sahib and I both appreciate very much that you are risking your life remaining loyal. You may be assured that this will not be forgotten, Rissaldar-Major—and you too, Daffadar. Nor will Karim's activities.''

Sikander Khan looked steadfastly at him. ''It is my duty, sahib. The Company Bahadur is my life. It had made me what I am, a man of standing and substance in my village by the sweet waters of the Sutlej. When I retire in two years' time, I wish to look back with honour on my service. If I fall doing my duty, so be it.

Inshallah.''

"Inshallah. Two last things, Rissaldar-Major. Firstly, ensure that the sentry roster on the compound gate is made up with the sowars you can trust. Karim may well notice this but he will have to show his hand very openly if he tries to challenge your authority on a purely military matter. Secondly, and most important, if you sense danger, if you suspect that trouble is about to break out, come to us in good time.''

Lalor shook hands with the two NCOs and returned their salutes, as did Meadows, and he and the subaltern walked back through the bivouac lines of the cavalry troop. Sunset was now near and the light filtering down between the tall forest trees was fading. Smoke drifted up from the cooking fires of the sowars but none stood up as they passed and all averted their gaze. Lalor looked hard for Karim but he could not see him anywhere in the wood. He was rapidly coming to the conclusion that the simplest solution was to arrest Karim, even at the risk of stimulating sudden violence, and send him packing down the road to Saugor under a trusted escort commanded by Sikander Khan. Once the ringleader was summarily removed, he knew, from his long Indian experience, that the unrest would fizzle out.

When a very young sowar at the gate saluted him and Meadows stiffly, Lalor knew that shrewd old Sikander Khan had already anticipated him. In the bungalow, where Joseph Evans sat in a cane chair on the verandah with a rifle across his knees, he called for Amin to bring him some hot water and he stripped off to sit in the tin tub positioned in a bedroom to scour the dust and grease of the hot day from him. For several minutes, he soaked and luxuriated there, sipping a whisky pani that the attentive Amin brought him, and the weariness of the day gradually ebbed from him. Then he dressed and armed quickly as he wanted Meadows and himself to join Evans on the verandah for a precautionary stand-to at the now imminent dusk.

The three of them were sitting there, armed and silent, when Wentworth and Alicia emerged dressed in fresh clothes and looking more relaxed after their rest and a bath. However, Wentworth looked grave when Lalor told him about his talk with Sikander Khan.

"Do you agree, Joseph, with what Sikander Khan says?" Lalor said to Evans, "that the next few hours could be crucial whether they shake off the Jhansi infection or allow it to bite further?"

The Anglo-Indian stiffened in his chair. Though he was of officer status, his retiring and deferential nature had always compelled him to avoid a dak bungalow where the rest of the party stayed overnight. He preferred to sleep outside in his tent where he could keep an eye on the natives and the baggage'. Now their crisis had precipitated him into their close, intimate circle.

"Well, sir, as you know, I hear the men in the baggage train talking. Though they are all aware that I speak several of the main languages, for some reason—especially when they're excited or frightened—they forget or don't care. Perhaps, sometimes, they wish me to hear things without having the burden of telling me directly. There is no doubt about it—the drivers, sweepers, cooks, all of them—are expecting trouble. They can smell it in the air. You've probably noticed how jumpy the bearers are—even yours, sir, Amin, who I think has been with you for many years and on campaign, too. Sikander Khan is certainly right—tonight and tomorrow are the danger periods. After that, with some luck on our part, the hysteria from Jhansi might die away."

"That settles it," Wentworth said firmly, "I insist that I do a watch tonight. I have a pistol and I know how to use it."

Lalor accepted his offer appreciatively. Four men would allow double sentries which was realistic. He thought that Alicia was looking pale and worried. When she caught his gaze, she gave him a faint, reassuring smile.

"And we have a spare pistol from the ammunition wagon which you can have," he told her gently. "Just for your self-defence. Nothing will probably happen at all, especially if we cry wolf loud enough. Adrian will show you how to use it."

Dusk was now setting in and Adrian Meadows walked forward to the gate, spoke to the sentry and then closed it, positioning its two heavy crossbars. They all sat on the verandah, armed and expectant, as the darkness slowly enshrouded them.

They sat in the twilight for a long hour, barely talking and then only in whispers. All about them was still and quiet, except from the nocturnal life of the forest stirring. Gradually, they relaxed. Wentworth called his bearer and insisted that they each had a burra whisky pani. Alicia had a glass of white wine. They talked quietly, watchful of the gate and the nearby walls.

When they had finished the drink, they went into dinner, leaving Adrian Meadows, who had insisted he should remain as the sentry on the verandah. The meal was excellent, well-cooked roast mutton, and they were all hungry after the exertions and tensions of the long day, but conversation was subdued as they ate from the fine china, white gleaming tablecloth and elegant glassware that was so typical of the faceless efficiency of trained Indian servants in the field. Then Evans went out to the verandah to relieve Meadows and the subaltern's presence, his normal bonhomie recovered from the knocks of the morning, did stimulate talk.

Afterwards all of them drifted back out to the verandah with their coffee and sat there again in the warm gloom. The scene could not have been more tranquil. Gradually, moods relaxed and the conversation became animated and general. Occasionally, the whooping, discordant howling of jackals came through the other cries of the forest but, otherwise, the night was still and placid.

They had been on the verandah for about two hours when, just as Wentworth was consulting a heavy gold watch and Lalor was thinking of starting their guard roster, wild cheering and shouting erupted outside the compound from the woods where Meadows's troop was bivouaced. They froze and listened. The tumult went on for several minutes, then a ragged volley of shots rent the air. Lalor stood up, as did the other three men, gripping their weapons. As the firing continued, he motioned Meadows and Evans and walked quickly to the compound gate. His two companions slid away the crossbars. He stood with drawn pistol while the gate was opened a man's width.

The sentry, a tall, lean young man, was standing outside, his rifle at the ready. The whites of his eyes gleamed askance at Lalor in the dark.

"What is the noise about?" Lalor asked him in Urdu.

"A horseman has arrived in camp, sahib. From the north."

From the direction of Jhansi, Lalor thought grimly. "And who was this horseman?"

"A sowar of the 14th Cavalry, sahib."

Lalor did not hesitate. "Go to the Rissaldar-Major and tell him I wish to see him here at once. I will guard your post."

The sentry disappeared into the night. Lalor turned to Meadows and Evans who stood covering him with their rifles. "Well, you heard that?"

"It all sounds like good news for Karim," Adrian Meadows said bleakly, "and bad news for us."

They stood in the darkness, tense and alert, listening intently. The noise from the sowars' camp died away. The resulting silence seemed even more sinister and menacing. Not a sound now came from the encampment. Lalor stood with his loaded pistol in the narrow gap of the slightly-opened gate which Joseph Evans, his rifle slung, held ready to slam shut. Meadows was a couple of yards behind with a levelled rifle.

Several minutes later, they heard running footsteps approaching and they stiffened. To Lalor's challenge, a familiar voice answered hoarsely: "It is I, Sikander Khan, sahib. I have seven men with me."

"Advance, Rissaldar-Major, but only one man at a time."

The burly figure of the veteran NCO came out of the night and he moved wordlessly through the slightly-ajar gate. One by one, in quick intervals, his companions slipped in after him. Daffadars Nurus Salam and Jahangir were there, with five young sowars, including the erstwhile sentry. Joseph Evans closed the gate sharply after the last man and thrust the two bars into position.

Sikander Khan, with his men crowding silently about him in the blackness, spoke at once without waiting to be questioned. "I have come, captain sahib, with our true men as you have told me. A messenger from the 14th Cavalry has just ridden in from Jhansi. Today, Captain Dunlop sahib, Lieutenants Campbell and Turnbull have been killed by the sepoys. Lieutenant Taylor has been badly wounded. All the English sahibs, their memsahibs and children, and other loyal people, have taken refuge in Jhansi fort."

5

Mutiny

About an hour elapsed before they heard Karim's voice calling in English from beyond the compound wall.

Lalor was sitting with Adrian Meadows in the darkness of the open hall of the bungalow, watching the barred gate. He had disposed Sikander with his loyal men in the two front bedrooms whose windows covered both the front and the flanks, while Julian Wentworth and Joseph Evans watched the back wall from the two rear bedrooms. Alicia was with her father.

"Meadows sahib, it is I, Karim. I wish to speak with you."

"I hear you, daffadar," Meadows shouted back, "Say what you have to say."

"The time has come to join the heroes in Delhi. Our brothers in Jhansi have sent us the word. Give us the ammunition and we will be gone."

"You are talking mutiny, Daffadar Karim. This could mean your being blown away from a cannon. I will pretend this once that my ears have not heard you."

Karim's mocking laugh came over the still night air. "But it is I who have the power of the gun now, Meadows sahib. I wish you no harm as long as you do not interfere with our destiny. Let us in the gate to take the ammunition and we will leave you in peace. If not, I cannot answer for the ardour that seizes our soldiers who only want to serve the Emperor Bahadur Shah, the restorer of our greatness. Remember you have Wentworth sahib and the young memsahib in your care.''

Meadows looked quickly at Lalor who shook his head. ''I warn you, Karim. Anyone trying to enter this compound from now on will be shot. And I will deal with you tomorrow morning.''

The unseen Karim laughed. He shouted out in Urdu obviously to men about him and cries of derision came from them. He called back in English again: ''It is I who must deal with you, Meadows sahib. Do not worry about any lack of sleep tonight. Everlasting sleep will come to you soon.''

Adrian Meadows leaned against the doorway suddenly drained. ''Well, that's it. My own men.''

Before Lalor could say anything, the bulky figure of Sikander Khan appeared by them. ''The running dog! He has eaten Company Bahadur's salt for fifteen years.''

''Do you think he will attack tonight?'' Lalor asked.

''All things are possible to a sick mind, sahib. But I think he will wait until daylight. It is one thing to talk the men into insubordination but quite another to persuade them to attack you. They will probably celebrate into the night which will allow him to sway them into doing what he wants.''

They stood together, listening and looking out into the darkness but now there was only silence. Karim and his men had retired from the wall. Lalor went to the rear bedroom where Wentworth and Alicia were. He found them sitting in the unlighted gloom, with Wentworth watching out the open window. The night visibility was still clear, with the compound wall gleaming whitely over the open grass, but it was going to be a dark, moonless night.

Alicia was in a chair by the bed and she stirred when he came in. He picked up a wicker chair and sat by Wentworth at the window.

''You heard all that, sir?''

''Yes, clearly. Karim has a fine parade ground voice and quite good English.''

''We think—or, more accurately, we hope—that they won't trouble us tonight. They'll probably have a party, chewing bhang while Karim works on them so that they should be fairly bad-tempered and aggressive tomorrow morning. We can certainly expect trouble then. Then again, in their unpredictable way, they might just pull out and ignore us completely. They've got quite a lot of loot already in the wagons outside. They could easily decide to clear off to Jhansi and join their friends there as soon as possible.''

''Oh, those poor people in Jhansi,'' Alicia murmured. ''I keep thinking about Captain Dunlop and those young men. And the families. Felicity and her daughters.''

''At least we know that the Skenes and the other families are in the Fort.''

''What do these men want from us?'' Wentworth said wearily. ''Surely not to take our lives, merely out of some blind blood-lust?''

''They want, without any shadow of a doubt, the ammunition. Though modest—it's only reserve stocks for fifty men—it's like gold-dust if you have a rebellion in mind. Already Karim has now done enough to be tried and hanged for mutiny and he knows that. I don't think he's a fellow that does things by halves. In for a penny, in for a pound. If the real purpose of this extraordinary neurosis that seems to be creeping about the countryside is to kill as many Feringhees as possible, our eradication could be several feathers in his pugri. He's an ambitious man, I would guess, and we know that he's very capable. Many successful mutinies have been led by intelligent, disgruntled NCOs and Karim fills that bill. He could go far—or at least I'm sure that this is how he reckons it—in any national rebellious movement, if that's what in fact we're contending with.''

''Admirable military advice, as always, Captain. Again, I think you are right—at least I fear so.''

''I'm sorry. Sound military advice doesn't always mean that it should be paraded without some tact and forethought. I certainly shouldn't have spoken so gloomily in front of Alicia.''

She said, almost heatedly: ''We must be told the truth, Martin. You are not to hide unpalatable facts from us, so don't blame yourself. Perhaps our real hope is that if we can defy them for two or three days, they may go away.''

''It's possible,'' he said unconvincingly. ''Especially if we can inflict casualties on them. More exciting news from Jhansi could also draw them off, though this could be at the expense of our people there.''

He sat talking with them, attempting to take their minds away from the awful situation confronting them in this dark, still night in the middle of an Indian forest. But he found it hard to divert his own mind. Alicia, with her wavy, fair hair, colouring and boyish figure reminded him of Cecilia, though she was several years older, and a certain dryness of fear for her cloyed his mouth. Both the Director and his daughter, from the ordered surrounds of a house in Westminster and a country house among the leafy glades of Surrey, could be slaughtered like animals by bhang-crazed mutineers before they saw another Indian dawn.

After a while, he excused himself and rose, gripping his rifle. He crossed over to the other rear bedroom where Joseph Evans sat by the window, his own rifle resting against the sill, watching out. The Anglo-Indian stood up respectfully but he thrust him down and took a chair himself.

"Well, what do you reckon, Joseph?"

"I heard Sikander Khan talking to you and I agree with him. Karim will have no qualms about attacking us as he knows he has dug his own grave already. He's the only committed mutineer that we've got proof against at present. He now has to persuade the sowars to join him irrevocably by murdering us and he will need a little time to do this."

They chatted on in a relaxed, desultory way. Lalor's liking for this reserved, self-contained man grew. When he stood up to go, he said: "Are you sure you don't want one or two of Sikander Khan's men here with you to spell you for a drop of sleep?"

"I would feel better if I was alone. I'll catch up with some sleep tomorrow morning."

"Joseph, I'd be obliged if you'd keep an eye on Sir Julian and Alicia as well as covering your own arc of observation and fire here. We assume we'll be engaged by a rush through the main gate but there will probably be a subsidiary attack from the rear or flank also."

"I am honoured by the task, sir," Evans said stiffly. "You may rely on me to do my duty."

Lalor knew he would, too. He turned to go but Evans spoke again. "Whatever is to happen to us, sir, I would like to take this opportunity to say how deeply I appreciate the courteous way in which you have always treated me."

Lalor was strangely moved. All the many humiliations that the Anglo-Indian official had stoically endured in the tight, hothouse protocol of John Company's India were behind those words. He nodded and left.

He went out the back to the small enclosed area of the kitchen outhouse and the servants' quarters. Here, in the small quadrangle, lay the precious well, now covered with its wooden top. He entered the kitchen where, by the light of a dying wood fire, Amin, Peter Rosario, the Goan cook loaned from Government House, Bombay, and the four other bearers squatted. They stood up when he appeared. Amin gave his slow smile, Peter, a tall, thin, solemn man with white grizzled hair and dark, dignified features, was his usual grave self, but the others looked almost numb with fear.

After some small talk to try to thaw them out, he said quietly: "You know that there may be trouble tonight or tomorrow morning. If there is, stay in here away from open windows and doors and you have nothing to fear. These thick walls will protect you from any bullets. Keep the chattis inside the house full of water. And those on guard will need tea during the night."

"Of course, sir," said Peter in his measured English.

"*Je, sahib,*" said Amin. The others remained frozenly silent.

"*Tek hey?*"

"*Tek hey, sahib,*" Amin assured him.

"Tea will be served, sir," said Peter again in English, rather as if he was still in Government House, Bombay. "What time do you wish breakfast in the morning?"

Good old Peter, Lalor thought. The best of three cultures had rubbed off on him admirably. The Rosarios from distant Portugal whose name his family had taken from some gravestone had been instrumental in giving him a faith which regarded this life as a passage through some joys and some tribulations before reaching final peace, the English had given him phelgm and a sense of the occasion, and his own Mother India that mysterious art of improvisation common to all cooks and bearers in coping in all conditions.

"About two hours after first light. Before then we will be standing to."

Back in the bungalow he walked through the darkened hall to find Adrian Meadows sitting in a cane chair, a rifle cradled across his knees, looking out at the compound gate and the front wall.

"And are you *tek hey*, young Adrian?"

"*Tek hey*, old soldier. And you?"

"Also *tek*. Mind you, I'd much prefer to be sitting in the Mess at Bombay contemplating the old 86th's imminent return home. However, let's you and me now get down to thinking how we're going to organise the night."

It seemed to Lalor that he had barely sunk into a deep sleep after Meadows had relieved him towards the end of a long night when he felt his arm being vigorously shaken. He heard the subaltern's voice coming distantly but urgently to him.

"Martin! The gate's burning!"

He sprang up with his rifle from the floor by the bungalow doorway where he had been lying and saw the flames licking up the gate. Meadows was already shouting the stand-to. He ran to the bedroom where the Wentworths were. The Director stood grimly by his window with his pistol at the ready. Alicia sat on the bed taut-faced, gripping the heavy Service pistol that Meadows had found for her with both hands. She looked so young. He could only grip her shoulder reassuringly before he hurried next across the passage to the room where Joseph Evans now crouched by his window, his rifle at his shoulder. He called hurriedly to him that he would be needed at the front if the assault was heavy and no threat came from the rear. Lalor then rejoined Meadows at the doorway and they waited to bring their rifles up in the standing position. He had seen that Sikander Khan and his men were manning the windows of the two front bedrooms on either side, ready and alert.

The sun-dried timber of the gate roared into a sheet of flame, sending sparks cascading upwards. It was still dark, at least half an hour before dawn. The blackness of the forest loomed about the compound wall and only the fiercely-crackling fire disturbed the quiet, ebbing night. As he stood there, Lalor grudgingly admitted the dramatic psychological effect of Karim's destruction of the gate by fire. He also worried whether the fire was a diversion to draw them fixedly to the front. He looked anxiously beyond the verandah roof at the dark sky, hoping for the first flush of light from an approaching dawn.

The last timbers of the gate fell down in a haze of glowing remnants and smoke. An eerie silence of several minutes was shattered by wild cries and screams coming from outside the compound on the road. A shadowy press of bodies surged through the gutted gateway, gripping rifles and sabres. In the dim light it was difficult to pick out individual targets but while they were still packed just inside the gate, beginning to run forward, Lalor shouted: "Fire!"

Their ten rifles roared in unison and their balls thudded into the charging mutineers. The close, leading ranks of the attackers crumpled or spun backwards. Lalor called for Joseph Evans, abandoned his empty rifle and sprang forward to the verandah steps with drawn sword and pistol in each hand. Meadows joined him, similarly armed.

The volley at fifty yards had caused the charge to waver. Some sowars paused to grab their wounded comrades, others halted to bring their rifles up to the aim while a few ran on towards the verandah with drawn sabres. Lalor could now see their hate-distorted faces as they came at him and Meadows. He and the subaltern could only try to buy time while Sikander Khan and his men reloaded.

The halted mutineers with their rifles at the shoulder now began to fire raggedly and the balls whistled by. Fortunately, they fired at the windows as the leading ranks of the charge had now almost closed on Lalor and Meadows. As he and Meadows fired their pistols at point-blank range, dropping two attackers, he heard a rifle and a pistol fire by his shoulder. Evans and Wentworth had arrived.

The survivors of the charge were then on them, snarling with exertion and battle fear. Lalor fleetingly realised that they were fighting to the death with men wearing red tunics. He parried the violent, downward-slashing sabre stroke of a big, heavy-moustachioed mutineer and drove forward with his own sword. The sowar shuddered and gurgled, his eyes starting from his head, and he fell limply away. Lalor clubbed blindly about him with his pistol while he dragged his sword out of the dying man's body. The fight became a bloody, hacking melee. Another full volley rolled out from the bungalow windows. Sikander Khan's men had reloaded. A few seconds later, Wentworth, followed by Evans, fired again also.

This renewed burst of defending fire, savagely effective at such close range, destroyed the attack. More mutineers fell, screaming. Through the noise and confusion, somebody shouted and the survivors began running away. Lalor and Meadows suddenly found themselves leaning on their swords, panting, no longer fighting for their lives. In the poor light, through the sweat pouring down his face and smarting his eyes, Lalor thought that he saw Karim lurching away, clutching an arm, but he could not be sure.

When the last mutineer disappeared out the gate, Adrian Meadows swung on him, his blue eyes sparkling with exhilaration. "We're unbloodied and unbowed, Martin," he cried panting, "and we hold the field."

Lalor stared at the scene before them. Six dead bodies lay there, still and inert while ten wounded writhed about, groaning. Four of the wounded began dragging themselves painfully away to the open gate. He looked behind him. Julian Wentworth stood on the verandah, still gripping his empty pistol rather dazedly. Joseph, holding his rifle proudly, smiled easily. He had liberated himself from something.

"Check on your lads, Adrian. Then get some out to collect the weapons, covered by the others. We all ought to get under cover again as soon as possible. This is not the time to stop a lucky potshot from somebody who hasn't given up."

Alicia stood in the hall when he went in, looking deathly pale. Her father embraced her and she clung to him, burying her face in his chest like a small girl.

"We did it, Alicia," Lalor said gently. "Everything is going to be all right."

She looked at him, still clutching her father. Her eyes were brimming with tears. "It's a miracle that you've all survived," she said.

Lalor looked at himself, then at Meadows standing by him. Apart from one slashed tunic sleeve, from which a thin trickle of blood ran down his arm to his hand from the graze of a sabre tip, he was unharmed. Meadows was completely unscathed.

Sikander Khan appeared from his bedroom firing position. He looked even more grey and old. He stood to attention before Adrian Meadows, gravely composed.

"Daffadar Nurus Salam is dead, sahib," he said calmly, as if he was delivering a parade state. Lalor liked the way he reported to his own officer, rather than to himself as the senior. One of the troop had fallen in battle and this was a regimental family matter.

All the intoxication of his first action fled from the subaltern. "Oh, God," he muttered, and hurried into the bedroom.

Lalor followed him. Nurus Salam lay stiffly on the floor, his face shattered where a ball had hit him squarely. Not a pretty sight, thought Lalor, very much bloodied and bowed. He glanced at Meadows who stared down at the smashed features of a very loyal, if not very bright, NCO of his first command.

He pulled a sheet off the nearby bed and covered up the body. "Requiescat in pace, old son," he said privately to himself. He said aloud to Meadows. "Now we must do something about the enemy's dead and wounded."

"We are ready to shoot the wounded, sahib," Sikander Khan said stonily.

"Rissaldar-Major!" Adrian Meadows gasped, glaring at him.

Lalor took the subaltern's arm. "Don't worry. It's a way they do things out here, especially if a friend turns into an enemy." He turned to the old senior NCO. "I don't think we should waste ammunition on them, Rissaldar-Major. They're no use to Karim any more. And also, he'll have to look after them."

Outside the room of Nurus Salam's death, Alicia clutched gently at his flapping sleeve where a steady stream of blood was now running down from the shallow slash on his arm.

"Martin, let me attend to that arm."

"In a moment, dear."

He walked past Joseph Evans, standing watchfully in the doorway, and went down the verandah steps along the path to the gate. He stood in the faint light of the coming dawn among the corpses and moaning wounded. He shouted out in Urdu. "Karim! Karim! It is I, Lalor. I must speak with you. You want your dead and wounded. If we can speak together, you shall have them."

He called out his message patiently several times. He knew that rifles in the bungalow covered him fully. Eventually, Karim's voice answered him hoarsely within a close range. He sounded just outside the compound wall by the destroyed gate.

"This is Karim. Speak!"

"We must meet face to face, Karim. Only you and I."

A pause.

"Why?"

"I've been telling you, Karim. You can take your wounded away, otherwise we will have to kill them. And we have one dead man, your comrade, Nurus Salam. We want to be able to bury him here in the compound in peace. I am proposing a truce. But let us not talk over a wall."

Silence. Lalor was about twenty yards from the compound entrance. He could hear that Karim had men with him as he could hear faintly some excited conversation. They only had to appear at the entrance firing and he knew that he did not stand a chance. His hope was that they were confused and shaken by the repulse of the pre-dawn attack.

At last Karim spoke again. "You and I will meet and talk. By the gate. But neither of us will be armed."

Lalor swore softly to himself. His first plan had failed. He had coldly intended to kill Karim as soon as they met. He was convinced that if Karim was destroyed, the mutiny within the troop disintegrate.

"Then I will meet you outside the gate without weapons. But none of your men must be nearer than the corner of the compound wall. Is this agreed."

"Yes."

Lalor reluctantly returned to the verandah to lay down his pistol and sword and walked back down the path to the charred remains of the gate. The crawling wounded had the greyness of deep shock and pain as he came by them. They halted their laborious retreat to lie back suppliantly to beg for the mercy that they knew that they would never get from Sikander Khan. Though it was not in his nature to ignore suffering, he barely gave them a glance. Perhaps it was their uniforms, their red tunics, that quite simply tipped any balance against sympathy.

He went forward to the gateway, feeling very exposed. But only Karim was outside the wall, leaning against it, looking shocked and sick. He nursed a bloody left arm. A shot had rent through the muscle.

The mutineer leader glared at him, defiance and hatred in his bloodshot, pain-filled dark eyes. "Well, we meet. What are your terms?"

"Only what I have said already. You recover your wounded and dead. Allow us to bury Nurus Salam."

Karim said through gritted teeth. "I agree."

Even in his detestation for the mutineer, Lalor grudgingly admired the implacable hostility. The man was a leader.

"Then we must have a truce for three hours."

"Three hours. After that we will come at you again. And this time we will destroy you all."

"Only unarmed servants are to enter the compound to bring out your casualties."

"Three hours only." Karim snarled as Lalor turned away. "Then we will truly avenge our dead."

As the new morning gathered heat as well as stark light, Sikander Khan's sowars dug a grave near the back wall of the compound under the shade of its solitary tree, a krishnachura, incongruously cheerful with its bright red blossom standing out against its verdantly green, delicately tapering leaves. Into the hole near its base was lowered the sheet-wrapped body of Daffadar Nurus Salam, 1st Bombay Cavalry, from an obscure village in the Punjab, killed in the service of Company Bahadur, loyally fighting for his pay and the pension he would now never enjoy. Sikander Khan intoned verses from the Koran over the grave, answered by Jahangir and the other sowars. Lalor and Meadows attended the burial and so did the bearers. Wentworth, Alicia and Joseph Evans remained in the bungalow, on guard against the uneasy truce.

Exactly three hours after his meeting with Karim, for Lalor had just consulted his watch, the mutineers poured through the gate again, yelling and screaming their fury. There must be about twenty of them, he calculated, as he opened fire. They halted and fired their rifles from the standing aim. Their volley crashed into the front of the bungalow and Lalor, by the doorway, thought he heard deep groans from one of the front bedrooms. But none of the assaulting mutineers attempted to close with the bungalow. There was no spirited charge with sabres. Nor did they try to re-load laboriously in the open. Five of them had fallen from the defenders' fire and they began withdrawing hurriedly, dragging their casualties with them.

A chilling thought suddenly struck Lalor. Where was Karim? He was not with this frontal attack. And where were the others of the mutinous troop?

He ran down the hall to the rear bedrooms. He entered the Wentworths' post as the Director fired his pistol and hit the bearded, sweating face of the mutineer clambering up through their window. Alicia screamed as the man fell back, his features squelched into red pulp. Lalor could see through the window a stream of attackers running across the dry brown grass and others dropping over the wall. He heard Joseph Evans' rifle fire resoundingly in the other room across the hall.

As another mutineer swung up to the window about to climb in, Lalor leapt across and smashed his rifle butt into his face. The sowar dropped away limply. He stood by the window and fired his pistol into the sea of faces jostling to get up at the window. He dropped his pistol and drew his sabre. He shouted: "Adrian! Adrian!"

He was hacking away with the furious dementia of a desperate man when he was hit by what seemed a tremendous thump and he found himself crashing drunkenly back across the room. He fell down. Instinctively he clutched his left shoulder and became hazily aware that his hand was sodden with sticky, warm blood. He heard Alicia screaming again. Her fear-filled blue eyes stared down at him as she bent over, trying to gather him in her arms. He was vaguely conscious of men running into the room and knew with great relief that Adrian Meadows was now countering the assault through the window. Then he passed into a deep, black oblivion.

6

The Siege

When Lalor regained consciousness, he gradually realised that he was lying on a bed. Alicia Wentworth's features came slowly into his blurred vision. She was sitting by the bed, gazing anxiously at him. As his scattered wits slowly collected and he was able to focus, his immediate impression was that she looked utterly tired and strained. Her normally vibrant blue eyes were dulled and had shadows of fatigue, and her clothes were stained with perspiration. As he stared at her, she smiled slowly. A burden of worry and weariness seemed to lift from her.

"Oh, thank God, Martin. You've pulled through."

His mind struggled to come out of its limbo. He became aware that he was in the rear bedroom that she and her father manned but there was no sign of Wentworth. It was quiet and hot, probably mid-morning.

"How long have I been like this?"

"This is the third day. We thought you were going to die."

He groaned. Though his shoulder wound was throbbing painfully, his cry came from sheer mental anguish. He sought out her hand and she eagerly grasped his.

"What has happened?"

She bit her lip. He could see that she was almost exhausted.

"Daffadar Jahangir and one of the troopers were killed in the same attack when you were wounded. The mutineers made another assault later that day but we just held on again. But Sikander Khan soon died of wounds after that. Sikander Khan bravely rushed out and fought with his sword until he was struck down. It was almost as if he was inviting death. Adrian said the old man was so shamed by the mutiny that he was heartbroken. Since then the mutineers have been content to snipe away at us—they have made firesteps about the walls. All the bearers have deserted us, except your Amin. Peter, the cook, is still with us. They have both been helping me to nurse you—to change your bandages, to wash you, to give you water."

She dipped a glass into a chatti of water nearby, cradled his head with her other arm and held the glass to his lips. He drank several glasses greedily. He had a burning thirst and as he swallowed the cool water, confused memories came back of lost, delirious hours when his wound caused fever to consume him. The green serene landscape of his beloved Ireland, the dusty plains and searing heat of the Punjab of his youth in the Sikh Wars and the freezing trenches and bloody chaos of Sevastopol had all been there, jumbled and distorted. More disturbing were the long-dead faces of old comrades, with whom he had toiled and fought, who came flooding back into his disordered mind, trying to say something to him.

He lay back, wiping his unshaven face with the back of his hand.

"We've managed to bury our dead each night," she told him in a small, tight voice, "and we let their sweepers come in again to take away their casualties after the last attack."

"You're a brave girl, Alicia," he told her softly.

She smiled tremulously. "I'm not, you know. I'm almost sick with fear. The only thing that holds me together is that I know I mustn't let you all down. But enough about me. I must tell the others you're back with us."

She called out to her father. A few seconds later, Wentworth came into the room, a belted pistol at his waist. He was gaunt and haggard-looking. He gave Lalor a faint, warm smile.

"I told them you were too tough to expire on us."

"I'm sorry to be lying here so uselessly."

"Don't worry. We're holding our own. They're now content to retain their distance."

"How's the food and water?"

"No problem. Peter is imperturbable and our emergency stock of food is going well, especially as, regrettably, we have fewer mouths to feed. Alicia probably told you about Sikander Khan? A gallant old soldier to the end. And your bearer has been first class."

Wentworth sat wearily down on a chair and went on: "I wonder how long Karim intends to bottle us here? He's lost quite a few men allegedly for a few boxes of ammunition, though probably he meant to kill us all the time."

Adrian Meadows entered, carrying his rifle. Though he looked tired also, he gave Lalor a cheery, affectionate grin. Lalor found himself oddly pleased that the young subaltern was clean-shaven and as presentable as his sweat-stained uniform allowed.

"Well, old soldier, you've fooled us again."

"It's this fellow who's feeling the fool."

"And you yourself warned about those lucky potshots."

"Never one to practise what I preach. Far too difficult."

"Alicia says you were pretty lucky for all that—I mean, if you do have to be hit. The ball passed right through you, and not all that far above your heart."

"I'm sorry to hear about Sikander Khan, Adrian. I hear that he was determined to go out splendidly and he did. Also about Jahangir and the sowars."

Meadows nodded sombrely but said nothing. He sat down in a cane chair, holding his rifle upright between his knees. Julian Wentworth was also silent, deep in his own thoughts.

From the bed, Lalor studied the three anxious-looking people about him. Each sat nervously on the edge of their chair, tense and apprehensive. He could see that sheer tiredness was beginning to dull and slow down their mental processes. A certain despair from the hopeless feeling of being trapped, with no apparent way out, was also probably affecting them. Was there no way out? He tried to get his own somewhat bewildered mind to think through their predicament.

He asked Alicia for some more water. When she propped his head against her breast, he drew some strength from her comforting nearness. When he lay back, the despondent silence went on. Eventually he said: "You must try to smuggle Amin over the wall tonight with a note to the Rani at Jhansi. With Dunlop dead, Skene shut up in the Fort, she is our only possible source of help."

They stared at him. Julian Wentworth said: "Will he go?"

Lalor nodded. "Of course we don't know how well Karim covers the wall at night but I would suspect, at this stage, not very well. They'll regard us as being cornered here and reserve the daylight hours for their maximum effort as this means good shooting. Amin is sensible and reliable and has a very good chance of getting through. Joseph would be the best choice, he speaks the language and could disguise himself—but you need every rifle here."

"How do we know that Amin won't cut and run, if we do get him over the wall?" Meadows asked. "I'm sorry to say that, Martin. I think Amin is a good chap but human nature is what it is."

"That's a fair question which, of course, has no proved answer. But I do feel that Amin is our only hope. So is the Rani at the other end."

"Perhaps the Rani's in the same difficulties as Skene from the sepoys," Wentworth said cautiously. "We may just be pinning all our hopes on an illusion."

"True, sir, but what other option have we? Jhansi is our only possibility. Saugor is just too far away. If Amin could get over the wall in the early hours of tomorrow morning, with money to buy a horse, he could be in Jhansi by noon. If relief could be organised right away, this could be here no later than first light next morning. Assuming the Rani can and will help us, she has enough men to handle Karim's casualty-stricken lot."

When Lalor saw the hope in Alicia's blue eyes, almost transforming her features to their old enthusiasm as she looked excitedly at her father, he wondered if he had gone too far. Wentworth sat in his chair, gripping its arms tautly, staring at Lalor on his bed. In his feverish, light-headed condition, Lalor watched him with some tolerance. This was a board meeting on policy that the Director of the East India Company had not experienced before.

"I think you're right, Lalor," Wentworth said finally, "an appeal to the Rani is not only an excellent idea but our only one. This is really a chance for her to prove herself—if she's able. I'll write to her at once."

"Then you're agreed that Amin goes over the wall tonight?"

Wentworth looked at Meadows who quickly glanced at Lalor.

"You're the military commander now, old son," Lalor told the subaltern. "Sir Julian is consulting you for your opinion. I'm laid low for a while. But give me a couple of loaded pistols. I want to contribute something."

He suddenly felt very tired. It was the heat, the strain of thinking coherently and talking and also the fever burning through him. He closed his eyes, vaguely aware that Alicia was watching him intently. For a while, he could hear Wentworth and Meadows discussing his proposal about Amin until, gradually, their voices drifted faintly away.

Again, his sleep was delirium-ridden and nightmarish. He awoke once when the room was in darkness, bathed in perspiration and disorientated as to where he was and what was happening to him. Then he saw the slim, slight figure of Alicia in a chair by the window with her back to him, watching out. He wanted to call to her, to talk with her, but somehow the words would not come. He gazed at her for what seemed a long time. She did not stir from her vigil. He slipped again into the healing, soothing nether world of sleep.

When he awoke again, pale light was seeping into the room and the sounds of noisy bird life in the surrounding forest told it was dawn. Alicia was curled up in the chair by his bed, asleep. Adrian Meadows had taken over the post by the window, his rifle propped ready on the sill as he stared out into the new day.

Lalor lay there silently. If only he was not such a helpless burden. He began to convince himself that he was now feeling much better. His mind did seem clearer. Perhaps the fever had now consumed itself. But his shoulder wound still ached sickeningly and he felt so weak.

Meadows shifted in his seat and glanced back. When he saw that Lalor was conscious, he grinned wanly. "Well, I suppose we should say good morning, Martin. I hope it will be for us. Have you come to for good now?"

"I think so. Let us say that I've every intention of trying to remain on duty without falling asleep."

"You slept through quite a bit of firing yesterday afternoon. We try to return their fire when we can—if we've got a target—just to remind them we still mean business very much."

"Then you must give me those pistols I asked for. If you move the bed by the window and prop me up, I can cover part of the side wall and some of the back."

"Well spoken, old chap. Fighting talk from the 86th. You'll be a great help if you could do this. We're all getting rather short of sleep."

"Did you get Amin away?"

Meadows's fatigue-drawn features brightened. "I knew there

was something good to tell you. Yes, we did, a couple of hours ago. It took ages but I think he's made it. With a bit of luck, he should be on the road to Jhansi now."

"If we don't get his head thrown back over the wall this morning."

"That's still very much on the cards." Meadows looked reflectively out into the sunlit compound. "What are we going to do if no help arrives from Jhansi, Martin? Just stick it out?"

"What else? I only hope Karim gets tired of the game before we do."

Meadows was silent for a while, then he looked back at Lalor in a guilty, embarrassed way. "Do you think we should do a deal with Karim? If we gave him the ammunition, he might well go away. I'm only thinking of her."

Lalor looked at the sleeping Alicia. She seemed so young and vulnerable. He saw the dark circles about her eyes, her tousled hair, her stained clothing.

"We've been over this ground once or twice before, Adrian. Both Karim and we have gone too far down the road for compromise now. It's no longer a matter of six boxes of ammunition—indeed, if it ever was. Karim has murdered Sikander Khan and other former comrades, we have killed a number of his followers. It's far too late for either side to turn back, or even sideways."

Meadows flinched visibly. "I'm sorry, Martin, I deserved that."

Lalor regretted his curtness. "No, you're right as a soldier to consider all the options. And you're more than right to give full emphasis to what could happen to Alicia if we're overrun. I'm sure this pre-occupies each of our minds most of all. We can imagine the worry to her father. But what you suggest is not a practical solution, whether we like it or not."

"You know I'm not thinking of my own skin, Martin," Meadows said to him huskily.

"I know that, Adrian old son."

Fortunately, Joseph Evans appeared in the door and came forward, smiling as he grasped Lalor's good right hand. Lalor was taken by his air of easy confidence. He wore an open-necked, slightly soiled white shirt tucked into white duck trousers with a certain nonchalance enhanced by the purposeful way he carried his rifle. Gone was the stiff, withdrawn Anglo-Indian minor official who remained discreetly in the background. Joseph Evans was now an integral part of the tenuous defence of the dak bungalow, he knew he was fully accepted as that and he was content, even buoyant. Though as an intelligent man he must know, Lalor thought, that death was probably the only outcome

A Soldier of India

for them all.

As they spoke, Alicia awakened and smiled faintly. Joseph Evans went away and Julian Wentworth came in, looking visibly relieved to see Lalor's recovery. Adrian Meadows left also to allow the four surviving loyal sowars to see him. As his hand was pressed between both of their hands each time and their young, dark faces smiled simply through their fatigue, Lalor knew that somehow he had to find a way out of this trap Karim had them in. Quite apart from Alicia, he realised that they owed it to their loyal dead, to Sikander Khan and the others, to find some solution to save these young soldiers.

When the sowars had filed out, Julian Wentworth asked him seriously the same question that Adrian Meadows had posed. "What should we do, Lalor, if relief from Jhansi does not come?"

"I suggest, sir, that we cross that bridge in the usual way. Let's give Amin at least seventy-two hours from this morning. He may not have been able to get a horse."

"Lalor, you Irish are noted for your optimism. We must think about the realities that could happen."

"Then I will think, sir," Lalor said evenly, "and I will come up with a plan in the worst case. We all, at least, have plenty of time to think."

He did have the germ of a plan stirring in his mind but it was such a desperate, final throw that he preferred to keep it to himself for the time being. Instead, he went on to say: "Could you ask Peter to come in and give me a shave? If we are to go down, I'd like to be as well turned-out as possible. The old 86th would wish it that way."

The long hot hours of daylight gave way to a moistly-humid night. Then another day dawned on the dak bungalow. The pattern of that day was broadly the same as before: a random succession of sniping shots crashing into the side of the bungalow and the responding roar of a defender's rifle as he tried to hit fleetingly-exposed target ducking below the compound wall. But no assault came from the mutineers. It was both Lalor's guess and fervent hope that Karim was also ill from his wound and this accounted for the apathetic conduct of the siege.

Lalor was again a defender, though bedridden and immobile, armed with two pistols. He had his bed carefully sited broadside on to the window where he could watch a section of the wall obliquely. By pressing back on his propped up pillows he could shrink from observation and aimed fire from the wall.

Another night came and went and soon that morning five enemy shots had already hurtled through the open window to thud resoundingly into the far wall. One bullet shattered with dramatic effect a glass-framed print of young Queen Victoria hanging there, watching remotely with unseeing eyes the travail of her beleaguered subjects. As if in sympathy, a woodcut of snow-capped Scottish mountains and cool glens on another wall, upset by the vibration of the impact, crashed to the floor also. Poor Queen Victoria, Lalor pondered as he looked at the debris of broken glass and bullet-ridden print, it was to be hoped that her fall was not symbolic. Against these shots, he managed to return the fire once at the dark face and red-tuniced shoulders of a rifleman aiming over the wall but his aim was wild and he knew he had no hope, anyway, of hitting anybody with a pistol at that range. Still, it was important, he reflected, as Cornet Meadows had said to him, to show that they meant business to the last.

He rather enjoyed the occasional excitements of bullets thumping into the bungalow side or whistling through his window. It kept him alert and keen-witted. Moreover, he felt his strength coming back slowly. Alicia changed the dressing on his wound daily, cleaning it carefully with hot water supplied by the ubiquitous Peter Rosario, and he saw that the wound was a neat round hole where the bullet had passed straight through him, again as Cornet Meadows had informed him, just below the collarbone. He had been very lucky. If the wound stayed clear of infection, he could be on his feet soon.

From where he lay, with the others coming to see him from time to time, he was in a central position to observe the effects of the siege on his fellow defenders. For the first twenty-four hours after Amin's escape, morale in the bungalow rose infectiously. The bearer's apparently successful departure, Lalor's recovery and the desultory conduct of the siege all contributed to hopes of ultimate delivery. Adrian Meadows and Joseph Evans had each taken two of the loyal sowars under their wing and their effective mixture of leadership and comradeship lifted the young soldiers out of the depression that the deaths of their comrades, especially of Sikander Khan, and their continuing isolation against their own hostile countrymen had caused. Alicia smiled more easily now and was almost her former cheerful self. Only Julian Wentworth remained sombre and withdrawn and he worried Lalor. The incessant strain, with the heat, was wearing him down. At the bottom of it all, Lalor knew, was the awful fear eating away at him about what could happen to Alicia.

The watershed where half-founded hopes turned greyly back to realisation of the stark facts confronting them came at sunset on the third night after Amin had gone.

"He's done a bunk," Adrian Meadows said quietly as he sat

with him. "I don't blame him. He's a servant, we're of another race and religion, and this sort of thing is just not in his contract."

"Well, I've know him on and off for thirteen years, Adrian. He followed me all through the Sikh Wars, including Ferozeshah where we very well bloody-near lost that first day. The Sikhs are not known to be kind to Mussulmans. Except for two years in the Crimea and a year at home after that, he's been with me all the time and he's never let me down. Mind you, he's gone to save me, not the Director, or you, or Joseph. Possibly Alicia also."

Meadows shook his head in wonderment. "Martin, you're an incredible optimist."

"That's more or less what the Director told me."

"Martin, the chips are down. We're all coming to the end of our tether. You can't believe we're going to get out of this—except by one of those miracles you obviously believe in."

"Despair is a sin, Adrian. Something will turn up."

"Oh, really, Martin, there you go again. You sound like something out of that novelist, that new fellow, Dickens. Mr Micawber, wasn't it, in David Copperfield? Except this is not London with a few footpads, old boy, this is Madhupur dak bungalow surrounded by fanatical mutineers."

"Yes, I enjoyed that book. The Agent in Aden gave it to me because he thought that the 86th had acquitted themselves fairly well in that bloody awful place and I read it several times on the ship coming back to Bombay."

Lalor knew, however, that Joseph Evans, with the dark suspicions of his mixed blood, also thought like Adrian Meadows, though he was too polite to say so. Alicia, clearly affected by both of them, grew quieter and became introspective again. Fortunately, Julian Wentworth did not come near him but maintained his own solitary watch elsewhere.

He made a point of staying on guard all night. The darkness that obscured their observation and fire created the most vulnerable time for the defenders and he was puzzled why the mutineers did not try to take them then. Karim must be prostrate like him. To get the strength for his all-night watch, he slept for a couple of hours during the afternoon whose scorching heat made the mutineers comatose and inactive, and Alicia usually came to sit watch for him then.

That night, after Adrian Meadows had left him and he had eaten the vegetable curry and tea that Peter Rosario brought him, he sat alone again in his darkened bedroom, looking and listening out during the long night hours. A faint breeze rustled its way during most of the night through the forest but he knew it was too early for the rains. Somewhere, nearby in the forest, a frangipani tree with its white, yellow-hearted flowers, drifted a heavy scent over the night air and he was appreciative. He thought heavily about Amin. As he had told Meadows, the Kashmiri Mussulman had always been faithful to him and they had been in some tight spots together, though never any as desperate as this. He had trust in his bearer. However, he realised that other factors could prevent Amin from winning through. Jhansi was in the throes of mutiny and he could have been recognised by the sepoys.

With the long-awaited dawn they all stood-to and though this usually brought on a wild barrage of shots from various parts of the compound wall, as if the besiegers felt that they had to justify themselves with the new day, that morning was silent except for the birdcalls from the surrounding treetops. They waited in the silence tensely. When the light was strong, a voice called hoarsely to them from beyond the wall. It was Karim's, speaking in English.

"My patience has gone. I have been waiting for you to surrender and grant you mercy. Now I give you one last chance. Lay down your arms, give me the ammunition and you may go your own way."

Lalor heard Meadows shout back defiantly from the front of the bungalow. "Your leadership has gone, Karim. You're a wounded and sick man, as much use to those men out there as an old woman. If you have any wisdom left, you will go before loyal troops come to our aid." Meadows raised his voice. "Hear me, sowars. This man is leading you to your death, either at our hands or you will be hanged outright when we are rescued."

Karim quickly came back, almost choking into incoherence as he spat the words out. "You do not know the news from Jhansi as we do. Skene and all those who fled to the Fort are now dead. The patriotic sepoys and sowars are now in control of the cantonment and city. You are without hope. Surrender to me and I will be merciful."

Lalor took a deep breath. He believed Karim's tragic news. It was what he had been expecting but could hardly bring himself to admit it. Amin could hardly fare successfully in that turmoil. The Rani herself would be hard pressed.

After a pause while he obviously absorbed the shock of Karim's announcement, Meadows shouted back again. "There is no surrender here, Karim, just as we know there is no mercy with you. You must come and take us. We would welcome an assault led personally by yourself. Ayub, Khalique, Sattar and Ali Noab and I are waiting for you. We wish to avenge the deaths of Rissaldar-Major Sikander Khan and our other true comrades on you, you running dog, progeny of swine! Come and get us!"

Silence. Except for footsteps striding down the hall of the bungalow and Lalor found himself looking up at Julian Wentworth. The Director was even whiter than his normal sallow self. He was almost shaking with rage.

"Lalor, has Meadows gone mad? He's deliberately provoking that fellow out there!"

"Sir, I thought Adrian spoke splendidly. That's a young man of only twelve months' regimental service, in his first operational situation and one of some desperation, too, and he has not only acquitted himself in a first-class manner so far but that exchange with Karim—in my book—was excellent. We understood it, Karim understood it. My only concern is that I don't think many of Karim's men understand English. But we can soon rectify that."

Lalor spoke quietly but he was on the brink of aggression. The raw nerves of a sleepless night, Wentworth's outburst and the taut drama of their situation could easily have also pushed him into heated emotion but with some effort he restrained himself. Wentworth looked ill and exhausted, with dark shadows below his eyes. His clothes hung more limply than ever over what had already been a very spare frame. Not only was he feeling the heat but he probably now had dysentery, too.

"Have we all gone mad?" Wentworth asked, almost talking to himself. He spoke with some difficulty. Tiredness was slurring his words. "We want those fellow to go away. We don't want to challenge them to attack us again."

"True, sir, that is the best solution. Except that I know, Joseph Evans knows, and—to my great delight—a beardless young subaltern also clearly knows, that Karim has no intention whatsoever of granting us mercy. Look at his casualty list, consider what will happen to him even if he lets us go. This is how he sees it all. Sir Julian, these are the hard facts."

Wentworth turned away abruptly and left wordlessly. Lalor thought for a short while, then called: "Joseph!"

Evans appeared, carrying his rifle, looking sharp and alert though untypically unshaven, but it was the hour of stand-to.

"Joseph, I want you to repeat exactly what Adrian had said in Urdu, Hindi, Punjabi—any language you think appropriate. Lay on the shortcomings of Karim and the insults—you can probably think of many more. Particularly stress that we want Karim to lead the next attack, for there surely must be one soon. If we can drop him, the whole thing will fizzle out."

He was lying wearily back against his pillows, still watching a section of the wall, when Alicia came in. She slumped into the chair by his bed, looking very subdued.

"You've upset father badly, Martin. I realise that's not too hard to do. He is very run down, rather more than most of us."

"I know. But I did try to be objective. It's just that all Adrian said is so right."

She bit her lip and swallowed. He could see that she was rapidly coming to the end of her resilience. He leaned over and rubbed her back reassuringly. She smiled gratefully and took his hand in both of hers.

"What makes it so horrible for him is that I'm here. It distracts him terribly."

"I know that, too. We all know it—even our sowars, I'm sure."

"You're an understanding man, Martin. Try to bear with him."

"Of course I will—we all will. And I know you'll look after him. If it's as well as you've cared for me, then he will surmount all trials and tribulations. There I go again, sounding like someone else, my cousin, Bernard, who's a priest—he knows all about trials and tribulations. But look after yourself, too, my dear. Get as much rest as you can and try not to worry. That's how you probably can help your father best. Keep your pecker up, as I once heard a soldier of the 62nd say at Ferozeshah after they had just marched into the fire of the massed Sikh artillery and had been decimated, and the whole Army spent that night thinking we were losing. But we won on the second day."

"You heard what that man Karim said about Captain Skene and the others?" She looked at him searchingly.

"Yes, I did."

"Do you believe that?"

He took a while to answer. "Yes, I think I do. I got the impression some such news had arrived that had revived his own flagging morale."

"Does that mean," she asked tremulously, "that the families—the women and little children—have been murdered, too?"

"I honestly don't think the mutineers would harm women and children. They have probably turned them over to the care of the Rani. There's not much manly glory to be gained in massacring women and children. At least, that's what I pray."

A strained silence set in between them. She released his hand and buried her face in hers, hunched forward in her chair.

"Could you be a real angel of mercy?" he asked her casually." Could you call on that co-religionist of mine out in the kitchen to get some tea around as soon as possible, closely followed by breakfast. I feel we're going to have an active morning."

She stood up, almost with relief, and left. Soon he was sipping a large mug of sweet black tea, listening to Evans calling out to the unseen mutineers in Urdu. He seemed to go on for a long time.

Meadows's words were getting some lively embellishment.

They remained standing-to alertly but an inertia followed the exchange with Karim. The tireless Peter brought around a breakfast of his own baked bread and honey to each post and Lalor ate ravenously after the long night watch, now that the fever had spent itself and his weakened body was recovering. Peter reappeared later and with some deliberation, scrupulously shaved and washed him. He always felt the soldier's traditional revival after a morning shave.

Peter was gone and he was settling down to await the events of the morning with two loaded pistols and his bared sword when Julian Wentworth came back into his room. The Director sat down heavily in the chair by him. He was still haggard and grave but the earlier emotional outburst had vanished.

"Lalor, I think we must begin discounting the hope that your bearer has got through to Jhansi or, if he has, that he has been successful in enlisting relief to come to our aid. We must now decide, in light of that, what we are going to do. Peter tells me we will run out of food in a day or so except for rice, hard biscuits and some tea."

"The 86th lived in the trenches during winter outside Sevastopol for weeks mainly on tea and biscuits. You'll have read that fellow, Charles Russell of *The Times*—the administration wasn't very good at all. In fact, I sometimes think that the reason we stormed and took the Great Redan with such desperation was that we really wanted to get at the food inside the besieged city."

"Lalor," Wentworth said with more than a touch of asperity," you do have this occasional irritating mannerism of lapsing into levity when a matter of some importance is being discussed. I wish to be serious."

"I am, sir. We can live on rice, biscuits and tea. We have our own assured water supply. We can hold off these attacks against us, and we've been doing more than well so far. Help must come from somewhere soon. Or Karim may just pull out."

The tired, dejected Director did not appear to be listening to him. "As I see it, we have only two options. The first, and obvious, is to try to hold out here indefinitely. The other—and I hope this slanging match with Karim hasn't ruled it out beyond recovery—is to surrender on a promise of safe conduct."

"If you do that—give yourself up to them—they will kill us all," Lalor said patiently. "You don't know how these people think. They're quite without mercy in these circumstances. We've killed a number of them and so they'll have our blood. They know that the British are ruthless too in these conditions and will hunt them down for retribution. If the story about Skene is true, I suspect very much that he did exactly what you propose, he gave in on the promise of safe conduct. Those sepoys at Jhansi could never have taken that Fort without a very sizeable siege train.'' He paused, then went on with some deliberation. ''Besides, sir, I wouldn't let you do such a thing.''

Wentworth stiffened in his chair. A faint flush of anger rose into his pallid cheeks. ''Lalor, I have enought to contend with in this frightful crisis without having to be confronted now with insubordination.''

''There is no question or intention of insubordination, sir. I'm sorry that you should take it that way. But we're in a military situation where you must follow the military appreciation—the military advice. Meadows and Evans know that and will follow what I say.''

''I find your words shocking and distasteful.''

''No doubt you do, sir, perhaps with good reason. But this is a time to be frank. A wrong decision could mean all our lives, including Alicia's.''

Wentworth gave a groaning sigh and buried his face in his hands. Lalor felt very sorry for him. To be frank was also to be brutal.

''However, in case you think that I'm bereft of ideas other than making a stand here until we die, I do have an alternative plan to offer—one I would strongly advise you to take.''

Wentworth's bloodshot pale blue eyes stared at him. He sat upright again, bewildered. Lalor went on: ''If we don't get help by tonight, all of you should go over the wall in the early hours of the morning as Amin did. If Adrian and Joseph plan it carefully, I'm sure you will all make it. Once you're in the forest they'll never find you at night, even if the alarm is given as the last man gets over. You're armed and you have money—you can reach safety in the south easily.''

Wentworth was aghast. ''What are you saying, man? That we escape and abandon you here?''

''What I'm saying is that I'm quite unfit to travel. I would be a complete burden to you and the exertion would probably kill me anyway. It's better I stay here in some comfort until the last. You might call it the luck of the soldier's game. Mine has run out.''

''You're talking madness,'' Wentworth said thickly. Lalor had seen him display real emotion only once before, when he had comforted Alicia after Karim's first attack. ''I understood the fever was leaving you.''

''It is. I'm talking military sense again. I would say almost logic, except that's a luxury we Irish don't indulge in outside of study for the priesthood.''

"The others would never agree to it."

"They will, if you and I both order Adrian and Joseph. You will personally have to handle Alicia. As your military adviser, I've given you my considered opinion on the line of action you should take. If you can't refute it—and I really don't think you can—you should enforce it. I will give Meadows and Evans a direct order. As you say, in the circumstances they may choose to disobey but you must intervene and see that they come to heel. Sentiment is no longer a factor—survival is. I'm useless now and you must get away from here without me. It's your responsibility to preserve the lives of the others, including the loyal sowars. They all have their lives before them."

"You're asking too much of me, Lalor," Wentworth almost whispered. "How could I ever live with myself afterwards if I condoned such a terrible solution to this business?"

"Just look at your daughter in later years and that will be all the justification you'll need. In any case, this is what I want personally."

Before Wentworth could speak again, the noise of rifles firing from the front of the bungalow shattered the morning calm. Wentworth sprang up from his chair and stumbled from the room. Through his window Lalor saw three red-tuniced mutineers drop down from the compound wall one by one and run towards him carrying rifles. He sank back against his pillows, hugging the wall, a loaded pistol in his right hand.

He heard the mutineers arrive panting outside the window. A few seconds later, the first sweating assailant hauled himself up into the window frame, about to climb in, Lalor fired. His point-blank shot blasted the man away, his brown bearded face smashed to pulp by the bullet. Much shouting went on outside after the body hit the ground. Then another wild-eyed face peered apprehensively over the sill. Lalor fired with his other pistol and the bullet tore off the mutineer's pugri, grazing his scalp with a livid red streak through his black hair. The man screamed and lurched out of sight. Lalor reloaded as urgently as he could, glancing up at the window as often as he could, ready to drop the pistol and grab his sword. But the third assailant never appeared. As he lay in wait, he heard footsteps running away and the shouting drifted off. He watched the section of wall he could see but the mutineers had retreated out of his line of vision.

The steady volleys at the front of the bungalow, three rifles firing at a time while the other three re-loaded, interspersed with Wentworth's pistol, with ragged and random firing coming from the attackers, continued for a few minutes, then it suddenly stilled. Someone came running down the hall to his room. Adrian

Meadows hurried in, gripping his rifle, his face streaked with black powder and perspiration.

"How are you, Martin?" Without waiting for a reply, he moved quickly over to the open window and looked cautiously out, careful not to expose himself. "Well done, old soldier! You've got a very dead body out there."

"And there's another somewhere with a bad headache."

"Capital! We dropped four and the others soon turned and ran. Two of them are wounded and are crawling to the gate."

"Any sign of Karim?"

"No. He seems to be leading from the back, and from behind the wall, too, damn him! He's smart enough to know we'd love to get him in our sights."

"I think he must be having some difficulty working up these fellows to come against us. There's no real guts in them. And it hardly helps their morale if he remains behind the wall."

Two rifle shots blasted out again in quick succession. Meadows rushed from the room. Lalor heard him shouting angrily. When the subaltern came back a few minutes later, his features were still flushed and his blue eyes snapped anger.

"Don't tell me," Lalor said mildly, "let me guess. The two wounded are no longer crawling to the gate."

"No, they're not! Ayub and Khaleque have finished them off. Quite apart from not getting a proper fire order to open fire, it's hardly cricket, old man."

"Perhaps Ayub and Khaleque know that we're not playing cricket."

"Martin, one does not kill the wounded! Of course, you will say we're in India where local rules apply. But it's up to us to maintain standards. We can't condone that sort of barbarism."

"Adrian, the unanswerable cry of the British in India to cover both their virtues and peccadilloes is that they have to maintain standards. Look at it another way. Both Ayub and Khaleque know that they can expect no mercy if they're taken."

"Well, we've now got even more bodies lying in the sun about us, polluting the air as well as bring the vultures and crows. I hope Karim sends in the sweepers again."

"They've probably bolted by now. There's only one real answer to our whole problem, Adrian, to Karim and his snipers and assaults, to our dwindling food, to the smell of decomposing bodies. If relief doesn't come by sunset tonight, you must be out of this deathtrap by first light tomorrow morning. You must all go over the wall as Amin did."

Meadows stared at him in blank astonishment as Wentworth had done. "What are you saying, Martin?" he asked incredulously.

"Exactly what I said to Sir Julian before Karim interrupted us. It's the Director's decision but if he agrees, I'm ordering you and Joseph to support him all the way. And that's one order which is not going to be a basis for discussion."

Before the open-mouthed subaltern could speak again, Wentworth and Alicia came into the room. When Lalor saw how drained and exhausted she looked, it was all the easier to say as harshly and forcefully as he could:

"Sir, you owe it to your daughter and all members of our party to take the urgent advice I've just given you. The early stage is dangerous but if Amin can do it, so can all of you with some thorough planning. Once you're in the forest, you'll be safe. Joseph and the sowars will guide and see you through. If you stay here longer than tonight, all of us will die."

It was 2 o'clock on Lalor's watch as he lay in the darkened room. He had arranged for his bed to be pushed back to its old position so that he again faced the door. His two pistols and sword were by his side, ready at hand. He could no longer see any part of the compound wall.

Beside him on the bed sat Alicia, sobbing quietly and uncontrollably. Her father stood by her, his hand resting consolingly on her quivering shoulders. Meadows stood there also, but even in the dim light, Lalor could see that he was near to breaking down. Lalor was not feeling too composed himself. The whole day had been full of emotional, even bitter, argument when he had been alternately assailed and pleaded with in separate and repetitive sessions with Alicia and Adrian Meadows. The disciplined Joseph Evans became the most virulent of all, demanding that he must not sacrifice himself, that they all 'must stick it out to the end together.' He had remained good-humoured and tolerant but adamant. Eventually his phlegm wore them down. They dispiritedly gave up their rebellion against Julian Wentworth's decision, announced at noon, after what was clearly for him some agonising hours of reflection.

"It's time you all went," Lalor said bluntly.

Alicia stood up slowly. Tears welled in her red-rimmed eyes and trickled down the black staining they had used on their faces. The whole escape party was also wearing dark clothing.

She bent down and kissed him softly and fully on the lips. She then tried to say something but broke down and turned away. Adrian Meadows placed a comforting arm about her shoulders while Wentworth grasped Lalor's hand and looked down on him ashen-faced.

"You will never be forgotten for this, Lalor."

He almost smiled in sheer relief from the tension in the room. Spoken like a true pro-consul of empire, he thought. *Ave Caesar, morituri te salutant* . . .

"It's always best on these occasions, sir, to have a plan which is objective and not affected by emotion. You've made the right decision, have no fear about that."

How smug and sanctimonious he sounded. And he had organised his own death warrant.

Wentworth took Alicia from the room. She gave him a last distraught glance and he smiled his gratitude. After an awkward pause, Adrian Meadows came forward and took his hand in a vice-like grip. The subaltern's tired, sunburnt face was taut and strained.

"You're a fool to do this, Martin," he said almost inaudibly.

"If one has to be a fool, it's best to do it well."

"We could have looked after you if you'd only come with us!" Meadows burst out impassionedly. "We should be looking after you! In fact, I honestly don't know why we're going, why we're abandoning you! It's the worst order, the worst decision, I've ever had to follow in my whole life!"

"And see that you do follow it, my lad," Lalor told him curtly. "You're now the commander of the party and that will give you enough to think about." He paused and then smiled wryly at his young distressed comrade-in-arms. "Goodbye, Adrian. Look after Alicia and the Director well. I know you will. And yourself too. Remember me to the old 86th when you see them. Now you'd better be going."

Meadows's blue eyes became suspiciously moist. He wrung Lalor's hand vigorously. "Goodbye, old soldier," he mumbled and hurried from the room.

Joseph Evans came in a few moments later, his rifle slung over his shoulder. The usually-urbane, unruffled Anglo-Indian was also nervously upset. Like the others, his features were drawn with strain, with sleepless shadows about his grey eyes, and his clothes were sweat-stained. He smiled wearily but warmly as he came to grip Lalor's outstretched hand.

"Goodbye, sir. And may your guardian angel watch over you."

Lalor was able to smile again. "I'm sure he's with me but he may shortly be rather overworked."

Evans quickly became emotional. "I don't want to walk out on you here, sir, any more than Mr Meadows! We both discussed disobeying Sir Julian."

"Joseph, Sir Julian is only carrying out, under considerable duress, advice that I gave him. You and Adrian Meadows must back him up in every way and not make an already extremely difficult situation any more difficult. I know I can count on you to do your duty—you've always done it so well. Goodbye, Joseph. Look after them all. You know the country and the language. I know also that you're a very good shot."

They shook hands finally. Evans reverted back to his stiff, formal self.

"God be with you, sir."

"And with you, too, Joseph."

Evans turned and abruptly left the room. After him came the four loyal young sowars, crowding into the room awkwardly two at a time. They saluted smartly and came forward to press his hand between their two outstretched hands. He thanked each of them feelingly for their courage and faithfulness. Each young soldier saluted stiffly in return and went.

He was now alone. He lay thankfully back on his pillows, suddenly very tired. Despite the comparative coolness of the early hours of the still black morning, he was perspiring freely. Soon he would be the only occupant of the whole bungalow. As if to remind him, his wound started to ache painfully again or, perhaps, he had only now become aware of it.

He stared into the gloom of the empty room, listening. Soon they would be slipping away through the darkness to the wall near the rear far corner. He had discussed the plan several times with Meadows and Evans. Meadows and his four sowars would gain the wall first, get over stealthily one by one and secure a small defensive ring on the far side. Evans would follow with Wentworth, Alicia and Peter Rosario, see them over and finally go himself. They would then disappear into the protection of the enveloping forest and keep moving as quickly as they could in the black night.

He lay there, gripping one of his pistols for security, and he found himself gnawing his bottom lip in anxiety, a habit, he recalled ruefully, he had teased Cecilia about when she was younger. Oh God, he worried sickeningly, what if they were detected and shot down on the wall? He seemed to become even more soaked in perspiration.

He listened intently but the still calm of the night prevailed. A half-hour went by, then an hour, but no shot or cries of an alarm being raised broke the benign silence. As that hour moved with agonising slowness towards another, he looked anxiously at the window. Dawn could not be too far away now and soon the sky would be lightening. He could smell the heavy scent of the frangipani tree by the wall near the mutineers' camp.

They must have got away by now, he thought exultantly. He tried to blink away his weariness but he now felt completely exhausted, both mentally as well as physically. It was not only the long vigil of the night watch but the emotional stress of the day's arguments, the farewells and the strain of waiting for the success or tragedy of the escape bid. His grip tightened on the pistol in his hand as he looked at the open door through which his friends had departed. There was now little else to do but await his death.

7

Salvation and Tragedy

When he awoke, it took him some considerable time to orientate himself. He was lying slumped on his bed, his pistols and sword still with him and so was the fruit and water chatti placed on his table. But something was different. He slowly realised that it must be near mid-morning. He stared through the open window at the sunlight coming through the window and felt the heat. He must have fallen asleep before dawn and had lain undisturbed for hours. He even sensed a strange peace and calm about the empty bungalow and its surroundings.

He got up slowly and moved unsteadily to the window. He felt weak but his wound, well-bandaged from Alicia's dressing, did not pain as long as he moved carefully. He peered out cautiously but all the compound wall that he could see was deserted. What had happened to the dawn fusillade at least, he wondered? He could not have possibly slept through that. Moreover, the answering fire from the defenders was all part of the daily ritual. The mutineers could only have become suspicious if a passive silence had come from the bungalow.

From his position at the window he could see the firegold tree beginning to spread some shade over the freshly-turned earth of the graves. Sleep well, Sikander Khan and the others, he thought, I may well be joining you there soon.

He picked his way to the door and then edged his way along the hall to the bungalow entrance. The front bedrooms, showing the disorder and debris of hastily-evacuated defensive positions, were empty. At the threshold, he looked over the barricade of solid heavy furniture that had been Adrian Meadows's firing position. The front area before the bungalow to the charred remains of the gate was as quiet as a grave, to coin a phrase, he pondered. The six corpses of the dead mutineers lay crumpled in grotesque poses and were becoming black and bloated with vultures about them. But apart from the obscene-looking big birds, hopping about attacking the bodies, there was no sign of movement. The sickening stench of the dead came to him from that revolting spectacle.

He was standing there, puzzled, when a familiar voice in English came from behind him.

"Good morning, sir. I have tea ready."

He spun round, causing a white sheet of flame to sear through his left shoulder. He brought his pistol up to the aim at waist level, then relaxed completely from his nerve-taut reaction. Before him stood, in a slightly-soiled, crumpled white shirt and trousers, the gaunt, dignified figure of Peter Rosario.

"Good God, Peter! You frightened the life out of me!"

"I am sorry, sir, I should have worn my sandals."

He lowered his pistol and leaned against the hall wall with some relief. He glared at the elderly Goan as fiercely as he could.

"Now what are you doing here? You were to go with Sir Julian and the escape party."

Peter Rosario gave an embarrassed, apologetic smile. "I know, sir. But I am really too old to be leaping over walls in the dead of night and plunging through the forest like a hunted animal. And all the countryside about here is full of savages. This is no way for an old man to die. I begged Sir Julian to allow me stay with you. I would prefer to find heavenly peace here, sir, not out in the wilderness."

So, according to Peter Rosario, Lalor pondered, death was to come in a last stand under the aegis, and ultimate recovery, presumably, of St Patrick and St Francis Xavier.

Curiously, despite his slightly irreverent thoughts, he felt lost for words. He also did not feel too well, either. Peter Rosario reached out a thin brown arm and gripped his right elbow.

"Come, sir, I can see that you need this tea. Let me take you back to your room where you can enjoy it."

Dear Mother Mary, Lalor's mind rambled in a light-headed way, *Peter, you sound as if you were are going to the aid of an elderly memsahib who is feeling faint at a garden party at Government House, Bombay*. But like that hypothetical old lady, he was feeling giddiness. And so it was that Captain Martin Patrick Lalor, 86th Regiment, veteran of two wars and now wounded for the third time, was assisted to his room by a Goan cook who abhorred violence but was totally loyal to his masters who perpetrated it.

In the room he stubbornly refused to lie down on the bed but sat down in a cane chair that faced the door. Peter brought him a large mug of sweet black tea which he sipped appreciatively. His head soon cleared.

"Peter, get your tea and sit down here. If we're both going to die, let's do it together—not you out in your kitchen and me in here."

The tea rapidly revived him. When Peter returned to sit awkwardly on a cane stool by the door, with his tea in a chipped, battered mug, the Goan said to him: "We are alone, sir."

"Yes, I know, Peter, and it pleases me. It means our escape party has got away."

"Sir, what I mean is that we are really alone. The bad soldiers, except for their sick men lying in the trees out there, are gone."

Lalor set down his tea on the floor, astounded. "What are you saying?"

"At dawn there was no shooting. Instead, there was a lot of shouting and noise of movement from the camp. Then, with much excitement, they rode past the gate at great speed. I saw them."

Fear chilled through Lalor. The mutineers had ridden towards Madhupur, not Jhansi.

"I waited," Peter went on solemnly, "then I took a small table to the wall to stand on and look over at the camp. Only men in their blankets were there, sick men. I could even hear several groaning. All the drivers and servants seem to have run away. I watched for a long time but could not see anybody moving about."

Lalor thought quickly. There must be spare horses in the camp belonging to the casualties, perhaps even his Paddy still. But the vision of Karim riding off furiously to the south with every able-bodied man, completely ignoring the bungalow, numbed him.

"Help me on with my boots, Peter. I want to speak with my fellow-wounded."

Ten minutes later, Lalor had inched his way along the outside of the front compound wall, a loaded pistol in each hand. He stood at its corner, looking into the forest at the mutineers' encampment. Peter had insisted on coming and waited several yards behind him, unarmed. Lalor watched motionless for several minutes. Not far from the road he could see three bandaged men lying incongruously swathed in blankets on the hot morning and, in the distance, horses tethered to a picquet line.

He advanced into the wood, his pistols held at the ready. He soon came on another group of bodies wrapped in crude bloody bandages who, grey-faced with pain and with half-closed glazed eyes, ignored him in their misery. As he moved through the trees more, he came on two sowars, unshaven and haggard, each with an arm in a dirty bandage, sitting against treetrunks. Their dark, bloodshot eyes, when they saw him appear, started in sheer terror. They struggled abjectly to their feet. The aim of Lalor's pistols followed them.

"Where has Karim gone so suddenly with everybody?" he asked coldly in Urdu.

A petrified silence answered him. He allowed the two mutineers to sweat it out. Patiently he waited. Then one, a tall young fellow with a straggling moustache that showed up blackly against his sick, pallid features, licked his lips nervously and glanced at his companion, an older thickset man stunned into a paralysed stare at Lalor's apparition.

"If you don't tell me the truth very quickly," Lalor said grimly, "I will kill you both. I may well do that anyway."

"Sahib, a horse dealer from Madhupur rode in here at first light and told us that a party of Feringhee had awoken him while it was still dark and had bought all his horses. He knew of the fight here at the dak bungalow. The whole town knows it. So he came to tell Karim. Karim became very angry and hot in the head. He ordered every man who could ride to saddle up and mount. Even though he too is wounded and has the fever, he led them away himself."

Lalor felt cold fear grip him. If only the escape party had by-passed Madhupur. "But why did not Karim first search the dak bungalow, or at least secure it?"

The callow young mutineer gulped and looked wildly at his comrade who still stared wordlessly and fixedly at the barrel of one of Lalor's pistols pointing at his stomach.

"Karim has a troubled head from his wound, sahib. He did not give any clear orders. Though I think Abdullah and myself, who are the only two sick men who can walk, were meant to go there at once. We did intend to do this. But, sahib, we are very ill. We have been resting to get our strength. We were about to go in there when you came like a ghost."

As he listened, Lalor's mind was awhirl with conflicting thoughts. What should he do next? He knew depressingly that he was quite unfit to gallop off down the road after both Karim and Julian Wentworth's fleeing band. The main hope could only be that Karim would fail to find the fugitives. Both Adrian Meadows and Joseph Evans would have the instinctive sense to keep away from the main road and follow forest and rural tracks that went roughly south. But one thing he did appreciate clearly. He and Peter could not miss this chance to escape from the dak bungalow themselves.

"What is the news from Jhansi?" he questioned further.

Both mutineers stared at the ground.

"So there has been much trouble? You had better tell me about it. Otherwise I will shoot you dead now."

Again the downcast, tongue-tied silence. He knew that their reasoning was that any utterance of tragedy to him would certainly end their lives and that they would not talk.

"Perhaps I will kill you disloyal swine anyway. If you wish to try to save your lives, obey me closely. You will now gather in all the rifles here. Carefully unload any that are loaded and with the muzzle pointed away from me. I will be right behind you both, waiting for an excuse to shoot you. Then we will go to the horse lines where you will saddle two horses for us. One had better be my own, and in good condition too, or that may cause your death also. Now, jeldi!"

Twenty minutes later, they were back at the bungalow, with, to his joy, Joseph leading his big red Paddy as well as another saddled horse, and the two mutineers struggling with armfuls of rifles. He ordered them to stack the rifles inside the house, then curtly dismissed them, still covering them with his pistols. They set off at a shambling run, casting terrified glances behind them until they reached the haven of the gate, but he did not fire. He lowered his pistols, feeling slightly dizzy from the heat and his exertions, to face Peter Rosario who had tethered the two horses to the verandah rail.

"What now, sir? You look like you could do with a good pot of tea."

Somehow, he thought admiringly, Peter, whether unwittingly or not, always seemed to be able to retrieve normality from threatening disaster. "Peter, I'm sure you're right but we must get going. Fill a couple of chaguls of water and get some fruit for our saddlebags, then we'll ride out. I'm going to prepare the bungalow for burning. Then I want you to help me into my tunic. If I'm to meet Daffadar Karim, I'd like to look like an officer of the 86th."

"I must warn you, sir, I'm not a horseman. My family are all fishermen and sailors."

"Don't worry. In my present state, neither am I. We'll go at a steady walking pace. All you have to do is sit in the saddle and stay on."

Flames were licking up the tinder-dry wooden bungalow when

they rode out the gate. Lalor halted on the deserted road to have one last look at the burning house, the scene of their staunch defence and of many anguished hours. After he and Peter had mounted, he had gone around to the rear of the compound to the firegold tree and had paid one last tribute to Sikander Khan and their other dead with a final salute. As they went on down the dirt road, he felt that the fire devouring the bungalow was a suitable pyre, a Viking's funeral, for their fallen. They had barely gone a thousand yards, to the near bank of the river beyond which the town of Madhupur lay, when an explosion thudded distantly behind them. The ammunition had been enveloped by the encroaching fire.

A crowd awaited them on the far bank as they splashed through the ford. Lalor was relieved to see that they were mostly unarmed countrymen, backed by intensely curious women and children. The river had clearly been a demarcation line beyond which these simple townspeople and peasants had not dared to venture while the violence at the dak bungalow expended itself. As he rode through the serried ranks, he realised what an extraordinary sight he must present to all those wide, staring eyes. He had managed, with Peter's help, to get his right arm into his red tunic but the left sleeve hung empty. He wore his white helmet with its white puggaree, both now rather soiled, and his blue trousers with their red stripe were also stained with blood and grime. Across his saddle he nursed a sowar's rifle, mainly for effect as he doubted if he had the strength in his left arm to bring it up to the aim. His pistols and sword were at his waist. Behind him, refusing stubbornly to ride alongside him, came Peter Rosario who seemed blissfully unperturbed.

They moved out of Madhupur and journeyed down the hard-baked rutted road that led between cultivated fields, with the forest again stretching ahead. None of the silent, expressionless crowd followed them beyond the fringe of the town. He wondered grimly if the treacherous horse-dealer was among those who watched them go by. He realised that he was doing exactly what he had criticised the escape party for—passing through Madhupur. And now he was moving openly down the road. Maleesh, as the Arabs had said in Aden. What did it matter? Suddenly he was beyond caring. It was now well into the morning and the sun was scorching down. He began to feel weak and faint again but he steeled himself. His sense of humour helped him, for he could see the irony of his situation. He and Peter could only equate, surely, to Don Quixote and Sancha Panza. Their motives were of the highest but also impracticable. What could he, in his condition, and one non-violent Goan hope to achieve?

They had been travelling for some interminate time when he distantly heard Peter Rosario's voice coming to him quietly but insistently. "Don't you think you should rest, sir?"

When he halted Paddy, or perhaps Paddy had halted himself, he found himself hunched over his horse's neck in a semi-stupor. He shook his head to clear his dulled senses. He knew that Peter was right. He turned Paddy into the inviting cool shade of the forest. Peter was by him, helping him as he lurched and half-fell out of his saddle. He slumped down against a treetrunk gratefully and closed his eyes. He seemed to be on fire from the heat and he was bathed in perspiration. He touched his bandaged shoulder which was now sodden with sweat and some blood seeping through and was also throbbing painfully. What a pathetic performance he was giving, he groaned to himself, helpless on his back in some nameless wood while Karim and his murderers were hunting down Alicia, her father and his friends and comrades.

Peter tilted a chagul to his lips and he drank the cool water deeply. He wiped his lips appreciatively and fumbled in his inner tunic pocket. He pressed all the money he found there into Peter's scrawny brown hand.

"Carry this with you from now on, Peter. If there is trouble, as there is sure to be, keep yourself out of it. Fade away quietly. It's most important that you get back to our own people and tell them what has happened. I'm a betting man, Peter, and I reckon you'll be the only one of us who will survive. And remember, that's an order. No attempts at martyrdom, please."

He became only vaguely aware of what Peter was saying to him in reply and he heard himself talking back repetitiously. The sleep of exhaustion soon came on him.

When he awoke, he gradually became aware that Peter and he were not alone. Squatting near him were several heavily-armed men talking quietly as their horses cropped the grass under the trees. His rifle was still lying by him and he also had his sword and pistols. He struggled up to a sitting position against a nearby tree, gripping his rifle, and found Peter by him.

"It's all right, sir. These fellows are from the Rani."

The Goan saw his bewilderment and went on: "They came down the road from Madhupur soon after you fell asleep. I spoke to their leader who said that the Rani had heard that we were in great trouble and she sent him with most of her men to rescue us. He has gone off to try to save Wentworth sahib and the young memsahib from Karim."

Lalor sank back against the tree trunk, barely able to believe the miracle. When his confused mind came around to accepting it, he did so fervently. But euphoria left him quickly.

"What is the news from Jhansi?" he called in Hindi to the Rohillas who had now stopped talking and were watching him.

They looked at each other and one or two laughed. One tough-looking individual with light-coloured eyes and a straggling beard answered him with malevolent amusement. "The sepoys have killed all the Feringhees."

Lalor felt his mouth go dry with fear. "Not the women and children, too?"

The fellow grinned crookedly. "All are dead. The sepoys fell on them after Skene had surrendered. No one was spared."

Lalor felt sick. He closed his eyes in anguish and he found himself praying. Poor little Megan and Katie Skene, their mother . . . He saw again in his mind's eye that pathetic, forlorn group standing on the road waving finally to them before they had departed through the cantonment gate only a few days ago.

"Are the sepoys still there?" he asked again, after a while.

"Yes."

"Yet the Rani has extended her protection to us?"

The Rohilla shrugged and stared back at him enigmatically. "Well, she has sent us for you."

Lalor did not pursue the conversation any further. The Rani's bodyguard were obviously just as puzzled as he was why they had been despatched away from Jhansi at this time.

Peter gave him a cool drink of water from their chagul again. When he had wiped his unshaven face with the back of his hand, he said to the patient Goan: "Peter, remember what I said. You are to slip away if you can. But we won't try that just now. These fellows are without their leader and it's also not the right moment."

He was still darkly contemplating the tragic massacre at Jhansi when the Rohillas sprang up, gripping their ancient matchlocks, and ran out on the road. Lalor struggled to his feet and moved after them, his heart pounding with both fear and hope.

A large body of horsemen came galloping up the dusty road. Lalor recognised at their head the big leader of the Rani's body-guard whom they had seen with her at the farewell at the Betwa. Then he saw, to his utter joy and relief, the slight figure of Alicia Wentworth riding beside him. No one else from their party was in the galloping ranks. He saw Karim, looking sullen, as they neared but his eyes were only for Alicia. She looked pathetic, almost broken, as she hunched in the saddle.

He pushed through the Rohillas as the wild-looking cavalcade drew up in a flurry of dust. He shouted hoarsely: "Alicia! Alicia!"

Haunted blue eyes from a drawn, shocked face stared dully at him for a few moments. Then she burst into tears. She slid out of the saddle and stumbled forward sobbing to his outstretched arm. He held her slim, shaking body to him and kissed her tangled hair. "Thank God you are alive," he whispered.

He led her through the silent, watching Rohillas into the seclusion of the trees. He let her sob on for a while. Then he asked the question he was dreading to ask. "What about your father? And Adrian and Joseph? And the sowars?"

Her body stiffened under her embrace. Strangely, she stopped crying. She did not look up but said in a small, flat voice, her head downcast: "They are dead, all of them. These men saved me just in time."

Before he could react in blind rage and hatred against Karim, the leader of the Rohilla bodyguard stood squarely before him. Though his mind was shocked from what Alicia had just told him, he carefully took in the big hulking man who was being so instrumental in their survival. The full red-hennaed beard, the rapacious-looking broken nose, the weathered yet light-skinned features, hard grey eyes and strong physique could have placed him as a soldier of fortune, a condottiere, of a bygone era. An air of authority and ruthlessness was stamped about him.

"I am Ghulam Muhammad, the commander of the Rani's soldiers," the Rohilla said gruffly in Hindi. "The Rani sent me for you."

Lalor thrust Alicia gently behind him. He answered formally. "I thank you and the Rani with all my heart. I am Captain Lalor."

He held out his hand. Ghulam Muhammad, eyeing him coldly, clasped it strongly with a big, calloused hand.

"You will be well rewarded for this. The British have two notable virtues—they never forget their friends and they never forget their enemies."

"I have done this because the Rani told me. I obey because I earn my pay. I do not like Feringhees."

Lalor had no time to digest this blunt retort. Karim came storming through the ring of listening Rohillas, pushing them aside with his one good arm. He was livid with rage, his eyes popping with emotion. His wounded arm was in a dirty sling and his strong, heavy features were sickly, almost yellowish.

"You are treating with the accursed enemy," he roared at Ghulam Muhammad in Hindi, choking on his words. "Kill him, not talk to him!"

The big mercenary stared stonily at him. "The Rani has told me to find the Feringhees who visited her court and to give them her protection. I follow my orders.''

Karim glared at Lalor. The foam of passion whitened the corners of his thick lips. ''That man will have us all blown from the guns if he is allowed to live.''

''He may do so for you,'' Ghulam Muhammad said dourly, ''but I have no concern.''

''I would gladly kill you now, Karim,'' Lalor said. He also was seething with fury. ''You bloody murderer! It would save a lot of trouble later on. But be assured. One day I will kill you.''

Karim's bloodshot dark eyes flickered uneasily. He glanced again wildly at Ghulam Muhammad. ''You heard that! Do you encourage such a threat against a fellow member of the true faith?''

''I am sure you have the Rani's protection as much as he has,'' Ghulam Muhammad said almost wearily. ''As for the future, that is between the two of you.''

''You are betraying your religion, Rohilla!''

Lalor saw Ghulam Muhammad's craggy features darken with sudden anger and his right hand move to the hilt of the big tulwar at his waist. Karim had overstepped himself by spitting out that accusation. Yet Lalor had to admire him again. He stood his ground solidly.

Ghulam Muhammad checked himself and his hand strayed away from his sword. But his eyes were coldly implacable as he looked at Karim. ''In my trade I must take a broad view of religion. Now a Hindu princess pays me well and I obey her. You followed the Feringhees for years, taking their money, food and shelter but now you have turned on them. Does this make you a better believer under Allah than I?''

Splendid stuff, thought Lalor savagely. Sikander Khan could not have phrased it more succinctly. Karim looked uncomfortable and licked his lips nervously. He was alone among hostile Rohillas pressing about him. His religious appeal had gone badly wrong and his own out-numbered men were away from him on the road.

''You're a running dog, Karim,'' Lalor said vehemently to him. ''That is how we will know you now on and how you will come to know yourself.''

Several of the Rohillas laughed outright. Karim did not say a word. He stood there, his sunken eyes full of hate for Lalor, his broad shoulders stooped with fatigue. He is in almost the same state as I am, Lalor thought.

''We have talked enough,'' Ghulam Muhammad said with some finality. ''We have a long journey back to Jhansi. Karim, you may travel with us to your camp to collect your wounded but then you will depart in any direction except Jhansi. I speak with the words of the Rani. Now let us go.''

Karim strode away abruptly and the gathering of Rohillas broke up. Lalor turned quickly to Alicia who was clutching his waist as if he was a vital sheet anchor she was terrified to lose. He held her closely again. She clung to him, her face buried in his chest.

''Don't worry any more,'' he murmured. ''Everything is going to be all right. This fellow Ghulam Muhammad knows what he is doing. Soon we'll be at Jhansi and the Rani will look after us.''

She agitatedly wiped away her tears and walked with him composedly through the trees to where the Rohillas were noisily mounting in front of the sullen and subdued mutineers. One of the Rohillas held Paddy for him. He saw Alicia into her saddle and it was when he was trying to mount, with pain stabbing through his left shoulder, that he realised that Peter Rosario was not helping him. When he finally mounted, perspiration streaming down his face, he looked back into the trees and among the milling horsemen behind them. With a surge of joy, he realised that Peter had gone.

The isolated presence of a spare horse soon alerted the Rohillas. Ghulam Muhammad had just arranged the order of march for his column, with Karim and his mutineers ominously sandwiched between two groups of his own men who outnumbered them two to one, when a cry went up from one of the guards who had been with them in the glade during the morning. ''The Christian from the south has fled!''

Lalor quickly intervened to Ghulam Muhammad who was mounted by his side. ''He is an old man who was very frightened. Just a cook. But at least you have gained a good horse.''

Ghulam Muhammad cast a sharply acquisitive eye over the big cavalry charger being led forward and grunted appreciatively. He gave a curt wave of his hand and the cavalcade moved off.

Alicia rode alongside Lalor with Ghulam Muhammad at the head of the column. She gave him a brave smile as soon as they started and he knew that she had now got a grip of herself after the horrendous events of the day. Again, his heart went out to her. She was exhausted, both mentally and physically, dust-covered and stained with perspiration, but she was holding on determinedly. He desperately wanted to talk to her, to find out what had happened, how Karim and his men had come on them, but the taciturn Ghulam Muhammad suddenly decided to become talkative.

''You should not have burned the dak bungalow. Your ammunition would have been very valuable to me.''

"At the time I started the fire, it would have been even more valuable to Karim."

"The Rani told me that if I was successful in rescuing you, I could have all your carts and their contents, except your personal baggage."

"You can have these indeed—with my full consent. A small payment for saving our lives. Take Karim's horses as well if you like. They're British property."

The mercenary chieftain bared uneven yellow teeth in the semblance of a smile. "I have thought of that but it would be too much."

"You are wise to make him ride away from Jhansi. If the sepoys are still there, he could cause trouble for the Rani."

Ghulam Muhammad nodded but said nothing. He lapsed into his own dour meditation and Lalor was able to talk to Alicia. She told him in a barely audible voice, as they rode along, that their party had been sighted by Karim and his men as they were crossing a large, open field away from the main road and ridden down. Adrian, Joseph and the loyal sowars had time only to get one shot away before the mutineers were on them with drawn sabres. She was saved from being hacked to death by her father throwing himself to the ground and protecting her with his own body. Then he was dragged away and shot before her eyes. The mutineers finally killed Adrian, Joseph and the sowars, who had all been felled to the ground by sabre slashes, with more shooting. For some reason, nobody shot her and Karim merely took her prisoner. They rode away, leaving the bodies, stripped of their weapons and valuables, lying abandoned in the field. The whole tragedy, with seven lives, including her father's, brutally murdered, was all over in a matter of minutes. Karim had been infuriated when he realised he had missed Lalor, and became almost hysterical when she told him that he was still back at the dak bungalow. Fortunately, Ghulam Muhammad had then come on them.

Lalor stared grimly ahead as they moved down the forest road to Madhupur. His mourning of the death of his comrades was made worse by the grief-crushed, red-eyed Alicia at his side. Cheerful, effervescent Adrian Meadows, not yet twenty-one years old and so full of promise, correct, reticent Joseph Evans, conscientious in all he undertook, were no more. Stiff, rather humourless Julian Wentworth would never see the City of London again and had died knowing that his only child and daughter had fallen into the hands of mutineers and murderers. And for their loyalty, Ayub, Khaleque, Ali Noab and Sattar had died like Sikander Khan and their comrades buried under the shade of the firegold tree at the dak bungalow. All were now lying forsaken in some unknown field with vultures tearing and rending their broken and bloodied bodies into shreds and scattered bones.

He glanced up at the sun boiling down on them. It was possible that they could be back in Jhansi late that night. He pondered what reception would be waiting for Alicia and himself if the sepoys were still there and the Rani was powerless against them. However, he brooded philosophically, it was the only haven now to which they could retreat.

8

Sanctuary

In the darkness of night, in a covered cart lumbering along in a convoy that was now Ghulam Muhammad's booty, Lalor and Alicia returned to Jhansi city.

The night before, after Ghulam Muhammad had secured the former British baggage train, the mercenary chieftain had moved north and made camp for the night in another wood. After eating some fruit and drinking some of the Rohillas' strong tea, Lalor and Alicia slept the deep mindless sleep of the exhausted. Both were drained, both mentally and physically, with Alicia still in a state of numbed shock from the brutal death of her father. She lay with her head resting on his good shoulder and his arm protectively about here. Fortunately, she soon fell asleep, her hair brushing against his cheek and her warm softness by him. About them in the dark wood he heard the Rohillas moving about and talking by their campfires, on the alert against a surprise attack by Karim. Next morning, they travelled on to the Betwa where the messenger Ghulam Muhammad had sent on to the Rani met the column. He brought instructions that they were not to enter the city until after sunset as the sepoys were still there. For the long hot afternoon, they lay up in another wood.

Now they bumped along the narrow streets of the city, amid its noise and smells, after coming through the walls at the Saugor Gate. They sat precariously together in two chairs side by side in the black anonymity of the closed-in cart as it rolled slowly along.

They sat silently and he held her hand for comfort. About them the Rohilla escort clattered, shouting abuse at anybody who blocked their movement through the winding streets. He thought ironically how different had been their previous progress to the Rani's palace, led by a Director of the East India Company with all the trappings of imperial power. Now two survivors from that august party, tired, dirty and dishevelled, were brought back under her protection to beseech her further help. Alicia probably had the same bitter thoughts.

The cart jerked abruptly and swung hard right. He guessed that they were now entering the archway of the palace into its large courtyard. Their cart seemed to move on its own now, with the horsemen and other wagons left outside. The dark, handsome features of Rao Chaudri looked in when it halted. The courtier looked taut and anxious.

"Please put these garments over your clothes. When you are ready, let me know. Then follow me quickly."

He thrust some robes across to them, and then withdrew, closing the canvas flap abruptly. They sorted out the clothes as quickly as they could. Alicia's was a one piece Muslim purdah burkah which amply covered her from head to toe, with a laced square across her eyes. Lalor's was a loose Arab-style ghalibiya which he slid over himself with her help, and a pugri which she wrapped about his head in a fashion. When they called out to Rao Chaudri, the flap was opened and they stumbled out of the cart. The courtyard, significantly, was completely darkened. They followed the slim, swiftly-moving Mahratta a few yards over the flagstones into a doorway and then picked their way down a narrow stone staircase. They were soon in a long open room, well lit by oil lamps, furnished with cushions and divans and profusely decorated with brass vases of flowers. Rao Chaudri awaited them, tense and ill at ease. Lalor was struck by the change in him.

"The Rani has instructed me to welcome you again to her palace, to her home which she hopes will regard as much yours as hers. She deeply regrets the death of your beloved father, Miss Wentworth, and all your comrades, Captain Lalor. However, she trusts you will now be safe and comfortable with her after your terrible experiences."

"What is happening in Jhansi at this moment?" Lalor asked.

"I would prefer that the Rani told you that herself," Chaudri answered stiffly.

"Where is the Rani now?"

"She and Mazumdar are talking with the sepoys. These are difficult times for us also."

"I hope we'll see her soon, if she's the only one who will give us news of our friends here in Jhansi. We can only think there must be bad news."

Did he see a flicker of satisfaction go through those dark, luminous eyes? Why did he dislike Rao Chaudri? Because he was too smooth and sharp-witted? Except the Palace official was not himself to-night. He was frightened. The situation in the city must be dangerous, now threatening the Palace. Lalor regretted the opening that he had given Chaudri, for a slight smile strayed to the courtier's lips.

"The news is not good, shall I say that, Captain Lalor?"

"When can we expect to see the Rani?"

"Very soon, I should think. Please make yourself comfortable here in the meantime. One of the rooms beyond is a bathroom with hot water and clean clothes for you both. We will get your personal baggage from Ghulam Muhammad shortly, though you will realise that it will be necessary for you to wear our clothing. And here is somebody who we think is trustworthy enough to look after you."

In the passageway leading to the other rooms appeared a stocky, smiling figure in white with a familiar rakish flair to his pugri.

"Amin!" Lalor strode across the room and shook hands delightedly with his beaming bearer. "I knew you'd get through!"

The smiling Kashmiri Mussulman salaamed respectfully to Alicia.

"I am afraid, Miss Wentworth," Chaudri went on, "that we have not yet got a woman to look after you, for security reasons. But we will soon. I am sure that your bearer will look after both of you well. Now I must go. Goodbye."

When they were alone, Lalor said to Amin: "Is there any wine? If there are flowers here for memsahib, I hope there's wine for me. First, take this damned nightshirt off me."

Alicia had already slipped out of her all-enveloping burkah. When Amin left, he led her over to a divan by the wall and they sat down wearily.

"What are we in, Martin?" she asked quietly. "I know we're somewhere in the palace but this looks a well-furnished dungeon."

"It's the taikhana—underground rooms for family use in the hot weather. Ventilation comes through ducts at ground level. It's quite a sensible place to keep us out of the way."

"What is happening here about our friends? Remember Karim taunted us at the bungalow that they were all now dead. I'm sure he was only trying to frighten us.''

Lalor realised with a sharp shock that she did not know what the Rohillas in the wood past Madhupur had told him. He hesitated. The shocks to her had to be paced. ''The Rani will tell us the whole situation when she comes and we can trust her. Why don't you have a nice hot bath now and change into fresh clothes? You'll feel much better then. And we must show a brave face for the Rani. It sounds as if she has her problems, too.''

She nodded dully and they got up to explore the taikhana. They found the room set up as a bathroom, with a large earthen tum brimming with warm water and with clean clothes and towels draped nearby. There was another room beyond which could serve as her bedroom. He left her at the bathroom and went back to find Amin waiting with a flagon of wine and glasses on a silver tray.

''Now tell me, Amin. What has happened to our people in the Fort?''

''All dead, sahib. The sepoys killed them all three days ago.''

Lalor sat down again on the divan. Though he had been fully expecting that answer, it was some time before he could speak. Amin poured a glass of wine and gave it to him.

''How did it happen? Did the sepoys take the Fort?''

''Skene sahib surrendered. The sepoys attacked them outside the city and killed them.''

''Did no one survive?''

''No one, sahib, not even the memsahibs and their children.''

Lalor groaned aloud. He felt sick in his stomach. He gulped some wine and looked at the impassive, solemn Amin. He closed his eyes.

''Who is the leader of the mutiny?''

''Rissaldar Kala Khan, sahib.''

The senior NCO of the 14th Irregular Cavalry, Lalor remembered. He had also successfully suborned Karim, too.

''Many say that he is now threatening the Rani, sahib.''

''No doubt, Amin. Power is like this wine, Amin. Too much of it makes men drunk and most don't know when to stop.''

He closed his eyes and leaned tiredly against the wall, clutching his glass of wine. So Alicia and he were really all alone now, more than ever utterly dependent on the good will of the Rani. He wondered what the news was from Delhi. The re-capture of the old imperial Mughal city by the British, together with keeping the Punjab quiet, was the urgent key to stabilising the whole depressing, crumbling situation. If only he could get some news what was really happening elsewhere. Perhaps even Bombay and Bengal were also torn by insurrection.

He had been lost in his own thoughts for some time when he detected a perfume near him. He opened his eyes. The Rani was sitting on a cushion opposite him, watching him. Amin had gone. He made a move to stand up but she quickly waved him down.

"What were you going to say?" she asked drily in English. "Captain Lalor, 86th Regiment, at your service, madam?"

She also looked tired and strained. She was dressed as he had seen her at the Betwa, in riding breeches with an embroidered cotton jacket over a muslin blouse. She was bareheaded, with her thick black hair tied severely in a bun on the nape of her brown neck.

"Something like that."

"I knew you weren't asleep as you were holding your glass of wine so firmly."

"Not always a reliable sign. An Irishman is trained from birth never to spill a drop, asleep or awake."

"I heard you were badly wounded. Now I can see for myself."

"Getting better every day. At least, thanks to you, Alicia Wentworth and I are still alive."

"Miss Wentworth is bathing?"

He nodded. He again said deliberately: "We owe you our lives, Rani. I certainly will not forget that. It was brave, even foolish, to send Ghulam Muhammad and most of your men after us when you had your own troubles here."

She looked at him evenly. "Perhaps, unfortunately for you, Lalor, you may have ample opportunity to repay me."

"I'd appreciate your telling us just what has happened to our people. Chaudri more or less said that you wished to do so yourself. We know about Dunlop, Matthews and Campbell. My bearer has just told me that all who took refuge in the Fort have been murdered."

She stared at him grimly. "Yes, that is so. They came out of the Fort when Skene accepted a guarantee of safe conduct from Kala Khan but the sepoys fell on them at a garden called the Jokhan Bagh outside the city and killed them all. No one was spared."

She must have read his tense, bitter features well. She leaned across to him, gesticulating with a shapely hand, her eyes pleading with him.

"Lalor, what could I do? I have one hundred guards, armed with matchlocks, lances and swords, against nine hundred trained and well-armed sepoys and sowars. I am as much at their mercy now as your people have been—indeed, I am their current target. However, that is my problem and I will handle it somehow. Your friends were besieged in the Fort and I sent food in.

But I could do no more, Lalor. I liked Felicity Skene and her daughters as much as you did but when all this happened, I was as powerless as you were at Madhupur."

Was she acting, he wondered? He sipped his wine and regarded her earnest, vehement expression. He decided to press her hard.

"And where are the bodies of the our dead now?"

"Still lying in the open at the Jokhan Bagh. Everyone is too frightened to go near them. Including the Rani of Jhansi."

Her defiant tone was now almost aggressive. He reached for the wine flagon and refilled his glass.

"I have no doubt, Captain Lalor," she went on hotly, "that, in my position, you would have mounted at the head of your men, rode to the Jokhan Bagh and have brought away the bodies for what you term a proper Christian burial, whatever the consequences."

"Or for a proper Hindu or Muslim burial for that matter, whoever they may be. Perhaps I would have, Rani, but, then, I'm never going to be a general for exactly that reason. And, in this particular instance, I haven't the responsibilities of the Rani of Jhansi."

She sat back on her cushion, mollified but still taut and suspicious. "You can be tactful and understanding when you wish, Lalor. What sort of a man are you really?"

"An Irishman can never be two things at once. Tactful very occasionally, and understanding most of the time as he's usually a man of faults himself. Please, do have a glass of your own wine."

She inclined her head slightly in a gesture of assent. He called for Amin who appeared with his usual anticipation, bringing another glass on his tray. When the bearer had disappeared to whatever discreet nether regions he frequented, she regarded him almost coldly.

"You are ill, Lalor. You should not be drinking and talking, you should be washed and put to bed."

"My main worry, Rani, is whether you have kindly positioned enough wine to make me drunk tonight."

It was the wrong thing to say. Her features froze into a hostile dark mask and her body stiffened. She knew that he was thinking of the bodies lying abandoned at the Jokhan Bagh, just like Julian Wentworth, Adrian, Joseph and the four loyal sowars in some field south of Madhupur.

"It all depends on how much wine you need to get drunk, Captain Lalor. There is, I hope, enough but your bearer can always get you more."

He had walked into that one. He hung his head, studying his half-empty glass. When he looked up, he thought that her instant anger had quickly burned out thought she was still appraising him, almost in a hard, detached way. He wondered why. Perhaps she too was not quite clear why she had taken such a risk to send Ghulam Muhammad to find and rescue them, especially in her present situation with Kala Khan.

"I'm sorry, Rani. I've inbibed your wine and I'm tired. We've had a lot of tragedy in these past few days. But it's over and done now. Tell me about your difficulties."

She leaned forward again, her dark eyes gleaming with emotion. He caught her deep-laid sense of worry and fear as he sat there, red-eyed and weary but warmed by the wine. He was intrigued by the way she called him Lalor when she wished to be friendly and informal, Captain Lalor when formality or irritation and anger were setting in.

"Lalor, Kala Khan called on me today to say that he and his men will throw me out unless I pay them to march away to Delhi. They want eight lakhs of rupees! If I do not pay, they threaten to install a dubious relative of my late husband's, a cousin named Sadasheo Rao, on the throne of Jhansi! Lalor, I will die for my Jhansi! This is what I told the British, this is what I will tell Kala Khan!"

She suddenly lost control and began shouting. She tried to get up, her eyes blazing with passion, but he caught her free outstretched hand with his right hand and stayed her. When they clasped hands, she subsided and sank back, her breasts still heaving with emotion.

"Pay the demand," he said quietly, "assuming, of course, that your treasury has the money. Get rid of them to Delhi. Then you will be the real Rani of Jhansi."

"Are you thinking of your own skin?" she snapped at him.

"Of course. How else does a soldier survive?"

"The trouble with you, Lalor, is that you answer questions too honestly."

"Only those that should never be asked."

She disengaged her hand from his. Again, the swift burst of anger ebbed as quickly as it had appeared. She regained control of herself and looked at him, more in her old appraising self.

"I need your help, Lalor. These are dangerous days for us all. We must think and work together to survive, as you say. Mazumdar is a good man, a strong man in his way, but he is an administrator. You are a soldier and we are now in a time of violence and bloodshed where order will break down unless we ourselves are strong and defend what we believe in. You must help me.''

"Tell me what you want me to do. You don't have to ask."

"I am not yet clear in my own mind. First, I have to get rid of Kala Khan and the sepoys. That only I can do. Afterwards will come new challenges to authority. As law and order breaks down as the British come more and more under attack, we will revert back to our old ways of land wars and blood feuds. I intend to hold my Jhansi against all challenges, real or false, Lalor, you must believe that."

He did. Determination rang in every word she uttered, in her whole expression. He listened with keen interest. He knew that she had more to say.

"You must know, with the death of Skene and the destruction of the British here, I now regard myself as the lawful authority in Jhansi. When the sepoys go, I intend to write to Major Erskine at Saugor telling him that, also re-affirming my loyalty and asking for confirmation from Fort William of my position. When all this trouble is over, I believe I have strong grounds for my status to be reviewed—in my favour."

He admired her. She was playing for high stakes. He now knew, as he had suspected, why she had despatched Ghulam Muhammad to try to save the life of Sir Julian Wentworth.

"At least you expect the British to win through, then?"

"I am not really sure. To be frank, I am more than doubtful. However, despite my outburst a moment or so ago, I like to think that I take a problem objectively, as I said to Sir Julian at our farewell meeting at the Betwa. In the hard facts of who is likely to restore Jhansi to me, and in the fullness of time, to Damodar, at present I am prepared to back the British. I know they will not go down without a hard fight. But I must warn you, I think of Jhansi first and last, and I want to be with the winner in the end, whoever that may be."

"Fair enough. Then the British will have to make sure they win."

"And the Irish will help them?"

The disarmingly quick casualness of the question almost disconcerted him. She was now studying him with what he could only describe as a bland innocence.

"Yes, certainly. You see, we have taken their pay. This is how Ghulam Muhammad, in Madhupur forest yesterday, explained to his fellow Muslim, the mutineer, Daffadar Karim, why he obeyed the orders of a Hindu rani."

She was about to speak again when Alicia Wentworth came into the room. Lalor was astonished. Alicia looked a changed woman. The bath seemed to have washed away not only the dust of their journey but also her depression. She was dressed in a blue shapeless cotton robe and gold-tinted sandals and her normal aura of outdoor good health again glowed from her. Her blue eyes were clear and striking in her deeply tanned face and her short, cropped hair, though still damp, gleamed yellowish in the dull light of the oil lamps.

She sat down on a cushion beside the Rani and shook hands with her. He watched them in a detached way as they talked. The Rani suddenly looked much older and tired.

After Alicia had thanked her deeply for their rescue, the Rani glanced across at him and said: "Lalor, why do you not go to the bath? Miss Wentworth and I have much to talk about."

His dismissal was hardly subtle but predictable. He could see that the Rani was building up to tell Alicia about the massacre at the Jokhan Bagh. He heaved himself laboriously to his feet, perspiration streaming down his bearded cheeks. He was somehow conscious that this would be the last time for a long while that he would appear looking like an officer of the 86th, albeit now a somewhat filthy and unkempt one. The Rani looked at him but did not say a word. Alicia became alarmed.

"Martin, are you all right? Do you want me to look after you?"

"No, thank you, dear. A lot of soap and hot water is all I need and I'm sure that Amin has that under control. Excuse me, ladies."

In the bathroom, he undressed slowly and gingerly with Amin's help and lowered himself gratefully into the warm, soothing water. He soaped himself thoroughly and luxuriously with his mobile right arm, scouring his matted hair. Then he lay back and soaked. He could not erase from his mind the stark vision of the bodies at the Jokhan Bagh. And he thought of their own dead south of Madhupur. Somehow, Alicia and he had been spared. But for how long, he wondered.

When the water cooled, he got out and dried himself. He dressed into the white cotton native tunic and breeches laid out for him. When he combed his hair, he noticed in the mirror the reddish-brown growth of his several days' beard and decided not to shave it off. A beard went with the native garb.

Both women were sitting silently when he rejoined them. His new appearance slightly startled them both.

"Perhaps we can pass you off as a Pathan," the Rani said thoughtfully. Have your bearer tie your pugri, when you wear one, in that loose, untidy way they have."

"At least I'm a clean Pathan now. That bath was splendid."

Alicia said nothing. He could see that she was looking subdued and downcast again. He knew she had been told about the massacre.

"Until I can rid Jhansi of the sepoys," the Rani told them, "I must ask you both, for all our sakes, not to leave this taikhana. Your bearer has my personal instructions to fetch you anything you want. I now have another meeting with Mazumder and my council and must go. Goodnight, and sleep well."

Lalor rose as she did. She gave him a non-committal glance and left the room. When he sat down again, Alicia came over to him and laid her head on his shoulder. He placed his arm about her and held her reassuringly.

"Oh, Martin, I keep thinking of Felicity Skene and those two dear little girls."

"So do I. It's hard not to."

They sat together wordlessly for several minutes, each deep in their own thoughts. Eventually, she spoke again. "I've a feeling that we're going to be well cared-for prisoners here."

"Perhaps refugees would be a better expression. We must count small mercies—and the Rani has given us a big one. In fact, she couldn't have gone any higher. She's saved our lives."

"But, Martin, what are we to do now?"

"We must wait for the sepoys to march away. Then I'm sure she'll see that we can escape."

"You use the word escape. What are we escaping from if the sepoys go away? Surely she is meant to be loyal and on our side?"

"It's not only the Rani we have to contend with, dear, but those about her—her officials, her nobles. Probably many, though now frightened of the sepoys, rejoiced when disaster struck us."

"But do you really trust her, Martin?"

"You asked me that once before. Yes, I do. At least, at present. Her aims and ours are the same. She believes that the British, the conquerors of all who have resisted them in India, will win through. If we don't retake Delhi soon, her attitude could well change. But, Alicia, let's not forget that already we owe her much."

"Where can we go if we can get away?"

"Gwalior is a possibility, and certainly not too far away. Though I think it would be better to try to go south again to Saugor, where the Rani intends to send a letter of allegiance."

Amin entered the room from the stair, bearing a tray of hot, appetising roast chicken. They disposed themselves as he set out the meal and ate ravenously after the rigours and privations of the past days.

After the meal, when Amin had cleared away, Alicia went away to the bathroom and he sat there, nursing a glass of wine, thinking of the questions she had put to them. Gwalior, 80 miles to the north-west, was the nearest possible haven but no Company garrison was there; they would have to journey on the same distance again to Agra. But he instinctively felt they would be heading into more danger by going north-west, just as north-east to Cawnpore and Lucknow did not appeal to him, though they had garrisons. It would be wiser to head south to Saugor and he could give Erskine, the tragic Skene's immediate superior, a first hand account of the traumatic happenings since 4 June at Jhansi and Madhupur.

He looked up and found Alicia standing there, holding a bowl of warm water and a roll of white cloth.

"I'm going to change your dressing, Martin. It's now been rather a long time."

He nodded and began to peel off his native tunic. He dutifully submitted while she cut away his soiled bandage, cleaned the wound and rebandaged him. For the first time, he became very aware of her sexually. He had always admired her attractiveness and vivacity but had rather regarded her distantly as a young woman, just out of her teens, some ten years younger than him and the daughter of a Director of John Company. Now he smelled her clean womanly scent and felt the soft but insidious pressure of her small, firm breasts, loose under her garment, as she leaned across him to dress his shoulder wound.

When she was finished, she stood up, looking down at him. He read the fright and misery in her eyes.

"Martin, I'm not sleeping alone in that room at the back. If we are also to die, we should do so together. Martin, don't leave me alone!"

He struggled to his feet and held her slim, slight but strong body to him. He could feel the sheer relief with which she clung to him.

They re-arranged the divans and cushions about them. He went about the taikhana, extinguishing the spirit lamps all except one by their makeshift sleeping area and came back to lie beside her. He lay on his back with his wounded left shoulder away from her and reached out to take her hand which she clutched.

Later that night, he awoke to find that she had snuggled up to him, her head resting on his intact shoulder, rather like a child seeking solace and security. He reached out protectingly with his right arm and held her to him. She stirred slightly in her deep exhausted sleep and buried her face more in his chest.

Again, during another part of the night, he got the strange impression that someone was in the room looking at them. Or was he merely dreaming? If he was not, he vaguely thought it could have been either the Rani or Amin. But he never did ask either of them.

9

The Two Survivors

The Rani came to see them each night, staying one or two hours, and she gave Lalor the news he keenly sought. Delhi was still firmly held by the mutineers but the British had established siege lines about the city. To the north-east, mutiny had broken out at Cawnpore and there were strong rumours of disturbances at Lucknow and Benares. North-west, disorders had occurred at Gwalior but she assured them that Maharaja Sindhia was known to be loyal to the British. Further on, towards Delhi, the sepoys at Agra had been disarmed. To the south she was not sure what was happening but again more rumours and counter-rumours of rebellion and disaffection were rife.

As she spoke during these visits, Lalor saw how tired and strained she was but there was nothing he could do to help her. As she had said herself, Rissaldar Kala Khan was her problem.

On the third night, however, she appeared smiling. She was now dressed in a sari of the white muslin that she favoured so much. Her dark eyes gleamed with happiness.

"They have gone! I have paid Kala Khan half my treasury but it was worth it. I am now mistress not only in my own house but also of the whole of Jhansi."

"And they moved off in good military order, with band playing?"

"Yes, they did. Why do you ask?"

"The British may have their faults but they can train native soldiers well. They're heading for Delhi?"

The Rani nodded and turned to Alicia who was sitting silently. "You can now leave this place for my guest rooms. Tonight I am having a gathering of my thakurs and leading citizens to mark our deliverance from the sepoys."

Alicia listened in a lack-lustre way. Lalor was becoming concerned about her. The shock of the Jokhan Bagh massacre, coming directly on her own personal tragedy and experiences, still bore down heavily on her. Their confinement in the subterranean taikhana had not cheered her low spirits and she tended to stay close to him, subdued and withdrawn. He longed to take her fully in his arms, and he sensed that this was what she yearned for, but he dare not. He found her nearness, in her loose native garb, disturbing. He was relieved that they were leaving the taikhana.

"Rani," Alicia said quietly. "We are of course most appreciative of all you are doing for us but when can we get back to our own people?"

The Rani hesitated. "I cannot say. I still don't know where to send you. There is talk of much trouble everywhere. You will have to be patient until I get some firm information. Now let me take you to your apartments."

She led them up the narrow stone staircase to the courtyard, now softly-lit in the moist darkness with oil lamps. Already, groups of people were standing about talking and more were arriving through the gate arch. The sky was cloaked and black with a canopy of cloud. Lalor breathed the night air appreciatively. Perhaps the monsoon rains, for which the burnt land parched, were now near and about to break.

They entered a corner of the palace behind the Rani and followed her up lighted, carpeted stairs to the first floor. Servants squatting in the corridors gossiping stood up respectfully and made their obeisance. She took them into a richly furnished apartment. Amin stood there waiting. He salaamed as they came into the room.

"Your rooms are here, Captain Lalor. Miss Wentworth, yours and mine are nearby. I now have women to look after you. You both only have to ask for what you want."

Lalor thanked her and she took the silent Alicia away. A few minutes later, when he was still talking to Amin, listening to what he knew of the departure of the sepoys, the Rani suddenly re-entered the room. While Amin hastily withdrew, he again wondered about this woman. She had come in boldly and confidently, quite unlike any Indian woman he had known before. He could see that she was brimming over with a certain excitement, yet she was cool and controlled. There was something vital about her.

"Lalor, you must pass yourself off as a Pathan tonight—and from now on. Have your bearer dress you in that way."

He stared at her incredulously. "But I don't speak Pushtu."

"But you speak Hindi and Urdu. People about here are very simple. They will believe what I tell them to believe."

He asked simply: "Why?"

"Because British officers are a dangerous issue. You must not blame all on Kala Khan and the sepoys. There are many here who wished the British gone."

"Such as yourself?"

He regretted his words as soon as he had uttered them. She stiffened. "That was unfair, Lalor."

"Yes, it was. Forgive me."

"You are right, in a way. I did wish the British to be gone. But I do regret the means of causing their departure. Perhaps I can convince you by saying that tomorrow I want you to help me to write a letter to Major Erskine at Saugor re-affirming my loyalty."

A tense silence set in between them. All he could say defensively was: "But what about Alicia? She looks very English."

"There is no problem compared to you. Honourable men in our land do not build their reputation by attacking women."

"It's not the honourable men I'm concerned about. It's all the others."

"My thakurs, my townspeople, will not be concerned about Miss Wentworth."

"But what about the Jokhan Bagh? Your people stood by and allowed that to happen."

Anger flared in her eyes. He had touched on a raw nerve. "You must not try to provoke me, Lalor."

"I don't wish to. It's just that I can't get the Jokhan Bagh out of my mind. What is worse—it's affecting Alicia terribly. She could have borne the death of her father as one of those private personal tragedies that comes to us all in this life but the massacre, coming on top of his murder, is becoming too much for her."

Her retort came back like a whiplash. "Do you consider that I don't think about the Jokhan Bagh? What kind of a woman do you take me for, Lalor?"

He remained silent. She was taut with fury.

"If it will make you feel better," she snapped, "I ordered the burial of the bodies as soon as the sepoys marched away today."

"Thank you, Rani."

She studied him in that deep, enigmatic way of hers. "You should be careful not to offend me, Lalor. We need each other."

She made a move to go, then looked back at him abruptly. "Are you and the English girl lovers?"

He almost smiled. "Regretfully, for me I mean, no."

"I could arrange for you to live together. You only have to speak."

He shook his head. He hoped that he looked as bland as she could be on occasions. "She wants someone she knows to be near her because she's frightened and shocked still. She didn't like the underground existence of the taikhana. Now that she is up here in these pleasant rooms near both of us, I'm sure she'll be all right."

Her smile was deceptive. "I have heard of the gallantry—if that is the right word—of English officers towards their ladies and now I hear and see this for myself. But what if she was an Indian?"

Anger now stirred in him. Her smile lingered. Whether this was from the cynicism of her own words or her enjoyment of his discomfiture, he was not sure. He became stiffly formal, though he felt slightly ludicrous as he made his rebuttal. "Rani, I have lived with several Indian ladies during my long service in this country. This was of their choosing as well as mine. I am told that a virgin always remembers her first man. I think this applies also to a man. I lived with Yasmin in Lahore after the Sikh War. She was no virgin. I was—I was twenty—and she was a lovely girl. Whoever I knew, I certainly did not force my attentions on them or rape them."

Her smile faded. She said expressionlessly: "I believe you, Lalor."

"And I am an Irish officer, not English." Why did he say that, he suddenly wondered.

"I well know it, Lalor. If things go badly wrong for me, I may have to depend on that."

"What do you mean? Go wrong in what way?"

Her smile returned wryly, almost sadly he thought. "That must be my secret for the present. I will tell you when the time comes."

They stood there, looking at each other. For want of something to say, he motioned the divan awkwardly. "Won't you sit down? If you wish to talk more, it would be more comfortable and relaxing for both of us."

She shook her head. "Bring Miss Wentworth down to the courtyard as soon as you are both ready. We are outside because many people are coming and it should be less warm than indoors. Come to me and Mazumdar. Go through the pretence of being Lal Bahadur, a Pathan, who rescued Miss Wentworth when she was fleeing from rebellious sowars who had murdered her father. You have brought her here for her protection. We must try to go through this pretence. Your height, beard and sunburn, together with your Hindi, might just carry this off."

She walked out of the room as abruptly as she had entered. As Lalor stood pondering, Amin made another of his timely reappearances and he said to him: "Amin, you must make me into a

Pathan, one who speaks Hindi with an Irish accent.''

An hour later, he began to believe more in his sudden incarnation as Lal Bahadur. Amin produced the loose shirt and flowing breeches of the Pathans and tied his pugri in their distinctly loose and brigandish fashion. A tulwar with a bejewelled hilt, denoting a man of rank, was even given to him to buckle about his waist. The Rani had thought of everything.

When he was fully dressed, Alicia came into the room. They stood taken back by each other. She looked very attractive in a dark blue sari trimmed with gold thread.

He was first to recover from their mutual shock. ''I didn't know that you knew how to wear a sari.''

''I took some lessons in Bombay, just for the fun of it. Fortunately, it would seem. And who are you meant to be?''

''A character called Lal Bahadur, a gallant Pathan who rescued you from the mutineers.''

He told her what the Rani had advised. She eyed him curiously. ''You could play that part, though I don't think I've ever seen a Pathan. You want to be careful you don't live the role too well.''

He was strangely disturbed by her last remark. He said, almost sharply: ''But I must play, even overplay, the part. It's all towards our survival.''

She glanced away from him. ''Let's go down to the Rani and her celebration. The open air will be a change and a relief.''

The great courtyard was packed when they entered it and late arrivals were still streaming through the archway of the main gate. More oil lamps had been placed about the central fountain, lighting the soft, warm darkness, and the watered shrubs and flowering bushes gave off an earthy, pleasant smell. As Lalor led Alicia through the throng to where the Rani stood receiving her guests, he thought that they got some curious glances. Alicia had drawn the drape of her sari over her blonde hair to make a discreet, concealing cowl.

The Rani was deep in conversation with a tall, elderly thakur with a sweeping grey moustache and hook nose. Mazumdar stood near her, thickset and impassively hard-eyed, and Lalor shook hands with him. The Vizer relaxed when he saw Alicia and salaamed. ''I am sorry to hear about your father. But at least you have escaped death or injury, for which I give thanks.''

''Thank you,'' she said in her subdued way, ''and we are most grateful to the Rani for saving our lives.''

Mazumdar turned to Lalor and began speaking in Hindi. ''I think I have told you that I do not like the British. We should rule our own country. But I did not wish their death.''

"But many have died. One cannot forget this. The British won't."

"It was not our doing."

"I know. Surely, though, you must have been aware of what was happening, or about to happen, in the cantonment. Why didn't you warn Skene and Dunlop?"

Mazumdar regarded him evenly. "It was not our business, whether we knew or not. It was a matter between the British and their sepoys."

"But you are meant to be friends of the British. The Rani has confirmed this several times since we've been here."

"And I suggest that this is fairly proved by the presence of yourself and Miss Wentworth here tonight."

Lalor liked the Vizer, despite his rather bleak neutrality. He was no fool. The Rani had a sensible, tough man by her side, though he could never credit him with the decision to despatch Ghulam Muhammad to their rescue at Madhupur. That was the Rani's own decision, he was sure. As a pragmatic man, Mazumdar, with Jhansi in the grip of the mutinous sepoys, had probably argued strongly against such a move.

"The Rani has her rightful heritage at last," Mazumdar went on. "She now has command of her domain of Jhansi. This is a day of rejoicing for all the people, high born and low."

"I know. Miss Wentworth and I are glad for her. And not only for saving our lives."

"Are you sure?"

"Yes, I am sure." Mazumdar's quick retort annoyed Lalor. "Many of the British sympathised with the Rani's case, including Alexander Skene, Francis Gordon and Frederick Dunlop, but they were only junior officers. Calcutta, and then London, decided otherwise. You may not like the British, but you should believe that."

"But now we rule our own country."

"The Rani is ruling in the name of the British, Mazumdar. She was very careful to stress that to me, whatever she may say to you."

"The men in Fort William do not govern too much of India now. And it can only get worse."

"You're doubtlessly right. But be sure of one thing. The British won't go down without a very bloody fight, especially as their women and children have been killed. There'll be a lot of blood spilt in the months to come, and not only theirs. You want to make sure, as the Rani's principal adviser, that this does not include yours and hers."

Mazumdar blinked his slightly protuberant brown eyes.

"What do you mean? Why do you say that?"

"Because you are talking differently from her. Don't lead her down a dangerous path."

Mazumdar stood, open-mouthed. He was both shaken and furious. "Are you threatening me? You are in no position to threaten anybody!"

"I also know that. I am merely advising you—you, the adviser to the Rani. Because you may be assured that the British will come back and they will do some accounting."

The Vizer's stiff composure broke. His voice became a choked whisper. "I am the faithful servant of the Rani. I do not need you to tell me what I should do, where my duty lies."

"Then you should not get so emotional about the events of today. Emotions are for women, and so far the Rani herself has denied herself this luxury in the full. She realises what is ahead. The happenings of the past few days here at Jhansi, as elsewhere, are merely the opening shots in a great battle that is going to consume us all."

Mazumdar glared at him, speechless. Then he turned away and walked into the crowd without another word. Lalor felt his sleeve plucked and Alicia, standing by his side, said to him nervously: "I have no idea what you were both saying but I can see that you have offended that man terribly. He's important, too, isn't he?"

"Very. And you're right, I did upset him badly. It was some frank talk that I only hope that he's big enough to take. I felt it was important that I spelled out certain things to him. The paradox now is that the Rani, trying very hard, is just keeping both feet on the ground while he, tonight, has all the euphoria. In a short time, I suspect that the Rani, carried away by her newly-restored power, will start gathering euphoria too whereas I hope that Mazumdar, after reflecting on my few heavy words—delivered more in optimism that expectation—will sober her down."

"Good evening, Miss Wentworth," a liquid voice said softly and discreetly behind them in English. "And you too, Captain Lalor."

Rao Chaudri stood before them there, resplendent in a high-collared silver-embroidered tunic and tight white breeches. A blue sapphire glittered prominently at the front of his white pugri. His dark, handsome features smiled in a charming and relaxed way.

"Good evening, Mr Chaudri," Alicia said smilingly. She seemed genuinely pleased to see him. "How nice to meet a friend here."

"I am so delighted that you think of me as a friend, Miss

Wentworth, and honoured. How do you feel now, after your rest with us?''

''Much better, thank you. It's so nice to get out into the fresh air and the open again.''

''And you, Captain Lalor? How are you?''

''I'm trying to feel like a Pathan, rather unsuccessfully I fear. However, as it's on the Rani's instructions, I'm trying hard.''

Rao Chaudri laughed, his even white teeth gleaming. ''You under-estimate yourself. I was most surprised to see you dressed like this, so much so that I had to think hard who you were.''

''You encourage me.''

''Come, let us take some refreshments away from this crowd where we can talk.''

The courtier led them through the throng to some chairs in the dim light by the colonnaded verandah that surrounded the courtyard. As they moved, they passed the Rani. She glanced across to catch Lalor's eye and he thought that he saw the glimmer of a smile as she went on talking without pausing. She had good reason indeed to feel pleased with herself tonight, and good luck to her. He believed her story that she was not implicated in the massacre at the Jokhan Bagh and was in reality at the mercy of the mutineers too. Or was that simply what he wanted to believe? He suddenly got an uneasy feeling, as he walked thoughtfully behind Chaudri and Alicia, that he was becoming part of the Rani's plans. And what was that strange remark Alicia had just made to him? Don't enter into your role too well, or something like that?

They sat down on the chair at the outskirts of the assembly and ate delicacies from a silver tray deposited before them by a servant. Rao Chaudri chatted assiduously and lightly to Alicia who responded easily. This pleased Lalor and he warmed to the good-looking young Mahratta. He took no part in the conversation and was content to study the scene before them. He watched the Rani moving about, speaking to her leading citizens, standing in respectful groups, and he found himself again admiring her. She had poise and presence. Style was too trite a word but it came somewhere near what he was thinking.

After about an hour, a servant came to Rao Chaudri and whispered in his ear. Chaudri leaned across Alicia and said to Lalor: ''The Rani is now about to withdraw from the reception. She wishes us to join her in her private apartments for dinner.''

Lalor and Alicia were admiring the inlaid panelling of the small dining apartment, delicately painted with peacocks and flowers, with Rao Chaudri when the Rani entered the room from the courtyard below. She was dressed in a silk sari of red and yellow with its effect heightened by a ruby necklace and ruby ear-rings. Lalor had to admit again that she looked a very desirable woman. Her whole personality exuded triumph and exultation. Though she was endeavouring to appear calm and composed, he could see that she was again repressing exhilaration.

"Miss Wentworth—and Captain Lalor—I am so sorry to have kept you waiting! You must be hungry. But my people detained me. Today has been a great occasion. But let us sit down now and we will have some food and talk."

As they settled cross-legged on cushions in a small intimate circle, the Rani tinkled a silver bell and a whiteclad servant appeared noiselessly from the inner door.

"First, bring some wine! We must celebrate!"

"Where is Muzumdar?" Lalor asked. He hoped that he had not offended the Vizer irrevocably.

The Rani smiled. "Mazumdar, like all of us, has had some hard days. He is growing old. Also, his wife would be nervous in the presence of a British officer."

"And, no doubt, of a Pathan also."

The Rani laughed. "And of a Pathan, too."

Rao Chaudri smiled dutifully but Alicia stared soberly at the Rani. "What do your people think about the future, Rani?" she asked in a flat voice. "Where do they see the way ahead?"

With a swift change of mood, the Rani became serious. "They see the future—their future—firmly with me, Miss Wentworth. With who else? They rejoice in the return to the old days. I have had many expressions of loyalty and good-will tonight."

"They don't fear that Jhansi may become a battlefield between the British and the sepoys?" Lalor asked casually.

The Rani turned her gaze to him. "Perhaps they do. But freedom and honour have been rarely achieved without some suffering or pain, or even the losing of blood. And I am their princess. They will follow me and put their trust in the wisdom and powers that the great lord Krishna has given me. Tomorrow I am holding a durbar and we will discuss the course we should take. What I must do as a matter of urgency is to hire many more soldiers of my own. We do now live in dangerous times."

"But your extra soldiers will not be used against the British when they come back?" Alicia probed persistently. Lalor was surprised again at the near-surface hostility that crept into her voice and the set of her features sometimes when she addressed the Rani. Some feeling of apprehension stirred vaguely in him. Alicia was a changing—or, perhaps more to the point, a changed—woman. He could hardly blame her.

The Rani was slightly taken aback by her bluntness. "Why do you ask such a question, Miss Wentworth? Am I not your friend, and therefore the friend of your country?"

"In the last century in our country, Rani, a famous man once said that the greater the power, the more dangerous the abuse. Another saying is that he who sows the wind, reaps the whirlwind."

Lalor took up the glass of wine that the silent, obsequious servant had poured and sipped it in some embarrassment. What was Alicia up to, antagonising the Rani? He found Rao Chaudri looking across at him, smiling sardonically.

"I draw my power from the people, Miss Wentworth. I will have this confirmed tomorrow at my durbar. About my soldiers, these will be used against any who threaten Jhansi, be it the Rajas of Datia and Orchha, the sepoys, or, if they chose not to believe in me, not to support me, then the British also."

Alicia glanced at Lalor. He merely said: "I am sure that you are looking at an extreme case there, Rani—about the British, I mean."

"I hope so, Captain Lalor."

"I'm ready to help you with that letter to Major Erskine at any time."

"We will do it after the durbar tomorrow. I want to carry the people with me first. They will listen to me but I wish to be certain. I assure you, Miss Wentworth, that I really believe that you must have the will of the people behind you if you are to rule wisely and well."

"Martin and I will be delighted to deliver your letter to Major Erskine," Alicia said quietly, but she had the same intense earnestness about her. "And, better still, we can explain in person all that has happened here and what you are doing."

A hush fell on the small room. Even Rao Chaudri stared with some askance at the Rani who studied her untouched glass of wine. She toyed with it with a bejewelled hand. After several long moments, she looked up at Alicia sitting opposite her.

"If you would deliver the letter, Miss Wentworth, and speak for me, I would be both grateful and honoured. A suitable escort will be arranged to ensure your safety to the best of my ability. But I regret that Captain Lalor must stay here in Jhansi."

Alicia gasped. She looked wildly at Lalor. He drained his glass of wine and set it down deliberately, avoiding her eyes. Somehow, he was not taken back by the Rani's pronouncement. She was playing her cards well. He anticipated her words fully when she spoke again to Alicia, ignoring him entirely.

"You see, I need Captain Lalor here with me as he will be

record of what I have tried to do in the absence of English rule, of my loyalty and good purpose."

"But both he and I can say this with more than full enthusiasm and appreciation when we reach Major Erskine! He will be so much better value than I as he knows the whole military background."

Lalor thought that the Rani lost some of her tenseness. She shook her head slowly, smiled slightly and looked down at her glass of wine again. She spoke as if talking aloud to herself.

"I wish that my decision was as simple as that, Miss Wentworth. Please do not think that I am unsympathetic to all the suffering you have been through. I am determined to get you away to your own people as soon as possible. I will admit, also, that it is in my interests that you talk direct to Major Erskine at Saugor—assuming that he is still in control. This is another great difficulty. We don't know exactly what is happening anywhere at present. As for my letter to Erskine, you must also see my problem there. Should I sent this by your hand with an escort which can be seen for miles around through the countryside, whose progress will be followed, and which could be waylaid and cut down by superior hostile forces or do I send it with a half-naked man whose back is black from the sun, who will hide it in his bamboo staff and who will never be stopped? I obviously would prefer you to take my letter, as the black man will be speechless and illiterate. On the other issue, you must bear with me. I know that you have a close association with Captain Lalor, perhaps even an affectionate one, but you must understand that his continuing presence here in Jhansi is vital to me, to my survival."

"Why?" Alicia Wentworth snapped out the word.

"Because only he, a British officer, can properly account for my actions," the Rani said mildly, "to the British when they come back. They will not believe me alone. After the Jokhan Bagh, they will be after blood. What is that saying you have from your Bible—an eye for an eye? I want to keep my eyes."

"But if we both went to Major Erskine now, the impact would be so great and could put what obviously is a confused story straight right away. Martin could inform him about the whole situation here in full military terms. Don't you see that?"

"I am not thinking merely about the present, or even next week or the week after. You may well think that everything is as bad as it could be, will ever be. You have much justification for that view. But I must take a much longer look. By another four weeks the rains will come and nobody will move, not on campaign anyway. All the warring factions will build up, plan and prepare for the coming of the dry weather in October. In the meantime, I know, I feel it, that gossiping tongues in Calcutta will be speaking against me because of the terrible happening at the Jokhan Bagh. I need someone like Captain Lalor to answer for me when the British come back, just as I want you to do this for me now—what I tried to do, what my motives for this and that were. He is my insurance policy, as I believe you say in the City of London.''

"And what if the British don't come back?'' Alicia asked sharply. "What if they fail?''

The Rani looked across at Lalor. "Then I will be his insurance policy. He will be free to go at any time he pleases and with the fullest protection I can provide.''

"When can Alicia get away?'' Lalor put to her quickly.

"Within two weeks, I hope. As soon as we know it is reasonably safe to travel and where she should go to. Saugor may not be the right place.''

"Who will look after her—command her escort?''

The Rani made a slight gesture and said: "My cousin here, Rao Chaudri.''

Lalor's face must have mirrored his shock and apprehension, for the Rani smiled slightly again. "You do not seem to be happy with my choice, Captain Lalor. I assure you that my cousin is a young man of some intelligence and discretion, and he is well known in this region. He will also have my best men with him.''

He looked across at Chaudri. The courtier stared back at him impersonally but his dark eyes were alert and watchful.

"I mean no offence to Rao Chaudri but I consider he's too young and inexperienced for the task,'' he said curtly to the Rani. "To take Alicia over some distance through what we must assume is hostile territory to the British authorities requires qualities of a special kind, related to the field rather than to the office or drawing room.''

"Which you have in abundance,'' she said drily.

"Which I think I have more in abundance than your cousin.''

A deprecating, even cynical smile came to Rao Chaudri's lips: "My dear Captain Lalor, nobody—certainly not I—doubts the veracity of what you say. But what is that other excellent English saying? One should not look a gift horse in the mouth? I, the gift horse in this case, am the only horse in the race. The Rani has said, for very serious reasons of state, that she requires you here. So you must repose your trust in me. You have little or no choice. Besides I do think I would make a much more personable travelling companion than, say, Ghulam Muhammad, whom, I am sure, Rani also needs here.''

Lalor said nothing as he looked at the elegant, handsome

young Mahratta. Alicia leaned forward and said to the Rani, almost brokenly: "I'm sure Mr Chaudri will be most satisfactory to look after me but I can't bear to leave Martin behind, after all we have been through together. Isn't there some other way?"

The Rani shook her head slowly. Her features were implacable. "No, Miss Wentworth, there is not. I have told you that Captain Lalor must be my insurance policy. I know you wish him to go with you but this is how it must be. You must accept this as a small payment, penalty or whatever you choose to regard it as, for what I have done for you."

A long silence set in. Lalor reached for his newly-filled wine glass and sipped it. Alicia stared tautly at the Rani. Eventually, she said: "Then there isn't any more anybody can say?"

"I regret not," the Rani said deliberately. "Lalor, what do you say? You have been very quiet."

Lalor looked at her. She was almost matter-of-fact and casual but it was all so posed. He saw the questioning look in her dark, intelligent eyes.

"I agree with all you say, Rani," he found himself saying easily. "It is, firstly, important to get Alicia to the safety and surroundings of a British community. Secondly, I am more than willing to stay to help you with any negotiations you have with the authorities. You've done much for us. I will do all I can for you in return."

The Rani studied him, now almost in a calculating way. "You are saying that your duty requires you to stay?"

"Yes, I am. I surely can't be wrong if I speak from a sense of duty? I know I may sound pompous but duty is duty."

"Martin," Alicia asked imploringly. "Just where, in what direction, does your real duty lie?"

Lalor was disturbed by the strained, hollow-cheeked look about her, a girl who had been bursting with vitality and cheerfulness throughout their long progression through central India. He saw again her desperation, her fear, her bewilderment in being in such an alien environment. He was also conscious that the Rani and Rao Chaudri were watching him, listening avidly.

"My immediate concern, Alicia, is to get you to Erskine, or where ever the flag is still flying, as soon as possible. My long term duty must be to see that the Rani is well represented to Fort William."

Alicia buried her face in her hands. "Oh, my God," she said weakly.

Lalor felt her misery as keenly as he savoured the emptiness of his own words. Awful doubts gnawed away at him. He said to the Rani bitterly: "But I should be escorting Alicia. I am not thinking of myself. I'm responsible for her."

"I know, Captain Lalor. I am sure that you are a good officer and a skilled soldier but what can you really do by your presence in Miss Wentworth's escort? You are, in the end, one man. Indeed, if your identity was detected, this could cause trouble for the journey. But the main issue, as I have spoken, is that I need you here. You see that. I only hope that Miss Wentworth, over the next few days, will also. Come, here is the food. We are becoming too serious. Let us enjoy that and each other's company."

Later, Lalor and Alicia sat alone in the dim lighting of her room. The dinner had been eaten in an atmosphere charged with suppressed emotion and tensions, at least on their part. Alicia did not utter another word but, tight-lipped, picked away at the food. The Rani and Rao Chaudri lapsed into conversing in Hindi, and Lalor said very little, deep in his own somewhat confused and gloomy thoughts, though the Rani, in a diffident way, did try to draw him out. When the meal was over, he had asked the Rani that they might be excused 'as they had much to talk about'.

As he now looked at Alicia, sitting by him on a divan as he leaned against the wall, he felt sick. She seemed to have gone back into a state of shock. They had walked back to her apartment in an icy silence and now she sat staring numbly at the carpeted floor. As if to join his mental misery, his bandaged shoulder wound started throbbing painfully again.

"I know you think that I am letting you down, Alicia," he said after a while. The nettle had to be grasped.

He saw the hurt accusation in her eyes before she spoke. "Aren't you?"

He could only give one answer. "Yes, I am."

Tears glimmered in those accusing eyes. *Oh, God, what am I doing to us both*? he groaned inwardly. It was some time before she could say huskily: "Then why, Martin? Why are you deserting me now, after all we've been through. Speaking of duty at this place! Don't you have some duty to me, to my dead father? Why are you abandoning me?"

"Because I have to."

He was almost relieved when, after a look of disbelief, gradual anger crept on to her face. Blinking away her tears, she said tersely: "At the risk of appearing stupid, I don't understand you. I haven't done so all night."

"Alicia, the Rani won't let us go together. It's as simple as that. She's determined that I stay here as her insurance policy, as she calls it. I know you didn't see the veiled threat but that's how it is. She's more than willing that you should go as then she gets the best return from her plan—you give a first hand account to Erskine, or whoever you get to, about her loyalty. I stay as a witness for whatever develops in the months to come. But we don't go together. It's quite clear that she's adamant about that."

Shocked surprise again left her speechless for several seconds. He knew also what she was going to say next.

"Then there is no question of my going without you. We stay here together."

He shook his head and smiled ruefully. "No, you can't, dear."

"But it is I who am really deserting you!"

"Desertion doesn't come into it, in either case. What each of us has to do, in our own separate way, is the only course of action."

"You can't force me to go if I don't choose to! I suppose she can, by tying me up and delivering me as a virtual prisoner, but that would hardly do her cause much good. I'm not leaving you under these conditions."

He reached out and took her hands in his. Some of her old fire and spirit was coming back. "Alicia dear, you must do so—for both our sakes. You could be here for a very long time otherwise, and if this mutiny succeeds, we may never get out. You've been through some terrible experiences over the past days and you must get back to our own people. This is a cruel, ruthless life here, another world, another culture, another set of values. I know it, I'm used to it and I'm paid to be used to it. For my sake, particularly, you must go when you can. This I do owe to you and your father."

"Martin," she said in a small voice, "you're telling me a second time to leave you to die. There's a limit to asking such things."

He laughed. He was feeling better now that she realised the truth of what he was saying. "Now come on! All this means is that I will have to eat local food for six months or so, the Company will come marching back after the rains, the Rani will be officially restored for her good work and we'll all live happily ever after."

"You seem to trust that woman. I don't."

"She did save our lives. If another few hours had been on our side, she probably would have saved your father and the others. We must never forget that."

"I do know that and I'm most grateful to her. I've told her so with the greatest sincerity. But there is something about her. We seem to be pawns in some game she's playing, to be used up when it suits her."

"She's a woman after her own ends. She's more or less told us that."

"Martin, you're a fine man, generous and true, but you're too gullible."

"My dear, I'm afraid we haven't much choice. We have just got to be gullible. And forever hopeful."

It was all beginning to sound like a similar conversation he had with Adrian Meadows at Madhupur dak bungalow, he thought wearily. His plan then had gone badly awry and this realisation was beginning to weigh heavily on his mind. If he had not persuaded Wentworth and his comrades to go over the wall that night to hurry through the forest and fields like the hunted animals they were to become, if they all could have held out at the bungalow for another mere twelve hours, Ghulam Muhammad could have rescued them all. Was he now making another calamitous blunder, sending Alicia off by herself through a dangerous countryside with an escort commanded by a man he could not bring himself to trust?

Alicia lay down on the divan and gently tugged him down with her. He stretched out thankfully as his wound was hurting and he felt tired. He slipped his good right arm about her and she nestled into him, her head on his chest.

"What are you thinking about, Martin?"

"You."

"Truly?"

"You're never out of my mind." He smelled with appreciation the fragrance of her hair and he kissed the top of the head gently. He felt her soft body stir against him.

"Oh, Martin, I do need you so," she whispered.

"We need each other, dear."

"Stay with me tonight. We haven't been separated yet."

"Of course." He was feeling drowsy, as a sudden exhaustion came over him. Yet he was sensuously aware of her nearness and he tried to think through his fuzziness.

"What I really mean, Martin, is properly as man and wife."

Before he could speak, she leaned over him and kissed his lips deeply and passionately. He responded fiercely. He clutched her head to him. After she had gasped from the first long encounter of their lips, he kissed her over and over again on the cheeks, eyes and neck. Then he thrust her away almost roughly and they lay staring at each other, panting.

"Alicia, what am I doing to you?"

"It's what we are doing to each other."

He struggled up to prop himself on his good right elbow. He gazed down at her as she lay there. He knew he was looking at a woman inviting him to take her, not the laughing, skylarking girl he used to know. He had to fight desperately against himself.

"Alicia dear, this is not the time or the place."

"Meaning, to take my virginity?"

"Yes, exactly."

"It's all right to risk losing my life," she said mockingly, "but not that."

"It was you who reminded me of my duty to you and your father. As much as I'd like to, I'm not going to forget that conveniently now."

"I'm a woman, Martin! You can't go on trying to ignore that forever."

"Alicia, I've been a soldier since I was seventeen. I don't know much about love, only a lot about lust, but I do think I could be in love with you. And that's why I am not going to hurt you now."

"Oh, my God, Martin," she breathed. "I do love you so." Her arms came up entwined his neck. He bent down and they kissed again and again. He gently but firmly disentangled her arms and sat upright again.

"Stay with me, Martin!"

"I can't, Alicia. I don't trust myself."

"I don't want you to trust yourself! I don't intend to trust myself!"

"Both of us would regret this for the rest of our lives."

"For the rest of our lives! How long is that?"

He ignored her vehemence. "Alicia, we're both near the end of our tether. There is nothing more in the world—especially this crazy, uncertain world we now seem to live in—I would wish more than to spend the night, fully, with you. I want you very much. But I know it's not right. I'm sure you do, too."

"Thank you for the sermon," she said bitterly. She lay there, arms resting behind her neck, studying him with a new, strange sort of hardness.

"I'm sorry about that. But there's a reason for sermons, whether we like them or not."

"It's your damned Roman Catholic conscience, isn't it?"

Against his better judgement, he became angry. "Let's just say it's my conscience."

"And now you're going?"

"Yes. It's best for both of us."

He stood up and gazed down at her. She looked at him in a defiant, wounded way. Was he being a complete fool in leaving her like this? He certainly felt a fool.

He leaned down to kiss her but she turned abruptly on her side, averting her face to the wall. His lips brushed her cheek.

"Goodnight, dearest."

He picked up his pugri and went out the door. As he closed it behind him, he thought that he heard her burst into tears. He stood in the dim silent corridor and listened. He then heard clearly her sobbing. He remained there for almost a minute, beset with worry and indecision. Then he walked away to his own room, angry and bitter against himself.

10

Lal Bahadur

The days went by, hot and sultry. The sun burned from a molten sky that still tortured the dried cracked land and denied the delivering coolness of rain. Lalor and Alicia stayed confined to their apartments and waited for what news the Rani could give them. They ate with her each evening but never saw her by day. Time and uncertainty hung heavily, especially as the atmosphere between Lalor and Alicia after the night of his desertion of her was strained. She dressed his wound carefully each day but though he tried hard to jolly her and himself back to the old camaraderie, she was now distant and withdrawn. He did not press her.

On the fourth night of their move from the taikhana, the Rani suddenly said to Alicia as they sat down to eat: "I have just had information from some merchants that Major Erskine is still in control at Saugor. You may go there whenever you wish."

Alicia gasped with delight. "Oh, what wonderful news! How soon can I go? Tomorrow?"

"If you like. I can give instructions now."

"That is, if it's convenient to Mr Chaudri. I don't want to cause a lot of trouble."

The young Mahratta smiled. "I am honoured, as always, to be of service to you, Miss Wentworth. We could, and should, start tomorrow. Let us strike while the iron is hot, as you say. The countryside now seems quiet. Also, the rains are not too far away."

"What do you think, Lalor?" the Rani asked quietly.

Lalor again had that sickening feeling of apprehension somewhere in the stomach. Yet he found himself saying, almost without hesitation: "I fully agree that Alicia should go as soon as she can, and why not tomorrow?"

He thought that Alicia looked at him oddly, with that same

hurt look that he was now beginning to know. The Rani spared him further contemplation. "Then we are decided. Tomorrow it will be, though you should leave well before dawn when it is both cool and discreet."

The meal, an excellent mutton curry, became a lively, spontaneous affair, especially between Alicia and Rao Chaudri who were talking and laughing, and the Rani joined in easily. Lalor tried to but he found it hard going. He lapsed moodily into sipping his wine.

"I also have some news for you, Captain Lalor," the Rani said after the servants had cleared away. "My spies inform me that Raja of Orchha is about to attack me before the rains come. It seems that he thinks that I and my Jhansi are fair game—is that how you say it?—now that the British are no more."

They all stared at her, astonished. Even Rao Chaudri appeared surprised.

"You don't appear to be too concerned," Lalor said.

"In a few more days I will have five hundred armed men of my own. And I know my thakurs are loyal. We also have six big guns which we buried when the British came and an artillery expert, Ghulam Gaus Khan, is coming to restore these and train men to attend them."

"When about the escort for Miss Wentworth, Highness?" Rao Chaudri asked hesitantly. "There will now be no guards you can spare."

"It is even more important that Miss Wentworth gets away before Orchha attacks. You will have thirty of my best men as I promised."

"Isn't it also just as urgent now that Martin gets away with me?" Alicia said worriedly. "Such trouble has nothing to do with him."

"That is where you are sadly wrong, Miss Wentworth. I have assumed responsibility for law and order in Jhansi on behalf of the absent British. I need Captain Lalor to help me uphold that task against Orchha who is after my lands because he thinks the rule of law has broken down."

"What do you want me to do?" Lalor asked.

"Drill and train my army. They will be brave fellows but wild. They will require direction and strong handling. Perhaps you could also command them for me."

"But he's still suffering from that wound!" Alicia said tersely, anger in her eyes. "He's not fit!"

"I am aware of that. I am hoping that Orchha's natural idleness and incompetence will give us two or three weeks to make all things ready, such as Lalor's health, the training of my army, our plan how we should meet the enemy. We may even have your escort from Saugor back.''

Alicia looked helplessly at Lalor. He could see that she was imploring him to extricate himself. ''I thought I heard Alexander Skene say once that the Raja of Orchha was very loyal to the British,'' he said rather lamely.

The Rani's dark eyes regarded him. ''I am also loyal, Lalor. You have heard me say this to your face several times. Orchha's loyalty was spoken in good times for the British. I speak mine in the bad times.''

''You want me to report this to Major Erskine?'' Alicia asked her challengingly.

''Yes, I would be pleased if you would do this for me, Miss Wentworth. He will not be able to help but at least he can judge between Orchha and myself. I am for peace, Orchha is for blood and strife.''

''Will you be giving me a letter for him?''

''No, I will depend on my messenger. I know you will give him a full and unbiased account of all that has happened here, especially of my actions. Now I suggest you leave here early in the morning well before dawn when we have both darkness and coolness. This means an early night for us all.''

They rose and Rao Chaudri salaamed. ''I go, Highness, to make all arrangements for the journey. Miss Wentworth, we should leave about 3 o'clock, as the Rani advises. I wish you all a peaceful night's rest.''

When he had left the room, Lalor said to the Rani: ''I would like to send three letters with Alicia—one to my family in Ireland, one to my colonel and the other to Erskine. You are welcome to read their contents if you wish.''

The Rani smiled. ''No, why should I wish to? I trust you, Lalor. Goodnight, and to you, too, Miss Wentworth.''

Later, outside Alicia's door, he said ruefully: ''I'm beginning to feel like the condemned man, about to write my last letters.''

He saw the suspicion of tears in her eyes.

''That is certainly how I regard you, Martin. And what depresses me terribly is that you have done so little to save yourself. Goodnight.''

''Goodnight, dear. And God be with you.''

She did not resist him when he took her in his arms and kissed her. Though she clung to him mutely for a long while, their lips conveyed no passion. She abruptly disengaged and left him, closing her door silently behind her. He realised rather dismally that they were really two forlorn, pathetic characters who had been through much together and who were now separating, with the unknown still before them.

He walked moodily along the darkened passage to where the faithful Amin rose from his patient squatting to greet him. As he entered his room, he wondered how he should tell his brothers and Cecilia that he would never see them again. He felt sick and miserable and he knew that his healing wound was not causing his low spirits. Alicia had been so brutally right when she had said that he had done so little to save himself. He knew also that he would miss her acutely. He was now to be alone.

In the balmy, pre-dawn darkness of early morning, he stood with the Rani among guards and the servants under the archway of the entrance to the palace. Alicia and Rao Chaudri had mounted their horses. Outside on the road, the horses of the escort snuffled and shifted on the cobbles.

While the Rani said farewell to Alicia, he moved over to Rao Chaudri. "Look after her well. Get her safely to the British and you may depend on me for anything in my power for the rest of your life."

The young courtier's dark face was gravely serious. "By the waters of the holy Ganges, I will deliver Miss Wentworth to Saugor or lay down my life in the attempt. This I assure you, Captain Lalor."

Lalor shook his hand warmly and went across to Alicia. The Rani looked at him obliquely and discreetly left to speak to Rao Chaudri.

"Well, it almost all over now, Alicia. A swift journey unencumbered by baggage carts—you'll soon be talking with Erskine and all the others at Saugor."

"Will I, Martin? I suppose I will, if all goes well for a change. What is that expression the Muslims use—inshallah? And what do we say about you?"

She was rigidly composed as she looked down at him from the saddle but he saw again the taut strain, the anguish that was near breaking point. He said awkwardly: "I think we say that I'm the unlucky soldier who has to remain at his post when he would dearly love to be going with you."

"Martin, what frightens me—and hurts me," she said in a low, tight voice, "is that you have made no attempt to fight for yourself. You seem to accept what is happening to you with the fatalism we laugh at the Indians for. It's surely not too late to tell her even now that you've changed your mind—that you must come with me. If you make a scene, the worst she can do is put you in prison. She may even realise that there's no point in detaining you if you're not going to be co-operative."

"The worst that could happen to me, dear, is that we would probably both be put in prison."

She looked quickly ahead, biting her lip. As she sat in the saddle, she had that same look of desperate loneliness and abandonment he had seen on the road at Madhupur when she appeared with Ghulam Muhammad. He felt her misery bitterly.

"Look after my letters," he said gently. "And yourself. We'll meet again before very long. You may depend on the luck of the Irish."

Rao Chaudri moved his horse slowly through the archway to the road to join the waiting escort. Lalor was aware that the Rani was standing nearby, watching silently. He took Alicia's hand, which was cold and trembling, and she leaned down. They kissed softly on the lips.

"Goodbye, Martin," she said brokenly.

"Goodbye, Alicia dear. And God go with you."

He watched her urge her mount forward to the road. Before she disappeared beyond the archway she looked back and he caught a glimpse, despite the cowl of the cloak that she had pulled over her head, of her white, tear-stained face. Then she was gone.

A mood of even blacker depression settled over him. He stared dumbly at the ranks of the wild-looking Rohilla escort moving by until they also had departed and only the echoing hooves on the cobbles, gradually growing fainter, came back to him.

He turned away to find the Rani by his side. "You must feel very lonely now, Lalor. I am sorry for you."

He looked at her abstractly. "I'm paid to endure lonely stations, Rani. It's Alicia I'm worried about. It's a dangerous journey to Saugor and if anything happens to her—"

"I have given up my best men for the escort. You heard me say that and I am a woman of my word."

"Yes," he said, again rather absently, "you have been very good to us."

"Also, Rao Chaudri knows not to return to Jhansi if he fails. That is the importance I attach to the safe arrival of Miss Alicia Wentworth to Saugor. You may say I am probably doing this for my own political ends. You may think anything you like. But at least I am doing what I am doing."

He nodded wordlessly. He studied her more perceptively. Why was it he continued to be so impressed by this woman? Because, he answered himself quickly, she was quite unlike any Indian woman he had ever met or even heard about. She confronted him in the dim light of the archway, a ragged circle of servants and guards standing respectfully some distance from them. She had a light Kashmiri shawl draped about her head and shoulders against the slight cool and the heavy dew of the open air. Her dark, handsome features had that bland mask he also now knew so well.

"But do you know that I am doing?" he said at length, "or meant to be doing?"

"Yes, I know that too. You are to protect the Rani of Jhansi."

Despite himself, he smiled slightly. "Rani, you must not pin your hopes in me. I am a chota sahib in the eyes of Fort William, and of many others far less august."

"In my eyes, you are a burra sahib, Lalor. And I will ensure that you are one in your own eyes. From today, I wish you to command and train my army against Orchha. Within the next few days, the thakurs and their levies will begin assembling here at Jhansi. Gaus Khan, the artilleryman, arrives about the same time. Our guns have already been dug up and are being cleaned and their carriages made. I want you to be my general, Lalor."

"I will protect you against the Raja of Orchha," he said, almost harshly, "and against anybody else. I owe you so much. But you must know that this can never be if mutinous sepoys are in your forces or British are on the opposite side. I am sorry to be so simplistic, Rani, but we both must know where we stand."

The impressive mask did not falter. Her dark eyes met his. "I once said to you what kind of a woman do you think I am, Lalor. Do I have to repeat that? I don't think I'm stupid and, moreover, I don't think you regard me as stupid."

No, I certainly don't, he thought. Before he could speak, she said: "Come, we cannot stand out here until dawn. Let us take some tea and I will tell you all the latest information I have from my spies about Orchha."

Curiously, she led him up the nearby stone steps into the durbar hall where Sir Julian Wentworth had his audience with her. They sat in a corner, all alone except for servants who slipped noiselessly in and out, near where her purdah screen was on that day. He drank several cups of tea and leaned against the wall, studying her with some fascination. How incongruous it all was, he meditated. But he had never seen her so animated as she spoke passionately, sometimes in English, sometimes in Hindi. Though her talk was mainly about the threatened invasion and her counter-measures, she ranged further about her plans for Jhansi. He said very little and soon knew that he was not expected to. She was trying hard to take his mind off Alicia and while Orchha was possibly a poor substitute, he was grateful. Yet, apart from that obvious deduction, he had never seen her unbend before so much. Soon, before he realised the passage of time, the dawn came slowly and golden through the windows and the palace came to life about them.

They breakfasted on fresh fruit together in the same corner of the empty durbar hall. When they parted after the meal, she smiled and said softly: "I know you feel alone and abandoned, Lalor. This is how I have felt for too many years. Now I no longer do. I have you at my side."

On 12 July 1857, Lalor, now known as Lal Bahadur, the Pathan, sat astride his horse, Paddy, watching the approach of the Raja of Orchha's host towards the far bank of the Betwa river. He was on the same long ridge where the Rani had waited for the departing column of Sir Julian Wentworth what now seemed an aeon ago. With him was Gaus Khan, the gunner, and the leading thakurs of Jhansi. Below them were sited six heavy cannons, dug in and ranged on the river, and on either flank of the battery, strung across the lower slopes, was the motley array of the Rani's army, matchlockmen and spearmen. On the plain at the northern end of the ridge were massed one thousand horsemen on whom, with the guns, Lalor was depending so much. As he studied the distant advancing enemy he could see that it was also very much an Asian feudal army that swarmed and straggled towards the river. With some irony, he had belatedly realised that morning that it was the anniversary of the Battle of the Boyne.

"How many do you think there are?" he asked Gaus Khan.

"Two or three times our strength, by the size of the dust cloud."

"How many guns?"

"I have seen ten elephants so far. Each will be pulling a gun. There are probably more we cannot see."

Lalor nodded. He liked the short, dark, ugly man with his pock-marked face, large nose and scruffy, wispy beard who had soon showed his professional competence once the Rani's hidden guns had been mounted on their new carriages.

"Then what all this means, Gaus Khan, that there are more of the enemy to be hit with your shot. As soon as their leading cavalry is in the water, open fire while they're still disorganised crossing. Jawahur Singh, I'm relying on the chivalry of Jhansi to strike home the final blow when the time comes."

The elderly, dignified thakur with the big sweeping white moustache and fine brown eyes, mounted nearby and dressed for war in his finely-chased cuirass and spiked steel cap, nodded gravely. "We will fulfil that honour, Lal Bahadur. When you give the word, we will ride straight and true at the enemy. Either they will be buried on Jhansi soil or we will."

"So be it. Now take up your battle positions."

Jawahur Singh and the thakurs had barely moved off along the ridge line when Gaus Khan said gruffly: "The Rani comes."

Lalor turned in his saddle and looked westwards across the plain. Galloping along the dirt road in a flurry of trailing dust was a group of horsemen. The leading rider was muffled in white from head to toe except for a cuirass that flashed in the sun.

He urged Paddy down the loose shale of the rear slopes of the ridge and cantered towards the oncoming party.

The Rani pulled up her sweating, wild-eyed brown mare with a flourish when they met. She was veiled against the dust and the sun but her eyes gleamed her exhilaration. Her escort, again commanded by the formidable, pugnacious-looking Ghulam Muhammad, milled about her as they steadied their mounts.

"Lal Bahadur, I greet you! What news of Orchha?"

"You've arrived at an opportune time, Highness. The enemy's leading elements are barely a mile from the river."

"Then I will be with my army for the battle!"

"Well, part of it, perhaps," he said guardedly. "We expect the action to go well into tomorrow. What I would like you to do is to ride in review of your army. The guns won't be opening fire for a few minutes yet. It will give the men much heart to see you in the field with them."

Her eyes again mirrored her pleasure. "I will be delighted to do as I am commanded, general."

They rode together to the ridge. When they rounded the southern end and began to trot before the forward slopes, she drew the slender, bejewelled sword belted about her waist. He dropped behind her with Ghulam Muhammad and the body-guard.

Standing in the stirrups and waving her sword aloft, she rode slowly along, uttering what Lalor assumed was an old Mahratta war cry. The bearded, polygot massed ranks, gripping round shields, spears, ancient muskets and clad in a variety of venerable armour and steel caps, roared back the same cry in unison. The six guns, sinisterly black and menacing with their open snouts aimed at the riverline, looked down inanimately at the passing cavalcade, attended by their watching gunners. Ahead waited the thousand horse in some barbaric splendour, serried ranks of chain mail, spike-crowned steel caps, lances and tulwars. They were probably as good as any light cavalry in India, Lalor thought. If he could maintain control of them, he knew he would win the battle.

The Rani rode headlong at their dense ranks which parted as she approached and soon they were threading their way through a scene of deafening noise, dust and heat as every horsemen jostled to get a glimpse of her, shouting salutations and war cries. Eventually they emerged out of the rear and he guided her back up on to the high ground of the ridge and they halted there.

She pulled away the white muslin scarf veiling the lower half of her face and sat her horse wordlessly for a minute or so, trying to get her breath back. Her features glistened with perspiration and a film of dust powdered the bridge of her nose and her forehead. She gazed at him, her lips still parted from exertion. She was hoarse when she spoke. "We are going to win this battle, Lalor!"

He smiled. "Now that you have appeared, Rani, I think we are, too."

He looked across to the Betwa and the slowly advancing enemy army. A large unwieldy body of horsemen were moving over the last few hundred yards to the far bank. Behind billowed the obscuring dust cloud. Their position must have been well sighted now, yet there was no urgency of galloping messengers or commanders or any pause in the ponderous advance. Gaus Khan's guns would be opening fire soon.

"My plan, Rani, is to use the river as an obstacle to help us in our defence and as an aid when we attack. Our guns can just reach the far bank, though the solid shot on this hard ground will go bouncing for some distance. I'm told that the ford here is only about two hundred yards wide. This will make the enemy crossing concentrated and so a prime target for Gaus Khan's guns. However, I expect he'll get much of his cavalry advance guard across, accepting casualties, and these we will take out with Jawahur's Singh's cavalry. Today, until sunset, we will be content to disrupt them, to prevent them making a major crossing of the river, and wear down their morale. From my own experience, and Gaus Khan and Jawahur Singh agree, it's very unlikely that they will attempt any major action during the night, though I'll have patrols along the riverline. Tonight, if all goes well, I'm taking our horse on a night march to the south where we will lie up behind that hill you can see about a mile or so away, with the village on its near edge. Tomorrow, when the enemy should have organised himself to make a concerted attack across the ford, we will charge, after Gaus Khan has done his best—or worst—with his guns—from that unexpected flank with the whole one thousand horse. I hope that the surprise and shock of this will throw him back across the river, and in some disorder."

"And all our leaders know this?"

"Yes, this had to be, to give them confidence. I'm a new man, and a strange one too, to all of them. We've been out here two days now rehearsing what we will do. No plan survives contact with battle but it's equally important to have a concept of how you want the encounter to go—and that everybody knows this—rather than just worrying about reacting to the enemy's moves. Do you approve that I've told the senior thakurs? Do you suspect we have a possible traitor who will send word, or perhaps cross the river himself, to Orchha?''

"No, I believe all are loyal to me." She looked at him deeply and said simply: "I am impressed, Lalor."

He smiled again, broadly. "I only hope that your enemy, Orchha, will be."

"Our enemy, Lalor. I do not want you crossing the river. How is your shoulder? You have been out here so long and probably mostly in the saddle."

"The wound is healed, thank you. I'm well and fit."

Gaus Khan's guns roared out in a ragged salvo, belching black smoke. Steadying their startled horses, the Rani and Lalor looked through the clear late afternoon sunlight to the river. The leading enemy horsemen were wading through the waters of the ford and he watched for the fall of shot. A great cheer came from the squatting ranks on either side of the battery. Gaus Khan's earlier ranging rounds had been more than worthwhile. Four balls hit the far bank and went careering and scything through the advancing mass of horsemen; the other two plunged into the ford with plumes of spray among the middle of the battery, shouting out corrections and orders to his sweating, half-naked gunners. Another salvo boomed out gun by gun and Lalor saw with some satisfaction the disruption that the bounding shot was causing among the packed enemy on the far bank. As the heavy pungent smell of gunpowder drifted up to them, the Rani clapped her hands delightedly.

By the time the third bombardment had crashed out, about two hundred enemy horsemen had forced their way across the hazard of the ford and stood reined in indecisively on the near bank staring at the defended position before them. He was about to turn away on Paddy when the Rani grasped his forearm.

"Where are you going?" she asked.

"It's time to clear this lot from the home bank with a brisk charge by Jawahur Singh's cavalry."

"You are not to go with them," she said sharply. "You are now the general, not the captain. I need your military brains, not the strength of your right arm."

"If you say so, Rani, so be it. But you must allow your general to make his own decisions. A commander is only as good as his soldiers see him."

He called up a young thakur whom Jawahur Singh had posted

with him as a liaison officer, gave him the order and the Bundela galloped away along the ridgeline and down to the waiting cavalry. Within minutes the mailed mass of horsemen moved off and in a gathering dust cloud, cantered in an arc to the river to come down on the enemy bridgehead from the north. More enemy horsemen had struggled across the ford but the flank approach of the Jhansi cavalry allowed Gaus Khan's guns to fire until they had turned south, reformed and slowly began to pick up the momentum and full gallop of the charge.

The whole operation was over in less than thirty minutes. The overwhelming numbers and weight of the Jhansi cavalry pounding down swept over the disorganised enemy bridgehead and shattered it. Some sporadic hand-to-hand fighting went on but soon it became a desperate struggle for the enemy survivors to fight their way back into the river for survival. True to his orders, Jawahur Singh did not permit any hot blooded pursuit across the river but set about rounding-up prisoners and riderless horses and stripping the dead of their armour and weapons. The Orchha artillery was still not in action and his clearing-up of the battlefield went unmolested.

The Rani, who had been watching the spectacle in rapt silence, turned to Lalor. Her striking features were animated. "All the signs are that we will indeed have a great victory, Lalor! You have planned it so well."

"The victory is yet to be won, Rani. We have a long way to go. Now if I am your general, you must listen to me. Orchha's artillery must deploy soon and they will get the range of this ridge just as we have the far bank. I will then move the infantry back on the reverse slope out of harm's way but your safety will be an embarrassment to me. Also, soon it will be dusk and I have many tactical and administrative matters to attend to in preparation for tomorrow, the decisive day. What I am saying is that you should now return to Jhansi and await news of our final victory. I will send a fast rider to you as soon as this is assured."

"I am old enough to know when a request is an order, Lalor."

She took one last look at Jawahur Singh's horsemen streaming back from the riverline where scattered bodies and carcasses of dead horses lay and turned her horse down the rear slope. Lalor accompanied her, followed by Ghulam Muhammad and the bodyguard.

"Ten wagonloads of shot are coming to you," she said as they picked their way down. "I passed them on the way."

"Good. It's going to be hot work for Gaus Khan and his men from now on—and for the enemy too, I hope."

At the foot of the slope, she halted. He clasped the hand she held out, feeling both its softness and strength. She looked at him seriously and deeply.

"May the gods watch over you in this battle, Lalor."

One only will do, he thought. She made no attempt to withdraw her hand.

"You hold the future of Jhansi in your hands. Jhansi is at stake, and so is your own life. Both are important to me."

She took away her hand abruptly. He saluted and said: "You may depend on the old 86th doing their best, both for you and themselves, Rani."

She wheeled her mount without another word and rode away, followed by her Rohillas. He watched her for a long while until her cavalcade disappeared into its own dust and the folds of the ground. He urged Paddy rather wearily back up the slopes of the ridge again. What was he doing here, he asked himself yet again, an officer of H.M. 86th Regiment of Foot, commanding one Asian host pitted against another in central India. Because the year was 1857 and one had to survive. Even the Rani had to survive.

A distant muffled roar made him urge Paddy up to the ridge crest hastily. The enemy guns across the river had now come into action. He had fresh dispositions to make urgently.

The rains broke as Lalor rode back from the Betwa the following evening. The skies unfolded with drumming torrents blown by a tearing wind but though he was drenched and bone-weary, hardly able to see the track in the poor light, he was elated. The victory, greatly helped by the ineptitude of Orchha's forces, had been complete. After Jawahur Singh's initial charge, they had repulsed two more blundering sorties across the river and then darkness had brought exhausted quiet. He had then led Jawahur Singh's horse south to their over-night lying-up position. When Orchha had forced the crossing of the ford next morning with a mass attack, they had charged from the unexpected flank. In the ensuing rout, they had pursued the fleeing enemy across the river and rode them down, spearing and hacking as they thundered along until, about some five miles from the river, he had regained some semblance of control and halted the pursuit. He had made sure of one certain military prize: that Orchha's captured guns were hitched up to their elephants to be dragged off to Jhansi. He then left the prisoners and the booty to the gallant Jawahur Singh who, in company with three of his sons, seemed to have physically rejuvenated himself during the whole battle. Riding with Lalor, in the middle of his small escort, was a son of the Raja of Orchha who had led the main attack that morning.

It was about two hours after sunset when he rode with his party through the Orchha Gate in the city walls. Despite the rain, the narrow streets were thronged with excited, cheering people as they clattered along. The news of the victory had spread from the messenger he had sent back to the Rani at noon and, coupled with the relief of the rains, the city was in a festive mood. At last he turned Paddy into the archway of the palace and dismounted stiffly. He gave his escort instructions to hold the Raja of Orchha's son until the Rani wished to see him, and even fuller instructions to the syces who came running across the road from the stables about the feeding and grooming of Paddy. As he trudged, sodden and mudstained up the stone stairs to the durbar hall to report to the Rani, he realised that he was more concerned about his horse than a young man, albeit an enemy, who had fought bravely. But, he again reasoned hazily, this was 1857, a year of blood, and the times were brutal.

He entered the durbar hall. The Rani was seated in a high-backed chair at the far end, flanked by a half moon of chairs occupied by court officials and leading citizens. He recognised only Mazumdar and Rao Chaudri as he strode across the long, soft Kashmiri carpets towards her. She rose to her feet, smiling, as soon as she sighted him, and the others hastily followed. She was dressed in what he called her campaigning kit: jodhpurs with riding boots, a white blouse and a white pugri. Except now she was wearing a huge red ruby which gleamed bloodlike in the centre of her pugri, a thick pearl necklace adorned her throat and she wore pearl earrings. Through his tiredness, he was slightly amused to surmise that she was determined, if the battle had gone against her, she was going to die both as a warrior and a woman.

"Welcome back, General Lal Bahadur! We have been waiting for you. All Jhansi rejoices in your victory."

He drew his tulwar, knelt before her and proffered it with both hands. She touched it symbolically.

He stood up and sheathed his sword. He said formally: "It is my duty to report, Your Highness, that your enemy, the Raja of Orchha, has been driven from the soil of Jhansi with heavy losses. The casualties of your own army have been light. We have captured fifteen guns, together with their elephants and ammunition train. About 500 prisoners have been taken, including the eldest son of the Raja. I have him outside for your disposal."

"Excellent! We will ransom him for a lakh of rupees which will go to the families of our dead and wounded."

"Jawahur Singh is bringing the army back and he should reach the city in about three hours. With your permission, Highness, I would now like to withdraw to bathe and change my clothing."

"Not before we drink some wine to toast our victorious army and their general."

She clapped her hands and a waiting white-clad servant came forward bearing an embossed silver flagon and glasses on a tray. The Rani and he stood looking at each other, holding their filled glasses. The radiance and elation of her mood permeated even through his weariness. She how had much to celebrate. The threat of the sepoys and their puppet, Sadasheo Rao, had been successfully fended off, she had resumed the throne of Jhansi with full power, and now she had a victory in battle while the rains were teeming down on the countryside. As the pouring of the wine went about the assembly with laborious slowness, he began to worry what Mazumdar and the others thought about him and the Rani as they stood close together. She was ignoring all of them.

To his relief, she at last raised her glass and cried: "To Jhansi and more victories for her!"

He repeated the toast and drained his glass in one appreciative gulp. Victories against whom, he wondered. He gave his glass to someone nearby.

"Go, Lal Bahadur," she said. "Food and wine will be sent to you. I await Jawahur Singh."

He went about her council, shaking hands. All made an obeisance to him, even the dour Mazumdar. Rao Chaudri looked uneasy when Lalor came to him, quite unlike the cockiness, even arrogance, he exuded since his return from escorting Alicia Wentworth to Saugor. Perhaps he resented, or even feared, Lalor's new found prestige and power. If so, why, Lalor pondered absently.

He saluted the Rani finally and left the durbar hall.

An hour later, he lay on his bed, bathed, fed and dressed in clean, dry clothes. Though he had been revived by the abundant hot water that Amin had ready for him, the strenuous activity of the past days still left him very weary.

As he rested drowsily, with a glass of wine by him, he brooded over the extraordinary circumstances in which he now found himself. He had just commanded an Asian army of feudal vintage in battle, he was living this charade of being a Pathan and he was now clearly elevated in the eyes of the Rani into being a major personality at her court. He wondered what Mazumdar and Rao Chaudri, who knew the real truth about him, quite apart from those who must be speculating, now thought.

Rao Chaudri. His mind dwelt heavily on the young Mahratta.

He had welcomed him back so enthusiastically after his success-ful mission delivering Alicia to Saugor. Rao Chaudri then had seemed so eminently pleased with himself and had basked in the congratulations showered on him by both the Rani and himself but what had disturbed Lalor was that Alicia had not written to him the briefest note to say that she had arrived safely with Erskine. Rao Chaudri had explained this quite simply. He had feared going into Saugor as anybody such as he was tainted not only with the mutiny at Jhansi but, far more dangerous, the massacre at the Jokhan Bagh. However, he had seen Alicia enter the gates of the fort. He had offered to swear to Lalor the most sacred Hindu oaths that this was so. Yet the old lingering distrust of the urbane young courtier nagged him still.

He must have dozed off for some time, for he awoke to find Amin bending over him, shaking his good shoulder gently.

"Sahib, one of the Rani's women has called. The Rani wishes to see you."

As he struggled to sit up on the side of the bed, he could hear the rain drumming down outside the window. Thunder rumbled distantly and a flash of lightning momentarily illuminated the close, packed houses by the palace.

"The name of Lal Bahadur, the conqueror, is on everybody's lips in Jhansi, sahib," Amin said again, smiling.

"I only wish it could be Captain Lalor, 86th Regiment, Amin."

He went outside to the passage where a slim, dark, anonymous female made obeisance to him and led him, to his surprise, not to the durbar hall but to the Rani's own apartments. As he followed his small, silent guide, he passed the door of Alicia's old room and he reflected bitterly.

The ayah ushered him into a room well-furnished with Persian carpets, divans and small carved tables, softly lit with tall brass oil lamps which illuminated exquisite batik work adorning the walls. Almost as soon as he heard the ayah wordlessly withdraw, he saw the small ironbound chest of jewels lying open on a round table in the middle of the room. He moved over to it and stared, fascinated. All kinds of precious stones lay packed in seductive opulence: rubies, sapphires, diamonds, pearls, gold bracelets.

He was still standing there, mesmerised by the treasure, when he heard the Rani's voice behind him. "You may take your choice."

He spun around, strangely startled, for subconsciously he had been expecting her. When he saw the woman who had emerged from the adjoining room, he knew that he was looking at a Lakshmi Bai, Rani of Jhansi, whom he had never known before. She stood there in the soft light, her black hair loose and brushed into a dark cascade, her handsome features set with a curious tension. She was dressed in a belted robe of yellow silk and without any jewelry. Only the ornate yellow slippers on her feet gave any aesthetic support to her robe.

"It is the custom, Lal Bahadur, to reward and honour victorious generals. You must not hold back because you are really Lalor. Remember Clive, Skinner, Hodson."

He took some time to answer. "I am so impressed with what I see that I find it hard to know what to say. A terrible admission for an Irishman. And I am looking at you."

She crossed slowly to the treasure chest, closed its lid and turned the key in its lock. He caught her perfume as she passed him. She slipped the key into the pocket of her robe and swung about to face him. He had never seen her looking so attractive. Gone was the aura of power and authority and the appreciation of that power which drove this remarkable woman along and which she enjoyed so much. Now she was a vulnerable, highly desirable woman.

"Now you must open the lock that has been about me these years, Lalor," she said almost inaudibly. "Only you have that key."

When he held out his arms, she slipped into his embrace. He kissed her passionately and she clung to him. He could feel her voluptuous but strong body writhing in his arms. When he began kissing her cheeks and neck, she gave a deep sigh and murmured in Hindi which he could not catch. They stayed held in each other's arms for a long time, their lips seeking each other's hungrily or buried in each other's neck. He caressed her long hair and firm back, intoxicated by her perfume and nearness. After a final lingering kiss, he picked her up and carried her, so sensually warm and yielding, to her bedroom.

When they had given each fully to the other and passion was temporarily spent, they lay nakedly in each other's arms, wet with perspiration from their exertions but, as lovers do, neither cared. Outside, the rains came steadily down and thunder grumbled against the occasional glint of lightning. She lay pillowed on his right shoulder and he stroked her hair gently. Her skin was like glistening brown satin.

Eventually she whispered: "Lalor, dearest one, you must stay here forever and be my prince. Everything is changing now. The whole of India is in turmoil."

"It's the coming of the monsoon rains. We Feringhees know that this affects the Indians as much as us."

"I really do not think that the British are going to win, Lalor beloved. I know Nana Sahib and Rao Saheb and the support they can muster, especially from the sepoys who come from Oudh. And the Muslims are rallying about Bahadur Shah for the restoration of the Mughals' glory—which is not really a problem as the Mughals were always tolerant to Hindus. Now that the sepoys have mutinied against the Company all over the north, every die is cast against you. Your sailing ships with more soldiers from England will never reach here in time."

"Lakshmi Bai, my dear—"

She interrupted him, running her hand lightly from his stomach to rest lightly about the healed wound on his left shoulder. "My family name is Manu, Lalor. You must call me that from now on."

"Manu, I hope that I may be your lover always, come what may. To be your prince is another matter. I think I said to you once that I've taken the salt of the British. I come from an Irish regiment who will not only be horrified to learn about what happened to British women and children at the Jokhan Bagh but will go almost mad—probably out of control of their officers. You must understand that."

She propped herself on an elbow, her full breasts with their dark nipples leaning over him. Her eyes flashed with her sudden anger.

"Lalor, sometimes I think you are what the British call a bloody fool!"

"I agree, dear. I shall never be a colonel, let alone a general, in the British Army. Haven't got the money even to buy a majority."

She gave him a firm reproving slap on his stomach. "Lalor, you must not joke all the time. You and I could make a kingdom together. Those jewels you saw were only my personal possessions. I will show you my whole treasury, my books that give the state revenue. I will share all I have with you. I care nothing for Nana Sahib, Bahadur Shah. I care only for my Jhansi and, now, for you. Together, with you as my general, we could conquer all Bundelkhand."

He gently lowered her beside him and began slowly stroking her breasts. He kissed her softly and he could feel the vehemence ebbing from her.

"Manu, I will be your general as long as those who are opposed to what my regiment are fighting for do not appear near you. That's as simply as I can put it. Certainly, that's how I see it. I'm sure you do too. Now, please, let me be your lover and we'll concern ourselves about my princely status later."

She drew him to her wordlessly. His lips sought, and easily found, hers. Their bodies became entwined in mindless, passionate sensuality.

Beyond the room, the rains lashed and tore, driven by a skirling wild wind, and thunder growled. Occasionally, distant lightning fleetingly glimmered across the storm-ridden sky. But Martin Lalor, 86th Regiment, and Lakshmi Bai, Rani of Jhansi, were lost, isolated and oblivious in their own world, one where two kindred spirits meet and give each to the other, mentally as well as physically.

BOOK TWO

RETRIBUTION

11

The Road Back

Though he was bone-weary from his many days in the saddle, Martin Lalor knew that he had rarely beheld a more exhilarating sight. He was sitting astride Paddy on the bare, rocky summit of a large wooded hill overlooking the River Chambal four miles from the rebel-held city of Mandesar. Below him, about six hundred yards away, a British force was approaching the river. He leaned forward on Paddy's strong, chestnut neck and took in the spectacle.

The Chambal had steep, verdant, shrub-covered banks, except for the ford crossing, and he watched the vanguard of cavalry splash and plunge into the quick-flowing, clear water. Across the plain, in a faint haze of dust, came a long thin column of infantry toiling forward. He could visualise behind them the artillery, obscured in the dust cloud, in a jingle of harness brass and creaking limbers. He could clearly imagine the trumpeting of the heavily-laden elephants and the grunting screams of the baggage camels. Before him lay the soft, blue-tinted horizon of a cloudless day with balmy winter warmth.

He was so engrossed that he failed to observe the mounted patrol emerge from the treeline behind him. He heard shouts in English and turned in the saddle to find six British cavalrymen urging their horses up the slope towards him. He did not move. Soon he was surrounded by a ring of sabres brandished by perspiring, red-faced Englishmen.

"Hands above your head," a big corporal with a heavy gingery moustache and sideburns ordered him roughly in a Newcastle accent, "and drop that rifle."

"That's a Company cavalry carbine he's got, corporal," one of the troopers shouted. "He's one of those bastards all right."

"I'm not really, corporal," Lalor said with some deliberation, his Irish accent as thick as he could make it. "I'm Captain Lalor, 86th Regiment, reporting back from Jhansi for duty."

If he had thrown a grenade, his words could not have had more effect. The ruddy-faced corporal's jaw dropped and he stared blankly in stunned silence. The other troopers looked on open-mouthed, also. The drawn sabres wavered uncertainly but remained levelled.

"Do me a kindness, corporal," he asked casually, "tell me, what is today? You see, I've been living like a native for so long that I've lost track of Christian ways."

The corporal still gazed at him dumb-founded. "Nineteenth November," one of the troopers muttered. The corporal repeated this hoarsely, as if giving the utterance official sanction.

"Now, I've told you who I am, corporal, even if you do find it hard to believe. But who are you? I can see you and your men are from the 14th Light Dragoons—you must have just returned from the Persian campaign—but what is this column you belong to?"

The corporal found his voice again. "The Malwa Field Force." He paused, his honest, stolid features still betraying nagging doubts. Then he grudgingly volunteered: "Brigadier Hasty is our commander."

"Then I request you to take me to him so that I can report myself. You may gladly have my rifle—only I'd like to retain my tulwar. It has a special significance for me."

The corporal thought laboriously for several long seconds. He decided as any good NCO in a quandary would.

"I'll take you to my officer," he said.

An hour later, Lalor sat in a canvas camp chair opposite Colonel Henry Mercier, Acting Political Agent for Central India, and Brigadier Charles Hasted in the shade of trees along the bank of the Chambal. Mercier, a big heavy man with shrewd brown eyes and blue jowls about a thick grey moustache, was dressed in a crumpled and dusty linen suit. Hasted, dark, neat and intense with deeply tanned, clean-shaven features, was in the uniform of the Bombay Infantry. Like the patrol, both had been considerably shaken by his identity but had recovered quickly to greet him warmly. While a knot of staff officers stood curiously by, Mercier and Hasted listened intently as he unfolded his tale.

Mercier spoke first after he had finished. "We knew of the murder of Sir Julian and the others, also of the survival of Miss Wentworth and yourself, from your Goan cook. He found us at Mwow in late August."

"Good old Peter. God bless him."

"What he told us about Jhansi as a whole was invaluable to our trying to fit the pieces together."

Lalor asked the question that was burning inside him. "What news of Alicia Wentworth? As you've just heard, she was escorted to Saugor but I believe trouble soon broke out there?"

Mercier nodded gravely. "We can only assume she's safe but locked up in the fort with many others, about one hundred and thirty including women and children. The place has been under siege by mutineers since mid-July, though the Thirty-First Bengal stayed firm. We've no real intelligence how they're faring, except we do know that they're still holding out."

Lalor stared at the Political Agent, shocked and speechless. When he found his tongue, dried in his mouth with fear, he said bitterly: "Oh God! From one tragedy to the makings of another."

"But at least she's with our own people," Hasted said soberly. "That's surely something."

"You must know even more than we do," Henry Mercier went on, "that almost all Central India is in revolt and now that the rains have come, both the rebels and ourselves are assembling for the final trial of strength."

"Yes, I do. That's why I came south-west from Jhansi and not south by way of Saugor. I had of course no idea that Alicia was still there."

"We're now moving on Prince Feruz Shah at Mandesar," Mercier went on, "and then our next objective will be Indore where the Holkar's army is badly disaffected. I don't trust him either. He's like several others of his ilk—waiting to see how the cat will jump. But, at least, the capture of Delhi in September has given us a beacon light of some success amid a lot of gloom. Next month we'll be much stronger with additional forces and Major-General Sir Hugh Rose arrives to take command. We'll then march to relieve Saugor and on to Jhansi to clear the whole of Central India."

Lalor nodded vaguely. He was not really listening. He was thinking about Alicia. What another disaster, again with the best intentions, he had perpetrated!

Hasted suddenly became sharp and blunt. "We've had intelligence reports about a heavy rumour that a British officer was acting as a general for the Rani of Jhansi's forces, disguised in native garb. We obviously deduced, from what your Goan cook said at his interrogation, that this was you, Lalor."

Lalor stirred in his chair. He felt the eyes of the circle of officers on him. "Yes, you're right, sir. After the sepoys marched away from Jhansi, the Rani assumed responsibility for law and order—quite rightly in my opinion—and went out of her way to say that she had done so in the name of the Company. I helped her draft a letter to Major Erskine at Saugor stating this and reaffirming her loyalty. You must know about this, Colonel?"

Mercier's eyes became heavy-lidded and impassive. "Erskine was ill-advised to forward her submission on with his recommendation that we back her."

Lalor became angry. He was tired and he recognised official-dom's negative, hostile mask with some irritation. Mercier pre-empted his outburst. "Fort William decided against her."

"Meaning that you decided against her and Erskine?"

Mercier mottled but he controlled himself. "The decision came from the Governor-General's Council at Calcutta, Lalor. That is all I wish to say to you or anybody else."

"Which also means that she's tainted with the massacre of Jhansi, whether there's evidence against her or not?"

Mercier and Hasted looked at each other. However, Mercier remained the objective political officer. "Why did you become her military commander, Lalor? Again, our intelligence sources tell us that you defeated the Raja of Orchha on her behalf."

"Yes, there was a battle. Orchha invaded her territory when she was representing the British suzerainty. Orchha lost."

"Orchha is a known friend of ours," Mercier said sharply.

Lalor leaned forward. He knew that he was going to transgress the bounds of discipline but his nerves were too raw. He was beyond caring to try to restrain himself. He said sarcastically: "Are you saying, Colonel, in this bloody awful situation we have all found ourselves in over the past six months that you really know who are our friends and who are our enemies? I suggest that until now you haven't been able to control anything beyond a stone's throw of Mwow and know little of what's going on beyond there! A couple of miles away from us now is a Mughal prince with ten thousand men and fifteen guns who, if you don't stop him, will go down the road to Bombay. You can't control Indore where your alleged man, the Holkar, is and you can't even give me any real news about Saugor where poor Alicia Went-worth, who's been through so much, is trapped yet again." He rose to his feet, tense with fury. "Colonel, I don't think you have the slightest bloody idea who our friends are! You can only identify the enemies who appear in the field against us, like Feruz Shah. Well, I did the same at Jhansi. Orchha was out for the traditional land grab when he thought the Rani was weak and vulnerable. Why shouldn't a declared loyal representative fight to repel whoever came against her?"

Mercier eyed him coldly, Hasted rather speculatively. The listening officers about the fringe closed in protectively and he sympathised fully. He was bearded and unkempt, burned almost black from the sun and his native dress travel-torn and dirty.

He sat down again. A silence, broken only by the twittering of happy, unseen birds in the great tree above them, set in. They were only a hundred yards from the crossing but even the noise and shouts from there were now muted. The head of the infantry column had now come up to the far bank after the cavalry had waded through and officers stood debating the depth of the ford.

Mercier slumped in his camp chair, studying him with a measured interest, and said nothing in retort to his outburst. Hasted spoke almost casually: "However, what made you leave her, Lalor?"

He did not hesitate. "Tantia Topi, the agent of Nana Sahib, visited Jhansi and the Rani entertained him."

Again Mercier and Hasted exchanged glances. Lalor remained nettled. He said bitterly: "By this time, Colonel, she knew that she had been abandoned by Fort William and her own particular die was well and truly cast. Can we blame her?"

"The circumstantial evidence against her was heavy," Mercier said stiffly, "Calcutta drew their own deductions."

"Or your deductions?"

"Lalor, I know you've been through a lot, that you're tired," Mercier countered with some asperity, "but I'm not used to being spoken to like this. I'm certainly not here to be interrogated. I only wish that the Rani could be."

"Like you, Colonel, I wasn't in Jhansi at the time of the massacre but I was a bloody sight closer. I was back there a matter of days afterwards. I spoke with her then, I knew the local situation. She had great problems with the sepoys whether she would survive herself—and she had to buy them off at some considerable cost. I tell you, she was ours then, ready to chance all for us. And what happens at the end of the day? She's been driven into the hands of the rebels."

"Then we will have to bear with that, won't we?" Mercier remarked icily.

A surge of anger went through Lalor again. Before he could speak, Charles Hasted intervened with quiet authority. "Lalor, to come to our immediate problem, I hope you've ridden through Feruz Shah's defences. Perhaps you've even been inside the walls of the city itself. Before we send you on to Mwow and some rest, I'd appreciate any intelligence you can give me about Mandesar and Feruz Shah's dispositions. You probably know that Mandesar has a reputation. Monson's column in '04 met disaster here retreating from the Holkar of Indore's army."

Lalor was almost grateful for the sharp little brigadier's intervention. He relaxed somewhat. "Yes, I've had a good look at the enemy and the city. I'll give you all the help I can, sir."

"Capital! After we've had a bite to eat, you and I will go on a reconnaissance. It'll take us a day or so to cross this river, especially to get the ammunition and baggage trains across, but I hope to attack as soon as possible."

Henry Mercier got heavily to his feet. Hasted and Lalor stood up also. The Acting Political Officer, whatever his Army rank, was a burra sahib by virtue of his appointment.

"I'm going to take a short rest, Charles. This evening we'll consult about the latest intelligence—of which Lalor may well be the main source—and then the plan of operations is yours entirely."

They shook hands. Mercier studied Lalor with some finality but his grip was warm and strong. When Lalor and Hasted sat down again, the brigadier leaned forward eagerly in his chair and began questioning him about Mandesar and the rebel force. He answered fully and willingly. This brought his seething anger back to normality. As his irritation eased away, he regretted in retrospect that he had almost blatantly insulted Henry Mercier who was also bearing many stresses. They were all trying to find the same victory. Yet that 'already proven' verdict on Manu rankled, and both Mercier and Hasted had noticed that.

The commander of the Malwa Field Force went on enthusiastically: "I haven't had the chance to tell you some real news. My infantry consists of 25th Bombay and—what will please you— two companies of the 86th."

Lalor smiled his delight. "Then not only can I get a good shave but I'll be properly kitted out again after so long. And enjoy some whisky after a very long drought."

He warmed to Hasted. He remembered that the 14th Dragoons patrol commander had called him 'Brigadier Hasty'. He reflected that the British now needed many Brigadier Hasty-ies.

Ten days later, Lalor reached Mwow. Over the long summer monsoon months, the station had been a tenuous linch pin for the Company in a crumbling Central India, held by Captain John Hungerford's Bengal European artillery battery until relieved by the Malwa Field Force in August.

At Mandesar, three days after the crossing of the Chambal, a sharp artillery engagement, followed by a charge by the 14th Light Dragoons and the Hyderabad Cavalry brought the British within a mile of the city. Next day, a hard fight developed but the superiorly-handled guns of Woolcombe's Horse Battery and the Bombay Artillery shattered the rebels and Feruz Shah slipped away with the remnants of his army. The British were too exhausted to pursue and Mercier and Hasted were content to hold the line of the Narbada river to prevent any reinforcement of Holkar's disaffected army at Indore.

Lalor had a joyous, if astounded, reunion with the officers,

NCOs and soldiers of the 86th companies with the Malwa Field Force and despite the busy preparatory period before going into battle, talked long into the night drinking with them. However, they resolutely refused to kit him out with any uniform, saying they were only carrying replacement clothing items for the soldiers. He saw that the 86th loved to see him dressed up as 'wun of them haythen Pathans' and he accepted his fate as regimentally-decreed. He had dearly wanted to go into action with the 86th on the final day but Charles Hasted crisply pointed out that the two companies had their full complement of officers and, anyway, Henry Mercier and he wanted him by their side.

At Mwow, however, Lalor did divest himself of his Pathan garb. He also shaved off his beard with almost a sensual feeling of achievement and was able to dress himself again as an officer of the 86th. Fortunately, Joe Morrow, the regimental Quartermaster, an engaging, roguish fellow whom Lalor had known since he was a young officer and Joe a sergeant, was at Mwow with his stores, as battalion headquarters and the other companies of the 86th were expected shortly from Bombay to join the concentration of troops assembling for the coming campaign.

He found that he had no inclination to journey to Bombay to take leave. Perhaps this was partially due to the expectation of the rest of the 86th coming up the road but really he knew that it was because Alicia Wentworth was besieged at Saugor. And soon Saugor would be relieved by both Company and Queen's troops now assembling at Mwow. Henry Mercier had stated that quite positively. Saugor was the first main objective, then the vengeance march on Jhansi, Lalor reflected soberly.

He did not have long to speculate. On 16 December, Sir Robert Murray, the Political Agent for Central India, arrived at Mwow, having sailed from England when news of the Mutiny reached there, and next day, Major-General Sir Hugh Rose assumed command of the newly-formed Central India Field Force. Within twenty-four hours, Lalor was summoned to report at noon next day to both Murray and Rose in Hungerford's former battery office. On Henry Mercier's direction, he had written a long, detailed account of his experiences as soon as he had settled in at Mwow.

Sir Robert Murray, after sitting him down informally in a cane arm chair, opened the conversation. He was tall and distinguished-looking with long thick silvery hair and an aquiline nose. He had an inquisitorial and penetrating calm about him as he regarded Lalor with his grey eyes. He wore a brown frock coat trousers that reminded Lalor of Julian Wentworth and the sartorial Joseph Evans.

"Captain Lalor, both the General and I read your report on Jhansi—and connected events—with absorbed interest. As you probably know, we have both only landed from England a short time ago and there has been much rumour and speculation about Jhansi, especially about that terrible massacre. You have set out the events, as you saw or heard about them at first hand, with admirable clarity. But of course you weren't there at that particular time—you had your own considerable troubles at Madhupur dak bungalow."

"What I have written is my honest assessment as one who was close, as you say, to the whole tragedy, which surely must mean something."

"Quite so. But you are very pro-Rani," Murray said swiftly, "if that is not too strong a term. I thought your otherwise excellent report was rather coloured by being almost an apologia for her."

"She rescued Alicia Wentworth and myself from what was almost certain death. Then she sheltered and protected us in her own palace, even when the sepoys were threatening her. I am sure, sir, you'll forgive me if I express some gratitude, even on behalf of the Company and the Crown. Is recognition and appreciation of such help 'colouring'?"

Murray pursed his lips and placed his long fingers together prayer-like. His eyes were hard and penetrating. "She wanted you—and, indeed, politely coerced you—to stay at Jhansi so that you could answer to us for her."

"But I don't understand. That seems to me to be an indication that she had nothing to hide or be ashamed of."

"What made you leave?"

Lalor was ready. Murray was determinedly going over much the same ground as Henry Mercier and Charles Hasted had. He wondered if Mercier had forwarded a report about him for Murray to read on arrival.

"Because she began treating with Nana Sahib," he said evenly, "through Tantia Topi, his agent. When she met Topi, I knew it was all up for her. I escaped as soon as I could."

"Then at least we are all agreed that she is now a rebel."

The slow fires of anger simmered again in Lalor. He stared at his urbane interrogator and spoke as coolly as he could. "I do think it is important, sir, that we get our dates and perspective right on all this. Tantia Topi did not appear until late October, by which time she knew that she had been abandoned by the British—indeed, condemned *in absentia* would possibly be more accurate—and so she cast in with the rebels as a matter of survival."

"I do think that you're making some sweeping assumptions

there, Lalor.''

''I think we all are, don't you, sir? You don't know what really went on at Jhansi—and neither does Fort William, least of all. I do think that I at least have a fair guess. Also, I do get the impression that the authorities are thinking of the Rani as they wish to think. As Ellis, Malcolm, Erskine, Skene, Gordon, all found in their day when they backed the Rani, their submissions were turned thumbs down.''

Murray was glacial. ''Are you implying a criticism of my office, Lalor?''

Lalor retreated into Irish irrelevance. He was not such a fool that he did not realise that he could not afford to confront the Agent for Central India as he had Mercier. ''I think I was only thinking out aloud how many Scots have been involved in the Rani's troubles, even to her advocate, John Lang. And now yourself and General Rose.''

His diversion caused Sir Hugh Rose to shift in his chair and smile. ''I suspect that the English always reserve the Scots for tasks where the going is hard, Lalor. I suppose it's rather complimentary.''

Lalor gave admiration grudgingly but Rose had made an immediate impression on him. The commander of the new Central India Field Force was slightly built but he had a wiry frame that suggested hardiness. His fair hair was tinged with grey and though he wore sideburns, he was clean shaven. His features were strong and maturely good looking and his blue-grey eyes were direct and discerning. There was a cool, confident presence about him. He was booted as if he had come from inspecting troops, and as a mild eccentricity from his general officer's uniform, he wore the trews of his old regiment, the 92nd Highlanders. Lalor had heard something about his record. He had commanded the 92nd in Malta and then fought with distinction in the Turkish-Egyptian War of 1841, later becoming the commander in Syria. As the Russian crisis grew, he had been seconded to the British Embassy at Constantinople and, when war broke out, he became the Queen's Commissioner with the French Army in the Crimea, 1854–55. To Lalor he looked a field soldier but his recent service was rather political. Was he merely another of those courtier generals so prevalent in the Crimea, Lalor wondered? Also, Rose had never served in India and its peculiar conditions before. As Peter Lalor in Australia would have said, he was a newchum.

''What are your plans, Lalor?'' Rose asked him. ''Some leave in Bombay? You deserve it.''

Lalor shook his head. ''Now that I've rehabilitated myself

somewhat, I'd like to rejoin the 86th for the campaign, sir. I hear that the rest of the Regiment will be joining the Force soon."

"Not for quite a while, I'm afraid. There's unrest in the Presidency south of Bombay and we'll have to hold them down there for at least another month or so. I'm as disappointed as you must be, as their delay affects my plans—I'm desperately short of British infantry." Rose paused and studied Lalor keenly. "If you're looking for employment and you can't serve with your Regiment—not even with the two companies with Hasted and more about that in a moment—I can offer you a post on my staff. As Chief of Intelligence."

"I'd be pleased to accept, sir," Lalor replied without hesitation.

"I've been briefed here by some officers who know you and I find that you're very experienced, especially in India, and well regarded. I have Sir Robert to advise me politically but I need all the first-hand local advice from all quarters I can get. You know much of the country we'll be advancing over, many of the personalities and when we get to Jhansi, you'll be invaluable. Wouldn't you agree, Sir Robert?"

The Political Agent nodded in a bland, pragmatic way. "Yes, very much so. An admirable selection. Even I'm well out of date after an absence of seven months."

Sir Hugh Rose leaned forward in his chair. "Let me tell you what we have to do, Lalor. The Commander-in-Chief's plan of campaign is that three columns will come up from the south to link up with his own operations to relieve Cawnpore and Lucknow. I am to advance to Kalpi on the Jumna, relieving Saugor and capturing Jhansi en route. I am to act in concert, on my right, with Major-General Whitlock's force from the Madras Army which will cross Bundelkhand from Jubbulpore to Banda. Well away on our left, Major-General Roberts, Bombay Army, will advance into Rajputana. To come back to ourselves, I intend to organise the Field Force into two brigade columns moving along widely-separated axes but we'll link up before Jhansi which is obviously going to be a very tough nut. The First Brigade will be more or less the old Malwa Field Force under Brigadier Hasted as you found them at Mandesar. The Second Brigade, which my own Headquarters will accompany, will be under Brigadier Archie Wilson of the 14th Dragoons and consist of the 14th Dragoons—less one squadron with the First Brigade—the Third Bombay Cavalry, the Third Bombay Europeans, the Twenty-Fourth Bombay Native Infantry, a battery of Horse Artillery and a battery of Bombay Artillery, the Bombay Sappers and Miners, and, later, we'll be joined by the siege train. The Second Brigade will relieve Saugor, so you can see why you can't—or, I assume, would not now wish to—go with the 86th companies on the other line of advance?"

Lalor nodded. He was further impressed by this general. He admired the ring of enthusiasm and determination in his quiet but forceful voice with its paradoxically soft Scots accent.

"Thank you, sir, for remembering me regarding Saugor."

"We can only hope and pray that Miss Wentworth—and indeed, all the women and children, the whole garrison—are safe and well. From reading your report she has had most harrowing experiences, and now Saugor. Have we had any fresh news, Sir Robert, how they're faring?"

"No," Murray said gravely, "but bad news travels faster in this part of the world than most. We can only assume, hopefully, that they're still holding out."

A silence fell over all three of them as their own thoughts consumed them.

Sir Hugh Rose looked across at Lalor again. "However, we've had the good news that Henry Mercier and Charles Hasted have disarmed the Holkar's army at Indore without bloodshed and now the stage is set for us to advance. We'll reach Saugor by the end of January. I'm totally committed to that."

Inshallah, Lalor, the old India hand, thought.

"Gentlemen, we all have much to do. Lalor, I'm pleased to have you on my staff. Report tomorrow morning. We're assembling a force of forty-five thousand—mostly Indians, I might say, and I find this most encouraging—and so an experienced fellow like yourself will find yourself very much a jack of all trades, just not intelligence."

Lalor stood up and placed on his sun helmet. The interview was at an end. He saluted and left the battery office.

That night he was invited, with Joe Morrow, to dine in the Mess of 3rd Bombay Europeans. The 3rd Europeans were a young Company regiment raised only in 1853 and were going on active service for the first time. A spirit of heady exhilaration, aided by ample wine and whisky, pervaded the great marquee tent pitched under the coolness of the winter stars and crowded with officers in uniforms of many hues. But though Lalor was caught up in the spirit of the crusade before them, he found that he was still moody and introspective, however much he drank. His fellow officers who knew him commented pointedly but still he could not rally to the festivities, though he did try half-heartedly.

He was thinking of Alicia Wentworth, awaiting rescue at Saugor from her lingering nightmare, and of Manu, at Jhansi, awaiting the vengeance of the British.

12

Saugor

With the General's ready approval, Lalor rode with the 14th Light Dragoons in their headlong rush on Saugor. The day before, 2 February, Sir Robert Murray's agents had brought information that the rebels had abandoned their siege of the fort and were now retreating before the approach of the Field Force. Soon after first light that morning, cavalry patrols had confirmed the reports. Sir Hugh Rose launched the Dragoons at once, followed by the 3rd Bombay Cavalry escorting the Horse Artillery battery and also ambulance and food carts. Behind trudged the 3rd Bombay Europeans in a forced march over the last miles. Well to the rear came the baggage train protected by the 24th Bombay Infantry.

Lalor galloped beside Simon Freeland, the Commanding Officer of the Dragoons, at the head of the pounding, dust-covered column. The excitement and anticipation that he knew gripped every trooper surged through him. More so, for he was going to rescue one who was dear to him: Alicia Wentworth. He muttered an anxious prayer as they thundered along. A splendid victory was seemingly in their grasp but was she safe and well, even alive? All the memories of the Madhupur dak bungalow, the meeting south of Madhupur when her father, Adrian and Joseph, together with the faithful young sowars, had been killed, and their tense days at Jhansi later kept whirling about in his mind.

The final advance on Saugor had been hard and bloody. On 24 January, the Second Brigade had come on Rathgarth, thirty miles from Saugor, whose fort, one of the strongest in Bundlekhand, was held by Afghan and Pathan mercenaries under Nawab Muhammad Fazal Khan. The fort was situated on the spur of a long, high hill with its east and south faces dropping down to the protection of a deep, fast-flowing river, its north wall covered by a dry mot and the west by bastioned gateways with guns sited in enfilade. Rathgarth had been a battle of cut and thrust with a brave and active enemy. The British had quickly driven the enemy picquets through the towns into the fort but the rebels had counter-attacked and re-occupied the town, aided by a surprise assault on the British base camp from the surrounding jungle. When the British set out next morning to clear their flank, the jungle had been fired and they had to turn back. But a determined main attack on the town again cleared it and breaching batteries were established opposite the north face of the fort. On 27 January, the batteries opened fire and by mid-morning, breaches had been made. As the British prepared to assault, another leading rebel, the Raja of Banpur, dramatically appeared in their rear with standards flying and bands playing. By the time Banpur had been driven off, another night had set in and many of the rebels in the fort escaped. But Nawab Fazal Khan was captured and he was hanged over the main gate of the Fort at sunset next day. Sir Hugh Rose pursued Banpur and the fleeing Rathgarth rebels and, three days later, came on them lining the banks of the River Bina at the village of Barodia. The British crossed the river further upstream and fought doggedly into and through Barodia, driving the rebels into flight again. Sir Hugh Rose then retired back to Rathgarth where the splendid news about Saugor reached him.

Soon the flying column of the 14th Dragoons was drumming across the deserted maidan which led to Saugor fort standing on the outskirts of the city. The whole countryside through which they had ridden appeared to be devoid of life. Fields were empty, houses were closed up and the road unnaturally vacant of any traffic. The avenging holocaust of the British had come and the local people trembled, Lalor pondered. Certainly blood would flow thickly if there was any resistance, even mere obstruction, for this was the dark mood of every British soldier in relieving columns throughout India.

When they drew rein on their lathered horses, the battlements of the fort were thronged with figures cheering raggedly. A faded and tattered Union Jack was being waved slowly and bravely from side to side. A great cheer went up from the Dragoons and they went on yelling. Lalor found himself cheering hoarsely alongside Simon Freeland who was standing in his stirrups, roaring away and waving his helmet as all his troopers were doing. More weak cheers came from the walls of the fort and handkerchiefs fluttered. Lalor scanned the distant faces keenly and anxiously.

Amid all the noise and confusion, Simon Freeland caught sight of one of his squadron leaders near them in the front ranks.

"Nigel, come here!"

Nigel, tall and languid-looking with a drooping fair moustache and a mop of blond hair sprouting from underneath his sun helmet, diffidently moved his horse towards his colonel, still looking at the battlements.

"Nigel, we must follow up the rebels," Simon Freeland shouted over the din. "You're to take your lot off and do that."

"Oh, God, Simon, do I have to do that right now?"

"It's the General's orders, Nigel. For Christ's sake, let's not have another argument over orders."

"But, Simon, look!"

The main gate of the fort had opened. A tall, bearded, gaunt man walked slowly out, followed by a veritable pied-piper rag-taggle of children jumping about and screaming excitedly, held by sobbing women trying to control them, and a silent concourse of men carrying rifles. More concerted cheers bellowed out from the Dragoons who dismounted and ran forward to pick up the children and shake hands with the men. Leading the rush, Lalor noted, was Simon Freeland, his military cares thrown to the wind, beating the recalcricant Nigel by a short head.

Lalor got down slowly from Paddy and he had to blink his eyes several times. He moved hesitantly through the press of bodies, embracing several sallow, crying women who clung to him as if they were afraid to believe that he was real. He eventually made his way over to the tall man who had led the joyful exodus and whom he now recognised, behind the full beard, as William Erskine, the Agent for Saugor.

"Martin Lalor, 86th," he said, holding out his hand. "I was acting as Military Assistant to Sir Julian Wentworth when we passed through here in May last."

Erskine's bloodshot brown eyes flickered tiredly. He seemed to be trying to focus. He gripped Lalor's hand. "Yes, of course, how stupid of me. I do remember. Things went badly wrong for you at Jhansi."

"That's exactly what I'm about to ask about. I believe you have Alicia, Sir Julian's daughter, here with you."

At that moment, Erskine was surrounded by his own people slapping his back and congratulating him on their deliverance. Lalor waited as patiently as he could. When he got a respite, Erskine turned back to him anxiously. "What did you say?"

"Alicia Wentworth."

"Oh, yes," Erskine said, nodding eagerly. "She's with us. She's been one of the best, quite tireless helping with anything, especially nursing sick children."

They both looked searchingly about the crowd but Lalor could not see Alicia anywhere. He felt Erskine's hand on his arm.

"But she's not well, Lalor. Very withdrawn. Always worked

terribly hard but never mixed. Kept to herself almost abnormally. Mind you, we're all rather run down and, no doubt, most of us have been acting rather peculiarly. I can hardly credit that you are all here today. We were beginning to think that it would never happen.''

Lalor pulled out his hip flask, unscrewed the cap and poured a nip of whisky into it. He was so relieved to know that Alicia was alive that he certainly needed a drink himself. He handed the filled cap to Erskine.

''Here, old son, celebrate your relief with me.''

Erskine was slightly bewildered. The shock of liberation after a long incarceration was still lingering with him. ''But it's only mid-morning.''

''And Saugor has been relieved.'' Lalor took a hearty swig from the flask himself and thrust it on Erskine. ''Your need is greater than mine. But do give the flask back to me later. It was given to me by my eldest brother, Matthew, when I returned home after the Crimea. Most of my letters had said I was freezing—which I was.''

He pushed gently through the milling throng of the relieved garrison and Dragoons but he still could not see Alicia anywhere. He walked slowly on through the shaded dimness of the great archway of the fort entrance into the sunlit square beyond. A certain foreboding gripped him. He knew that something was wrong.

Then he saw her. The square was hemmed in with tiered barrackrooms, offices and stores, set behind wide verandahs. In the almost eerie emptiness, as every occupant had poured out the gate to greet the Dragoons, he sighted a solitary figure standing alone and motionless between two stone pillars on the ground floor opposite him.

He shouted ''Alicia! Alicia!'' and began running across the square. He kept calling her name over and over again. ''It's me, Martin!''

She moved to the nearest pillar and touched it as if she needed support. Soon he was with her, holding his arms outstretched. She shrank rigidly against the pillar, staring white-faced at him. He was shocked when he saw her closely. She was not only drawn and washed-out looking, like all the women from the fort whom he had seen, but she had a tense, highly-strung expression as if she was fighting to control something within her that was about to snap. Her mouth was thin and pursed and her blue eyes were frightened.

She almost resisted his embrace. He felt her body stiffen under his hands but the spontaneity and strength of his grasp drew her to him. He tried to kiss her but she quickly averted her face and his lips buried in her hair.

"Alicia dearest! It's me, Martin Lalor! You're safe now. It's all over at last. The Army is outside the Fort. No more fighting and no more worries."

She clutched him about the body with surprising strength but still kept her face hidden. He pushed her gently away from him and took her chin in his hand to turn her face to him. Her eyes were brimming with tears. Her almost bloodless lips quivered and her taut, thin features showed every sign of severe strain.

"Alicia dearest, it's all over," he repeated softly. "You can go home now."

Tears trickled down her cheeks. She at last spoke in a halting, choking way.

"Oh, Martin, what have they done to me?"

Before he could answer, she began screaming and writhing in his arms. He held her firmly and tightly to him. He remained silent and let her scream. Gradually, she calmed down, sagging in his arms and sobbing compulsively. He picked her up and marched stony-faced across the square to the entrance. Her sobbing went on, her face buried in his chest, as he carried her and he was glad. She had to burn out all the repressed memories of her experiences.

Outside the fort, the excited groups of cavalrymen and the rescued community were still talking and laughing loudly in the exhilaration of the relief. He threaded his way through them, bearing Alicia. He sighted a banyantree with a shady grassy area and was about to move there away from the happy tumult when Erskine and another man, dressed in a crumpled, ragged white cotton suit and open-necked shirt, intercepted him.

"I'm so glad you've found her and are looking after her," Erskine said in his earnest way. "We've all been concerned about her for some time. This is Doctor Sanderson."

Sanderson peered at the sobbing Alicia and then turned his red-rimmed, tired eyes up to Lalor. He was a small man, with a trimmed, grey-flecked gingery beard and spiky red hair also streaked with grey.

"This breakdown has been coming for some time. I could see it. She worked closely with me and was simply splendid. Almost tireless, though she really wasn't. Just wouldn't give up. Erskine and I had to order her to rest. What really worried us was that she never really mingled, much as the other women tried to bring her out. Something seemed to be haunting her, preying on her mind. We'd all heard, of course, that her father had been murdered before her eyes but, then again, she never once mentioned it.

She's bottled everything up for so long."

"The ambulances with our medical supplies should be here soon," Lalor said. "They were moving at best speed."

"It's good you're with her now," Sanderson went on. "You're reassuring for her. Curiously, I think that's why she's broken down now. It's all being released, the whole pent-up emotional crisis."

"Here's your flask, Lalor," Erskine said. "Both Sanderson and I have sustained ourselves from it but we have left a drop for you."

Lalor thanked them and moved on. He sat down on the grass under the banyantree, cradling Alicia to him as he rested his back against its broad trunk. She had now stopped crying but was gulping in deep, rasping breaths, as if she was trying to expunge something from her. He unscrewed the cap of his flask and poured some whisky into it unsteadily. He held the brimming cap to her lips.

"Here, Alicia, have this. It will do you good."

He was able to get her to drink it all. She coughed as the raw whisky burned down her throat and then turned wordlessly back again to the comfort and security of his arms. He slowly began to feel better, after the initial shock of their meeting. Her eyes were closed and she was breathing normally again, though he knew she was not asleep. He was a safe, familiar refuge and he warmed to this realisation. He looked across to the front of the fort where the celebration of the relief went on with much laughing and even some sporadic singing. He glanced away across the long, empty maidan towards the road from Rathgarth. The ambulance convoy should arrive at any moment.

In the fields outside Saugor the Second Brigade erected a large tented camp and this included the field hospital to which Alicia and other sick and disturbed patients were admitted. The tented environment was a happy choice as it removed all the survivors of the siege away from the fort where they had endured for seven months. The General garrisoned the fort with four companies of the 3rd Bombay Europeans while the hard pressed AQ staff took over the offices and stores, but it was symptomatic of dark British suspicions of the time that the other companies of the 3rd Europeans were at the camp as well as the 14th Dragoons, even though the 3rd Bombay Cavalry and 24th Bombay Native Infantry had always fought loyally and well. The warm and blissful winter sunshine made existence under canvas pleasant, though the nights were sharply cold, demanding warm clothing and blankets.

The days were extremely busy for Lalor as much planning went on for both future military operations and the current civil administrative problems. The capture of Saugor had opened up the roads to the north and north-west and gave the prospect of an imminent juncture with the First Brigade now moving along the Mwow-Agra trunk road. Sir Robert Murray and William Erskine, now restored by rest and good food, were pre-occupied with the re-imposition of British administration in the Saugor district. Sir Hugh Rose listened understandingly. With his own difficulties regarding the collection of supplies and the repair of several elephant-drawn siege-gun carriages after the long march from Mwow, it was clear that the Second Brigade would be at Saugor for some days.

Though Lalor was flattered to notice that the General relied more and more on his advice at the many staff conferences, he was also aware, and appreciative, that he was released as much as possible to be with Alicia. After her initial breakdown, when she had slept deeply for twenty-four hours, she occupied her days sitting outside her tent in the hospital lines, enjoying the mild sunshine but doing nothing, just looking into the distance. At least, that was how it always seemed to Lalor when he came to see her. He found himself looking forward to their meetings with both keen anticipation and, conversely, a certain amount of apprehension. He also sat with her in the evenings and they dined together in the hospital Officers' Mess. Yet he always came away rather flat. She was now such a different person from the bright, slightly-mocking, vivacious lass whom he had known on the journey from Bombay to Jhansi. As he had seen signs during their refuge with Manu, she was now quiet to the stage of being withdrawn, seemingly immersed in her own thoughts, and when she did talk, she was distant and speculative. He found the atmosphere between them frustrating, even upsetting. Some kind of rapport between them still lingered but something about her shut him out, as if they were separated by a thick pane of glass. They could see each other, they could hear each other, but they could not reach out to each other as in the old days.

On the fourth evening after the relief, he was with her outside her tent in the fading light of sunset. The coolness of an imminent dew was already gathering.

"The General has decided that the convoy to take all the Saugor people to Bombay will leave the day after tomorrow," he told her.

She regarded him impassively. "Good. I will be pleased to get away from this place."

"Will you sail for England as soon as you can?"

"I don't know. I've come to hate this country. However, perhaps that would just be running away from this terrible situation we've all found ourselves in. If I can find some worthwhile work to do—connected with the situation—I'll probably stay. I don't suppose it matters really whether I go or stay. I'm all alone now. I'll just have to get used to that wherever I am."

The glimmer of tears came into her eyes and she looked hastily away. He felt her unhappiness and loneliness acutely.

"I hope that you'll always consider me a close friend, Alicia," he said, feeling how desperately inadequate his words were. "We must keep in touch."

She looked at him again with a curious, deep, almost fatalistic expression. "Yes, I hope so, too."

"Alicia, is there anything particularly troubling you? Other than the death of your father, I mean. I know that must weigh heavily on you still. I'm also conscious that you didn't think that I behaved particularly well in those latter days at Jhansi."

She avoided his eyes again. She hesitated for a long while. When she did speak, her voice was subdued, as if she was almost talking to herself.

"I can't cast out of my mind how he and Adrian and the others died. It is still so vivid that it seems only days ago."

"Try not to think back on all that," he urged her gently. "I know that's a trite thing to say but you must not let your mind keep dwelling on the tragedy of your father's death. You really aren't well, Alicia. You need a lot of rest in another environment. You've changed so much."

"You're much quieter, now," she said bluntly. "And harder."

He studied his hands reflectively. "I suppose we've all run out of jokes by now. How may did you bury during this siege—twenty?"

"Twenty-two. And a number of them were children."

Silence fell between them. The dusk was now closing in rapidly and from somewhere over the serried array of tents, a bugler blew Retreat. A bearer came with a lighted hurricane lamp, placed it on the small table between them and departed as noiselessly and anonymously as he had appeared.

"You haven't really told me much about Jhansi after I left," she said suddenly.

That jolted him. He was glad that the gathering darkness probably masked his surprise. The faint light of the hurricane lamp hid her expression also.

"I didn't want to remind you about Jhansi," he said defensively.

"I've really very interested."

"I suppose you got a rumour here that a British officer was fighting for the Rani, at least against the Raja of Orchha? It reached Mwow, so no doubt Erskine heard it too?"

"Yes, he was intensely interested. I had to tell him that it was you."

He slowly and deliberately gave her an account of those months. She sat with her legs curled up underneath her on her chair, arms folded, listening intently and not uttering a word to interrupt him. Did she suspect, had she heard through one of those tales that seemed to sweep through India so quickly, he wondered, that Manu and he had become lovers?

"I left, escaped, fled—call it what you like," he said in conclusion, "because she began dealing with Nana Sahib. But by then we'd abandoned her and she knew it. I told both Colonel Henry Mercier and Sir Robert Murray this and they don't like it very much."

"So now they're all firmly in the enemy camp? The Rani, Mazumdar, Rao Chaudri—the whole lot?"

He was struck by the bitter vehemence in her tone. "Yes, I suppose we should call it that."

"Then I hope they get a fair trial when they're captured and brought to justice! But captured they must be, and justice given!"

He listened, astonished. She had almost spat those words out. He saw how rigid with feeling her body had gone as she sat upright and the angry flash of her eyes. He was about to defend Manu again but he suddenly got the feeling that anything he said would be useless. Instead, he said blandly: "Alicia, let's go to the Mess tent for a drink before dinner. It's getting a wee bit nippy outside now."

In the large marquee tent that served as the hospital mess, various convivial characters jerked Lalor out of his worried preoccupation with Alicia. Most of the doctors were either Scots or Irish and he was well pressed with whisky. Alicia stayed quietly by his side and did try to join in the animated, if bucolic, conversation about them but gradually lapsed back into her own silences. They had a pleasant dinner with the doctors and afterwards, Lalor was inveigled into playing cards with the Irish fraternity, a bottle of whisky prominently on the table. Again, Alicia sat silently near but seemed content.

About ten o'clock, out of regard for her, he quit the Mess and walked with her back to her tent. When he tried to kiss her good-night in what he thought was a brotherly fashion, she again swiftly averted her face and his lips brushed her hair. She then almost fled into her tent.

As he walked slowly and thoughtfully through the lines to his own tent at Field Force Headquarters in the darkness, he tried to take some solace in remembering that Dougal Sanderson had buttonholed him in the Mess when Alicia was talking elsewhere.

"You're good for her, Lalor, y'know," the little Scot had said, clutching a neat whisky.

"No, I don't know, doctor," he had replied morosely. "I don't think I have any bloody effect at all. She seems to retreat into her own world all the time."

"Ah, you wouldn't see the improvement as we who've been with her in the fort do. She now talks a little, eats her food rather than just picking at it. You seem to have given her some new-found base of security. Women, like children, need this, y'know. Complex creatures, women."

"That's all I do know about them."

Sanderson had then eyed him carefully. "You can't go back with her to Bombay, I suppose?"

He had shaken his head emphatically. "I'd obviously like to, of course, but I can't."

"Pity. You're a kind of sheet anchor for her. She seems to be still in some kind of psychological shock. Extraordinary, how it lingers on after all this time."

Sanderson's last words stuck in his mind when he undressed in his tent and lay down in his bed. It depressed him deeply that he could do so little to help her. She had almost broken down again when she had told him that she was now alone.

He blew out the lamp by him but he lay wide awake for some time within the musty confines of his mosquito net, thinking. Outside, beyond the sleeping camp under the starlit sky, the discordant, eerie cries of jackals came distantly through the still night.

Sir Hugh Rose toyed absently with a paper knife on his field table and looked across at Lalor. They were sitting alone in his office tent.

"If I was a kinder and more humane man, Martin, I'd place you in charge of the convoy leaving tomorrow. Alicia Wentworth and yourself could then be together, especially in Bombay away from all this and you could assist her back to normal health. However, the Queen pays me to be hard and do what's best for the Service. I'm sure you understand that?"

Lalor nodded and said nothing.

"I need you here. The hard battles lie ahead. Once the convoy has gone, we'll march against Garkakota and clear the country to the east."

"The latest intelligence we have, sir, is that Garkakota fort—

which is another Rathgarth, very strong—is held by the Fifty-First and Fifty-Second Bengal. It could be a tough fight if they stand.''

"Yes, I agree. After Garkakota, we'll have to concentrate on gathering at least fifteen days' supplies and as much transport as possible from about the countryside here. Any news of the First Brigade?''

"The messenger we've been expecting rode into the Fort only an hour or so ago. Major Orr, Hyderabad Contingent Cavalry, commanding their scouts, has reached Goona on the Mwow-Agra road.''

"Excellent! Then get out orders from me that Orr is to reconnoitre those three passes that lie across our advance—Malton, Madanpur and Dhamoni. Also, direct the First Brigade on to Chanderi. We'll go north, cross the Betwa and link up before Jhansi. Still no word of Major-General Whitlock's column from Jubbulpore?''

"None, sir.''

"A slow coach, I fear. However, he's probably troubled with supply and transport problems as we are. We can only hope we can get through to Jhansi alone.''

"Bundelkhand is rugged country, sir, ideal for defence. Rocky hills, jungle, deep nullahs, many streams. Apart from its fort and passes, it's ideal for a mobile, lightly-equipped enemy.''

"Yes, my lack of infantry in terrain like that does concern me. But I do hope to have the whole of your Regiment with the First Brigade in a month or so's time. Tell me, pitching ourselves ahead to Jhansi, will the Rani fight?''

"I'm sure she will, sir. She'll defend Jhansi against all comers and that will include us.''

"But we could try to get her to talk with you?'' Sir Hugh Rose asked keenly. "You must have considerable influence with her.''

Lalor smiled wryly. "That's perhaps a little debatable now, General. You must remember that I deserted her without warning, though escaping from Jhansi is how I describe our parting. She's not the kind of woman—person—who will easily forget that. But I'm most willing to try. Anything to save bloodshed on both sides.''

"That's exactly my view. From what you've told me about the place, an assault on Jhansi could be a heavy and costly affair. Perhaps she'll listen to you if we guarantee her a fair hearing?''

A fair hearing, Lalor thought. Alicia had used a harsher word: trial.

Sir Hugh Rose laid down the paper knife, folded his arms on the table and studied Lalor. "Martin, I've been very pleased with your contribution to our efforts ever since we met at Mwow. We work well together and I'm appreciative. That's why I say I require you here, though possibly if the doctors had advised me that it was essential to Miss Wentworth's health that you accompanied her, I might well have been forced to yield to my better instincts and let you go. But you know how Colonel George Sherburn has been unwell for several weeks now, indeed you've been doing his work for him. The ADMS has now told me this morning that he has jaundice and so we must evacuate him with the convoy tomorrow morning. I want you to act officially as my Chief of Staff in his place. The Intelligence side can be handled fully by Sir Robert, now that he's back in the picture and it's so involved with the political anyway. I'll also see that the AQ stuff is kept away from you. I want you to concentrate entirely on current operations and operational planning for the future. Once we link up with the First Brigade, you're going to be even more hard-worked. However, to soften the blow, I'm promoting you Brevet-Major in the field and this will be published in Force Orders today."

"Thank you very much, sir," was all he could mumble.

"Don't thank me. You've earned it. As I've told you, I can be a hard man when it suits me—that's how you become a general. However, let us pass on to another hopefully pleasant event. Tonight I've arranged for a farewell dinner for the Saugor people. We'll have it in the square at the fort al fresco with the idea of eradicating some of the ghosts. Then again, it could be a disaster. Either way, I'm sure that Sam Wood and his AQ staff will lay on a very good dinner."

Next morning, Lalor lined the side of the Rathgarth road with many other officers and soldiers of the Field Force and watched the convoy of carts carrying the Saugor community trundle slowly away, escorted by a troop of the 14th Dragoons.

His last few minutes with Alicia had been poignantly emotional and he felt savagely angry with himself. He had caused her to break down again by saying that she would never be really alone while they were both in India. She had burst into tears and clung to him as desperately as she had when they had met in the fort. She was still weeping bitterly when he was forced to hand her over, as the convoy was already late in leaving, to Dougal Sanderson who had promised to watch over her during the journey. One of the Saugor wives helped the Scottish doctor calm her in the ambulance cart in which they were travelling. When the convoy jerked disjointedly forward, his last glimpse of her was a white, tear-stained face staring out the open back of the ambulance at him. He waved in farewell but she made no response. He looked after her until distance and the dust obscured her from sight.

Though he was lost in his own thoughts, he sensed a stir among the soldiers nearby. He turned to find Sir Hugh Rose standing by him.

"While I'm relieved to see them on their way," the General said thoughtfully, "I'm sorry also, for they were such splendid people. So much guts and cheerfulness after all they'd been through."

"They enjoyed the dinner last night," Lalor said absently. He was still thinking of Alicia. "I'm amazed how elegantly the ladies managed to dress."

Sir Hugh Rose laughed quietly. "Yes, women respond to a challenge like that. Between that and the cooks doing so well, I hope I achieved my aim of exorcising the ghosts of the fort and the siege from those poor people." He paused and then went on, a little hesitantly: "Though I think I failed with Alicia Wentworth. She doesn't say very much, does she?"

"No. She's quite unwell. I'm rather worried about her."

"Sanderson's a good man—he'll look after her. I hope she'll write to you so that we know how she's getting on. Tragic about her father. I met him at a Guild dinner in the City a couple of months before they came out here."

"I've asked her to write but she didn't answer. It's sometimes hard to get through to her, as you've just said, General."

"I'm sure she will. Well, Martin, you and I can't look backwards down the road towards Bombay all morning. Let's now go and talk about our digression to Garkakota. It will soon be time for us to look forward entirely to Jhansi."

13

Return to Jhansi

Dusk was setting in when Lalor rode into the compound of the requisitioned kutcherry which temporarily housed Field Force Headquarters at Chanchanpur. Andrew Gow, Sir Hugh Rose's ADC, a tall, gangling, broad-shouldered subaltern also from the

92nd Highlanders, hailed him from the verandah and Lalor urged Paddy over to him.

"The General's called a meeting, Martin. He wants you now."

Lalor dismounted and handed Paddy over to a syce who had come running. He mounted the verandah steps to join Gow.

"What's in the wind?"

"Much hot air. Important despatches from the burra sahibs themselves—the Governor-General and the Commander-in-Chief. The General doesn't look best pleased."

Lalor went along the verandah with Gow to the room that served as the General's office. They entered and he saluted. Sir Hugh Rose, Sir Robert Murray and Brigadier Archibald Wilson, 14th Light Dragoons and Commander, Second Brigade, were sitting informally in cane chairs about an occasional table. Under the soft light of a glowing spirit lamp, some letters in important-looking stiff blue paper lay on the table before the General.

"I'm sorry if I've kept you waiting, sir. I've been visiting units."

The General waved him to sit down with them. "*Pas de problème*, as our French allies in the Crimea used to say. You've arrived at the right time. We've just assembled." He leaned forward and picked up the letters. "The reason I've got you all here, gentlemen, at such short notice is that only an hour ago a messenger rode in from Erskine at Saugor with these despatches. The first is from Sir Colin Campbell and dated the 24th of January. He would then have just defeated Rao Saheb and Tantia Topi at Cawnpore and would be concentrating the Army of Oudh for his campaign to re-take Lucknow."

Sir Hugh Rose paused and glanced up at his ADC. "Andrew, organise some whisky for us, seeing the sun's gone down. And burra pegs too, laddie."

He placed on a pair of spectacles. "I'll read the Commander-in-Chief's first, as it's straight to the point, exactly what we want and what we are in fact doing. It's written by his Chief of Staff and I must say I'm taken with the fellow. His directive could be a model for all staff officers. Too much paper and quill-pushing these days. This is what he says:

> *Sir Colin will be glad to learn if Jhansi is to be fairly tackled during your present campaign. To us, it is all-important. Until it takes place, Sir Colin's rear will always be inconvenienced and he will be constantly obliged to look back over his shoulder as when he relieved Lucknow the first time in November. The stiff neck this gives the Commander-in-Chief and the increased difficulty of his operations in consequence you will understand.*

The General threw the letters back on the table, took off his spectacles and looked around. "Well, gentlemen, all I need to tell you about the other two is that one is from Lord Canning—an important matter in itself—and the other, with a much more recent date from his previous communication, from the C-in-C again. They both direct me to divert away from Jhansi to go to the aid of the loyal Raja of Charkeri who has been besieged by Tantia Topi and the rebel Gwalior Contingent for some time now."

Kader Bux, the General's elderly Punjabi bearer, appeared in the door with a tray of whiskies and a jug of water. A thoughtful silence set in as the drinks were dispensed. Kader Bux withdrew and they sipped meditatively.

"Charkeri is about eighty miles away, sir," Lalor said. "Jhansi, our main objective, a mere fourteen."

Rose nodded. "So I believe." He turned to Murray. "Sir Robert, what do you think?"

Lalor could see that the urbane Political Agent was taken back. His instinctive diplomatic outlook would see the issue from too many angles and he would want time to think it out.

"General, all I can say is a truism rather lamely. The Governor-General is the Governor-General."

"Archie?"

The brigade commander stirred himself in his chair. He was slight and sparsely built, with long brown hair which was greying like his full moustache. Despite the growing heat of late March and their many days in the field, his face remained sallow. He looked almost apologetically into the whisky he held in his hand before replying.

"Like Sir Robert, General, I also feel that I can only say that the Commander-in-Chief is the Commander-in-Chief." He cleared his throat embarrassedly. "Something on the lines of obeying the last order, y'know."

"Martin?"

"General, I don't have to remind anybody in this room that over the past four weeks since we left Saugor we've all had a hard time—especially the soldiers. The battle to clear Malton Pass was touch and go at times, and then there was the march on Maraura, Surshi, Banpur—"

"Yes," the General broke in drily, "I certainly enjoyed blowing up the forts and palaces of the Rajas of Shahgarth and Banpur, almost as much as Harry Boileau and his sappers."

"Here we are, General, on Jhansi's doorstep. Our soldiers are tired, the weather is now getting hot, and we certainly must husband our infantry who are getting thin on the ground. I would suggest, sir, that if we can press on and take Jhansi fairly expeditiously, Charkeri can probably then look after himself. The morale effect on both sides of our capturing Jhansi can only be considerable—inversely proportioned of course. I would hazard a guess that Tantia Topi, who's really no field soldier though he seems to be credited with a victory over General Wyndham at Cawnpore last November, would pull out rapidly and scuttle away. While I realise the political pressures, sir, I feel we must not stray away, at this stage, from what we are meant to do—retake Jhansi."

Sir Hugh Rose looked across at the Political Agent. "These are rather my thoughts, Sir Robert. Very simplistic and military. However, perhaps you should be the devil's advocate."

Murray shook his head. "No, I find it hard to confute the uncomplicated logic of that. On balance, I agree."

"Archie?"

"Naturally, General, I too would prefer a straight military solution—which is to go for Jhansi—if you feel you can convince the C-in-C."

"Yes, that's certainly my problem and I must take it on. Sir Robert, I'd be obliged if you would draft a reply on those lines to His Excellency also. We can take mild assurance that each despatch will take some time to reach their destinations and by then, please God, we will have Jhansi in our hands. I only hope that our gallant friend, Charkeri, does not have his throat cut in the meantime."

They drank their whisky in silence. Sir Robert Murray took some notes from inside his jacket. "If that's all about that particular problem, General, I can return you wholly to Jhansi. We've had in today two rather interesting intelligence reports."

"Good. Let's hear them."

"The first is from one of our agents inside Jhansi city, a fellow named Ganeshi Lal, and it's only five days old. I'll give a rough translation of his words:

Bala Bhao Pundit, Dulaji and Ganeshju, thakurs of Kerwa, who are in the service of the Rani, have returned to Jhansi with two thousand horse and foot and two guns after being away fighting at the side of the Raja of Shahgarth. Mardan Singh, Killadar of Tal Bahat, with sixty followers came to Jhansi and stated that Tal Bahat was occupied by the approaching British force. A report from the Pachor district says that the son of the Raja of Narwar with fifteen hundred men had come to the village of Mayra and intends to join Tantia Topi in the Charkeri area. All the inhabitants of Jhansi city want to get out of it but the Rani does not allow them to do so, acting on the proverb that a dying leper wishes to have companions."

The Political Agent stopped reading and glanced up at Sir Hugh Rose. "Well, morale about the Rani would appear not to be too high."

"But the indication is that she's going to fight."

"The other report is not high grade," Murray went on, "but it's useful and I'd say, quite true. A camelman from Datia came into camp this morning and told us that yesterday he saw two hundred of the Rani's horsemen at the village of Lohar. When he asked them what was going on at Jhansi, they told him that our old adversary, the Raja of Banpur, had reached the city."

"What strength do you estimate the Rani has to defend Jhansi city?" Sir Hugh asked him.

"I'd say about twelve thousand—about seven thousand Bundelas with some Afghan and Pathan mercenaries and five thousand sepoys sent to her by Tantia Topi."

"And we know she's well served with guns and has her own foundry to make ammunition. From what you've told me about that fortress, Martin, it sounds formidable. What a pity she's unlikely to venture into the open field against us."

"She's far from stupid, General."

"Well, if she prefers to bottle herself up behind those walls, that suits me nicely in another way. We must ensure we seal off the city thoroughly as too many of our other big fish have slipped away from us. Archie, you know I'm riding out with all the cavalry tomorrow? I want to reach Jhansi as soon as I can."

"Yes, General. Martin briefed me this morning. The orders are quite clear."

"You follow up with the main body at the best pace you can make. Martin, have we any word about the First Brigade's progress?"

"Yes, sir. I met the patrol we sent out from the Dragoons returning this evening as I was coming back myself. They made contact all right. The officer will be reporting to you personally any time now. The First Brigade have been going well along their axis after the battle they had at Chanderi and Brigadier Charles Hasted estimates he'll close up to Jhansi the day after tomorrow."

"Excellent. Then we'll be concentrated at last, with first class timing, to have a good crack at Jhansi—or, as Sir Colin's Chief of Staff has it—to fairly tackle it. Gentlemen, let's drink to that—our fortunes before Jhansi. Andrew, call Kader Bux. One sherry and four tunda whisky panis."

On a warm mid-afternoon under a clear blue sky on 20 March, 1858, Lalor set astride Paddy alongside Sir Hugh Rose on a ridge he knew well, gazing at Jhansi fort rearing before them in black granite massivity over open ground about a thousand yards distant. Away to their right was the southern wall of the city bastion, six hundred yards away. Behind them, in the protection of the dead ground made by the ridgeline, were echeloned the massed ranks of the 14th Light Dragoons, the 3rd Bombay Cavalry and the Hyderabad Contingent Cavalry, a forest of be-pennanted lances. With the General, Lalor and Andrew Gow were the commanding officers of the cavalry regiments, the two artillery battery commanders, Captains James Woolcombe and Anthony Lightfoot, the CRE, Captain Harry Boileau, all silently studying the formidable objective before them.

Again, they had ridden through a deserted countryside near the city. The great Jhansi plain, with its dark, frowning crags in the distance, was almost empty and bereft of life. Lalor had deliberately taken the whole mounted column through the burnt-out cantonment, pointing out the blackened ruins of the bungalows in the officers' lines where Sir Julian Wentworth, Alicia and their party had stayed and had been entertained by the ill-fated Skenes, Frederick Dunlop and Francis Gordon, and then the Jokhan Bagh, an innocently peaceful scene of Hindu shrines and groves of tamarind trees, where the mass grave of the butchered British and Anglo-Indian community lay. He could sense the murderous hostility of the troopers of the 14th Dragoons rising as they rode through the Jokhan Bagh. He knew that the 3rd Bombay Europeans, when they came marching through, would feel the same desire for bloody vengeance. Certainly his own regiment, the 86th, would. Again, he hoped that Manu would surrender, or better still, flee.

As he gazed at the fort with the others, he wondered what they made of it. Its site on a huge rocky outcrop looked down into the city which seemed to rest up against its solidity of 16 to 20 foot thick walls with almost pathetic reliance, even though the city's own walls were between 18 and 30 feet high and in a sound state of maintenance. The towers of the fort dominated the whole area and, with other outworks, were loopholed for artillery and small arms sited in both defilade and enfilade. He could see the black snouts of artillery bristling in the near towers and parapets. His erstwhile comrade of the battle on the Betwa, Ghulam Gaus Khan, against the Raja of Orchha, would be laying and supervising those guns. He wondered why he did not open fire on the tempting target on the ridge now.

"Well, I see what you mean, Martin," Sir Hugh Rose murmured, looking through a telescope. "Not even the siege train will make an impression on that. The best we can hope for is that the heavy mortars will be able to lob enough stuff inside to wear away at the spirit of the defence."

"You see that tower flying the yellow Mahratta flag, General? It's called the White Tower and the flag is the Rani's personal standard. It means she's in the fort."

"Yes, I've reluctantly come to the hard conclusion that taking the city, though her palace is there, doesn't mean taking her." Sir Hugh Rose handed the telescope back to Andrew Gow. "The battlements are thick with men, and so is the city wall down there. They give the impression they're spoiling for a fight. However, once the whole Field Force is here and we're deployed in strength, I'll send in the request to surrender that Sir Robert has prepared. If that fails, you're our second string, Martin. A personal appeal from you, pointing out the futility of her position and that we will ensure that she'll have the honour and privileges of her rank, also a full and objective investigation into her activities, might well save a lot of bloodshed, as we've discussed. As far as I'm concerned, despite those gardens where our people's grave lies, she's innocent until proved guilty."

Lalor remained silent. He knew the hopelessness of both appeals. He was saved from having to comment by the General turning to his AA&QMG, Lieutenant-Colonel Sam Wood, Bombay Sappers and Miners, a big heavy man with a fiery red complexion and a thick, white, untidy moustache, and Captain John Cairns, Bombay Artillery, an alert perky Scot, sandy-haired and freckled, who had a sharp sense of humour that Lalor liked.

"Sam, you take yourself off now with young Cairns with a suitable escort and site the camps for both brigades in the old cantonment area. The First Brigade should be left, as we look at the city and fort now, as they will go against the city from mainly about here. The 86th are fresher and more experienced than the 3rd Europeans. The Second Brigade will be right assault, going mainly for the northern city wall. The siege train is going to take several days to reach us and we'll just have to bear with that. What does matter is to seal off the city and fort and as quickly as possible with cavalry picquets. Gentlemen, the rest of us, including the regiments, are now going to ride around Jhansi both as a show of force and, most important, to reconnoitre the ground."

The General's evening conference sat down in his operations tent expectantly. Lalor could see that they had an inkling of the main news that would come from Sir Robert Murray. The tall, suave Political Agent had whispered to him as he entered: "The Rani has replied. She will fight."

It was a warm, sultry night and the spirit lamps about the tent seemed to compound the heat. Beyond the camp, the sporadic firing during the day of the guns of the fort and the answering field artillery with the two brigades had died away with the coming of darkness. The Field Force was now complete except for the approaching siege train and the conference was fully attended. With the General, Murray and Lalor about the long table were the two brigade commanders, Hasted and Wilson, and their respective brigade majors, James Todd and Ian Coley, the three cavalry commanding officers, Simon Freeland, William Orr, Hyderabad Contingent and Macormack Bonner, 3rd Bombay. James Woolcombe acting as CRA, Harry Boileau, CRE, Sam Wood and John Cairns were also there.

"Gentlemen, please smoke if you wish," Sir Hugh Rose said. "As usual, we'll lead off with the intelligence and political situation from Sir Robert."

The Political Agent cleared his throat. "Well, gentlemen, as I've already reported to the General, the Rani sent her answer to our request to lay down her arms. It's short and to the point and I can give her exact words from memory. This is the translation. *We fight for independence. In the words of the Lord Khrishna, we will, if we are victorious, enjoy the fruits of victory. If defeated and killed on the field of battle, we shall surely earn eternal glory and salvation.*"

"I'm all for ensuring she gains eternal glory and salvation," Macormack Bonner said shortly, and a laugh went up. Bonner was a big, blue-eyed Devonian with dark curly hair that showed some Irish blood.

"Yes, we may well have to ensure that," the General said non-committally. "But we'll come back to that. Anything else, Sir Robert?"

"Well, I must confess to feeling rather pleased with myself tonight as I've recruited an agent very close to the Rani—at some expense, of course. I got a approach from the fellow when we were at Chanchanpur and when he could clearly see the writing on the wall. Anyhow, he was proved himself tonight. He has sent word that the Rani has appealed to both Tantia Topi and Rao Saheb. Nana Sahib's nephew, for help."

"Rather to be expected. Do you think either or both will march to raise our siege?"

"I would be inclined to say definitely yes, General. The recapture of Jhansi by us would be a serious blow to the rebel cause and they know it. At least one of them should react, though of course we don't know how much cohesion and co-ordination exists in their higher command, if we can deign to grace it with that title. Certainly Tantia Topi is available if he drops his siege of

Charkeri. Rao Saheb, we could safely surmise, is too concerned with the present operations of the Commander-in-Chief.''

"It would be a happy occurrence if we could draw Tantia Topi away from our friend, Charkeri, though I don't welcome a battle on two fronts with our not-over-generous resources. However, let's take stock of our present position, bearing in mind we may have to contend with a relieving force. First, the cavalry flying picquets. I was quite impressed when I went about them today with the Chief of Staff. Martin, indicate these on the map for the brigade commanders.''

Lalor pointed out the red blobs dotted on the sketch map propped upon an easel behind him. "Here they are, gentlemen, seven cavalry flying columns, with horse artillery guns in support, each operating from a base camp protected by native infantry. The Fort and city have been effectively sealed off, as the General required, for both departures and unwanted arrivals.''

"I am appreciative, Simon, Macormack, William, of the prompt and efficient way you have set up these posts.'' The General turned to his two brigade commanders. "Charles, Archie, as we spoke today, these cavalry detachments will now be under my direct command. This will leave you free to concentrate without distraction on your sector of the city.''

Hasted and Wilson, both smoking pipes, nodded silently. Sir Hugh Rose turned to Sam Wood.

"Sam, what's the latest report on the siege train?''

"Duncan Hay-Newton, the commander, sent a young officer ahead this afternoon, sir. They're still two days' march away.''

"Then, in the next two days, when we have comparative inactivity, we'll try our last peaceful card.'' Sir Hugh Rose turned to Lalor. "Martin, as we've discussed, I now want you to write a personal letter to the Rani, based on your support of her when she was openly known to be loyal, requesting her to surrender. You may quote me as the guarantor that she will be treated as a person of rank, that she will have a proper and objective, if searching, inquiry. You should spell out to her exactly what the consequence will be if she ignores this last bid from us to prevent loss of life, especially for her own people who are bound to suffer most.''

"Very good, sir,'' Lalor answered. He felt the eyes of the officers in the tent staring askance at him. His association with Manu made him a figure of some fascination or, rather, as he had long admitted to himself, of much gossip. Sometimes, he felt that only the General's ready acceptance of him, the competence that he knew he had as Chief of Staff, and his past service managed to wash over these unvoiced doubts.

"General," Sir Robert Murray broke in, "if Lalor is to write this letter, he should do it now. He will have to get it to me urgently so that I can arrange its entry into the city by safe hands tonight and, particularly, that it gets to our new man who had the entrée to get it to the Rani. These things do take time and we need as much of the night as possible. Can you release him from the discussions now?"

Sir Hugh Rose nodded. "Yes, certainly. Get off with you now, Martin. John Cairns, laddie, take any notes for the Chief of Staff from now on."

Lalor got up, stood to attention before the General and left the conference. He walked a few yards through the soft darkness to his own tent where Amin stood waiting.

"A burra whisky pani, Amin, and then you go. Chai at first light tomorrow as usual."

He stood in the night looking towards Jhansi, hidden a mile away by ridges and groves of trees. All was quiet now as the British and Indian sentries in the siege lines and the rebels on the battlements of the city and fort silently and distantly confronted each other. It would all be so different when the siege train arrived.

Amin offered his whisky on a tray. He bade the bearer good-night and went inside the lighted tent to his working table. He took a large gulp of the whisky, laid out some paper carefully, dipped his pen in the inkstand and wrote without pause:

My dear Manu,

This is I, Lalor, also known to you as Lal Bahadur. I am now outside your walls with the army of Sir Hugh Rose who has you surrounded. I have been with him closely since the advance from Mwow in January. I have his confidence and he has mine.

Manu, dear friend, I am grieved that you have rejected the General's plea that you should surrender. We are about you in strength, certainly in trained soldiers, and shortly we will be joined by heavy guns. If you defy the General's peace offer, much devastation of your city and loss of blood from your people will follow.

Sir Hugh Rose is a just and humane man. He has authorised me to say that he will personally take you and your people under his protection. He also assures you that you will be treated according to your rank and titles and also, not least, he gives his word that an objective investigation will be held about any connection you may have with the rebel cause.

Manu, we know each other well and with affection. I beseech you to listen to my words and to cease your resistance. Otherwise, blood will flow as if it came from buckets and your city will be flattened to dust and rubble. You are alone and abandoned.

*I ask you with all my heart to heed my advice. You and the British
are not enemies. Let us come together again and build a new Jhansi free
from war and misery.*

I am, as always, your devoted Lal Bahadur.
                                             Lalor.

When he had scratched his signature, Lalor drank deeply of his
whisky and read through his letter. Had he got it right? He had to
steer her into submission, not stiffen the obstinacy that he knew
well.

He drained his whisky, tucked the letter into an envelope
which he addressed simply to 'H.H. The Rani of Jhansi', sealed it
and walked along the lines to Sir Robert Murray's tent. He was
not surprised to find the Political Agent writing at his table when
he entered.

"Ah, Lalor," Murray said smilingly, taking off his spectacles.
"I see you have the letter. Well done. I also excused myself from
the conference as I thought you would produce it rapidly."

"It's written in a personal vein, Sir Robert," Lalor said casually.
"So I've closed the envelope and there's no copy, not even for
myself."

The Political Agent's smile broadened indulgently. "That's
exactly how the General said to do it. *Pas de problème*, if I may
quote him. Well, I'll now get the organisation going to see that
delivery is made with some urgency. Can I offer you a peg?"

"No, thank you. We're all rather busy, especially you."

"This may save a lot of lives, Lalor. Think of that."

"I do, Sir Robert. I hope and pray also. Good night."

Outside the Political Agent's tent, he turned towards the
Officers' Mess tent. On impulse, he determined that he was not
going back to the General's conference which was still probably
going on. He felt strangely despondent, even disturbed. As he
strode along, absently returning the salutations of bearers and
chowkidars whom he normally answered cheerfully, he wondered if he had been a complete fool, writing to Manu in the way
he did. Murray, as the complete political and intelligence animal,
was sure to open the letter, read and copy it. He had doubtless
done himself no good at all but he knew, for Manu's sake, he had
to reach her somehow before the bloodbath occurred. He would
have written to her far more intimately and appealingly if he
could have been certain that the contents of his letter would not
end up on Murray's files.

As he neared the Mess tent, John Cairns, chirpy and cocky as
ever, appeared at his shoulder.

"Martin, whatever your mail priorities to catch the over-the-wall post, we needed you in there after you left. Wilson became somewhat confused about the inter-brigade boundary about the city."

"It's been spelled out to him. I walked him over the ground yesterday."

"I know. The General, who's usually very tolerant as y'know, was beginning to get a bit tetchy."

"Wilson's a cavalryman. You really don't expect him to get infantry tactics right, do you? Any more than a Gunner. Anyhow, I don't think he's very well."

"All right, 86th Foot. Well, let's get down to the operational issue of the evening. How did your letter writing to the Rani go?"

"It's done and handed in."

They were almost at the Mess entrance. John Cairns stopped him and said seriously: "That letter of yours, Martin, may save a lot of lives."

"So someone else has just said. It may cause a few, too. Who knows? Like a good staff officer, you're quoting your commander. Now look here, young Cairns, I badly need a drink, more than one, in fact. I'll even buy you the first."

Two mornings later, the siege train was reported three hours away on the route that the 1st Brigade had used and Lalor, James Woolcombe and John Cairns rode out to meet greet Lieutenant-Colonel Duncan Hay-Newton, its commander. After briefing Hay-Newton on the situation, he left his two Gunner companions to guide the column of big calibre guns and heavy mortars, drawn by elephants and tiers of yoked oxen, to their firing positions about the city which had already been sited. On his return to camp, he rode directly to the General's tent and found Sir Robert Murray seated with him.

After he had saluted, Sir Hugh Rose motioned him to sit down. Before he could report about the siege train, the General said: "We've just had the Rani's reply to your letter."

"It came my word of mouth," Murray said flatly, "via a merchant who issued from the Datia Gate under a white flag with his family and movable possessions. His reward for delivering the message was that the Rani had allowed him to evacuate—or flee, whatever is the right verb for the occasion—to Gwalior. Her answer is even shorter than the last communication, so the fellow, even though he was trembling all over, could not have got it wrong. The message he conveyed to us was that the Rani of Jhansi does not treat with a person who has deserted her."

Those last bare blunt words hurt Lalor sharply. But he merely

shrugged and refused to comment. He gazed stonily at the
Political Agent.

"At least that clears the air," the General said grimly. "And at
what an opportune time as the siege train approaches. Jhansi is
going to have a very noisy and destructive night and be it all on
her princely head. And many more days and nights—for however long she chooses and while our ammunition holds out. Well,
so be it. Martin, let's now get down to our contingency plan of
holding the ring here and yet extricating enough of the Force to
meet any intervention by Rao Saheb or Tantia Topi."

An hour before sunset that evening, Lalor stood with the
General and Hay-Newton on the ridge facing across open
ground to the Fort and City Bastion projecting from it as a
southern wall of the city. The Rani's yellow battle flag flew stiffly
from the White Tower in a strong breeze that swept across the
dusty, dry plain and again the battlements were thronged. Below
them, along the ridgeline, were dug in eight 32 and 24-pounders
and a hundred yards away, a siege train battery commander stood
watching the General. Behind them, sited some distance back in
the dead ground, was one 8-inch howitzer and several mortars.

The General looked towards the BC, raised his arm and then
dropped it. Within seconds, the whole ridge seemed to shake and
the air reverberated with noise as the guns roared out. The
pungent, acrid smell of gunpowder drifted down the ridge.
Shells crashed into the city wall about the chosen breaching area
and, after a longer time of flight, explosions came thuddingly
from the Fort as the bombs of the heavy mortars and the
howitzer's shell landed inside its great walls. The boom of siege
guns firing in the Second Brigade's sector also drifted over to
them. Belatedly, the guns of the Fort came into action and with
some difficulty, Lalor and Hay-Newton persuaded the General
that the exposed ridgeline was no place for any of them.

As they walked back to the grove of trees where they had left
their horses with the escort of Dragoons, Sir Hugh Rose said
almost savagely: "Well, I did invite her in my original proclama-
tion, if she refused my surrender terms, to let unarmed civilians
and their families through our lines before we are bombarded.
Now she is bringing all hell down on her people. And it won't
stop until we've entered the city and cleared it."

In the ensuing days and nights, Lalor often thought that the
General's description of a hell raining down on Jhansi was only
too apt. Steadily, remorselessly, the British guns and mortars
wore away through each twenty-four hours. With captured
stocks, the ammunition supply was plentiful, hauled forward to

the sweating, stripped-down Royal Artillery, Bombay Artillery and Hyderabad Contingent gunners by siege-train labourers. Even the nights were punctuated with the periodic but persistent firing of the mortars, half of which were now concentrating on the city, and by day, if no wind was blowing, a heavy pall of smoke hung in the air. The direct-fire guns gradually blasted their breaching gaps about the city walls but these were repaired by night with an energy and efficiency that drew the grudging admiration of the besieging Field Force. Lalor heard through Sir Robert Murray's intelligence reports that Manu was active everywhere in the city, encouraging and exhorting, and even women were toiling away, exposed to fire, filling in the breaches. Lalor smiled almost bitterly to himself. Manu was a natural leader but he realised, despite such treasonable thoughts, how much she must need him now.

On the sixth night since the siege train had opened fire, the General's nightly conference had gathered in his operations tent. In the distance came the dull thud of an artillery gun firing. The Political Agent ended his intelligence briefing: "To summarise, General, the time is now ready for your assault. The city is disintegrating from our bombardment, both materially and morally. Many fires are still burning and dead bodies and carcasses litter the streets. The people are mobbing the food storehouses and water is scarce. Despite the Rani's personal leadership, they are now unable to repair the breaches fully—all resistance is being knocked out of them. In the Fort the big gun they call the Kadak Bijli is still in action, as you will certainly have observed, but the Rani's chief artilleryman, Ghulam Gaus Khan, who manned it is dead and so is her general, Khuda Baksh, and his second-in-command, Motibai."

Sir Hugh Rose was about to speak when the sound of galloping hooves approaching the tent became louder and louder. The General checked himself and the whole company listened tensely with him. The horseman stopped outside and, after some unseen commotion, a sweat-stained, dust-covered young Hyderabad Contingent Cavalry cornet came abruptly into the tent. He halted, a chunky, red-faced young man with bloodshot blue eyes, blinking in the light through the haze of pipe and cheroot smoke.

"Yes, laddie, what is it?" the General asked calmly.

The young officer saluted hurriedly. He spoke urgently. "Major Orr's compliments, sir. I've been patrolling the Betwa and beg to report that a strong rebel force is moving on the fords from the east. We've run down some of their scouts and the prisoners we took say that the army is commanded by Tantia Topi and its strength is about twenty thousand with twenty-two guns. As I came to the city after reporting to the Major who sent me here at once, a great bonfire was on a hill near the river and there was an answering fire burning on one of the towers of the fortress. Near the city, I could even hear the people on the walls cheering.''

14

The Meeting

When he rode back with Sir Hugh Rose and Andrew Gow towards the setting sun of the following evening, Lalor had the same feeling of elation that he had seven months ago when he defeated the Raja of Orchha. He was again unshaven, drenched in sweat and almost aching with weariness. He knew how exhausted the General was as they cantered along with an escort from the 14th Light Dragoons riding behind them.

In a series of running engagements along the crossings over the Betwa, Sir Hugh Rose had defeated Tantia Topi decisively with his skilful handling of the cavalry against the enemy's flanks and the rapid deployment into action and shooting of Woolcombe's and Lightfoot's batteries. The infantry had marched and counter-marched with great endurance and had been splendidly steadfast in defence and relentless at close quarters in the attack. Tantia Topi had deserted the field during the day and his shattered forces fled across the Betwa in disorder, firing the dry grass of the plain beyond the river to deter cavalry pursuit and mask artillery observation. The Field Force was now marching triumphantly back to Jhansi with prisoners and booty from the battlefield.

"Thank God, she didn't make a sortie," Sir Hugh Rose shouted to him over the drumming hooves, his face grey with fatigue and his eyes blinking tiredly. "It was another near-run thing out there today, to quote the old Duke. She could have changed the whole balance of the game if she had come out."

"She probably intended to but nobody else wanted to hear the bugle. When are you going to assault, General?"

"As soon as the infantry have had a really good rest. Now's the time to strike. Their morale will be at rock bottom after Tantia

Topi's hurried exit. But our laddies must be fresh and in top form. Depending on Hay-Newton's progress with the breaching, I hope we can attack two mornings hence."

Half an hour later, they sat in the General's tent, drinking whisky appreciatively while Sir Robert Murray briefed in quiet, measured tones on the latest intelligence from the city. The Political Agent had little fresh information to give. He again stressed the growing deterioration of morale caused by casualties and destruction from the bombardment and he predicted that the flight of Tantia Topi's relief force would plummet the remaining shreds of that morale into near despair.

Lalor drained his whisky and Andrew Gow shouted for Kader Bux. "Make it three," the General said wearily, "and another sherry for Sir Robert."

They were slumped in the folding camp chairs, only half-listening through semi-exhaustion to the Political Agent's report. When Kader Bux had brought the new round of drinks, Lalor took advantage of the pause as the bearer left to speak to the General.

"Sir, all that Sir Robert has said confirms what we were talking about on the way back. Jhansi is now set for our assault. I'm sure we'll be successful but it will be, or could be, a bloody business. I'm saying the obvious—we all know that. I can think of only one last final move that just might save many lives, both British and Indian. If I could talk face to face with the Rani, possibly I could persuade her now that it's quite hopeless for her, that the only course to save her people is to surrender, and that you and Sir Robert will guarantee the fairness of any investigation into her conduct."

Sir Hugh Rose straightened up in his chair. So did the semi-comatose Andrew Gow. Murray looked at Lalor keenly.

"What do you mean, Martin?" the General asked him sharply. "How can you possibly do that?"

"It really depends if Sir Robert can do it, General. If a letter from me could reach the Rani tonight, and she replied by first light tomorrow, I could meet her tomorrow night at a breach or one of the city gates. The preparations for the assault can still go ahead. I'm only offering a last throw of the dice."

"I can't let you do that! What are you saying, man? That if this meeting is agreed, you're to walk up to the enemy, thinking that you're going to speak with the Rani? It would be a trap, laddie! You can surely guess their minds. They're in the depth of misery. We're giving them terrible punishment, we've driven Tantia Topi away. You could see how delighted they would be to use a British officer as ready-made target practice. I'll not allow you to throw your life away like that!"

"General, I know the Rani. Even now, when all is breaking up about her, she has the personality and presence to carry people, far less brave and resilient, with her. If she does decide to meet me, I'm sure I'll be safe. Unless of course, she wishes to shoot me herself—for my alleged desertion of her."

"Martin!" Andrew Gow exclaimed, shocked out of his ADC discretion. "What are you saying? You're joking, of course?"

Lalor laughed. The General and Murray were also staring at him. "Yes, I think I am, Andrew. At least, I hope so."

The General stirred uneasily in his chair. He was very tired but Lalor's abrupt and startling proposal had shaken him.

"Sir Robert?"

For several seconds, the Political Agent studied Lalor with some circumspection, then he glanced back at Sir Hugh Rose. "I rather agree with Lalor, General. It's worth that last roll of the dice. I do have that contact close to the Rani who, for possibly more money than usual, will see that she gets Lalor's letter tonight and he should be able to get her reaction, verbal or written, back to me by first light. I recommend we suck it and see."

"And when Brevet-Major Lalor is shot down in cold-blooded murder tomorrow night, who do we blame?" Sir Hugh Rose asked crisply. "Apart from the Rani?"

"Lalor," Murray replied blandly.

Lalor took up his glass of whisky and smiled wryly at the General. "I don't think there's much more to be said, sir."

As he picked his way in the dusk down the rocky slope of the ridge where the siege guns were dug in and sited against the City Bastion, Lalor felt cold fear about his heart. He had said a mock-cheery farewell to the General and the subdued knot of officers who had all looked at him with the commiseration usually extended to one condemned to a summary execution. Even the effervescent John Cairns had been stunned into silence. His nerves tingled rawly and his mouth was dry. The large white flag draped over his shoulder made him feel starkly conspicuous under the clear, starry sky.

He reached the bottom of the slope and began marching steadily to the city wall darkly outlined in the distance. The words he had penned hurriedly last night ran through his mind as he went forward.

My dear Manu,
You will now well know that Tantia Topi has been defeated by Sir

Hugh Rose and that he and his army have fled for their lives, abandoning you and your people. You are all alone and your situation is
hopeless. The British will now devote their fury to a full assault on
your beloved Jhansi. If they do this, many innocent people will lose
their lives. Once our soldiers get inside the city, the officers may not be
able to control them.

Manu, as your devoted friend, I again beg you to give up this futile
fight. I repeat, your cause is hopeless. Nana Sahib and Rao Saheb are
now confronted with the main British Army under Sir Colin
Campbell. Feruz Shah, Banpur and Shahgarth are fleeing the British
like hunted dogs.

I speak with the full authority of Sir Hugh Rose and Sir Robert
Murray to offer you, on their behalf, all courtesy according to your
rank and just treatment if you will surrender.

You know that I believe in you entirely, that I know you were not
implicated in the massacre at the Jokhan Bagh, that this was the
perpetration of Kala Khan and the mutinous sepoys, and I gladly
volunteer to give evidence on your behalf in respect of the events
surrounding the sepoys' mutiny at Jhansi and your assuming the
administration when the British responsibility for law and order broke
down.

I implore you, my dear friend, to save not only your own people but
yourself. Let us talk together, as we did in the old days. If you are
willing, we could meet at the breach in the south wall of the city at
seven o'clock tomorrow night. All the British guns will stop firing at
six o'clock. They will not resume at all if our meeting is favourable
regarding the peace proposal. At least, agree to meet me where we do
not have to deal through paper and faceless intermediaries.

                                             Lalor.

Before dawn that morning, her answer had come back verbally
through the Political Agent's spy organisation: "I will meet Lalor
at the place and time he states. Only he must come."

Lalor approached the breach, an ugly sore in the city wall
strewn with blasted rubble and only partially filled in. The white
flag over his shoulder seemed like a vast, obscene aiming mark.
Yet now he was quite calm, almost fatalistic. If he was going to
die, possibly shot down like a dog, he might as well accept it with
some style. As Murray had implied last night, this situation was
nobody's fault but his own. Also, he admitted a new excitement.
He realised suddenly that he was eagerly looking forward to
seeing Manu again.

As he came close, in the strange, disturbing silence of stilled
guns and the banished noise of battle, he could see heads and
shoulders cramming the embrasures on the wall and detect

figures lurking in the dim depths of the breach itself. He halted ten yards away, planted the staff of his white flag with all the flourish of a medieval herald that he was far from feeling, and took a deep breath. He could sense the hate and hostility breathing over him. Many eyes were watching him and he knew that weapons were aimed at him. He called out firmly in Hindi:

"I am Major Lalor, well known to the Princess of Jhansi. I come to speak with Her Highness by appointment and with her consent."

He saw a slight movement of white in the dark recesses of the breach. To his relief and joy, he saw Manu appear. She was clad in a burnished cuirass, jodhpurs and white pugri with a jewelled sword belted at her waist. He could not see her features in the shadows.

"I am here, Lalor," she said firmly and clearly in English.

He took another deep breath. He went on in English, but still formally: "Your Highness, it is my duty to state to you again the terms of surrender offered by my general, Sir Hugh Rose. The General and the Political Agent implore you to cease this needless bloodshed. Both are honourable men and will see that you are well treated."

"And that will be the fate of my soldiers, Lalor?" her voice, so familiar to him, came back bitterly. "Will they be despatched from the mouths of your guns? Or perhaps you're running too short of ammunition to be able to indulge in this pastime? After all, you are expending many shells on helpless women and children."

"All known murderers will get their just deserts. I personally would be delighted to find Rissaldar-Major Kala Khan and Daffadar Karim within your ranks."

"As for myself, I really do not think that existing in a dungeon in Fort William for many years is—how do you say it—my cup of tea? I think it is better to die on the field of battle. As a soldier, would you not agree with that?"

"Manu, for the love of Mary, don't be a bloody fool! Save yourself and your people while you have this chance. This will be the last time that the British will extend the hand of peace to you."

Silence. He glanced up at the wall about him and saw bearded faces, the whites of their eyes showing as they stared down at him.

"Lalor, in those days which now seem so long ago, when we were together," she said slowly, "I thought that you and I both would fight for my people. You did once, or do you try now to forget that? I also realise that I was stupid to have such dreams, just as I thought you could be my prince. I take some poor consolation that I am not the first woman to be deserted and betrayed by her man.''

"Manu," he said fiercely. "I would fight for you personally anywhere and at any time! Indeed, I'm trying to do that now with a white flag in my hand. But I can't fight for the cause you've drifted into. You know why I left Jhansi.''

"Lalor, you and I were one." She paused, and he thought her voice was slightly broken. He wished he could see her face. "You abandoned me and took away the only real happiness I have known.''

"Manu, we had to go our own separate ways. The time had come. You know that also, even if you don't wish to admit it.''

"And now you wish personally to deliver me into the hands of the British?''

"Only for your own good, dearest, and to save the unnecessary loss of lives. Why else do you think I would have come back in the service of Sir Hugh Rose's army? To attack you and Jhansi?''

"I have wondered often, once I got over the shock of hearing that you were among the enemy about my walls. Tell me, what happened to Alicia Wentworth? How is she?''

He stiffened. He was at a loss for words for several seconds, taken off guard by her sudden change of direction. "She was caught up in the siege at Saugor for seven months. We rescued her, with the others, two months ago. Her ordeal has affected her badly. She is not well, especially mentally.''

Another silence. He was again aware of the enmity bearing down on him from the nearby walls and from the breach about her.

"Manu, we must return to the main reason why I'm here and we're both talking. Raise a white flag over the towers of the fort and the gates of the city and there will be no more fighting, no more destruction and misery. I can assure you a peaceful re-occupation by the forces of the Company and the Crown.''

"Lalor," she cried angrily, "how can you judge me so lowly! You of all people, at least among the British, know that I will never forsake my Jhansi!''

"Manu," he retorted bluntly, "we are talking about the saving of lives, not your pride and personal power.''

Her answering words came back like a whiplash. "Lalor, I have always thought that you are a fool in some ways but neither you nor I have time now to discuss that any more. Don't you know that there are at least thirty rifles and muskets levelled at you, held by men I have had difficulty in restraining? You must know how you wounded me when you fled from me. Why should I not have you shot down now?''

"That thought has crossed my mind several times over the past twenty-four hours."

"Do you think I would do that, Lalor? Kill you?"

"I don't really know, Manu. I'm sure I'll find out soon. Whatever is to happen, let me see you. Come out into the light. It's a terrible thing to try to talk to a shadow."

Rather to his surprise, she did emerge from the darkness and stepped on to a forward pile of rubble. She stood there, a few yards distant, a slight but brave and defiant figure, her dark eyes and handsome features set off by her white pugri.

"I did not wish you to see me, Lalor. I am very weary and I now feel old."

"We are all very weary, Manu. And quickly getting older."

He felt an irresistible urge to go forward and take her in his arms. Not only did he feel again the subtle strong attraction she had for him but he sensed her emotions. She also wanted him, urgently. The crushing defeat of Tantia Topi had almost broken her spirit and she was now alone, isolated and, though she would not admit it even to herself, frightened. Jhansi no longer had a war party, Murray had told them that. She was the sole flickering flame of resistance and she now faced death or humiliating capture. He yearned to be able to help her, to comfort her.

As if to echo his thoughts, she said: "I need Lal Bahadur, the warrior I used to know and love, who shared my bed, my every thought, not Lalor of the British Army who surrounds my city with soldiers and destroys it house by house. What has happened to Lal Bahadur, Lalor? Can you tell me?"

"He rode out of the Saugor Gate the night you entertained Tantia Topi. Again, you know that."

"So it is all over between us, Lalor? This is the end?"

"No, Manu dearest, it isn't. You only have to walk with me now and meet my general. I'll be at your side again and won't leave you. I'll look after you, and so will he."

"And arrange my hanging?" The bitter, mocking tone again came into her voice. "Lalor, strangely enough, as much as you have hurt me, I do believe you because you are such an honest fool. But I know, and you know, that you have no power to protect me from those who want my blood and, indeed, neither has your general."

"Then, Manu, why are you and I here?" he asked tersely. "Why are we meeting like this? You must see the utter hopelessness of your position."

"I am here, Lalor, because I do see the hopelessness of my position. And so I wanted to see you again for the last time before I die."

He took another deep breath. She looked so poignantly lovely, standing there alone in the great scar of the breach.

"Come with me, Manu, and we will be together for ever."

"You come with me, Lal Bahadur, and we will die a glorious death, repelling our common enemy. We will die in each other's arms."

"Manu, I have taken the Queen's salt. I told you that once before, a long time ago."

"And you have taken me, Lalor. Am I not closer to your loyalty, even love?"

"I do love you, Manu. That's why I'm here, trying to save you from yourself. For the love of Mary, please see some reason!"

"The great Lord Krishna will give me what reason and wisdom I require. But include me in your prayers, Lalor. I am sure that I will need all the prayers I can get."

He realised it was futile to go on. They stood facing each other in the warm, still night, separated by a mere few yards which were now clearly an unbridgeable gulf, two solitary figures between two watching armies.

"Manu, dearest," he said with urgent finality, "the General is allowing me to take part with my Regiment in the attack—which, I must warn you, will not be too long in coming. I'll be leading the column that will strike for your palace. If you feel you have to be in the city for morale purposes, rather than the Fort, be there and I'll look for you."

"If I am there, Lalor," she answered mockingly, "I will have to try to shoot you."

"And don't do any bloody foolish Hindu act like doing away with yourself," he said harshly. "That is the act of a coward—which you are not."

"But what if you fall in battle, Lalor—as I certainly will? Perhaps this is the best solution. Surely we will meet as lovers in a paradise somewhere?"

"Manu, do see reality. Don't be so obstinate! Come with me now."

"Goodbye, Lalor," she said so softly that he could just hear her. "I would like to think that we will meet again on this earth but I doubt it. I fear that blackness is closing about me, that I will not see the sun very much from now on. I loved you, prince of my heart, and still do. May your God look after you."

She was suddenly gone. She turned, stepped down from the rubble and disappeared. He found himself looking at ranks of sepoys in red tunics who had moved into the open space of the breach and who stared at him with uneasy truculence, gripping their rifles. He shouldered his flag of truce, turned and walked away through the night.

His mind was awhirl and confused from his encounter with Manu. He felt so depressed and heavy-hearted as he trudged along that he was climbing the slope of the ridge, where the General and his staff stood waiting, before he realised that no fusillade of bullets had shattered his back when he had retreated from the breach.

The night was still silent, unnaturally so. But soon the bombardment would roar out again and in the early hours of the morning, the assault columns of infantry from both brigades would launch themselves. It was now impossible to save Manu and her Jhansi from the final retribution the British would exact with bullet, sword and bayonet, cannon and fire. He wondered, almost sickened, how she could possibly survive.

15

Assault

All that night, the heavy mortars kept up a desultory but remorseless fire on the city and the Fort, exploding their bombs inside the walls every ten minutes. At 2 a.m. the moon went down and the direct fire guns, the 32 and 24-pounders, roared into action, aimed at their breach target areas in the city walls. The guns pounded away in a fury of noise, smoke, dust and crashing masonry for a full thirty minutes.

Two hundred yards away on a flank from the breach where he had met Manu, Lalor lay flat on the ground. Fifty picked men from the two companies of the 86th that he was now temporarily commanding were lying prone on the earth behind him. They had crept there in the blackness when the moon had set and now watched as the breach area shuddered and reverberated from the impact of the shells. At 2.30 a.m., when the guns' pulverisation would cease, he would lead his storming party in a desperate charge to seize a bridgehead about the breach. The main body of his two companies, waiting back at the ridge, would then close up and pass through. Beyond him, well away to the right, Lieutenant-Colonel Patrick Drummond would be leading the rest of the 86th against the east wall with scaling ladders. Along the northern wall, the Second Brigade would be going for their breaches and also for the walls with ladders.

Precisely to the minute, the barrage stopped. Lalor sprang up, held his bared sword aloft and shouted to the soldiers scrambling to their feet with their rifles, bayonets fixed: "Come on, boys! For Ireland and the 86th! Let's have an Irish yell!" A cheer went up from his men, echoed by their waiting comrades on the ridge. He led his storming party doubling hard for the breach.

Soon they reached the great pile of shattered rubble that was the breach, heavy with the smell of cordite mingling with a dust haze. Bugles were now sounding along the walls and musket balls began whistling about them but they scrambled, stumbling and cursing, over the chaotic masonry of the breach. A counter-charge of rebel sepoys, ironically also clad in red tunics, soon came forward from either flank in the narrow alley behind the city wall but Lalor had got his first wave over. Rifles hastily aimed by both defenders and attackers blasted out at point blank range. Men sagged and dropped to the ground, to be trampled on and fought over in the press of close-quarter fighting that soon raged in the confined alleyway.

Miraculously, Lalor emerged unscathed from the murderous one-shot volley. He was quickly among the rebels, firing his pistol and hacking and thrusting with his sword. His soldiers, all still yelling wildly, drove hard at bayonet point about him. Now and then one would grunt shudderingly and fall but the 86th surged on irresistibly. He had attacked the breach in two files, one he now led right behind the wall while the other, headed by a big, strong subaltern named Sean Herlihy, went left.

After an exhausting hour, they had cleared a bridgehead area about the breach, including the nearby battlements and over-looking rooftops. His two companies were inside the walls in strength and had re-organised. From the right came the rolling muffled crackle of musketry which told that other points of attack were also heavily engaged. On their left, the guns of the Fort had begun a desperate bombardment of the open ground between the ridge and the breach to catch follow-up troops in the open. From the ridge and behind it, the guns and mortars of the siege train were replying.

Lalor was now ready to push forward into the city. The soldiers had been able to snatch a brief rest, the dead had been gathered in, the wounded given first aid, and ammunition replenished. He left a reliable subaltern, Michael Jefferies, with a strong platoon to hold the vital artery of the breach and evacuate the dead and wounded while he directed Captain Peter Hamill to advance along streets that he knew meandered roughly parallel to the route he intended to lead the other company towards the Palace. Fortunately for him, its real company commander had fallen ill with jaundice and his pleading, backed by Patrick Drummond, had persuaded Sir Hugh Rose to allow him to take part in the assault. Another factor had been his close knowledge of the city. He now desperately wanted to use that advantage to reach the Palace before Drummond's main column, just in case Manu was trapped there.

Dawn was still more than an hour away when he ordered his bugler, a freckled, gangling youth named Rooney, to sound the Advance. Rifle and musket fire rattled away in the darkness beyond and the distant glow of burning houses fused the sky with a red light. As he watched the leading platoon move by him, hugging the side of the narrow street, flanked by rambling two-storeyed houses, shuttered, broken and abandoned, he knew that it was going to be a long, hard and bitter fight to clear their way, house by house and rooftop by rooftop, to Manu's palace.

All day they fought, except for an hour's halt he ordered at 8 a.m. to re-organise, rest and devour a spartan breakfast of hard biscuits washed down by a plentiful supply of hot tea that had been brought forward. As Lalor had feared, their progress was slow, laborious and costly. With the daylight, rebel resistance hardened and became cohesive. Every yard of street had to be hotly contested against rooftop snipers, every house broken into and cleared with the bayonet. Most of the inhabitants who lived near the perimeter of the city walls had fled from their property but as his advance thrust deeper into the city, Lalor saw some pathetic sights in the houses that they smashed opened and rushed to gain the roof. Women and children crouched in corners, clutching each other in abject terror. Small naked brown infants, either lost or abandoned, wandered in the street crying amid the crossfire of bullets until grabbed by the Irish soldiers and thrust into the safety of a nearby building.

By mid-afternoon, Lalor was concerned about the number of his casualties. Fortunately, Daniel O'Regan, the regimental surgeon, with several medical orderlies and a train of stretcher-bearers, had joined him after being with Battalion Headquarters all morning and worked hard for several hours, treating and dressing the wounded who had been carried to Lalor's makeshift headquarters in an abandoned house. When the wounded had been borne away, he sat with Lalor and Colour-Sergeant Carmody, drinking whisky from a bottle that Lalor produced from his haversack. Lalor and Carmody, a big, hardbitten NCO, were soaked black with sweat and red-rimmed about the eyes from exertion and the heat. The stubble of beards proclaimed the long, hard day.

"The bullets have surely been coming like hailstones, Martin," Daniel O'Regan said, sipping at his metal pannikin appreciatively. He was a small, wiry man with bright blue eyes, large greying mutton-chop whiskers and an expensive complexion that was now even redder. He always reminded Lalor of an elderly but irrepressible leprechaun and he certainly had the best repertoire of Irish ballads and poems in the Officers' Mess. This made him much admired, and sought after, by the Sergeants' Mess. "It's the same on the Colonel's front," the medical leprechaun went on, "and they had the divil of a time, too, in the assault. The poor fellers that went for the walls had many ladders too short."

"How far are we from the palace now, sir?" Carmody asked Lalor.

"Only five hundred yards or so. Once the boys have had a blow from this phase, we'll go for it in one last rush."

"How is Captain Hamill doing, sir? I saw the runner you sent come back when I was down the street with Mister Herlihy's platoon."

"He says it's hot work. A Hamill understatement, I'd say. It means he's having at least as rough a time as we are. Daniel, old son, thank you for coming along and letting us see your smiling face. I'd be obliged if you'd see our casualties well bedded-down in hospital. Come on, Colour-Sergeant, it's time for you and me to capture the Rani. Tell Aloysius Rooney to prepare to blow his bugle."

Two hours later, after their detachment of the Bombay Sappers and Miners had blown in the gates of the Palace, Lalor, with the redoubtable Carmody and faithful Rooney, charged through the entrance with Sean Herlihy's platoon. They had gained the palace area with surprising ease. Rebel resistance had crumbled during that final thrust, though they had come under fierce, accurate fire from the stables opposite the Palace entrance and Lalor called up Hamill's company to deal with it.

They dashed into the shelter of the thick stone pillars about the ground-floor verandahs against the ragged fire coming from windows overlooking the large courtyard. While Herlihy's men filtered along the verandahs, returning the fire, Lalor ordered the Bombay sappers to lay pole charges against the stout wooden door leading to the durbar hall which he had first entered so long ago with Julian Wentworth and Alexander Skene. When the door was blown in, he led Edward Cassidy's and John Redmond's platoons up the narrow stone steps.

His mind was awhirl with conflicting thoughts as he ran through the deserted durbar hall to clear the other rooms of the rambling Palace. Again, victory was firmly in their grasp after a bloody, exhausting day of fighting. Too many of his soldiers had fallen and he knew that his men had, in turn, shot outright any rebel sepoys, 'Pandies', who were taken prisoner. As they had neared the Palace, many dead lay in the streets and the wounded begged for mercy. Now he was concerned about the Palace servants as his soldiers rushed through after him. His men were tired and short-tempered. The blood lust of battle adrenalin in them was surging. They would not be too particular who they shot or bayonetted, for the ghosts of the Jokhan Bagh, especially of the women and children, haunted their minds. He also knew that once the Palace was cleared of rebels, looting and a frantic search for liquor would set in. For both traditional Army activities, he had a certain amount of sympathy. He was only too aware of the appalling conditions the soldiers endured: poor pay, indifferent food, a harsh discipline enforced by fear of the lash, and in India, a climate and disease, such as cholera, which could decimate a regiment. Yet, despite all these privations, they would follow a good officer to the death. He never ceased to find that loyalty and devotion very touching.

Among all these apprehensions was his deep fear that Manu was in the Palace. He had to find her. He realised his anxiety was akin to the ride on Saugor, wondering whether Alicia was dead or alive.

The sun had set and dusk was gathering when he sat wearily on the balustrade about the fountain in the courtyard with his platoon commanders. They had taken the Palace expeditiously, as many of the defenders had fled by dropping out of the windows into the back streets. Nearby, terrified servants crouched on the flagstones, guarded by one tired, bearded 86th sentry who sat with his back to a wall, cradling his rifle. Lalor had questioned them but even from their petrified monosyllabic replies, he knew that Manu had retreated into the Fort as he hoped that she would. Another crucial aspect was that the resourceful Colour-Sergeant Bartholomonew Carmody had nosed out the Palace wine cellar and had promptly posted two abstemious Ulster Presbyterians to guard it. However, Lalor had ordered that an equal ration from the stocks should be given to all ranks and now they were drinking Manu's wine in a mixed feeling of post-battle euphoria and near exhaustion. Yet an atmosphere of crisis and urgency still hung in the air. From the direction of the stables, the sound of heavy firing came clearly to them.

They had barely finished their half-pannikin of wine when Kevin McCulloch from Peter Hamill's company came towards them. McCulloch, a tall, blond subaltern noted for his dandyish dress in Bombay, now had the stubble of a fair beard smudged with powder stains and his tunic and trousers were torn and sweat-stained.

"Captain Hamill's compliments, sir," he said haltingly, "but he would be obliged if you would join him. The stables are strongly held. We've tried one attack but had to call it off due to casualties. We can't get at them except only over the open court-yard which they cover every inch of. Captain Hamill wants to fire the stable and smoke them out."

"That sounds a very effective and simple solution, Kevin. Why ask me?"

"Because the rebels defending the stables are the Rani's body-guard. We know this, sir, because several of them have rushed out at us and we've shot them down. We reckon the whole lot's mad with bhang."

"So?" Lalor, in his tiredness, was becoming irritable. "Do your bloody duty, lad. You don't have to clear this with me. Peter Hamill knows this."

"He's worried that the Rani may be with them, sir. Their resistance is so desperate and fanatical. It can't be just the bhang."

Lalor stirred himself out of his lethargy and stood up. "Sean, take command here. There was a story that a tunnel ran from the Palace to the Fort. Have a good dekko for it. Colour, you come with me. All right, Kevin, lead on."

Across the road, in the dusk, he found Peter Hamill standing by the gateway to the stables. The soldiers of the 86th had con-structed makeshift firesteps about the wall and were returning the heavy fire that came from the ground floor and loft of the stables. Any rush across the cobbled forecourt would be savagely raked by the Rohillas' fire.

Peter Hamill, a tall man with slightly stooped shoulders and a shaggy brown moustache, had been with Lalor in Aden and they knew each other well. "I want to smoke them out, Martin. There appear to be no horses inside. Is this all right? As probably McCulloch told you, I'm worried that the Rani may be with them, making some last ditch stand. They're fighting like madmen."

"Go ahead, Peter. I'm sure the Rani's not there. She has too much style to die in a stable. But first let me talk with them. I know these fellows, especially their leader. Tell your boys to cease firing."

The silence brought about by the 86th lowering their hot rifles from the stable wall gradually drew a similar, if ragged, reaction from the trapped defenders.

Lalor .showed himself in the open gateway. He shouted in Hindi: "Ghulam Muhammad, it is I, Lal Bahadur. I must speak with you."

A long, tense, confused pause ensued, but there was no firing. Lalor repeated his call several times. Eventually, a gruff, snarling voice came from the main door of the stable. "What do you want, Feringhee?"

"You saved my life once, Ghulam Muhammad. I am how here to repay that debt."

"I am particular who I take money and favours from. You can do nothing for me."

"I can do much for you, man! I can save the lives of you and your men. Don't be a fool! Lay down your arms and surrender to me."

"I told you once that I earn my pay. I do that now, even when the times are bad."

"I warn you, Ghulam Muhammad. We are ready to fire this whole area and burn you out like rats. That's not the way for a man to die. Give yourself up to me and I will see that you and your men are fairly treated. You have nothing to fear—you're not mutinous sepoys."

"You fail to listen to me, Feringhee. I must make myself more understood."

A rifle fired from the stable door. Its bullet crashed into the stonework of the gateway entrance, inches from Lalor's head. Chips of stonework flew about and Lalor belatedly ducked, wincing as the near side of his face was stingingly cut. Hamill and Carmody both grabbed him and pulled him behind the wall.

"Are you all right, Martin?" Hamill asked anxiously, staring closely at him. "That was a near one."

"Thank God it's dark," Lalor murmured, feeling the blood trickling down from his forehead and near cheek. He was doubly thankful that his eyes seemed to have been spared. "Otherwise he certainly would have got me. Light your matches, Peter. We'll have to make our answer clear too."

Within twenty minutes, the sun-dried, aged timbers of the stables was a crackling red inferno, lighting up the immediate darkness of the early night. Soon, thick smoke came billowing out, drifting over the cordon of soldiers waiting watchfully with their rifles at the ready.

"They must come out soon," Peter Hamill murmured as they watched intently. That smoke means that the fire has reached the fodder.''

At that moment they did come out. About thirty Rohillas, screaming and shouting, surged out from the stables' main door. They stopped to fire a ragged voley, then dropped their firearms to run brandishing tulwars.

Many did not survive the halt to aim their matchlocks and rifles. The concerted fire of Hamill's company ripped through them. Bodies hurtled backwards from the impact of the bullets. Those who did dash on were shot down mercilessly. Only one man came on, waving his broad, gleaming tulwar aloft.

The sole survivor of the charge was Ghulam Muhammad. Lalor stood in the open gateway, pistol in one hand and sword in the other, watching the big mercenary leader bearing down on him, snarling and shouting with murderous rage. Yet he could not bring himself to fire his pistol. He braced himself, gripping his sword, to receive the Rohilla's assault.

A rifle roared out alongside him. Ghulam Muhammad spun about and staggered like a drunken man trying to regain his balance. He dropped his tulwar and clutched the gaping hole in his chest that the point blank shot had blasted. He pitched to the cobbles and lay there inert.

Colour-Sergeant Carmody stood by Lalor with his smoking rifle. Lalor, Hamill and the 86th soldiers stared silently at the carnage of the stables courtyard. Bodies lay about in grotesque positions, Ghulam Muhammad, his erstwhile saviour from Madhupur, only ten yards from him. Behind, as a fiery backdrop, roared the holocaust of the stable, now about to crash into blazing embers. The pungently-sweet stench of cordite and the stifling smell of smoke mingled in the air.

''What a waste of brave fellows,'' Lalor said, speaking almost to himself.

''Bluddy haythens,'' Carmody said uncompromisingly.

Lalor went forward to where Ghulam Muhammad lay doubled up, clutching his chest. The prostrate body started to writhe as he knelt and, surprised to find that the man was alive after the awful wound that blood-streaked hands pathetically tried to cover, he saw the eyes open, glazed with approaching death. He knew the dying man recognised him as a twisted grin, from which blood trickled, struggled to his lips. Summoning all his waning strength, Ghulam Muhammad began speaking to him in slurred Hindi, the blood from his mouth slavering over his beard. What he heard rooted Lalor to the spot. He was still crouching there, transfixed, almost paralysed mentally as well as physically, when the mercenary leader gave a shuddering gurgle and died. Dimly, he became aware of his shoulder being shaken and he stood up rather dazedly.

"Martin, for the second time tonight," Peter Hamill said to him, "are you all right? What was that fellow saying to you?"

"He was cursing me with some very foul obscenities. It wasn't very pleasant."

"You look done in."

"I feel a little sick, but it'll pass. Not fit enough after a soft life on the staff, that's the trouble. I'll be all right in a moment."

Lalor leaned dejectedly against the stables gateway and stared at the ground, trying to pull himself together. He slowly became aware that a perspiring Andrew Gow stood before him with Hamill.

"The General wants to see you, Martin," the ADC said breathlessly. "The Rani's surrendered. She's with him now."

When Lalor walked into Sir Hugh Rose's operations tent, the General was standing by the enlarged sketch map of the city, talking to Sam Wood. Wood saw him first.

"Good God, Martin, you are a mess."

Lalor saluted as the General came over to him, peering concernedly at his face in the dimlight thrown by the spirit lamps about the tent.

"Are you all right, boy?"

Lalor nodded. "I was in too much of a hurry for the medical orderly to clean me up properly after Andrew arrived with the news. Just superficial cuts. Where is she, General?"

"In my anteroom next door. Let's go there at once."

They moved out into the night and through several yards of darkness to the next tent where two 3rd European sentries stood guard. Lalor, Wood and Gow followed the General inside. The interior was carpeted and furnished with cane armchairs and an occasional table. Beyond was the General's sleeping tent. A woman sat with her back to them. The only other occupant was John Cairns who stood up.

Even before he saw her face, Lalor knew that the woman was not Manu. The simmering excitement and tense anticipation that had dried up his mouth during the long walk back with Andrew Gow through the desolate, dark streets, littered with corpses and the carcasses of dead animals, to the breach and then to the ridge, where the ADC had horses waiting, now left him.

The woman had started when Cairns got hurriedly to his feet. She stood up also and swung about to confront them. He could see that she was stiff with fear.

"Greetings, Aruna," he said softly in Hindi. "Do you know who I am?"

She stared at him. She had only known him as Lal Bahadur, the bearded Pathan, and now he was clean-shaven and in British Army uniform, but he knew that she recognised him. She was dressed in the Rani's martial garb, the white pugri, cuirass and jodhpurs, and even with the sword. She was an attractive, pale-skinned woman about twenty with high cheek bones and a long, slim aristocratic nose. Her dark eyes gleamed with apprehension.

"This is not the Rani, General," he said to Sir Hugh Rose. "She is Aruna Gupta, a companion, a lady-in-waiting you might say, of the Rani. The Rani saved her from the degradation of Hindu widowhood when her young husband was killed in the battle we had with the Raja of Orchha. The Rani took her into her household."

Sir Hugh Rose smiled wryly. "I thought she wasn't. I remembered you'd said that the Rani spoke quite good English. This lassie hasn't said a word in English and has given some strange replies when she was interrogated in Hindi. She also hardly has the swashbuckling presence I would expect of the Rani. However, she's got guts. She came out of the main gate of the Fort alone under a white flag when she must have known that more than a few guns were bearing on that area."

"What all this means, sir, is that something's afoot. The girl has been set up to distract us. It could mean that she's meant to be a diversion—that the Rani is escaping tonight while the British think that they really have her."

"Yes, that thought is rapidly occurring to me. Only two persons in the whole of the Field Force can recognise the Rani—Sir Robert and yourself. Only this morning I reluctantly agreed that Sir Robert should go off post haste to Gwalior as Sindhia is very worried and as I thought that I now had merely a military problem on my hands, I sent him off. It's uncanny how these people seem to get wind of these things. And with you, you did tell the Rani herself that you were attacking with your regiment? A clever woman. However, if she is slipping out of the Fort and through the city at this moment, I don't think we can do any more than that we're already doing. We expected break-outs once we assaulted and the cavalry picquets will be doubly alert to-night."

Lalor took Aruna Gupta's arm. He could feel her trembling. "Aruna, you knew me once as Lala Bahadur. I am now an officer of the British Army. My general wants to spare Jhansi further bloodshed and now only the Rani can do this for him. If she surrenders, all the fighting will stop at once. My general will protect the Rani and you need have no fear about her treatment.

You must tell me where she is now.''

Aruna Gupta gazed at him, rather like a rabbit before a snake, he thought. ''In the Fort,'' she answered hesitantly, after a long pause.

''Then why are you here, dressed as she does and pretending to be her?''

Silence. Lalor waited patiently. It was a somewhat incongruous scene, he reflected, five British officers, including one general, surrounding one lone Indian girl who had knowledge vital to them. He increased his grip on her forearm slightly.

''Aruna, you must give us the information we need. Where is the Rani now? What is she doing?''

She swallowed in sheer nervousness. He got the impression that he was supporting her. Aruna Gupta, despite her attire, was no warrior but she was brave.

''Aruna,'' he pressed on ruthlessly, ''we are hard men here. We've had a bad day of fighting in which too many of our men have fallen. Our patience is running thin. Now speak the truth we want or you will be given to the soldiers.''

He thought that she was going faint. Her eyes closed and she swayed but his grip held her firmly. When she opened her eyes, he noticed the circles of exhaustion.

''I will never betray my princess, and you must believe this, Lal Bahadur—or whoever you may be.''

A chord of memory came back when she whispered those words. Manu had once said something like that: Lal Bahadur, or whoever you may be. He released her arm and turned to Sir Hugh Rose.

''She won't say anything, General, and I feel there's little point in questioning her further. We could settle for the obvious: that the Rani is probably now trying to escape from Jhansi and that we can only hope that our cavalry patrols will intercept her.''

Sir Hugh Rose nodded mildly. ''Then what do we do with her?''

''We should keep her for some interrogation in depth by Sir Robert when he returns. She can probably give a lot of background on what has happened here after I left. Then I suggest we set her free.''

''I agree. Cairns, see that she has comfortable quarters and refreshments now, and as soon as possible a woman to attend to her. You're responsible for her welfare and security. Until we capture the Rani, she could be our most important prisoner.''

''Very good, sir,'' John Cairns said briskly. He motioned his captive forward. Aruna Gupta moved, eyes downcast, towards the tent entrance.

"You have much courage, Aruna," Lalor said to her finally, again in Hindi, "Lakshmi Bai would be proud of you."

She stopped and looked at him with a direct gaze that was now devoid of fright.

"I love my princess, Lal Bahadur, and I thought you did, too. My princess certainly thought you loved her. But we were all wrong about you. You are now the sword of the enemy determined to achieve her destruction."

After John Cairns had ushered her from the tent, Sir Hugh Rose asked Lalor curiously: "What did she say to you then?"

He made a discreet paraphrase, though he guessed that Sam Wood probably understood Hindi. "She said how devoted she was to the Rani, how her loyalty to her would never falter, unlike some near her who have not shown that."

"Come, let's have a drink, even if only to drown our disappointment about the missing lady." The General motioned them to the chairs. After they had settled down and the indefatigable Gow had shouted out into the night, he looked at Lalor keenly. "Martin, you look all in. I congratulate you on taking the Palace, even if our bird had flown the nest. After this drink, you must get your face attended to and have a good clean-up. I know you'll want to get back to your laddies tonight but, first, you'll stay to dinner with me. Tell me, how's it gone?"

Lalor gave him a brief summary of the day's operations. He said finally: "We've had quite a few casualties, mostly wounded I'm glad to say, but that's street fighting. Just before I left, Colonel Patrick Drummond's main column linked up with us at the Palace."

"Good. Reports from the Second Brigade's sector are encouraging. Both the 3rd Europeans and the 24th Bombay are well into the city—the northern wall was where Sir Robert's high-placed traitor advised were the weakest defences. I've now given orders for all units to go firm and consolidate where they reached at last light and resume operations tomorrow morning. I'm going forward then with the 25th Bombay. How long do you think it will take to clear the city?"

"All tomorrow, I should think, sir."

"Then we'll have the Fort to contend with. All we can do it is starve the garrison out and this could take more time than I can afford."

"If Aruna Gupta is the distraction to mask the Rani's flight tonight, then the Fort, without the Rani's presence, will be no problem. Thick walls are no substitute for guts, especially in this country."

The bearer came in with the tray of whisky panis and Sir Hugh

Rose took his thoughtfully. "Yes, I almost forgot. We're probably in for an interesting night. It's now up to the cavalry to apprehend the lady if she does make a dash for it. But they can't cover every track, especially in the dark. However, to come back to today, Sam, you were about to give me the casualty figures from the brigades and the ADMS's report when Martin arrived. Let's have these now."

While the big, bluff AA&QMG briefed his commander in his deliberate manner, Lalor thankfully took a large gulp of his whisky and leaned back in his chair. He was very tired but so was everybody. He wondered where Manu was now, how she was feeling, what her plans were, who was supporting her. The one man she could really trust, a Muslim mercenary, he had been more or less instrumental is destroying. Ghulam Muhammad now lay dead, like Gaus Khan and others who had fought stoutly for her merely for their pay. He sensed that she was now surrounded only by those who wanted to save their own skins. Who was the well-placed traitor Murray had manipulated so brilliantly, he speculated over his last mouthful of whisky. Whoever he was, the fellow had operated with some efficiency for his emoluments. His mind went back to Manu. The appearance of the heroic Aruna Gupta cheered him greatly. He knew, somehow, that Manu was not staying to allow the trap to close about her.

As he sat there, his mind wandered back to Ghulam Muhammad and the mercenary's dying, salacious taunts. The sickening shock came slowly over him again.

The General and Sam Wood were still discussing administrative problems when he quietly took his leave. Outside the tent in the darkness among the sentries and bearers, he found the faithful Amin with hurricane lamp, waiting for him. Soon he was in his own tent, shedding his filthy uniform and soaking in a tin tub of hot, soapy water, gripping a whisky pani poured by Amin. After he had dressed, a RAMC sergeant was waiting to clean up and treat the many small cuts over his face.

That evening he ate hungrily at the General's table in his anteroom with Sam Wood and Andrew Gow. It was an interrupted meal as messengers arrived from the two brigades inside the city and from the cavalry regiments ringing the black countryside. Near midnight, as they sat talking and drinking and he was about to set off back to the Palace, they heard the drumming of hooves of another hard-riding galloper coming down the lines of tents towards them. Conversation stopped. They watched the tent entrance expectantly as the horseman reined in and halted outside.

The same cornet of the Hyderabad Contingent Cavalry who had brought the news of Tantia Topi's approach and whom Lalor now knew slightly as Jack Redfern burst into the tent, sweat-stained and dust-covered. He stumbled through a hurried salute.

"The Rani's bolted, sir!" he exclaimed, panting. "Our patrol gave chase but she's shown us a clean pair of heels. They lost her in the night. Bob Bowker stopped an unlucky shot in the shoulder and his men gave up the hunt to look after him."

"Now let me see," the General said calmly. "Lieutenant Bowker was stationed to the north-east of the city. Which means she must have slipped through a gate in the city wall about that direction. The 24th Bombay were attacking there." He stopped and glanced at Lalor. "I hope there has been no laissez-faire."

Lalor said nothing. His mind was full of Manu's successful escape.

"How is Bowker?" the General asked Redfern evenly. "Perhaps his well-being is the main thing I should be concerned with in this incident."

"He's not too good, sir, but our surgeon says he should pull through."

"Splendid. Andrew, see that this young man has a glass of whatever he requires to refresh himself. I'm much obliged to you, laddie."

Sir Hugh Rose took Lalor's arm and walked with him to the tent entrance. His blue-grey eyes regarded him quizzically. "Y'know, Martin, I'm almost glad she's got away—that we haven't caught her. Though I fear that her freedom means much more trouble for us. Where do you reckon she's heading for?"

"To Kunch and Kalpi, if she's passed through Bowker's area. Tantia Topi is probably now up that way, and others of the same ilk, too. It's nearer to be in touch with Nana Sahib and Cawnpore, though Sir colin must now be sorting all that out."

Sir Hugh Rose held out his hand. "Goodnight to you, boy. You need some rest badly. I'll be with you and Patrick Drummond at the Palace about 0700 hours tomorrow with the 25th Bombay at my back and we'll clean up this whole mess finally."

When he rode back, with a section of the 14th Light Dragoons cantering behind him, from the camp to the ridge and the breach, now being cleared and widened by the Bombay Sappers and Miners, through the dark, empty alleyways to the Palace, Lalor kept thinking of Manu. Somewhere, out in the night, she was probably still riding hard, her young adopted son, Damodar, strapped to her, with a few faithful retainers striving to reach some distant haven of safety. He thought bitterly that she would have a very long way to go before the relentless arm of the British, thinking of their murdered women and children, was unable to reach her again. But he took much solace that she was, at this moment, safe and free.

16

Pursuit

As Lalor had forecast, the Field Force, less the cavalry still holding the ring, took another day to clear the last pockets of resistance and, by this time, the heavy, sickening stench of death permeated the whole defeated, battered city. The leaderless, depleted garrison of the Fort quickly capitulated and inside its great walls, he found the grave, among many others, of Gaus Khan. In some of the rooms the 86th came on articles of clothing, baggage trunks and other personal possessions of the victims of the Jokhan Bagh massacre and this instantly drove the soldiers, nerves raw after their days of battle, into a murderous fury. Lalor and his officers were barely able to hold them from an outright slaughter of the surrendered garrison.

Six more days elapsed before the short-tempered soldiers had finally herded the surviving inhabitants to collect the many corpses into the various city squares where the bodies were stacked, covered in wood and burned in huge pyres. Lalor heard Sam Wood, anxious about the health of the troops, say as he organised the vast cremations that he estimated some 5,000 had died. The carcasses of many animals killed by the days and nights of bombardment, even some elephants, were dragged outside the walls and buried in massive pits. Jhansi was a morbid scene of death and destruction and Lalor, like every other officer and soldier, was relieved when they were withdrawn to the tented camp pitched in the old cantonment area. The two companies of the 86th that he had commanded remained in the Fort.

While the clearing-up of Jhansi went on, Sir Hugh Rose held a meeting of all his commanding officers and informed them that the Field Force would stay for at least another fortnight. Any immediate pursuit was out of the question, not only because of a grave shortage of ammunition and supplies but also due to the condition of the troops. Sam Wood and the ADMS, a tall, angular, laconic Scot named Kincaid, reported that the two field hospitals, already strained with battle casualties, were now overflowing with sickness cases. It was as if soldiers had steeled themselves for the assault, knowing that every bayonet was direly needed, but once the driving motivation of battle had gone, many had now quickly succumbed to the illnesses racking their run-down bodies: dysentery, heat exhaustion, skin disorders and general debility.

Lalor recognised the military necessity of the decision but he dearly would have preferred to continue the advance within a few days. Jhansi, with the burned cantonment and the city, held too many memories for him.

During the later rest and recuperation period, the General gave a dinner night in the small Headquarters mess for his brigade commanders, commanding officers and staff officers. All dressed and sweltered in their best, if now somewhat frayed and patched, uniforms. The food was excellent after days of field rations and the conversation flowed as easily as the wine. After the Queen's health had been drunk and coffee and liqueurs served, Sir Hugh Rose stood up amid many cheers and made a brief speech through the thickening swathes of cigar smoke. The Field Force would soon march on Kalpi on the Jumna to join hands with the Commander-in-Chief who had re-taken Lucknow on 21 March and after dispersing the rebels throughout Oudh, would now be turning his operations towards Rohilkhand. Once they had reached Kalpi, the Field Force would have done its task after advancing several hundreds of miles over very difficult terrain against spirited enemy opposition, and it would then disband. The great mutiny, apart from running to earth any wanted leaders who had escaped the net, would then be at an end.

By 1 o'clock, all the guests had bibulously departed and Lalor sat with the General, Sir Robert Murray, Sam Wood and Andrew Gow outside the mess tent in the open air under the stars. It was a clear, calm night, with the many rows of darkened tents distantly about them, and in the early morning air, they now felt cool. They were enjoying a last brandy.

Suddenly, Sir Robert Murray cleared his throat and said importantly: "I couldn't of course tell you in there tonight, General, but just as I finished dressing for dinner, I had a communication from our man with the Rani."

Lalor sat upright, as did the Sir Hugh Rose. Murray inhaled his cigar, savouring both it and the occasion. Lalor now saw that he was tight. More than one sherry tonight. The General leaned forward and said softly, his Scottish accent coming through: "Then you must tell me now, Sir Robert."

"The Rani is safely at Kalpi. She has met there with Nana Sahib, Rao Saheb and Tantia Topi. A dispute of some bitterness developed. She wants their main defensive stand to be at Kalpi which is apparently very strong, and to win or die there. Tantia Topi argued for halting us at Kunch. The Rani also objected strongly to Tantia Topi being made the field commander. However, it seems Tantia Topi has won on both counts. Kunch it is and he has got command."

"Kunch," Sir Hugh Rose said reflectively. "About sixty miles from here and Kalpi is a hundred. I rather think that Tantia Topi is again proving our best—if fortuitous—ally. He completely destroyed their morale and resistance here by his abject failure in the relief operation and now he could help us to defeat the enemy in detail by meeting us at Kunch. They must keep some force back at Kalpi which controls that important crossing over the Jumna. Also, I do hope my rather laggard colleague, Whitlock, has at least an advanced guard moving along the Jumna to meet us there."

Hamilton's cigar smoke wafted over Lalor as he stared thoughtfully at the starlit sky above. He was brought back to earth by Sam Wood.

"Martin, did you ever meet Tantia Topi?"

It sounded like his several; interrogations again. Hamilton looked at him quizzically, gripping his dying cigar.

"No, Sam, I didn't. I nearly did. The reason I left Jhansi, or escaped—call it what you like—was that he was coming to visit the Rani. I knew then that she had ultimately thrown in her hand with the rebels. But, I repeat again what I've said to many people who have asked me about her—including you, Sam—that in my opinion she has been a hard-tried woman. She wanted to be known as a loyal supporter of the British—naturally, with certain benefits to herself in view and why not, she was taking considerable risks—but she was spurned by us. She had to get help from somewhere."

Murray frowned. The borderline between tipsy mellowness and irritation had tilted for him. "Lalor, you are being repetitious on a well-known theme."

"But you must have seen signs, Martin," Sir Hugh Rose asked in his quiet, speculative way, "that her allegiance, policy, sympathies—whatever—were changing?"

Dear God, had he not, Lalor reflected. The pleadings and arguments that had gone on between them, though never affecting their devotion to each other. "Yes, General, for some weeks. That allowed me time to plan my departure carefully."

They sipped their brandy. Lalor studied Murray, picking his

moment.

"Sir Robert, I know you don't like talking about sources in your part-time business," he said casually, "but I think we're all rather secure here. Seeing I am an old Jhansi hand, for want of a better description, could I ask who is your inside man near the Rani?"

Murray looked at him sharply. Then he smiled slightly. "Now why don't you tell me, Lalor?"

Lalor got up without a word and went back into the marquee mess tent where servants were still clearing away. He picked up his own name card from his dinner place, went over to the visitors' book on the table by the entrance and dipped its pen in the ink stand. He scratched a name on the back of the card.

He returned outside and handed the card to Hamilton. As he sat down, he saw the Political Agent glance up quickly from the card at the General.

"So he's still close to the Rani," he said matter-of-factly, "and we may look forward to more first-class intelligence?"

Hamilton realised he had been led into an indiscretion, though retrieved by Lalor's gesture of maintaining security. "I hope so," he said coldly. "The man is not only well-paid but he is also very efficient."

Sir Hugh Rose stood up. The others got up also.

"Nobody likes traitors but anything to save lives. This, as always, must be our guiding light. Sir Robert, we'll go into this Kunch business tomorrow morning. With you too, Martin, Sam. Goodnight, gentlemen."

Lalor walked away with Sam Wood and they parted outside his tent where a hurricane lamp burned dimly. He went over to his charpoy, sat down on its edge against the mosquito net and stared grimly in the dim light at the name that he had written on the card. Apart from his own instincts, his deduction had been very easy. In the past sordid week of clearing away the dead, he had identified the bodies of Mazumdar, the Diwan and the Kotwal. Each had killed his wife and had committed suicide. Gaus Khan, Ghulam Muhammad and other military figures close to the Rani had all fallen in action.

He tore up the card very slowly and minutely. But Rao Chaudri's name burned into his very being.

On 25 April, the Field Force marched away from Jhansi in the vast, straggling column that an army on the move in India was. To escape the scorching heat of the day, the start was made soon after midnight. The cavalry led, their scouting patrols well ahead and out on the flanks, followed by the infantry, some marching, some carried in lurching horse and bullock-drawn carts. The guns came next, with horses drawing the lighter field guns and elephants hauling along with stolid placidity the heavier-calibre cannon. Finally came the baggage and ammunition trains and the commissariat wagons and pack animals, attended by a horde of camp followers who, despite their seeming disorganisation, had a vital role to play in support of the fighting troops. The advance would ponderously go forward on its north-eastern route until 10 o'clock that morning when the sun would be burning down and the air would be almost breathless and stifling. Camp would then be made for the day and the tormented, dehydrated British would try to get some rest and respite from the heat in tents, under carts and in the shade of trees. That night, the advance would resume between midnight and 0200 hours and this routine would be the pattern until the Field Force closed with the enemy.

Ten days later, Lalor, almost burned black by the sun, sat astride Paddy alongside the General with the Field Force deployed before them, ready to attack the rebel positions about Kunch. As he licked his cracked lips, he wondered, not for the first time in the campaign, if they would succeed. Their reconnaissance had shown that the town was surrounded by woods and temples which were bristling with mutineers. The town itself had a strong wall and further entrenchments lay about it.

He looked about him at the assault columns of infantry sitting on the ground with their rifles, bayonets fixed, propped against their shoulders, waiting patiently for the bugle calls that would summon some of them to death or a gory wound. The ranks of the British infantry on whom the day depended so much, the 86th and the 3rd Bombay Europeans in their grey collarless shirts, khaki canvas campaigning trousers and pillbox caps with white cotton cover and neck shades, were dangerously thin and depleted. With them were the 24th and 25th Bombay Native Infantry who had performed so well during the long advance from Mwow and Sehore, also the three engineer contingents, the Bombay, the Bengal, and the Madras Sappers and Miners with their assault equipment in support.

Again the General was attacking from a flank, with most of the cavalry, the 14th Light Dragoons and the 3rd Bombay, massed behind them, poised to support the infantry, counter any intervention by the enemy cavalry or move to a cut-off and pursuit position in the rear of Kunch. The whole assault force was concealed by broken ground but across the plain away on their left in gun positions were Woolcombe's and Lightfoot's Horse Batteries and the Bombay and Hyderabad batteries, protected by the Hyderabad Contingent cavalry and infantry. Because of the sickness and casualty rate, the talkative, irrepressible John Cairns was commanding one of the Bombay batteries and Lalor knew that he would be revelling in his escape from the staff. While he was looking gazing at the artillery, the whole gun line erupted, belching smoke, and its muffled roar carried to them. Sir Hugh Rose, drawn and tired-looking, turned to him and said: "Well, the game's on again."

By sunset, the game was exhaustingly over for both attackers and defenders. The Field Force, under a broiling, relentless sun, had fought through the outlying defence works and broken into the town with the Horse Batteries galloping up, unlimbering and firing point blank at the gates and crumbling walls. By late afternoon, rebel survivors were streaming north along the road and through the fields to Kalpi but the cavalry was able to pursue only for a few miles through the poor condition of their horses and the prisoners they captured gave up abjectly, pleading for water. Quite a few of the rebel sepoy dead wore the white facings of the 12th Bengal Native Infantry which gave Lalor a certain grim satisfaction.

It had been a terrible day. The General had tumbled out of his saddle twice from dizziness and heat exhaustion. Though Lalor had implored him to rest, he had himself doused in water and stubbornly mounted again. Brigadier Archibald Wilson collapsed completely and at the General's command, Patrick Drummond hastily took over the command of the 2nd Brigade. Lalor would have dearly loved to have commanded the 86th in action but he did not offer himself in lieu of Drummond as he knew he must remain with the gallant, almost exhausted Sir Hugh Rose.

As the day wore on and they moved through the assault area, Lalor saw with some apprehension that as many men had fallen with heat exhaustion as from gunshot or sword wounds. He got an urgent message galloped back to Sam Wood to hurry along ambulance carts and water right up to the firing lines. That evening, after some rudimentary defence measures against a counter-attack that all knew would never come, the Field Force slept on their arms virtually where they found themselves at dusk. Many soldiers were too dehydrated to stomach food, crying out only for water. The dark-skinned, half-naked scrawny bhistis padded through the night, somehow finding isolated detachments to dole out their precious water, and again Lalor wondered about India. They could not survive without the support of such lowly folk, despised by their own countrymen and often abused by his. Yet the loyalty, even affection, that the bhistis gave was remarkable.

While the regiments slept the drugged slumber of the exhausted, Lalor, though drenched with sweat and aching with tiredness himself, drove himself to work with the indefatigable Sam Wood and the capable ADMS, Angus Kincaid, to brief them about the locations of units for the delivery of water, rations and ammunition and the collection of casualties. It was well after midnight when he climbed stiffly down from Paddy in a clump of trees that was the open-air bivouac for the Force tactical head-quarters. Several hurricane lamps burned softly about the grove as he walked Paddy slowly in and Amin and a syce hurried forward to meet him. He stripped himself out of his sodden, dust-covered uniform down to his underpants and had a refresh-ing birdbath in a basin of water. Then he lay down gratefully on the charpoy ready for him under a tree. On the far side, he saw the General inert, sleeping deeply.

As he lay among the luxury of clean cotton sheets after the heat and grime of the day, gulping a pannikin of water, he thought about the strong rumour that only Tantia Topi had been in command and that Manu was at Kalpi. But it would be some days before the Field Force would advance on Kalpi. They were currently in no condition to do anything.

For five days after its arrival on 15 May, the Field Force remained at Gulauli on the home bank of the Jumna to the east of Kalpi, resting after the long gruelling march, establishing the artillery batteries and preparing for the attack. On the night before the preliminary bombardment was due to begin, the General held a co-ordinating conference in his operations tent. Again, Sir Robert Murray led off with the intelligence summary and Lalor saw that the Political Agent was in an unusually buoyant mood.

"General, as we surmised, there have been great recrimin-ations within the hierarchy of the rebel camp. This has been a mixture of the Rani saying I told you so about the futile attempt to defeat us at Kunch, the infantry accusing the cavalry of leaving them in the lurch by withdrawing somewhat precipitately and finally, but certainly not least, that Tantia Topi also quitted the field rather early—as he did at the Betwa."

Laughter broke out. The sunburnt, bewhiskered faces exchanged amused glances.

"We have 'em, Sir Hugh!" Simon Freeland shouted. "They're now fighting with a river at their back. They're as good as in the bag."

Cheering erupted but Sir Hugh Rose held up a hand for silence. He said gravely: "I believe so too, gentlemen. At least, I hope so. What's the word you often use, Martin—inshallah? We've done a lot of hard marching and a lot of hard fighting. We're all getting rather tired, I know, but final victory is now within our grasp. However, let us not get over-confident or complacent. There's many a slip betwixt. I don't think the soldiers can sustain the campaign much longer, and I mean our sepoys as well as the British regiments. Units are so under-strength—I certainly don't have to tell you commanding officers that. I am not being pessimistic as that's no way for a general to talk before a battle but we must be realistic. I'm only saying what you all know in your hearts. We must go at Kalpi as we've never done before—even at Malton Pass where the situation was des-perate for a long while, or at Jhansi and the Betwa. It's our last throw and rather like the desperate gambler who stakes all on that throw, we must win. And we will win, for unlike that gambler, we have the means—our splendid soldiers, both British and Indian—to divorce us from the fickleness of luck. You must instill this sense of ultimate victory into them. In reality, though, it is a case of do or die."

A sobered, subdued silence followed. Lalor glanced at Simon Freeland and saw with slight amusement that the likeable *beau sabreur* had sunk into his chair, his big fair moustache seeming to droop visibly.

"But I'm sorry, Sir Robert, we've interrupted you. Do go on."

"I regret that's all the good news I can give you, General. Not so good is the fact that the Nawab of Banda, with two thousand cavalry, some infantry and guns, has joined Rao Saheb, Tantia Topi and the Rani at Kalpi. His arrival has restored morale con-siderably, despite the squabbles, charges and counter-charges about Kunch—you know how mercurial these people are. Also, the Rani has forced Nana Saheb to have a council of war in which it was solemnly agreed to defend Kalpi to the last man. She made them swear an oath on the sacred waters of the Jumna. I quote: we will win or perish but never leave the field."

"We've heard that before," Sam Wood said contemptuously.

"How many sacred waters are there around here?" Macormack Bonner, sitting at the back, asked wearily.

"They'll leave the field—Rao Saheb and Tantia Topi—but she won't," William Orr, Hyderabad Cavalry, said quietly but emphatically. He was a lanky, fair-headed, rather reserved man who had done excellent scouting before the two brigades had linked up. "She's got guts which the other two haven't and, I fear, brains as well."

"Martin," the General said. "I think you'd agree with that? Certainly I regard her as our main threat. Strangely enough, not because she has any real forces to command now but she seems to have a personality that makes men follow her into battle—true leadership."

Once again, Lalor felt all eyes on him once Manu's name was mentioned. He had even trained himself to ignore Murray's oblique, searching glances whenever her name or title came up in conversation.

"General, you're right in a way but you're also wrong in a way. It's true that she will sway them with her personality. That is, for a while, but in the end, nothing will happen. She's a woman in India and they'll choose to ignore her. Even though they really know what she says is the best course, the best plan, there's too much loss of *izzat* in being seen to be dominated by a woman."

"But she could motivate them to fight well at Kalpi, Martin?" Charles Hasted asked. Lalor thought suddenly that the 1st Brigade commander now looked older, even greyer, that the sharp, intense officer he had met on the banks of the Chambal six months ago.

"Yes, she will, Brigadier, if she can get about to address the rank and file. But she'll be excluded from the real command structure which will be Rao Saheb and Tantia Topi."

"Then that should make our task much easier," Patrick Drummond said drily. He was a big, bulky man in his forties with a thick black moustache and dark blue eyes who had taken over command of the 86th when Harry ffrench-Blake had been promoted to a brigade operating south of Bombay. Lalor had always got on well with him.

When the laughter had died away, Macormack Bonner asked innocently: "Do you pay Tantia Topi to be on our side, Sir Robert?"

The Agent for Central India smiled thinly as more mirth broke out. Sir Hugh Rose maintained a straight composure when he spoke again but his eyes showed appreciation of Bonner's sally. "Well, gentlemen, apart from Banda's appearance—driven on by General Whitlock's column I'm sure and out to save his own skin—the intelligence picture looks cheerful. Martin, let us now move to our proposed operations against Kalpi."

Lalor got up and moved over to the sketch map of Kalpi and the surrounding terrain pinned on an easel. He picked up a long twig that he had trimmed as a pointer and faced the veteran, whiskery faces staring at him.

"General, Sir Robert, gentlemen, Kalpi is another Kunch but rather in a reverse order. Kunch had outworks among temples and baghs but it was walled and we had to break into it—though of course very small beer compared to Jhansi. Kalpi goes the other way. The town is not fortified but the approaches are broken up by many deep ravines. Our cavalry patrols have seen extensive entrenchments commanding the ravines, despite the fact that we have avoided the obvious frontal approach along the road from Kunch and have moved distantly to this flank. No doubt, once the enemy are driven from these forward positions, they'll fight back through the clumps of trees, the temples, the walled gardens in the pattern we met at Kunch. However, I do feel they'll fight harder, much harder. The Rani, as we've discussed, will rally and inspire the rebel sepoys, her Bundelas, the Walayatis, whoever is there. The Jumna is behind them and they well know it.

"That's the outline picture so far. The General will give out his detailed orders tomorrow once we've seen the effects and reactions from the bombardment. However, to balance the perhaps unwelcome news of the arrival of the Nawab of Banda, our deep-ranging cavalry patrols on our right flank have only this afternoon brought back news of a British column approaching along the Jumna from the east and this can only be Colonel Arthur Robertson's force from General Whitlock's column, bringing, apart from much needed reinforcements, more artillery ammunition. Gentlemen, the jaws are closing. As Colonel Simon Freeland said earlier, we have them in the bag!"

A concerted roar and cheering burst out as he sat down. Sir Hugh Rose stood up again and silence gradually returned. The General's intelligent, appraising blue-grey eyes ranged thoughtfully over the assembly of officers as he spoke.

"Gentlemen, Kalpi is our final test. We must fight and be prepared to die to take this place—whatever the odds, whatever the difficulties. That is rather a trite thing for me to say, I realise that very much. I've always known that's how the Field Force tackles its operational tasks. But now there can be no turning back, not the slightest consideration or admission of defeat. We must succeed or die in the field—ironically, rather what the Rani is saying now to our adversaries. Once we have captured Kalpi— and who knows, perhaps the rebel leaders as well—the Central India Field Force will have accomplished all it set out to do. And I say this with all humility, looking to you, my brigade commanders, my commanding officers and, indeed, to my own staff who, I know, have supported you fellows as well as they have me."

Spontaneous clapping, almost unheard of in an operational gathering, followed his words. The General was about to speak again when a distant drumming of hooves gradually became louder. All in the tent listened intently. Lalor saw the strained, tense look on the faces of his brother officers. They were all worn out, overworked through a dire shortage of subordinate officers and NCOs from casualties and sickness, and living on their nerves.

Only one horseman was approaching, he quickly deduced. The rider halted outside amid total silence in the tent. A few moments later, a dusty, dishevelled figure burst through the entrance and straightened himself up hurriedly with a wild, excited glint in his blue eyes when he sighted the General. Lalor blinked when the identity of the visitor came to him.

"It's young Redfern, isn't it?" the General inquired mildly.

The young cornet of the Hyderabad Cavalry smiled his delight and saluted with crashing emphasis.

"Sir!"

"Well, Mister Redfern, you're looking as if you've something to tell me yet again. Get on with it, laddie."

"Sir, I beg to report that Captain Brian Dalby's patrol which established contact with Colonel Robertson's column today is bringing on the Colonel ahead of the marching troops to meet you. They are just behind me. They should be here within the hour."

"Capital! What does the column consist of, laddie?"

"Six companies of the 88th, sir, a Camel Corps of one hundred and fifty Rifle Brigade and 88th, and three hundred Sikhs. And an ammunition train."

The tent erupted to more cheering that went on and on. The General, smiling, shook Jack Redfern's hand and the others surrounded the cornet to pummel his back appreciatively.

When Lalor stood up to join the milling throng, the General said to him wryly: "More Irish, then, with the 88th, eh?"

"What you are really saying, General, is that the appearance of the 88th will more than compensate for the Nawab of Banda and others."

With approval, Lalor observed that the perceptive Andrew Gow had hurried out of the tent, crying in the night for the bearers. Obviously, whisky in some quantity would be needed soon.

Three days later, with a deeply russet sunset before them, many officers, NCOs and soldiers of the Field Force, British and Indian, crowded into the square of Kalpi fort. They were all tattered and grimy, and many had bloody bandages. They stood gazing up at the flagpole sited on the battlements over the fort gateway. Six buglers of the 86th sounded off and all officers saluted as the Drum-Major began slowly raising a large Union Jack. When the flag reached the truck and streamed away in the evening breeze, the clear notes of the silver bugles were drowned by a concerted roar from the watching ranks. Pipe-Major George Taylor of the

71st Highlanders, a regiment that had recently joined the Force, began pacing the battlements by the flagpole with his bagpipes, playing the piobaireachd, *The Desperate Battle*. The cheering died away as the plaintive skirl of the pipes echoed about the square.

"Well, we've done it, Martin," Sir Hugh Rose said to Lalor quietly as they stood in the rear on a stone-flagged verandah. "And such good timing too. On the Queen's birthday."

Lalor was quite affected by the setting and emotion of the occasion. He knew that the General was also. It had been a long, hard march back, littered with death, wounds, sickness and much misery.

"A pity though, sir, that we've failed to catch Rao Saheb and Tantia Topi."

"You haven't mentioned the Rani. And I quite agree. She would be an embarrassment if we captured her."

"The final clearance and search of the town is still going on and this may turn up something, or someone, yet. I've just come from the river. The ferrying across of the cavalry for the pursuit is going well, if slowly."

"Good. I'm sure I was right to give the overall coordination of the cavalry to Hasted as he'll press the pursuit hard. It would be a great bonus if he could flush one or two of our high-priced birds."

The tall, forbidding figure of Angus Kincaid appeared out of the throng of staff officers about them. "General, I trust now that this final battle is over," the ADMS of the Field Force said reproachfully, "that you will at last allow yourself to come under my medical orders."

Sir Hugh Rose smiled faintly. Yet Lalor could see, as he had done for weeks now, that he was extremely tired. He looked almost frail.

"That I will, Angus. You will have no more insubordination from me. I am in your hands, at your mercy."

"Your ADC has found quarters for you here in the Fort and has them ready. He seems to think that Rao Saheb himself may have occupied the rooms previously and have made a hurried exit a few hours ago."

"I am indeed honoured. I hope that underneath my bed has been searched—he may still be there."

"General, you must go there now and rest. You've been in that saddle since dawn for the last three days."

"I will, Angus. But first I must speak to my soldiers."

When the Pipe-Major had ceased playing, the General stepped up on to the broad edge of a stone tub holding a flowering shrub. Lalor shouted to the 86th buglers to sound a 'G'. The bearded faces who had been watching the flagpole and the Pipe-Major turned about when the bugles rang out.

The General, a slight figure, began speaking, pitching his voice across the dense, jumbled ranks with a hoarseness that betrayed his innate weariness. He gave a simple, sincere address, devoid of any pomposity that was the measure of the man in the eyes of Lalor who admired him greatly, both professionally and personally. He expressed his deep appreciation to all his soldiers, British and Indian, of whatever creed or background, for the victories that the Central India Field Force had gained in the campaign. Though regrettably the main leaders had eluded them, in his opinion not only was their task over, so was the whole mutiny. Despatches to him recently had brought news of decisive victories in Oudh, Rohilkhand and Rajputana. The King of Nepal had sent 10,000 Gurkhas to the Commander-in-Chief. All that remained was to apprehend the fleeing leaders of the revolt but the main fighting effort was almost certainly at an end. Sadly, this would mean the imminent disbandment of the Field Force but that fact in itself indicated that the great mutiny was crushed and final victory was now complete.

Six hundred throats cheered in unison when the General ended and went on in waves of exultation. He stood there, smiling, but Lalor could see that he was visibly affected. He felt a nudge at his elbow. Kincaid stood there.

"You must get him out, Martin. He now needs a lot of rest."

Ten minutes later, Lalor sat with the General, Kincaid and Sam Wood in a large cavernous room at the top of the Fort which overlooked the Jumna flowing through its ravine below. Andrew Gow hovered about his master anxiously.

"The sweepers have given the palace a good clean-out, General. Kader Bux has been on their tail."

"Good. And we still haven't found Rao Saheb?"

"What, sir?" The tall, freckled subaltern was startled.

"Nothing, laddie. A small joke I'm perhaps overdoing. If my baggage has arrived, I'd like Kader Bux to produce a good cheroot for me. I feel like relaxing and celebrating."

Angus Kincaid held up a deprecating hand. "I'm afraid I must forbid smoking, General. Your whole system, which is now very run down, needs thorough rest and recuperation. Smoking will not help your lungs or heart at all."

The General spoke in broad Scots: "Man, ye'll be killing me with the cure. I was next about to call for a wee dram for my friends here and myself."

Sam Wood and Lalor laughed. A rare half-smile strayed reluctantly to the ADMS's lips. "A wee dram has never done any man harm, Sir Hugh. But in moderation, mind you."

Sir Hugh Rose looked at Sam Wood and Lalor in more serious vein. "However, though I hate to admit it, the ADMS is right and I must lie up for a while. I haven't been feeling too grand lately, as you will have well noticed. As there's nothing worse than an unfit general, because that makes him an incompetent general, I'm going to take the medical advice in full—except for that wee dram occasionally. Sam, you'll now have much to do, clearing up the field, sorting out prisoners, replenishing our rather thin supplies. With the prisoners, perhaps we should be fairly circumspect about the Bundelas and others who have followed their traditional leaders into this business, but with known and identified mutineers, we should obviously look hardly. Martin, I'd be obliged, among your many other tasks over the next few days— coordinating Charles Hasted's search and pursuit operation and sorting out the re-deployment of our units for the disbandment of the Force—if you'd write an account of our operations since Jhansi for me to sign and submit to the Commander-in-Chief. You should work closely with Sir Robert who is sure to come up from the base camp tomorrow to begin his political report. I think you told me that our situation report, stating that we have taken Kalpi and giving the first estimate of our losses and gains, is going to the C-in-C with the first cavalry patrol to cross the river?"

"Yes, General," Lalor replied blandly. "With William Orr's agreement, I selected Jack Redfern to convey our news. I felt he had the greatest facility in finding the Commander-in-Chief, wherever he may be now, with the greatest speed."

Sam Wood laughed heartily again and Sir Hugh Rose smiled. "Yes, an admirable choice. A veritable persona dramatis who appears to thrive on night movement. I hope he startles Sir Colin as much as he has done me."

Kader Bux appeared with his tray of whisky panis. Sir Hugh Rose took a glass and looked about him in a deep, grave way. Lalor saw again how tired, almost shrunken, he looked.

"Gentlemen, the battle is over but we are old soldiers and know that the work of the staff goes on—even increases. We also know that the role of the staff is to ease the burden on the general. This, Sam, Angus, Martin, you have done for me admirably and I'm very appreciative. However, I've never believed that the staff should have to prop up their general but, in this one instance, you'll have to bear with me for a few days while I am under command of the ADMS. All I can say, finally, is that I'm most confident you will carry on for me—you know my mind, my policies—and this means that I can gladly succumb to what the ADMS has in mind for me."

Sam Wood cut through the ensuing embarrassment. He held up his own glass and said forcefully: "To the regiments and us, sir—the Central India Field Force!"

The room echoed to his toast, led by the General, and they drank deeply. Lalor caught Kincaid's eye and nodded across to Sam Wood. Sir Hugh Rose was leaning back in his chair, gripping his half-glass of whisky, looking drained both physically and mentally. They finished their drink and stood up. Despite the General's mild protestations, they said goodnight, saluted and left. Andrew Gow remained with the ever-vigilant Kader Bux.

Soon afterwards, Lalor stood on the home bank of the Jumna with Brigadier Charles Hasted, Simon Freeland, Macormack Bonner and William Orr, watching the cavalry horses and troopers being ferried across the river on makeshift rafts of planking lashed on country boats made by the Sappers and Miners. As he stood there, chatting, he looked over the river into the darkness beyond and wondered where Manu was now. He prayed that the cavalry would not capture her.

Ten days later, Lalor was sitting in his office on the ground floor of Kalpi fort, discussing the dispersal of the Force with Sam Wood and John Cairns, now back at his staff appointment, when Sir Robert Murray entered abruptly. He was carrying an official brown envelope covered in broken red seals. Lalor saw the shaken look on the Political Agent's clean-shaven, patrician features.

"I've just had this despatch by special messenger," Murray said rather dazedly. "It's from Macpherson, the Agent at Gwalior. The rebels have taken Gwalior."

"Which rebels?" Lalor asked quickly.

"Rao Saheb, Tantia Topi and the Rani," Murray answered in a slow, shocked litany. "It's incredible."

But brilliant too, Lalor thought, a master-stroke worthy of Manu, not the other two.

Sam Wood's red face deepened in colour and his blue eyes popped with indignation. His large moustache seemed to bristle. "But we've been working for days on the disbandment of the Force! The campaign is over! Both the C-in-C and the General have said so!"

"Perhaps the rebels weren't aware of that, Colonel," John Cairns said innocently. "Or worse still, they did know and they've deliberately captured Gwalior to make us look silly."

The near-apoplectic AA&QMG was about to round on his staff captain when Murray said: "All of you come with me while I inform the General. Some sharp decisions have to be taken."

Sir Hugh Rose was writing at his desk when the Political Agent knocked on his open office door and they entered. He looked up in some surprise, then laid down his pen and took off his spectacles. He motioned them to be seated.

"Gentlemen, I fear you have more bad news than good to tell me."

"General," Murray said huskily as he sat down, "I regret to say that I bear very ill tidings. Rao Saheb, Tantia Topi and the Rani of Jhansi defeated Maharaja Sindhia's forces at Morar five days ago and now have Gwalior in their complete possession. Sindhia has fled to Agra with his bodyguard—all his other troops deserted to the rebels—and Major Macpherson, the Agent, is with him. Macpherson has written to me from Agra."

"Bad news indeed," the General murmured. He picked up a paperknife and began tapping the desk gently, an old habit.

"It's almost shattering news," the Political Agent emphasised hoarsely. "In one move they've undone all we have achieved. Rao Saheb has proclaimed himself Peshwa of the old Mahratta dominions and he's obviously hoping to rally the princes of the Deccan to him. They have Sindhia's treasury to pay the sepoys, and much more over. And of course, the prestige of staging this most successful and dramatic comeback from their train of disasters."

The General looked across at Lalor. "I now regret we didn't capture the Rani. I detect her hand in this. She's the best and bravest of them all. Sir Robert, does Macpherson give what strength Rao Saheb has?"

"Yes, he does." Murray rifled hurriedly through the pages of the letter. "Here we are. About seven thousand infantry, four thousand cavalry and twelve guns. And another fifteen hundred horse and eight guns who deserted from Sindhia."

"Martin, the Field Force is intact? Our redeployments have not yet started?"

"We're still concentrated, sir. The 71st are due to march away tomorrow to join General Whitlock."

"Cancel that. We have greater need of them."

The General picked up the sheet of paper that he had been writing on, studied it for a few moments and then slowly tore it up into small pieces which he dropped into a wastepaper basket with equal deliberation. He looked about him, smiling slightly.

"That, gentlemen, was a draft of my Special Order of the Day marking the imminent disbandment of the Field Force in two days' time. However, let us be thankful to Macpherson for his prompt information. I will resume its composition after Gwalior."

"But, sir," Sam Wood protested in some agitation, "apart from the disbandment of the Force which the Commander-in-Chief has already approved, the ADMS has said that you must go up to the hills for sick leave."

"Sam, you must tell Angus Kincaid that he has reverted to being under my orders again. Gwalior comes first, then, *inshallah*, Simla."

The reflective drumming of the paperknife went on. Then it ceased. The General dropped the paperknife and straightened up in his chair. His tanned but gaunt features and tired blue-grey eyes were determined.

"Gentlemen, it's clear to me that the Field Force cannot disband and that we must march on Gwalior as soon as administratively possible. Sir Robert, I'd be grateful if you would prepare a full account of Macpherson's report for both Governor-General and the Commander-in-Chief. Perhaps the news has been telegraphed but we should fill in what we can. I'll write now to Sir Colin, informing him of my decision and intentions. Sam, do a staff check on our administrative position to see when is the earliest we can march. Martin, send out a warning order placing the whole Force at twenty-four-hours notice to move. Call in the brigade commanders and the cavalry COs for a meeting at five o'clock tonight when all of us have had time to digest the full implications of a move on Gwalior. Stop all cavalry patrols except for our immediate security and summon in those who are already out. I seem to keep saying we are entering on our last throw. I assure you, gentlemen, that the dice is going to roll finally at Gwalior and it will not be against us."

17

Gwalior

The Field Force moved on Gwalior by forced marches at night and reached Morar, a cantonment five miles to the east of the city, by 16 June. Sir Hugh Rose, accompanied by Lalor, galloped a swift reconnaissance. The rapidity of the approach from Kalpi had surprised the rebels and the General was determined to capture the cantonment, so inviting as a logistic base and, almost as important, for shade and shelter from the scorching sun, before its buildings and stores were fired. A quick attack was mounted with the 1st Brigade, supported by the remnants of the 2nd who had not been left garrisoning Kalpi. With the 25th Bombay left, the 86th right, Woolcombe's and Lightfoot's batteries going into action from gun position to gun position in the centre, and the 14th Light Dragoons covering the flanks, the Field Force advanced on the cantonment and cleared it at the point of the bayonet.

"A very satisfying day," Sir Hugh Rose said to Lalor as they sat drinking large pannikins of tea in the comparative cool of the verandah of an abandoned married quarter that Andrew Gow had seized after the battle was over. It was early afternoon and beyond the protecting latticework, the heat and stark, glaring sunlight bore down on mind and body like a white-hot hammer. "We've given the enemy a sharp, bloody nose at very light cost to us, we've taken a lot of his supplies which we can well use ourselves, and I hope that the men can now get some rest and recuperation here after their great efforts over the past days—or rather, nights."

Lalor sipped his tea. He knew that the General was worried about the condition of the soldiers. The whole campaign must end at Gwalior. Soon the fighting strength of units would be too low to go on.

He was spared from any comment by Sir Robert Murray, led by Andrew Gow, striding up the path to the verandah. The Political Agent sat down wearily, mopping his perspiring face with a large red and white spotted handkerchief as he took off his helmet.

"Have a really good brew of Army *chai*, Sir Robert," the General said cheerfully, "made by my Dragoon escort."

Murray reached for the pannikin of tea that Andrew Gow had scooped unceremoniously out of the nearby metal dixie and he drank a gulp appreciatively.

"I've just come from interrogating the rebel commander whom the Dragoons snared so efficiently when he was bolting. Very fascinating stuff from him. He was a high officer in Sindhia's army and, I would hazard, probably the chap who instigated the mass desertion of Sindhia's troops to Rao Saheb. Of course, he's now terrified and sweating all over. It seems he was privy to the rebels' inner council that debated policy and future strategy. In his gibbering state about the imminence of Sindhia's vengeance, the words are pouring out."

"Do go on, Sir Robert. You make a tired man extremely interested."

"Firstly, and this will delight you both, while all the euphoria about taking Gwalior was still lingering on, the Rani publicly accused Rao Saheb of making sweetmeats instead of cannon-balls."

Sir Hugh Rose laughed softly. "Splendid! And I hope she's right. I'm sure she is. Somehow I have trust in the woman."

Lalor smiled and thought back. He could easily visualise the outburst. That was authentic Manu.

"Finally, she got so exasperated that she withdrew from the council altogether. However, when wind of our approach did reach Gwalior, she was hurriedly consulted by Tantia Topi who, whatever his other limitations, is no fool. Our prisoner was present, also obviously worried. She so impressed him that he was able to remember word for word her reply to Tantia Topi. I was also so impressed that I began to write it down as he recounted it. This is what she said. *Rao Saheb has destroyed all hope of victory by deliberately ignoring the warnings I gave him and by neglecting his war preparations and giving all his attention to trivial-ities. The enemy is on us and our army is not ready. Everywhere I see nothing but disorder and chaos. How can you expect to win the battle? However, I shall not lose heart. The thing you can do now is it to take out all your troops for one glorious attack on the English without caring for the result. You must see that the attack is sudden and determined and overwhelming. The enemy must be rolled back.*"

"Stout lassie," Sir Hugh Rose murmured. "Have their main forces issued from Gwalior as she advised? What does this fellow say about their present dispositions?"

"He hints that they have moved in some strength to meet Brigadier Leeper's column from the Rajputana Field Force closing in from the south. Our march from the east was quite un-expected."

"Where would Leeper be now, Martin?"

"From our last message from him, a rough guess would be Kote ki Serai, about twenty miles from here."

"We must get a strong officer-led patrol from the Dragoons or 3rd Bombay to make contact with him."

Lalor stood up. "I'll do that now, sir. If you and Sir Robert will excuse me, I want also to tie up our re-organisation here with the brigade commanders and check that Sam Wood knows that his ordnance park and the hospital can now move up to join us."

The heat seared him like a torch when he left the bungalow and walked across the hard-baked brown earth square to the bashars where Field Force Headquarters was setting up. He had to stop several times to wait for files of infantry and jogging horse artillery with their guns and limbers to pass as the organised movement of a well-trained and tried formation re-deployed after the confusion of battle. His eyes were half-closed from the glare and the dust and he was only a few yards from the Headquarters when he saw the troop of British cavalry, the dust-covered troopers dismounted and holding their sweating horses. He quickly noticed the regimental insignia on the troopers' uniforms and the pennants on their lances.

John Cairns was talking to the troop commander when he saw Lalor and waved excitedly. "Martin, I was just about to fetch you!"

Lalor studied the cavalry officer. "And it's the 8th Royal Irish Hussars if I'm not mistaken, all the way from the Rajputana Field Force. You're a sight to gladden our sore eyes."

The young officer saluted and shook Lalor's proffered hand. He was tall and thin with a straggling fair moustache and red-rimmed blue eyes. He looked tired. "James Purcell, at your service, sir. Brigadier Leeper has sent me to inform the General that he has come up against a very strong rebel position well-posted in high ground blocking his advance. Though the brigade has made some initial progress, he feels that he must request reinforcement from the General urgently. Our intelligence from prisoners is that more rebels are coming out from Gwalior for a concerted attack on the brigade. They also say that the Rani of Jhansi is commanding in the area."

When Lalor reported Cornet Purcell's message from Kote ki Serai, Sir Hugh Rose had said firmly: "I'm determined that our laddies will have a night's sleep tonight, Martin. We'll march at first light tomorrow. The 86th, 25th Bombay, three companies of the 71st and Lightfoot's battery will form the column with two troops of the Dragoons to cover us."

The decision to have a night's rest was much appreciated by the regiments but the sun exacted a severe penalty as the sweating infantry toiled their way to the south-west next morning. About a hundred men from the 71st and 86th collapsed and had to be carried along in dhoolies. Lalor saw that the General, suffering himself from the heat, was shaken by the number of sunstroke casualties and he hastened to reassure him.

"They'll be all right, sir. We've brought plenty of water and when they've had a good rest at our destination, you'll find that they'll be fit for action tomorrow. They're that sort of men."

During late afternoon they came on Kote ki Serai, a straggling town on an almost bare plain before a range of hills. About a mile outside the town, sitting their horses under the shade of a clump of laburnum trees, was Brigadier Anthony Leeper and his brigade major with a troop of the 8th Hussars. After an exchange of salutes and introductions, the General, Lalor and Andrew Gow dismounted and were led to a circle of camp chairs.

While bearers dispensed mugs of tea, Leeper came quickly to the point. He was a very tall man, about six foot five inches, lean, hardy and clean-shaven with a coldly-appraising direct gaze.

"General, we attacked yesterday and made some gains near the pass but we just can't get on without more infantry. The 95th and our sepoys have done very well but they can't persevere without more support which I knew you would provide. If we can break through the pass, I'm told the door to Gwalior is then open. We have before us, and are continuing to draw, what I believe are their main forces. You have unhinged them by suddenly appearing to take Morar but I suggest, sir, with respect, that the real battle for Gwalior lies here."

"I agree with you entirely. Indeed, we can end this whole thing here if they are brave enough—or rash enough—to meet us in the open field. I have no desire to be involved in some lengthy investment of Gwalior which I'm told makes Jhansi look like some minor laird's keep—a fortress that covers about four miles of a mountain with great walls and wells and reservoirs inside. Of course we can bottle the rebels up there but I just haven't the troops to do it properly. I hear also that Feruz Shah is in the vicinity. We British think we have now crushed the mutiny, rebellion, call it what you like, but a reverse, or even inactivity, before Gwalior could be catastrophic. However, to come back to the immediate issue before us, you will appreciate that we are in no condition to mount a main attack before tomorrow?"

"Fully understood, sir. When you've had a rest, I'll take you forward on a reconnaissance of the enemy positions. But all this is almost of secondary importance to the news I must give you now."

Both Sir Hugh Rose and Lalor stared at Leeper who went on almost casually.

"We think we have killed the Rani. Or, at least, badly wounded her."

Lalor felt his hand clutch the tea mug that he was holding until his knuckles whitened. He gazed almost unseeingly at Leeper. He had a sickening presentiment of the probable truth that lay behind that simple, bare statement. Why was he so shocked when he had subconsciously been expecting such a fate for Manu for a long time now?

"Good God!" the General ejaculated in his surprise. He sat up and looked across at Lalor.

"In the action this morning when we again attacked the mouth of the pass, I had the 8th Hussars out on our open left flank—the right, as you will see, General, is protected by a dry canal. It's wild, broken country, full of nullahs, with a few stands of timber and some sparse scrub. One of the squadrons surprised a rebel cavalry detachment which was obviously reconnoitring our flank. The squadron charged and got among them. In the melee, the rebel leader was clearly recognised as a woman, though she was dressed as a warrior. She wore a cuirass and wielded a sword with the best of 'em. When the Hussars were beginning to cut them up, her bodyguard hustled her away but she was seen to be hit by a shot as she rode off. Somehow, she stayed in the saddle. That was only a matter of hours ago but I'm told by my Intelligence Officer that already Kote ki Serai is buzzing with rumour that the Rani of Jhansi has died in action and has been burned according to their rites."

"Jesus, Mary and Joseph," Lalor muttered to himself. He put down his tea mug, clasped his hands and looked down at the dry, sandy soil at his feet.

"Martin, you seem to believe that?" the General asked, after a while.

"I'm afraid I do. It could only be her."

The General said to Leeper: "Martin Lalor knows the Rani very well."

Anthony Leeper looked across at Lalor. "The Hussars are still searching for her body, or, indeed, any evidence that this person several troopers in the fight swear was in fact a woman. Despite all the rumours and speculation, we have no real confirmation. If the General could spare you, would you join the Hussars now to identify the body if they do find it uncremated? Or perhaps she's just badly wounded and they may come on her somewhere."

The General was sitting back in his camp chair, studying Lalor, but he spoke without hesitation when he saw his inquiring glance.

"You must go, Martin. This is very important."

"But, General, there's your reconnaissance, your orders for the attack tomorrow, the deployment of our column."

"The Brigade Major here and John Cairns can cover all that. It's crucial to our fortunes whether we know the Rani has fallen or not. The morale factor, in inverse proportions to each side, is very considerable. And you know that, Martin. Now off with you, laddie."

An hour later, Lalor was with the Hussars squadron that had charged the rebel cavalry detachment. They were resting in a miserable village that stood among parched, dusty fields on a dried-up stream several miles from the hills that barred the way to Gwalior. The squadron leader, a young brown-eyed deeply-tanned captain named Gerald Fitzgerald, had summoned the troopers who were adamant that the wounded leader of the rebel horsemen was a woman. Lalor sat on the verandah of the village bania's house talking with them.

"Where did you hit her?" he asked Trooper Kiely, a stocky, sunburnt, bearded man who claimed that he had shot the rebel leader.

"In the neck, sir. It was the luckiest shot—certainly the best one—I've ever done in my whole service. It was a fleeting snap shot at about eighty yards. She had turned away and her people were beginning to follow her, so I didn't have too much of a target. I saw her reel as soon as I fired and she almost fell from the saddle but somehow she steadied herself. I saw the blood gush over her hand as she clutched the wound. A great cry went up from the others and they closed in fast about her, riding off. I saw no more of her then."

Kiely comes from Cork, Lalor thought dully and absently. A lucky shot he had said. Not too lucky for poor Manu. Lalor felt depressing, numbing shock coming over him. He knew it was all over now for Manu. All his nagging, only half-admitted fears about her ultimate end were now coming only too true. He realised that she was dead. She had probably died from loss of blood. Her followers would not have been able to staunch the neck wound, especially if they had to flee for some distance and she had managed to stay in the saddle.

"Unfortunately, I contributed greatly to her escape," Fitzgerald said ruefully. "At that stage we had been broken up by several nullahs in a running fight and were in penny packets all over the place. I suddenly became aware that I didn't know what other rebel strength might be in the area, that these fellows might have only been an advance guard. I had the recall sounded so that we could re-group and I could regain control. What that really achieved was that we lost the Rani."

"I suppose you've searched the village?"

"Every nook and cranny."

"And nothing from any of the villagers?"

"Not a syllable. Of course they're frozen with fear about us but you know how you get these funny feelings? They know something but they're not telling. Something big has happened. I can smell it like our mess contractor's curries."

"I'd like to say one thing, sir," the man from Cork broke in quietly. "I didn't know the rebel leader was a woman when I aimed that shot. It was Brophy and McCann here who saw her when the fighting was close. They've told me what a game 'un she was. But I don't think I would have tried that shot if I'd known that my target was a woman, whatever her rank in the rebels. You're an Irishman, sir. We have our faults but we don't make war on women and children and I pray we never will."

Lalor smiled faintly. Somehow, the honest, frank statement raised him slightly from his despair.

"I'm sure we never will, too, Kiely. However, the Rani of Jhansi is a very important leader in the rebel cause and it's our duty to capture her, or failing that, even kill her. I know her. She's very courageous and I've also heard from Captain Fitzgerald how she was seen wielding her tulwar with the best. I would say she would have wished to die in battle, though perhaps not in a skirmish in unmapped nullahs in this desolate countryside. She would have wanted to fall in the main battle for Gwalior, to go down gloriously in some last desperate charge. However, she was also philosophical and prepared to meet her destiny wherever that might be. Don't feel any remorse. You shot brilliantly and that's the end to it."

What hollow, hypocritical words, he thought as he turned to speak to Fitzgerald but he had to say something to console the earnest Trooper Kiely. The desperate optimist in him, however, groped for the slim possibility that Manu was still alive, though seriously wounded. Perhaps she was lying up not too far from where they were.

"Gerald, I know your boys have had a hard day. Also, my horse, like me, is not too fresh either. But would you mind continuing the search for the hour or so before darkness?"

"Not at all, sir. That is what we expected to do. It would be a great honour to the Regiment if we can capture the famous Rani of Jhansi. Anyway, as a hunting man, I don't like to think that somewhere near us a wounded fugitive is bleeding away. We'll mount up at once."

It was an arid, hostile, scarred landscape they rode over, through deep ravines and winding nullahs, relieved only by some straggling clumps of trees standing by barren water-courses. The whole countryside was gasping and crying out for the rains. The horses's hooves alternately clattered over stony gravel or stirred thick, cushioning dust and the Hussars rode with neckerchiefs to mask their faces from the billowing dust-cloud. The sun still bore down and their tunics and breeches, dried out from the rest period, again became soaked with sweat.

They had almost reached the hills when, riding in columns along a twisting nullah, they came into a shallow wide ravine with intermittent pools of water joining by straggling trickles that Lalor guessed was the Morar river wandering its dying way from the scene of their battle yesterday. Downstream, several miles away, lay the Field Force waiting to attack through the pass in the morning. He had already decided that he could not ask the Hussars to ride any further when he saw the Hindu shrine under the spreading arms of a large banyantree and the sadhu sitting crosslegged on a smoothly polished flat stone-slab before it. Something compelled him to lead the squadron to this lone, bizarre figure who was watching them fixedly. Perhaps it was because they had ridden through seemingly abandoned, uninhabited territory. If any peasants or shepherds had seen them, they had obviously hidden in fear.

With Fitzgerald, he reined in before the shrine. The troopers of the squadron crowded forward in a curious, dusty half-circle. While he looked at the sadhu who sat motionless as if carved in stone. The holy man's lean, scrawny, ash-covered body was clad only in a dirty loin cloth and he had long straggling plaits of hair, matted with cow dung and urine Lalor guessed, falling down to his shoulders. He had a long unkempt beard which strangely did not conceal gauntly handsome features daubed with white clay caste marks.

Before Lalor could speak, the sadhu did.

"I have been waiting for you," he said in Hindi.

Somehow Lalor was not surprised. This is India, he reminded himself. He felt the hate in the sadhu's cold, dark, dead eyes.

"You know me then?"

"It does not matter whether I know you or not."

"But you have something to say to me. So you must know who I am."

"I know you as a defiler of our illustrious womanhood, a traitor, a barbarian from the darkness beyond the seas."

"Then you must tell me your news quickly, parasite on your people, especially about the illustrious womanhood you spoke of, before I stuff beef in your mouth and cast you among the sudhra houses for them and all of us to defile you also."

Real fear flickered in the sadhu's eyes. He seemed to become suddenly aware of the hundred British soldiers, leaning in their saddles, staring with some hostility at him. He got slowly, almost defensively, to his feet. He was quite tall, about six foot Lalor reckoned, and perhaps only in his early thirties.

"I am to tell you that Lakshmi Bai, the Queen of Jhansi, is dead. We have burned her and her ashes are scattered. Neither you nor anybody else will never find her."

The sadhu had quickly recovered from the shock of Lalor's threat. He delivered his words with malice. Lalor rested wearily on Paddy's neck and looked away. He could feel the eyes of the whole squadron watching him questioningly.

"For Christ's sake, Martin," Gerald Fitzgerald said to him urgently, "what's the evil-smelling thing saying? I got bits of it but that's only served to confuse me."

"Apart from expressing an instant dislike of me—which is fair enough—he says that the Rani is dead. I believe him."

"But," Fitzgerald protested in bewilderment, "do you mean to say that this filthy scarecrow has been sitting here, out in the bloody wilds, just waiting for us to come by to tell us that?"

Lalor could think of no more profound explanation than what he had told himself. "This is India, Gerald. I don't pretend to understand it any more than you do. I gave all that up a long time ago. Why don't you tell your boys what this is all about."

As Fitzgerald edged his horse away, Lalor returned his gaze to the sadhu who stared at him with an arrogant defiance.

"I see you have Ganesh, the elephant god, there. I believe he's a cheerful fellow to whom you pray for obstacles to be removed. It could be said that today the British did away with an obstacle—Lakshmi Bai. Do you think that Ganesh was listening to our prayers, not yours?"

Harsh, brutal words, and rather unnecessary. He was not entirely sure why he had said them. He realised that he not only wanted to upset the sadhu but to insult and wound him. He had tried to do so with a gibe at Manu's death, too.

The sadhu's eyes gleamed their hate again with a strange confidence. "She is dead but you, her helpmate who became her greatest obstacle, will perish as she did. You also will be consumed by fire and never seen again."

A fairly reasonable forecast anybody could make, Lalor thought philosophically. And it would probably take a lot of appeal to a god with a trunk on his face to change such an event. Suddenly Paddy became restive and started backing away. When Lalor had controlled him, he found himself closely alongside the sadhu.

"Who are you?" he asked him curtly.

"I am nothing but I see everything."

"You mean you were somebody, now are nothing and do nothing."

Lalor spurred Paddy away and rode into the Hussar squadron. Fitzgerald caught his mood and shouted a command to his sergeant-major.

Before they moved off, the squadron sergeant-major, a wiry, tough-looking man with a clipped gingery beard and hard blue eyes, said bluntly to Fitzgerald: "Why don't we put a bullet in him, sir? From what you've told us from the major, he's one of them."

Fitzgerald looked at Lalor inquiringly. He answered bitterly: "No, sa'r-major. While I agree entirely with that thought in a way, on the other hand he has done us a service. We now know that the Rani is dead. They've cremated her. The chase is over and the rebels have lost their best leader. Enough is enough. That thing is nothing as both he and I, strangely enough, have agreed on. He is something that India, with its obscene caste system, its millions of cattle roaming around while millions of its people starve, has to live with. It is not for us to change their ways. We can only try to give peaceful conditions, build roads, canals and railways. And, I suspect, when we are all long dead, gone and forgotten, we'll get little credit for that either. No, he belongs to India. Let him live, as India would wish him to live. To us, he's not worth the bullet."

Fitzgerald and he rode away back up the nullah from which they had emerged, without a backward glance at the sadhu, the squadron pounding behind them. Lalor was furious. What a way to hear of Manu's death, from a parody of a man such as that sadhu. He would have cheerfully killed him, as the SSM had suggested, but he knew, in quick hindsight despite his black mood, that he had been right in desisting. The sadhu was part of India and as he had persuaded both himself and Gerald Fitzgerald, this was India. There was no other answer. And he surrendered to that realisation.

At sunset, next day, the Field Force were streaming through the streets of Lashkar, the new city about Gwalior, with the guns of the massive fortress on its great rock towering over the old city unable to interfere. The attack on the pass that morning had gone well, despite the rebels being well served by 12-pounder and 18-pounder artillery fire. The 95th skirmished frontally in the mouth of the narrow pass while the 86th and 25th Bombay crossed the dry canai, scaled the heights and turned the enemy left. Beyond the final ridge, taken by the 86th, lay Gwalior and Sir Hugh Rose ordered a general advance. With the 8th Hussars deployed on either flank, the 86th and 95th, supported by the 25th Bombay, moved forward down the hillsides towards the tree-lined houses of Lashkar. The rebel artillery was still active but it was soon obvious to the British that many rebels were fleeing the field.

That night the old city and Sindhia's palace-fortress remained held by the rebels but next day the great fortress fell ignominiously to the daring of a young officer. Lieutenant Michael Rose, 25th Bombay, and his company, with some of Sindhia's police as guides and a local blacksmith to smash locks, slipped inside through a series of side entrances. In desperate hand-to-hand fighting, in which Rose lost his life, every man of the depleted garrison who had stayed was killed. Gwalior was wholly in British hands.

Lalor reported to Sir Hugh Rose at Field Force headquarters in the fortress that evening.

"General, from what we've been able to establish from the interrogation of officer prisoners, Tantia Topi withdrew this morning with about twelve thousand men and twenty-two guns. They say he was rather in a panic about which way he should go. He thought of Goona but then heard that was occupied by Colonel Herbert Lewis's force and he couldn't go north as Brigadier Underwood's column is coming down from Agra."

"Give Brigadier Sir Robert Napier my compliments and warn him that his column from the Rajputana Field Force is to follow up Tantia Topi with all urgency. He is to have Third Bombay as his cavalry. Macormack Bonner is just the chap to chase local difficulties." The General sighed tiredly and gazed abstractedly at the far wall of the spacious room in which they were sitting. "Now it really is all over, except to hunt down Tantia Topi and Feruz Shah. What a damnable pity and tragic waste of life to have young Rose, who achieved so much, killed in the final minutes of the campaign. No kin as far as I'm aware but what a keen laddie. And he'd survived the mutiny at Neemuch and collected two mentions in despatches so far. However, I suppose the rebels could say the same about the Rani. Though they didn't really appreciate her worth while she was alive, I'm sure that her death in a chance cavalry encounter completely demoralised them. They caved in abjectly yesterday, except for their gunners."

"Yes, it's tragic when the best fall during the last shots," Lalor murmured.

Sir Hugh Rose looked back at him. "I've just heard by special messenger that Maharaja Sindhia will be arriving back from Agra in two days' time. We must give him all the pomp and circumstance we can muster, subject to operational commitments. We'll despatch the 8th Hussars and the 14th Dragoons to meet and escort him and his household back to his own city. Once he's installed, I'll disband the Field Force and hand over to Sir Robert Napier as soon as I can." He paused and studied Lalor deeply for a few moments. "While we're alone, Martin, I'd like to express my appreciation of the splendid way you've carried out your duties and for all the support you've given me when the going was rough—which it was for most of the time. You'll get proper recognition when I write my final despatch at Simla."

"Thank you, sir. It's been an honour to serve with you."

"If you ever need a leg up anytime, don't hesitate to contact me. I don't believe in patronage except when it's deserved. I consider you in the deserving category."

"Thank you again, sir," Lalor said in some embarrassment. "It will be strange to go back to a quiet garrison life in the Regiment after all that's happened over the past twelve months. I don't suppose India will ever be quite the same for any of us now."

In the following weeks, the ordered routine of a peacetime garrison existence of which Lalor had spoken was still far distant. After the triumphant return of Maharaja Sindhia, the Central India Field Force paraded before Sir Hugh Rose for the last time. That night Sindhia held a magnificent banquet in his palace for the officers which was really the dining-out of the General. Next day, with the brigade commanders, the commanding officers and fellow staff officers, Lalor said good-bye to the slight, elderly, handsome Scot who had led them so calmly and successfully through the hard campaign.

Lalor returned to the 86th, billeted at Morar cantonment, and settled easily into the family circle that a good regiment is. He was soon out in the field leading a column of several companies mounted on horses, searching for armed rebel bands and individual stragglers. Sir Robert Napier, in his pursuit, had caught and defeated Tantia Topi at Jawra Alipur. Tantia Topi escaped and the countryside was infested with the fleeing remnants of his shattered army. The rains then broke, bringing down the severe temperatures and cooling the parched, baked land which sucked in the healing water avidly, but movement soon became difficult as the rivers and streams rose and mud now choked the once dust-deep roads and tracks.

One afternoon in late July, when the black sky was being torn by an electrical storm and rain was teeming down, Lalor was at the head of his drenched mounted column as they approached the cantonment after an operation lasting five days. At the main gate, he was surprised to find the Adjutant, Tony Dewhurst, in a dripping oilskin coat, sitting astride his horse.

Dewhurst urged his horse over to him as he drew near. "Sir, the Colonel requires to see you urgently. He'd be obliged if you would report to him as soon as possible."

Lalor stared at Dewhurst, a good-looking, personable man with a dark moustache who was a few years younger than himself. There was a strange, stiff formality about him. They had know each other in the Regiment for years and were close friends.

"What's in the wind?" he asked casually. "You haven't found Tantia Topi hiding in my company lines, have you? He probably can't stand this bloody rain any more than we can. What a country! Fried to a cinder just the other day and now we're like drowned rats."

Even through the rain that was cascading down their faces, driven by a tearing wind, he could see that Dewhurst was ill at ease.

"I'm afraid that the Colonel must tell you himself, Martin."

Dewhurst had relaxed slightly but he still sensed the official barrier. He decided not to press further. "Righto, Tony old son. Tell himself that I'll be there within the hour, as soon as I've seen my boys dried out and fed."

Lalor's puzzlement had not lessened by the time he had washed and changed into dry uniform. The storm had passed when he walked gingerly around the puddles on the square across to Battalion Headquarters. Again he was confronted by the strained formality of Tony Dewhurst who was hovering about the entrance to the verandah waiting for him. He caught a glimpse of the Orderly Room Sergeant, Milton, an old soldier whom he had known as far back as the Sikh Wars, who gave him a tense, worried glance before disappearing quickly into the room where his clerks were.

It was now Lalor's turn to become uneasy. He could read the atmosphere clearly when Dewhurst, in a subdued voice, asked him to wait outside the Commanding Officer's door while he went inside. Lalor stood patiently. He now had a foreboding which he curiously matched with that morning at Jhansi when he had waited for Adrian Meadows to return from his sowars' lines. More bad news than good, he surmised, as Sir Hugh Rose had said recently at Kalpi.

The door opened. Dewhurst stood aside, holding it.

"Major Lalor," he said in a flat, suppressed voice.

Gripping his sword with his left hand, Lalor marched in, halted, and saluted Patrick Drummond who was at his makeshift desk looking down at an open letter. Dewhurst closed the door. There were only the three of them in the room. Lalor stood to attention and waited. He could now divine the nature of the interview. He was not going to be asked to sit down.

Patrick Drummond looked up at him. His dark blue eyes had the same embarrassed expression as his Adjutant's. He spoke harshly and bluntly, after clearing his throat at some length.

"Major Lalor, it is my duty, as directed by the Commander-in-Chief of the Bombay Presidency, to charge you with the grave offence of giving aid and comfort to the enemy. I am further directed to inform you that you are to be tried for this alleged offence by general court-martial."

Lalor stood rigidly to attention, staring in disbelief at Drummond who lowered his eyes again to the paper before him. Deep anger soon surged through him, dispelling the shock. But he restrained himself. The two men in the room were brother officers, his friends and comrades of many years, both in the good days of easy garrison life and in the hard times of the dangers and privations of active service.

Drummond looked up again. His eyes were now not so much embarrassed as pained. He spoke quietly, as if he was almost delivering a reprimand to himself. "Major Lalor, I regret to say that you must now be confined to your quarters and you are not permitted to use the Mess. I must also tell you that your court-martial will be held in Bombay. Again, this is at the command of the Commander-in-Chief, but I must admit that I do agree it's a wise decision. From my own point of view, as Commanding Officer of this Regiment, I intend to move you on your journey to Bombay this very night. You're a well-known, popular and respected member of the Regiment, as I am the first to recognise, but once this news about you gets about, what with the situation in Ireland and your regimental record, there could be a lot of trouble from the NCOs and soldiers, even from the young officers, but especially from the Sergeants' Mess. I feel terrible about ejecting you so brutally from your own regiment like this but you must appreciate the circumstances I have to consider."

"You'll get no trouble from me, Colonel," Lalor found himself saying, also as if he was talking to himself. "I'll do whatever is good for the Regiment."

Drummond leaned on his elbows and interlocked the fingers of two large, brown, rather hairy hands before him. He contemplated this wall of fingers as if he had erected some kind of fortress or defence about himself.

"I knew you would say that, Martin," he said almost absently.

Drummond stared at his fingers again for some moments. Then he banged a great fist on his desk and stood up, livid with passion. He waved an admonishing finger violently at Lalor and Dewhurst.

"For Christ's sake, what is this charade we're putting ourselves through, all because of some high-priced and senile idiot in Bombay! Martin, we've served together for years! You saved my life at Sevastopol when I was hit. I know I would have died if you hadn't tended to me with your own field dressing and wrapped me in my only blanket! What the bloody hell are we talking about? What are our values? Who are we meant to look after?"

Lalor saw the strain of months of campaigning breaking through Drummond's disciplined reserve. Tony Dewhurst reacted quickly with the instincts of a capable, intelligent adjutant.

"Sir, Major Lalor has just been arraigned on a very serious charge. You must not be seen to be condoning the offence."

Patrick Drummond crashed his fist down on his table again with fresh fury, causing the ink well to jump precipitately and spill blackly over the grey army blanket covering.

"I don't care what the bloody hell I'm condoning! Martin Lalor is a member of the 86th and we're not going to abandon him."

"Should I get a wee drop to help our further discussions along, sir?" Dewhurst asked tentatively.

"You had better, young man," said Drummond menacingly," otherwise I may have to find another adjutant. And get a whole bottle, too. Martin, sit down, for pity's sake. What have the 86th found themselves into? You're one of the best!"

Drummond moved away from his table and began unbuckling his sword. He sat down heavily in a nearby cane chair and opened his tunic collar. He looked again at Lalor, still distraught.

"Martin, I'm sorry about this but the orders have come down from the all-highest in Bombay. If only Sir Hugh was still here!"

Lalor sat down also. He, too, laid aside his sword and undid his tunic collar. He looked hard at Drummond.

"Patrick, before Tony comes back, you must tell me who has laid this charge against me. Obviously it relates to my time at Jhansi. Who was it? I must know."

Drummond studied his fingers again. He took a while to reply. "I'll be needing a few drinks, Martin, before I divulge that."

"Patrick, come on. We've known each other for fifteen years. What have I meant to have done wrong? Certainly nothing against the Regiment! Who accuses me?"

Patrick Drummond looked at him, partly pityingly, partly searchingly. But he said nothing.

Lalor persisted. "Henry Mercier? Sir Robert Murray?"

Drummond's eyes bored into him.

"No. Alicia Wentworth."

BOOK THREE

THE RECKONING

18

Court-Martial

Martin Lalor stared through the near window of the court-martial room. Beyond, in a sharp morning downpour, lay Bombay cantonment and he was looking along a deserted, puddled avenue of firegold trees. Their flower had long wilted and vanished, for it was now September, and no glimmer of the orange-gold colour lingered among the dark green feathery leaves. He found himself thinking again of Jhansi and the dak bungalow at Madhupur.

Somewhat reluctantly, he dragged his mind back to the court. The Prosecuting Officer, Curtis, an awkward-looking, bespectacled Royal Engineers major with close-set blue eyes and a drooping reddish moustache, was outlining the case against him. He was only half-listening to the litany of events that had happened to him between June and November last year. The burden of the prosecution case had been predictable, as he had already warned his Defending Officer, Major Hamish Balgarnie, sitting beside him. His command of Manu's levies against the invading forces of the Raja of Orchha was its main prop.

While Curtis spoke in an unemotional monotone, Lalor again studied the officers who composed the court-martial trying him, as he had done searchingly during the ritual of their swearing-in. The President, Brigadier Kelsey, Royal Artillery, was a big, heavy man with an untidy grey moustache and a thick mane of iron grey hair. His full red face was set off by sagging jowls and a large purplish nose which Lalor had initially contemplated with some awe. His small muddy-coloured eyes stared bleakly at him when he was not distracted by speech or movement elsewhere in the courtroom. "A hanging judge," Tony Dewhurst, escorting officer, had whispered to Lalor apprehensively, if irreverently, earlier. The members of the court-martial were two lieutenant-colonels, Ashford, 9th Lancers, tall and elegant with a carefully tended blond moustache, and Barrett, Royal Artillery, dark, alert and dapper. The one major, Pemberton, 32nd Regiment, thickset with balding fair hair, reminded Lalor of tragic Frederick Dunlop at Jhansi. Captain Blair, 78th Highlanders, freckled and sandy-haired, completed the five officers who composed the General Court-Martial. They were all Queen's officers unknown to him and he had not objected to any of them, even though Hamish Balgarnie had whispered urgently to him that Kelsey had arrived in India only a few weeks ago and was ignorant of Indian conditions.

He glanced at Balgarnie who was listening intently to the prosecution. Balgarnie, sallow and brown-eyed, was a major in the Commissariat Corps who had introduced himself somewhat deprecatingly. "I've been ordered to take this job but it does interest me greatly. That is, of course, if I'm acceptable to you. My sole qualification, if I can flatter myself to that extent, is that I'm a failed law student from Edinburgh." He had sensed that he would get good service from this sharp, rather abrasive officer who soon showed that he had an acid turn of wit.

Lalor's attention was caught back by Curtis. The gangling Engineer laid down the sheaf of papers from which he was reading and looked across at the President. "That, sir, completes the outline of the case the Prosecution will lay before the court. I now wish, with your approval, to call my first witness."

Kelsey nodded. Curtis called across to the Court Orderly, an invalided sergeant from the 86th named Coady whom Lalor knew well, standing by the door at the back of the room.

"Captain Richard Meadows."

Lalor got a shock when he heard the name. He had forgotten that Adrian Meadows had an older brother in his regiment. He watched Richard Meadows, a clean-shaven, fair-headed man heavier and taller than Adrian, take the oath. Meadows looked solemnly at him when he sat down.

"You are Captain Richard Meadows, 1st Bombay Native Cavalry?" Curtis asked formally.

"I am."

"And you are the brother of the late Cornet Adrian Meadows who commanded the escort for Sir Julian Wentworth's tour of Central India early last year?"

"Yes."

"I believe you received a letter—the last one before his tragic death several days later—from your brother written from Jhansi and dated 2 June 1857?"

"Yes, I did."

"I also understand that in this letter your brother spoke of a certain spontaneous rapport, or affinity, or even attraction, between the Rani and the accused on their first meeting. Also that this meeting was not untinged with some political sentiment between them."

Meadows took out a carefully folded piece of paper from his tunic pocket and Lalor saw Adrian's bold boyish writing as his brother opened it up.

"Yes, I have it here."

"Please read it to the court."

"*My dear Dick,*" Meadows began quietly, "*It's late at night and I have a few grogs aboard, including a fair portion of the Rani's wine as well as a nightcap with Martin. However, Skene has a mail courier going to Saugor tomorrow and he's too good an opportunity to miss. Though my first bit of big news is that we too are turning back and heading that way also, our travelling circus will take many weeks to reach Bombay. However, this is really to tell you that I've had a simply fascinating evening at the palace. The Rani—and what a woman she is!—had the Boss and the whole gang of us to dinner. A fabulous time was had by all! Even dear old Sir Director unbent into the odd smile by the end of the night. The food, colour, even the noise of the so-called music—plus dancing girls, mark you!—were all splendid, a real eye-opener for Yours Truly. Alicia looked absolutely stunning, though pestered by a very smooth palace hanger-on type. But the remarkable thing about the evening was the extraordinary way the Rani and Martin Lalor took to each other. I'm sure it was simply because he's Irish, for as you've heard, she has a very big chip on both shoulders of her sari about us English and I did hear her say that she knew that the Irish are also oppressed by the English and that they had much in common. They went on to discuss the local situation but I'm sure Martin was just digging away to guess whether she knew anything. They certainly had their heads together rather confidentially for quite a while. As I've told you many times, Martin is a great chap but he can be funny about the Irish question and though he pretends to be your easy-going, casual Irishman, he's really quite deep. Well, must to bed now. Early rise tomorrow as we start the Great Retreat.*" Meadows paused there for a few seconds, staring down at the letter. Then he went on, his voice dropping. "*Any news from home, I wonder? That's the worst of all this wandering. However, see you and the mail from Mother and Father ere long. We'll have a wild party! Your affectionate brother, Adrian.*"

Richard Meadows remained looking down at the letter and an awkward silence fell on the room. Then Curtis walked over to him and took the letter gently from him.

"Sir, the Prosecution tables this letter as Exhibit A".

Hamish Balgarnie stood up immediately. "Sir, the Defence fails to see how this chatty letter from one brother to another, the writer a young and very inexperienced officer and by his own admission in his cups, is in any way relevant. The Court is surely not concerned with the Rani's social small talk or with Irish politics.''

Kelsey's bushy grey eyebrows rose and his small eyes looked questioningly at Curtis. ''This seems a reasonable submission to me.''

''I can assure the Court, sir, that this exhibit will be developed and justified as the prosecution case goes on.''

Kelsey looked about at the other members sitting on either side of him but none spoke. He sat brooding at the green blanket covering the table before him, then reached out and took the letter from Curtis's hand. ''Exhibit A.''

Balgarnie sat down and glanced at Lalor who shrugged impassively.

''Your witness,'' Curtis said to Balgarnie and took his seat.

Hamish Balgarnie rose again slowly. He drummed his fingers meditatively on the table that he shared with Lalor as he looked across at Richard Meadows and then stopped.

''Captain Meadows, you obviously had several letters from your brother while the tour was on, despite the distances and the unpredictability of the mails. No doubt he discussed and described the personalities in Sir Julian Wentworth's entourage. What was his considered opinion of the accused?''

Meadows spoke unhesitantly, his honest blue eyes looking directly at Lalor. ''He was clearly a great admirer of Captain Lalor, as he then was, both as a person and as a soldier. He got on very well with him socially and he liked him very much. On the military side, he was worried that he himself was so junior and inexperienced to have the responsibility of escorting such an important personage as Sir Julian and it was obvious to me, reading his letters, that Captain Lalor gave him much advice and help.''

''Thank you. That is all.''

Balgarnie sat down. Curtis declined to re-examine. After standing to attention and replacing his helmet, Richard Meadows saluted the President and strode away to the door, held open by Sergeant Coady. Curtis looked down at his papers and said to Coady: ''My next witness is Colonel Mercier.''

Henry Mercier settled into the witness chair after he had been sworn in. The big official was dressed formally in a grey suit with a blue cravat tied about a pristine, starched white collar which contrasted sharply with his swarthy, tanned features. Lalor thought that he also now looked much older, with his thick hair whiter than his grey moustache. We are all much older, he reflected. Mercier looked across at him but he only recognised the bland appraisal of officialdom which conveyed neither warm recognition nor hostility.

After Curtis had gone through the formality of identification, he asked: "I believe, Colonel, you were Acting Political Agent for Central India from February to November 1857 while Sir Robert Murray was on home leave?"

"I was."

"I am further to understand that you were accompanying the Malwa Field Force late that year when the accused made contact with you outside Mandesar."

Mercier stirred himself in his chair and his intelligent brown eyes gazed at Curtis wryly. "Perhaps it would be more accurate to say that we encountered each other. Captain Lalor rode into our camp, having more or less allowed himself to be intercepted by one of our cavalry patrols. You will realise, to effect his escape from Jhansi over hundreds of miles of hostile countryside, he was in native dress. And rather effectively, too."

"His sudden arrival, and physical appearance, must have been quite a shock?"

"Yes, frankly, it was. Though in those turbulent months last year, shocks and surprises were frequent and many."

"But would you not also agree that the re-emergence, the return to the fold—how shall I put it?—of Captain Lalor, one of the rare survivors of the Jhansi mutiny was rather a special shock?"

"Yes, it certainly was. If only from his appearance. He wore native garb convincingly, he was deeply sunburnt and bearded. It was only when you looked into his eyes that you realised he was a European."

"But I suggest, Colonel, there was a bigger impact on you personally. If I am correct, in your position you were building up an intelligence network for the eventual return of British administration to the disturbed areas. Did the accused feature in any information coming in to you?"

Mercier shifted heavily in his chair. He glanced across at Lalor who recognised the same embarrassed, worried expression he had seen in others recently. Mercier looked back at Curtis.

"We had got garbled, but cross-checking, reports that a British officer was assisting the Rani of Jhansi. From what Captain Lalor told me himself when he came to us outside Mandesar, these rumours—to which level I had discounted such reports—had obviously been only too true."

"And the Rani of Jhansi was then known to be an open enemy?"

"In November she was," Mercier answered sharply. "I'm not

qualified, and I very much doubt whether anybody else is, to pronounce what she was before then."

"But why do you say that?"

"Because Captain Lalor informed me, at that meeting on the banks of the Chambal near Mandesar, that the reason he left the Rani was that she was receiving for the first time a known rebel personality—Tantia Topi, Nana Sahib's agent. He knew then she had obviously thrown in her lot with the rebels."

"Colonel, I put it to you that another strong rumour—or perhaps report of some substance—was that the accused was acting as the Rani's general. That he commanded her army against the Raja of Orchha, a known loyal adherent of ours. From your intelligence and deductions from that intelligence, please tell the Court about this."

Mercier drew a large white handkerchief and dabbed his face and the back of his neck. He re-folded the handkerchief with care and looked across with some emphasis at Kelsey, the President.

"Orchha was loyal in that he was with us at the end. What went on between June last year and March this year, when Sir Hugh Rose and the Central India Field Force arrived at Jhansi, must be a matter of conjecture about which I am not prepared, on low intelligence reports—as they were in those days—to speculate."

"But you will agree, at least, that the Raja of Orchha was not an avowed enemy?"

"Yes."

"And the Rani's army that met him was commanded by the accused?"

"Again yes. Captain Lalor admitted that freely at the Mandesar meeting. But I do ask you to look at the whole time scale of those months."

"After that somewhat dramatic encounter, as you yourself call it, with the accused at Mandesar, Colonel, and once the dust of that successful battle had died down, you must have written a report on your interrogation of, or should I say, discussions with, the accused?"

"Yes, I did," Mercier answered heavily. He took out a thick official-looking brown envelope from the inside of his frock coat and laid it on his lap, almost like a sacrificial offering. "Sir Robert Murray was due to reach Mwow shortly with the new general, Sir Hugh Rose. It was part of my briefing and handover material."

"What does the report say, Colonel?"

"It has so many intelligence references to agents and sources that I cannot jeopardise these. You may take it for the court to examine but it must be treated with considerable confidentiality. The agents named cannot be exposed to any vengeance."

"Colonel, its handling will obviously be most discreet and secure. But I have to request you to tell the Court what are the salient points regarding the accused."

"You must realise that I wrote this report many months ago. I think we would agree that all of us have lived through traumatic times since June last year, even since November when I wrote the report, and the picture, the known facts, have been changing constantly."

"Agreed, Colonel. No one would dispute this with you. But you must give the Court the gist of this report pertaining to the accused, as seen by you, a highly experienced political officer, last November."

Henry Mercier took a deep breath. He looked questioningly at Kelsey but the President stared stonily back at him. He returned his gaze to Curtis and said coldly: "All right, I will say what you wish me to say—"

Kelsey broke in harshly. "Colonel, you must say what you wish to say, always assuming, between gentlemen, that this is the truth. There is no coercion. Perhaps you have phrased yourself wrongly?"

"Sir, I realise that. But I am being held to a report I wrote almost a year ago, certainly a good eight months before the rebellion was over."

Kelsey nodded sombrely. "Let me assure you that the Court appreciates this important aspect and notes it. But you must meet the Prosecution's request."

Mercier stared over Kelsey's head, as if he was consulting some blank deity on the damp-ravaged wall. "From the background reports I had from various agents about a British officer serving with the Rani of Jhansi, particularly regarding the defeat of Orchha by the Rani when he was clearly her commander in the field, I had formed a pre-judged picture of that officer which our meeting by the banks of the Chambal, in those days, only seemed to confirm."

"And what was that?" Curtis asked, with some urgency creeping into his monotone.

"By deduction, from what information we had about the mutiny at Jhansi and subsequent reports, we knew that the officer concerned must be Captain Lalor, the Military Assistant to Sir Julian Wentworth who was on tour in the area. This was later made very positive by another survivor who reported to us, Peter Rosario, a Goan cook. Captain Lalor was Irish, an Irish Catholic, with known strong political views about the Irish question, and perhaps one was led into a too-easy deduction that old, bitter political wounds and grudges, coupled with the temptation of riches that India holds for a forceful military personality—look at Hodson and Skinner—had taken him over the brink and into the rebel camp. Or at least into the Rani's camp. We had also heard stories of a close attraction between the two."

"Thank you, Colonel. We will take your report as Exhibit B for the prosecution case." Curtis looked across at Hamish Balgarnie. "Your witness."

Balgarnie rose when Curtis sat down.

"Colonel, on your own admission, I think I am right in saying that information you received in those somewhat dark days for us between, say, June and November last year, was mostly low grade. Indeed, you have said so yourself."

"Yes, that is right. Many areas were closed to us and complete blanks. We were desperate for whatever we could get. Much was rubbish but now and then something connected. It was a time when most of India thought that the British would lose and were not eager to come forward, even for money."

"And you were prepared to condemn Captain Lalor—or at least damn him in your own estimation, and certainly in a written report to your own superior and Sir Hugh Rose—on the basis of such bazaar gossip?"

"I repeat—all I deduced, suspected, was more or less confirmed by Captain Lalor when we debriefed him at Mandesar. Moreover, he was extremely virulent in defending the Rani, which did make me suspect him still, or at least his mental balance."

"And only served to confirm you also in your pre-judged assessment of the Rani?"

"I rather think," Mercier snapped, taut with anger, "That in regard to her, events from April to June this year, at least, have proved me right."

Balgarnie went through the motion of shuffling papers on the table and he thoughtfully looked down at this activity. Then he glanced up again at Mercier. "Colonel, in the short time you served with Captain Lalor in the Mandesar area, what was your impression of him as an officer?"

Mercier became slightly mollified. "First class. He was a considerable help to Brigadier Hasted, commander of the Field Force, because he had taken the trouble, and risk, to reconnoitre Feruz Shah's dispositions. He was also invaluable during the battle. Later I found him a great mine of information about the rebel situation in Central India generally."

"I believe at that time two companies of the 86th, Major Lalor's regiment, were serving in the Malwa Field Force?"

"Yes, they were."

"What was your impression of Major Lalor's reception back into his own regiment?"

"He was obviously very highly regarded. All ranks were delighted to see him. As well they might, for no doubt they thought that he had returned from the dead."

"And would you agree at least half the strength of those companies of the Royal County Down, as I believe the regiment is also known, would probably be North Irish Protestants? I mean, not just Irish Catholics like Major Lalor."

Mercier glowered at Balgarnie. He said stiffly: "I suppose you could be right."

"Thank you, Colonel, that is all."

Henry Mercier stood up, made a cursory bow to the President of the Court and walked slowly and heavily from the room, looking straight ahead.

"My next witness," Curtis said, "is Sir Robert Murray."

The Political Agent for Central India sat down in the witness chair after taking the oath and looked calmly about him. He was dressed impeccably in a white linen suit and his black cravat was tied with a flourish. His long silver-grey hair was brushed to the nape of his neck. Lalor thought, however, his handsome tanned features were now rather gaunt, almost hatchet-faced, and that he, too, had lost weight from the strain of the past months. He glanced at Lalor with the same bland impassivity as Mercier had and quickly returned his gaze to Curtis who began to go through the opening formalities.

"Sir Robert," Curtis said tentatively after a while, "I understand you know the accused well—that you both served closely together during the campaign in Central India in Sir Hugh Rose's headquarters."

"Yes, we served together from the assembly of the Field Force at Mwow last December until its disbandment at Gwalior in July this year."

"What is your assessment of the accused during this time when you necessarily saw much of each other?"

"An admirable officer. Sir Hugh Rose depended greatly on him. Not only was he efficient but he could get the fullest co-operation from other members of the staff. Also the brigade commanders and commanding officers thought highly of him. He was also an experienced observer of the native scene and of some considerable assistance to me, especially when our advance approached Jhansi."

"A very competent professional officer, then?"

"That is what I said. But an agreeable personality too. He could not have accomplished all he did without that aspect as well. The times were hard and everybody was under great pressure. Also, we had some difficult characters within the Field Force."

"But did you not start off with some considerable reservations about the accused, Sir Robert?"

"What do you mean?"

Curtis picked the envelope containing Mercier's report lying on the table before Kelsey, took out the bulky document and held it before Murray.

"I refer to Colonel Mercier's report to you, now before the Court as Exhibit B, giving you an account of his meeting with the accused before Mandesar and expressing some guarded comment about him. Do you recognise this as that report?"

"Yes, I do. It is a document of its time, no more and no less. Major Lalor, or Captain Lalor as he then was, was one of the many phenomena of India of those days and he naturally drew much comment—one who had escaped a bloody mutiny and massacre and who re-appeared later, having somehow survived. You must be aware of many accounts of such adventures, even of British women being sheltered in native villages."

"But we are talking of months in regard to the accused, Sir Robert. And apart from his journeying, he had not been roughing it or harried and hounded?"

"That is a question you should have discussed with Colonel Mercier. I was not there when Major Lalor reported to the Malwa Field Force. I am certainly in no position, certainly no legal one, to comment."

Curtis tucked the report back into its envleope almost sorrow-fully and returned it to the long table where the five members of the Court-Martial sat. He took off his spectacles which he cleaned with some deliberation with his handkerchief while his blue eyes studied Murray almost absently. Quite a good-looking, pleasant fellow, Lalor thought, watching him, and obviously clever.

Curtis replaced his spectacles and said to Murray: "But what of the accused commanding the forces of the Rani of Jhansi against the Raja of Orchha, which I don't think is in dispute, even from the defence. What did you make of that, Sir Robert?"

"It is not for me to elaborate on the Mercier report. You have it before you—take it or leave it. I was not even in India at the time. It would only be hearsay evidence for me to give an opinion."

"But as the Political Agent for Central India, Sir Robert, I do hope you can see your way clear to say that the Raja of Orchha was a known loyal adherent of the Company and the Crown."

"He was before June 1857 and he was in March 1858 when the Field Force approached Jhansi. What he was in the intervening time, only he knows, though I do admit there is no evidence of this throwing his hand in with the rebels or even of any collusion."

Lalor glanced wonderingly at Balgarnie and Dewhurst sitting with him. Balgarnie's brows were knit in puzzlement. Murray sounded almost a hostile witness.

"Sir Robert, am I right in saying that Colonel Mercier would have briefed you on the intelligence network he had built up and that you would have taken over its direction?"

"Yes. Disappointingly, much of it was nonsense sent in by cranks or liars, telling a story they thought we wished to hear for money. Mostly poor quality. However, we were desperate in those early days."

"But it did pick up as the advance of the Field Force got under way?"

"Yes, it improved dramatically after we re-took Saugor, which was the turning point. Nothing succeeds like success."

"You say dramatically. Was there a particularly startling break-through?"

"Yes, just before Jhansi, which was Sir Hugh Rose's major objective and obviously a formidable one, a courtier very close to the Rani made contact by letter, offering his services for money and immunity from arrest and trial. We snapped him up, naturally. He laid on a system of communication by trusted messenger even during the ensuing siege and he proved to be a brilliant and most valuable agent. Sir Hugh knew almost every-thing that was going on in the enemy camp—the Rani's problems, her reactions, the deployment of her forces, the weak spots in the defences, the state of morale."

"Was his information only operational intelligence? I mean, pertaining to your tactical problems of how to capture Jhansi? Did he volunteer any information about the accused regarding, shall we say, his stay at Jhansi after the massacre until his departure?"

Sir Robert Murray hesitated. He uncrossed his long legs with their perfectly pressed trousers and stuck them straight out before him. He slumped in the chair, his long brown fingers held prayer like before his face as he stared in a hard, speculative way at Curtis. Some moments elapsed until he sat upright and spoke.

"I asked him about Major Lalor. He of course had no idea—at least I'm almost sure he hadn't then—that Major Lalor was with the Field Force."

"Why did you now suddenly have doubts or misgivings about the accused? You have implied that you, and Sir Hugh Rose, accepted the accused seemingly without reservation."

"At Jhansi Major Lalor did an extraordinary thing. I say extraordinary because it was either an extremely brave act or a most foolhardy one, or possibly both. Sir Hugh's ultimatum to the Rani, after our siege lines were established, to surrender to save bloodshed had been rejected. Major Lalor offered to meet the Rani at a breach in the walls in a last attempt to persuade her into surrender and she accepted this offer. Much against his better judgement, Sir Hugh approved Lalor going ahead with this meeting, mainly talked into it by Lalor himself who persuaded the General that it was merely his life at stake as against possibly many soldiers if we had to assault. Everybody thought he was going to his death.''

"But, very obviously, he didn't.''

"No, he came back completely unscathed. It was then our turn to be even more completely amazed. He had talked with her— unsuccessfully, of course—under the guns of rebel sepoys and her retainers. We had been bombarding the city and causing destruction and casualties. The feeling, the hatred, against us must have been very high. Yet he walked back safe and un- harmed.''

"So? I mean, your deduction from all this?''

"Clearly, only the personal power of the Rani could have protected him from a summary and savage death. There must have been a very strong—er—understanding between them.''

"Sir Robert, exactly when did you decide to ask your well- placed informant within Jhansi city about the accused? This is rather important. Before or after this meeting?''

"Before.''

"Why?''

Murray shifted in his chair and looked across at Lalor. It was a frank, appraising gaze, almost absent as if his mind was else- where. He looked back at Curtis.

"In political and military intelligence, you have to examine all the possible options, every avenue. This includes being a devil's advocate, of trusting nobody, of inferring the worst motives for even an obstensibly praiseworthy, admirable act.''

"And how did you relate this philosophy to the accused's meeting with the Rani?''

"I had to weigh up the possible contingency that he would pass information to her about our intentions, our dispositions. Or in the worst case, desert to her, despite her seemingly hopeless situation. The riches of India have lured headstrong and deter- mined men, such as Major Lalor obviously is, to such adventures before.''

"That surely is a serious view, even as a contingency, to take of a key, important staff officer such as the accused then was?''

"I agree. I assure you that I was most disturbed, unhappy, to have to consider such possibilities. But that was my duty."

"And what did your Palace agent send back to you? Did it reassure you or, in fact, deepen your fears and overall concern?"

"The information I got back did worry me."

"And this was?" Curtis asked sharply.

Murray hesitated. He looked for several moments at the bucolic features of Kelsey, the President, staring at him and then glanced at the other members of the court. Lalor felt a tense atmosphere grip the room. Curtis stood almost nonchalantly by his table but Lalor saw his bespectacled eyes boring into Murray sitting in the witness chair a few yards away. He knew that Curtis sensed that he was 'on to something'.

At last Murray spoke, looking impassively at Kelsey.

"My agent said that the Rani of Jhansi and Major Lalor had been lovers."

An almost concerted gasp came from the members of the court-martial. Even Kelsey, slumped with folded arms on the table like an old bull elephant, was shaken out of his Buddha-like repose. His jaw dropped slightly. His eyes flicked from Murray to Lalor to stare again coldly.

"Christ!" Hamish Balgarnie muttered. He leaned towards Lalor and whispered: "True or false?"

"Very true," Lalor answered mildly.

Balgarnie became agitated and tried to keep his voice down. "But why didn't you tell me?"

"What's the point? Eighty per cent of British officers in India have native mistresses. Ask Dewhurst here."

"Oh, for Christ's sake, Martin!" Balgarnie's Scots accent became thicker as he became more emotional and struggled to control himself." She wasn't just any native mistress, was she? We're talking about the Rani of Jhansi, remember!"

Curtis effectively stopped any further discussion by saying simply, before he sat down, "Thank you, Sir Robert, that is all."

Hamish Balgarnie stood up slowly, almost disconsolately. He looked across at Murray and asked flatly: "I believe I am right in saying, Sir Robert, that apart from this extremely brave confrontation with the Rani—whatever his relations with her were, he obviously could not be sure that fanatics in her ranks would not shoot him down—the accused also acquitted himself with some dash and valour in the later assault on Jhansi. I mean, not as a mere staff officer in the rear but as one in the forefront of the battle, leading soldiers of his own regiment into action."

"Yes, you are entirely correct. It was his column who fought their way through the city to capture the palace."

Balgarnie thoughtfully traced an imaginary circle on the blanketed table where Lalor and Dewhurst sat, as if he was skirting some imaginary raw nerve. He again studied Murray.

"Sir Robert, doubtless it came as a considerable shock to you to learn that the Rani and the accused were allegedly lovers?"

"It did."

"But I do think that we must make it clear to the court that almost every British officer, at some time or other, has had a native mistress. Also, if I may respectfully say to the court, that it is not sitting in judgement on the accused's morals."

"How right you are. And I am pleased to make it clear that I am in no way attempting to criticise, to comment on, Major Lalor's morals. What did concern me, had to concern me, were the political implications, the pressure that his association with the Rani exerted on him. This was the whole crux of my worries at that stage."

Lalor admired Murray for the way he had turned Hamish Balgarnie's line. The Political Agent for Central India was too astute to go along baldly with it.

Balgarnie sought to retrieve the encounter. "Did the accused ever falter in his duties, ever give you cause for doubt or alarm otherwise? I am speaking now about the whole campaign."

"No, emphatically not. As I said at the outset, he was an exemplary officer and a great help to Sir Hugh Rose and myself."

"Thank you, Sir Robert."

Curtis rose quickly to re-examine.

"Sir Robert, no one in this court, I am sure, would wish to decry the obvious gallantry of the accused in the assault on Jhansi but would it not be a fair assumption to say that the accused fought his way to the palace so that he would be able to protect the Rani, his paramour, if she was to be captured there?"

"You must not try to put words into my mouth," Murray answered coldly. He looked at Kelsey. "I consider that to be a leading question."

No intervention came from Kelsey. Undeterred, Curtis persisted. "Then let me put it another way. Why do you think the accused fought his way to the Palace so expeditiously?"

"He is a determined, forceful leader."

"And?"

Murray hesitated again. He looked with some asperity at Curtis. Finally he said: "Because if anyone was going to capture the Rani, it would be him and no one else."

"Thank you, Sir Robert. That is all."

The Political Agent for Central India stood up, bowed curtly to the President and strode swiftly to the door. Lalor could sense his pent-up anger. Murray was an aloof, distant man, somewhat ambivalent because of his duties but one whom Lalor had grown to like. Nothing like a hard campaign to bring men of diverse personalities and interests together on a similar plane, he thought.

Curtis now addressed himself to Kelsey. "Sir, with your indulgence, I would like to call my next witness tomorrow morning. It is now noon. You may consider it is convenient to adjourn for the day."

Kelsey ponderously took out a heavy gold watch on a chain from his blue Royal Artillery tunic. He glanced briefly at it and looked across at Curtis.

"I agree. The Court has to consult and weigh up the evidence so far. The Court is adjourned until 0800 hours tomorrow morning. One last point, Prosecuting Officer. Who is your next witness?"

"Miss Alicia Wentworth, sir."

"Well, how do you think it went, Martin?" Tony Dewhurst asked anxiously. They were sitting in the living room of the bungalow they shared in the cantonment, tunics off, drinking a glass of beer that Amin had brought them on their return from the court. Hamish Balgarnie was staying to lunch with them.

"Strangely enough, I've a terrible feeling," Lalor said quietly, "that poor old Adrian's letter did me much harm. Henry Mercier and Robert Murray could have been very damaging but they did their best. The Mercier report on me was a fact of life, which Curtis of course knew about, and both had no choice but to be co-opted as prosecution witnesses. They spoke the truth as they saw they had done their job and one can't quarrel with that. But Adrian's letter will have had quite a psychological impact. It's written by one who died in the mutiny about one who not only survived but allegedly consorted with the enemy in more ways than one. It mentioned suspected political affinity, too. However, perhaps you should ask Hamish."

"Martin, you must not hold back from me," Balgarnie said reproachfully. "Your sharing the Rani's bed was an absolute bombshell. My middle stump went completely."

"Well, I was naturally hoping it wouldn't come out. But I underestimated Murray and his spy."

"Fair enough but I, who am meant to be on your side, must know all. Is there anything else you should tell me?"

"No. I'm in so deep now that I don't suppose even Curtis needs any more."

Balgarnie was silent for a while, then he leaned forward intently in his chair. "Martin, I need to have a real go at Alicia Wentworth tomorrow morning. She caused the charge against you and as a woman who lived through it all, who saw her father murdered before her eyes, whatever she says that court is going to swallow without even chewing. The previous testimonies will fade into insignificance against her words."

Lalor stiffened. He said curtly to Balgarnie. "You're not to be rough with her, Hamish. And that's an order which is not a basis for discussion."

"Martin, for Christ's sake," Dewhurst interrupted angrily, "you're on trial for your life! They'll shoot you for this if you're found guilty! Think clearly, man! You've gone all woolly and almost apathetic—fatalistic—lately. You used to be a fighter in all respects."

"She is a sick woman, Tony," Lalor answered stonily, "and she's to be left alone. She's been through enough."

Dewhurst grunted exasperatedly and grabbed his drink to drain it. Balgarnie said patiently and slowly in his soft Scots accent: "Martin, Tony has rather a point there. It's your life we must be concerned with. What has she got on you, why has she brought this charge?"

"Hamish, we've been all over this before the trial. The foundation of her charge, as far as I'm aware, anyway, is that she knew I was going to fight for the Rani—at least later known to be a proved enemy—against Orchha. Also that I, in her eyes, refused to accompany her when she left for Saugor and I remained at Jhansi. She just couldn't understand—and you must believe that there was nothing between me and the Rani at that stage—why I seemingly chose to remain. I suppose, as a woman, she put the usual female connotation on that. But I knew that in no way was I going to be allowed to go, as I was the Rani's insurance policy as she called it herself, if and when the British returned—which she certainly believed in then. It was either that Alicia went, or none of us, and if it was to be the latter situation, I did think that Alicia would crack up completely. However, in that splendid hindsight we all get, that was a terrible mistake. I should have gone with her. I don't know how I could have done that but somehow I should have."

"Why was it a terrible mistake?" Balgarnie asked quickly.

Lalor did not answer for a while. He slumped in his chair with legs straight out and clasping his hands behind his head, he studied the far wall. "Because otherwise, I wouldn't be where I am today. I'm beginning to feel sorry for myself."

"I've a feeling you're being just a little evasive, Martin. I'm the fellow who's meant to hold the cards close to the chest."

Lalor glanced across at Dewhurst. "But perhaps no longer apathetic."

"And about bloody time too. I've never seen you like this. And it's just come over you in the last few days."

"But what's that remark about the clearing of one's mind by an imminent hanging? I forget who said that."

"Oh, stow it, Martin!" snapped Dewhurst. "Bloody well concentrate."

"I am. That's what the saying is all about."

Balgarnie broke in quietly. "Martin, we have never really discussed your relationship with Alicia Wentworth. I plead that's not my fault as you've always shied off. But if we are indeed on the even of your imminent hanging or shooting, now might be the best, indeed the last, time we could discuss this."

"Alicia and I got on very well together during the whole tour. I liked her fresh approach to life and also her sense of humour—in my limited experience, rare in a woman—and she seemed to tolerate my jokes. Then, with the murder of her father, Adrian Meadows and the others before her eyes, she got a terrible shock from which she has never recovered—certainly not helped by walking straight into the siege at Saugor after Jhansi and incarceration there. I know she has never forgiven me for not going with her from Jhansi but I repeat, the Rani would never have permitted me to leave. Alicia could not, would not, understand that. I don't blame her at all. It was a very natural reaction."

"You seemed determined," Dewhurst said, still highly irritated, "to devote your time to defending women who have done you much harm, first the Rani and now the Wentworth girl."

"Martin, I agree that you've told me all that, more or less, before," Balgarnie said, resuming his restrained but persistent probing. "What I am really after is your close personal relationship, not just the joke-making. Why, really, has she done this thing to you after—to quote just one instance when you put everyone, including her, before yourself—that dak bungalow at Madhupur when you more or less ordered them all to abandon you while they escaped?"

"I've told you. She's mentally unwell."

Balgarnie stroked his clean-shaven chin reflectively as he stared at Lalor. "Yes, I'm also sure that is so. It's a promising line of attack, possibly our only one. Is that being rough on her, as you admonish me not to be? Can I use this line?"

"No. Leave her alone. The court will weigh her up for themselves."

Balgarnie looked with some desperation at Tony Dewhurst

who again exploded into vehement protest. "Martin, I'm not going to beat about the bush! The whole set-up looks to me very much like a matter of the woman scorned. And she's putting the knife into you."

"You're a good adjutant, Tony," Lalor said to Dewhurst coldly. He was beginning to get angry, even though he realised that his touchiness was unwarranted. "But I didn't know your knowledge of psychology was so deep."

"We're all good at psychology, Martin, including you. We've been soldiers for many years."

"So it's hands off Alicia Wentworth tomorrow?" Balgarnie asked with some asperity among his Scots tone. "If that's the right expression."

"Right or wrong expression, the answer to your question is yes. The Court can decide themselves without our attacking her. Now let's have some lunch."

Lalor felt the nervous, expectant atmosphere in the court-martial room next morning when Curtis called quietly to Sergeant Coady: "Miss Alicia Wentworth." The members were sitting stiffly, even the bulky Kelsey, staring fixedly at the door. Lalor himself was dry-mouthed and tense but he looked ahead with his back to the entrance.

After Coady left the room, several agonising minutes dragged away. Eventually, the door was flung open again. A slim, trim figure passed Lalor with a whiff of fragrance as Coady guided her to the witness chair. When Coady retreated with booted tread, he watched her avidly, like every person in the room.

She was clad entirely in black, her long sweeping dress relieved slightly from total severity by its ruffled neck and sleeves. After being sworn in, she sat upright facing the members. Though she did not even give him a glance, he could see much of her face from the defence table a few yards away. As he had seen at Saugor, she had aged considerably. She looked like a woman in her thirties rather than twenties. Her features, which he so remembered from happier times to be suntanned and youthful, were white and drawn and her lips were thin and compressed. Her eyes, merry and laughing in the old days, were humourless and almost cold. She seemed to be composed but her fingers picked away nervously at a black handbag resting in her lap when Curtis rose from his table.

As the Prosecuting Officer went through his formal opening questions, she answered unhesitatingly, as if she had been rehearsing herself for a certain role.

Yet Lalor got the eerie feeling, as he heard her speak, that she spiritually was elsewhere. She was transposing herself back to the dak bungalow, to the field where her father, Adrian, Joseph Evans and the loyal sowars were killed, to the palace at Jhansi.

Curtis soon came to the question which he knew she inwardly must be dreading.

"Miss Wentworth, do you know the accused?"

She had to look at him. She half-turned in the witness chair, gripping its wooden arms tightly as if she needed support. Her gaze, the set of her pale features, were implacably hostile. Yet, in an austere, daunting way, she was beautiful.

Oh, Alicia, you're so pathetically alone. You're probably a little deranged. What are you doing to both of us? You're not only destroying me but you're destroying yourself as well.

"Yes, I do," she answered in a dull, flat voice. "He was Military Assistant to my late father for his tour of Central India. I later met him again when Sir Hugh Rose relieved Saugor last January when I was a member of the besieged community."

As soon as she had spoken those words, she looked back at Curtis. Lalor felt that stark, impersonal dismissal deeply. *Alicia,* he almost cried out, *it's me, Martin. They're going to shoot me for this and it will be on your evidence. You don't know what you're doing. You'll crack up completely. It will be the end of you as well as me. You want to hurt me because I've hurt you, and I know you're unwell after all that has happened to you, but I'll be shot for what you've brought against me. Alicia, you're still ill.*

"Miss Wentworth," Curtis said gently, "the Court would be obliged if you would give in your own words an account of the events that occurred from your arrival at Jhansi with your father and his entourage until you were ultimately restored to safety with the relief of Saugor, particularly in respect of the involvement of the accused in those events and, indeed, his relations with the Rani of Jhansi."

Alicia Wentworth, after slight hesitation as if she was willing herself, began to speak in a firm voice. She stared fixedly at a point on the bare polished floor several yards ahead of her chair and the only sign of stress was a periodic clutching and unclutching of her hands. Lalor listened, fascinated, as everybody in the room did. The hushed attentive silence, broken only by her soft modulated voice, was almost stifling. As she got into her story, her voice trembled when she came to describe how the escaping party from Madhupur dak bungalow had to abandon him. When she got to their flight and apprehension by Karim and the mutineers, she faltered and for the first time, became slightly incoherent as she tried to grope for the right words. Kelsey broke in quickly.

"Miss Wentworth, you may wish to pause here and retire for a while. I know some ladies have come with you. I assure you that we are all fully conscious of how distressing it is for you to have to recall these tragic happenings."

"No, I'm all right, thank you," she replied in a choked voice. Lalor thought that he saw the hint of tears in her eyes. "But I would like a glass of water."

An uncomfortable silence of several minutes elapsed after Coady had shouted in Urdu down the outside corridor and a bearer hurried in with a jug of water on a tray. She drank a full glass slowly. When the bearer had left, she went on with her evidence.

Hamish Balgarnie thrust a note in front of Lalor. *Have you changed your mind about my riding instructions?* He picked up the pen at once and wrote: *no, she is only stating a true tale as she saw it and fairly too.*

Alicia Wentworth had been speaking for almost thirty minutes when she stopped. She took out a lace handkerchief and dabbed her face. Lalor noticed her shaking hands.

"Thank you, Miss Wentworth," Curtis said, standing up again by his table. "That was very clear. I must put to you several supplementary questions, if you could bear it. Firstly, to recapitulate on what you have said, you are quite certain that the accused, in your presence, agreed to train and command the troops of the Rani against the Raja of Orchha? From depositions we have, the accused does not dispute this."

"Yes, I am quite certain," she said faintly, her eyes still downcast and her hands tightly clasped on her lap.

"Also, would it be a fair description to say that you were bewildered, even deeply shocked, to hear him agree to stay behind in Jhansi when you had the possibility to leave for Saugor?"

"I was both shocked and horrified."

"Why do you think he stayed?"

"He said that the Rani would not let him go."

"Why?"

"Because he was regarded by the Rani as some form of insurance policy, as she called it, for when the British returned."

"You heard her say that—not just the accused?"

"Yes. I assumed that she was very conscious of any suspected involvement with the Jokhan Bagh massacre."

"Did you believe this? I mean, did it sound valid to you? Did the accused protest, get upset, remonstrate with the Rani?"

Alicia Wentworth looked up at Curtis. The strange hard look that Lalor had seen occasionally come into her eyes at Saugor during her convalescence was there again. She said bitterly: "I have long ceased believing in anything. To answer your last question, no, he didn't. He accepted the whole situation without a murmur. This was what I could not understand. This is what hurt me most."

Alicia, I was doing it all for you. I know you just couldn't take in all what I had to do. Manu could be a ruthless woman and she was fighting for survival in a situation which could have gone badly wrong either way. In the end it did, because she lost confidence in her insurance policy and I had in her. But, whatever happened later between Manu and me, Alicia, this early decision was all done to save you, dear.

Lalor could see that Curtis was sensing blood. The Prosecuting Officer quickly tried another approach.

"Miss Wentworth, what do you consider, as one present at that time, were the relations—or should I say, relationship?— between the Rani and the accused?"

The same taut expression seemed to consume her again. She snapped out: "The Rani had some kind of hold over him. He listened to her and ignored me. He became determined to pack me off to Saugor." Suddenly her voice rose hysterically and she leaned forward in the witness chair, rigid and wild-eyed. "He seemed to abandon me, to desert me! Yes, he deserted me, just when I needed him most! On the journey to Saugor! The road to Saugor! Saugor! Saugor and another imprisonment, another hell, all alone!"

She broke down, sobbing bitterly, burying her face in her hands, her shoulders shaking. Lalor started out of his chair but Tony Dewhurst and Hamish Balgarnie quickly thrust him back. Kelsey banged a large fist on his table and said loudly. "The Court is adjourned. Orderly, fetch the ladies quickly!"

"She's destroying you, Martin," Balgarnie said bluntly. They were sitting on the verandah outside the court-martial room, waiting to hear if the court was to be re-assembled that morning. "You must give me a free hand in cross-examination. I feel sorry for her, we all do, but it's your life against her tears. There are several openings I could attack with some promise."

Lalor was still thinking of the distressing, somewhat chaotic, scene in the courtroom when Coady crashed out the door to find the waiting women, with Alicia crumpled and sobbing uncontrollably and Curtis by her, a consoling hand on her heaving shoulders as he looked anxiously at the door. Kelsey and his members had stared aghast at her, embarrassed and fixed to their seats. Lalor had been still gripped firmly by Dewhurst and Balgarnie on either side of him. He had so wanted to rush over to her, to comfort her in his arms. He felt her recall of those tragic days acutely. Eventually feminine rescue had come swiftly with fast-moving short steps and the sweeping of dresses and Alicia was led away, supported by her friends. Her face was covered up by her hands as she passed him and all he got was a baleful glance from a stout, severe, middle-aged woman holding her.

"She's cooking your goose all right," Dewhurst said tersely, smoking a cheroot, "if she hasn't already cooked it. Did you see the faces of the members when she began her evidence? We worry, Martin, even if you don't."

"There's no point in harassing her," Lalor replied stubbornly. "You've seen yourself how she has the total sympathy of the members. Being rough with her will really just put their hackles up. Thank you for your concern, but that's the end of it."

The appearance of Sergeant Coady, his portly figure resplendent in ceremonial uniform, medals and red sash, made all three of them look up expectantly. Coady halted before Lalor and saluted rigidly.

"The Court is re-assembling now, sir."

"Good, sergeant, we'll be right there."

Coady lingered, his broad Irish face solemn and morose. "You'll be wishing to know, sir, the whole Regiment's behind you on this. There'll be some trouble from the boys if it goes against you. I had a few lines from Gwalior, from Carmody, yesterday. He, McIntyre, Brennan, Craig, Donnelly and the rest of the Sergeants' Mess send their best wishes to you."

"Thank you, Coady, and my deep appreciation to all. Tell them I really need their prayers as well. I know that's not quite their style but every little bit helps."

Alicia Wentworth looked remarkably composed after her breakdown when she came back into the re-filled courtroom and took her seat in the witness chair. Kelsey ponderously reminded her she was still on oath. She sat bolt upright and faced Curtis standing at his table. Lalor could see that she was steeling herself that there would be no more tears.

Curtis began hesitantly. "Miss Wentworth, I have one last question before the defence's cross-examination. It is a somewhat distasteful one and I apologise if it gives you offence but I must ask it to support my case. In the time you took refuge in the Rani's palace, were the accused and the Rani, to your knowledge or in your opinion, lovers?"

To Lalor's surprise, she answered calmly, if very quietly. "I don't know. But I really didn't know much at all in those days. I was completely shaken and bewildered. However, to answer your question to the best of my ability, I don't think so."

Curtis paused cautiously again. He stared down at the papers on his table before suddenly looking back at her. "We have had testimony given from an early witness, and which had not been refuted by the defence so far, that they did become lovers at some time before he left Jhansi."

Again, she took this with an almost unreal resignation. To Lalor watching her, she seemed to have lapsed into the apathy that he had found so unnerving at Saugor.

"I believe that," she murmured, almost to herself, looking at the floor before her again. "I knew it would happen. That is all I wish to say."

"Thank you, Miss Wentworth. We all realise how upsetting, how completely distressing, this has been for you. That is all."

As Curtis sat down, all eyes went on Hamish Balgarnie who rose with some deliberation to his feet. Balgarnie addressed himself to Kelsey.

"Sir, the defence does not wish to cross-examine this witness."

Lalor saw the astounded expressions on the five officers who were trying him. Curtis was also visibly surprised.

"We do not dispute the content of Miss Wentworth's testimony, which is true in fact as far as she saw the situation. The defence sees nothing to gain by requiring her to go over the same tragic ground again. Where we would, and must, differ from the witness is in her interpretation of these events. The accused will attempt to lay before the court another interpretation. In other words, the reasons that made him act under considerable duress the way he did."

Balgarnie took his seat. Curtis stood up again and said to Kelsey: "That completes the case for the prosecution, sir."

"Then you may step down, Miss Wentworth," Kelsey said quietly to her. "We are obliged to you for your valuable evidence."

Alicia Wentworth stood up and remained stationary for several moments, as if she had become dis-orientated. Then she quickly turned to walk to the door. As she did, she glanced at Lalor. He saw again that strained, haunted look he had seen so often at Saugor.

When the door had closed behind her, Hamish Balgarnie got to his feet again. "Sir, the case for the defence will open with the accused taking the witness stand and he has elected to give evidence on oath."

After he had been sworn in, Lalor studied the faces of the court-martial members from the witness chair yet again. He saw a mixture of incredulity, suspicion, even open hostility. Kelsey was again slumped forward on the table with folded arms on the table like some brooding malevolent deity.

"Sir," he started evenly, determined to keep his emotions under control, "I do not intend to take up the time of the court by retracing well-worn paths we've been over with the testimonies of Colonel Mercier, Sir Robert Murray and just now, Miss Wentworth. As Major Balgarnie has stated, the facts as presented by them are not challenged. But I earnestly ask you to realise the background, what the pressures were on me to cause me to take the decisions I did. I don't plead that these, on looking back, were necessarily the best or right decisions but in those days, they seemed to be the only choice to me. As two such decisions are the main burden of the prosecution's case against me, I will concentrate solely on answering these.

"The first principal accusation against me is that I ensured or allowed Alicia Wentworth to go to Saugor while I allegedly chose to remain at Jhansi with the Rani, either through political affiliation or sexual attraction or the hope of riches—I'm not sure what you are meant to think, possibly all these reasons. I'll simply re-iterate, as you will have read in the Mercier report, that in my considered opinion at the time, Miss Wentworth's mental and physical condition would not permit her to remain a refugee, a semi-prisoner, in a native court in Jhansi. I had to balance this up against the dangers of her journeying to Saugor but I decided that this was the lesser of two evils. Looking back, I now know I was wrong.

"The other and main accusation against me is that I commanded the Rani's forces against an alleged ally, the Raja of Orchha. I do not intend to go over this all again ad nauseam. It is all stated clearly in the Mercier report—I assume that he has taken down truly and accurately what I told him outside Mandesar. So I will now repeat simply that in July, when the battle against Orchha was fought, the Rani was a declared loyal adherent of British interests and she stated so in writing to Saugor. I know her letter got through because Erskine told me so when we relieved Saugor. However, she was rebuffed and left isolated and soon became conscious that she was being blamed for the mutineers'. massacre of the women and children at the Jokhan Bagh. So she drifted into the enemy camp for some form of survival. But if this trial can offer any defence or exoneration of her actions, I am happy that it should have occurred. To go back to Orchha's invasion that July, all I knew was that the Rani had taken over responsibility in the absence of the British for law and order in Jhansi territory and Orchha, a completely unknown quantity as far as I was concerned, had attacked her. Orchha, in my opinion then and now, was out to make capital out of British misfortune. And I'll say solemnly to you, as I have done to Colonel Mercier and Sir Robert Murray many times, we lost the Rani to our cause through unfounded rumour, prejudice and neglect.

"To the charge against me, my conscience is clear. I repeat that I am in no way guilty. I have served my Regiment, the Army and the Queen honourably and to the best of my ability for fifteen years. 1857 was no exception.

"However, I am more than ready to admit that I should shoulder blame for two decisions I made which, in hindsight, had appalling consequences. One was my sending Alicia Wentworth away alone to Saugor. We have discussed that enough and I'll say no more. The other was much earlier—when I talked Sir Julian Wentworth into escaping with the rest of the party from the dak bungalow at Madhupur. If this had not happened, they probably would all have been alive today. We only had to hang on until that following afternoon until the Rani's bodyguard arrived. And in passing, let me remind the court of that courageous and generous act, at a time when she was very much threatened by the mutineers herself. I've told myself many times, in desperate consolation, that these things happen, that if they had all remained at the bungalow, next morning Karim and his men would doubtless have stormed and taken the place but I do find it hard to persuade myself. I am quite willing to be punished for these blunders. They make a cross I'll have to bear for a very long time.

"That is my statement. I don't think there is much more I could—or would even wish to—say."

When he finished speaking, Lalor looked around almost casually, with a mere academic interest he now felt as he was so thankful that he had remained calm, into the eyes of his brother officers who were trying him for his life. Did he glean some comprehension, some new nagging doubts, even a little sympathy?

Hamish Balgarnie stood up. "I do not wish to examine, sir."

Curtis rose as Balgarnie resumed his seat. His blue eyes regarded Lalor through his polished spectacles. "Even if we accept a main tenor of the defence case that you had to remain in Jhansi when Miss Wentworth left because the Rani looked on you as her—er—insurance policy, didn't you stay an inordinately long time before making good your own departure? Miss Wentworth got away in July while you reached the Malwa Field Force in November. Surely it must have been clear to you very shortly that the Rani was moving into the rebel camp, even taking your premise that she was initially loyal?"

"You don't realise what my circumstances were. I was a semi-prisoner, watched closely all the time. All right, the Rani and I were lovers but she was a pragmatic woman. She knew that as soon as I detected that she had become disillusioned with the British and was throwing in her lot with the rebels, I would wish to go. As it was, it did take some time to plan my escape—the moment, the opportunity. And it took me almost four weeks to reach the Chambal. The countryside was hostile and alive with armed bands and I had to take a very circuitous route away from the roads and main tracks."

Curtis paused for a while to read a sheet of paper that he had extracted from the file before him. "Major Lalor, is it not true that your eldest brother, Matthew, by occupation a farmer in County Clare, was released last year after three years imprisonment for illegal Fenian activities—indeed, he narrowly missed transportation to Australia?"

Hamish Balgarnie leapt to his feet. "Sir, I fail to see, and I trust you do too," he said heatedly to Kelsey, "why the sins of a brother should be visited on the accused."

"I submit that the question is relevant, sir," Curtis said calmly. "You will recall that as early as Captain Meadows's evidence I said I would develop that the accused's political sympathies, affiliations, are suspect and have a bearing on the case."

"You must answer the question as posed," Kelsey said without hesitation to Lalor.

"Yes, that is so," Lalor replied tersely.

"And where exactly do your political loyalties lie, Major Lalor, concerning the Irish situation?"

"I believe in a united Ireland, won by peaceful political action, not force. I believe in proper rights for the Irish people to govern themselves by themselves and not by a planted alien gentry supported by an occupation force. That is also what Matthew Lalor believes in. He was not imprisoned for violence but for speaking his mind and that of many others. For what is called free speech in England, Scotland and Wales."

"But if you were part of that so-called occupation force, as you could be, what would be your reactions then?"

"I always obey what I consider to be a lawful order, as any soldier does. You can take that or leave it as an answer. I don't intend to try to answer a hypothetical question any other way."

To Lalor's surprise, Curtis turned to Kelsey and said: "No further cross-examination, sir."

The court-martial president looked across at Balgarnie. "If you do not wish to re-examine, it's now about time to close for the day. We will hear any other defence witnesses tomorrow. If you have none, then we will start with your closing address."

Again Lalor was astonished, for Balgarnie answered: "There may be one or two witnesses, sir. I regret that I must be so vague but it is all subject to their willingness to appear."

Kelsey grunted non-committally. "The court is adjourned until eight o'clock tomorrow morning."

"Where was Hamish rushing off to after the court?" Lalor asked Tony Dewhurst curiously. They were back at the bungalow, sitting out on the verandah in the soft, moist evening dusk drinking whisky pani. "He shot off like a ricochet—didn't say a word except goodbye. He had a rather strange look about him too, almost furtive. Is he all right?"

"Perhaps he was about to be ill," Dewhurst countered acidly, "having heard yet another spirited Lalor defence of the Rani from the shadow of the gallows or whatever it is, the firing squad."

"Who are these witnesses he may turn up? He might have enlightened me a little." Lalor began to get sarcastic also. They had been drinking for some time. "Who will these helpful and mysterious characters be? Peter Rosario? Amin? They really would carry great weight with Kelsey and his solemn, bewildered brood. Loyal servants are meant to lie honourably and cheerfully for their sahibs."

"Hamish has a family in the cantonment, Martin. He hasn't seen too much of them over the last week or so."

Lalor looked out into the black night about the dimly lit verandah and saw again the unhappy, tortured face of Alicia Wentworth. "It's now my turn to ask how did it go today? Alicia made great impact, of course."

"That's an under-statement. She was in no danger, either, because you tied Hamish's hands behind his back. However, you did well too. They sat up a bit. But as I've just said, you spoil the whole show by launching into another bloody eulogy about the Rani."

Amin came from inside the bungalow with a heavy brown envelope heavily adorned with red seals on his tray.

"A chaprassi has brought this from Bombay burra sahibs in Army, sahib."

Lalor scribbed his initials on the chit Amin proffered. He said to Dewhurst: "It's from Sir Hugh."

"About time we had a big gun like him brought to bear. But we need him in person to shake up old Kelsey, not his prose."

Lalor opened up the envelope as Amin departed. He read:

Simla
17 August 1858

My dear Martin,

I have just heard with some shock about your trouble. It seems that I am about the last to be informed about what I am belatedly told is a cause célèbre now holding the Messes and memsahibs of India in thrall. There appears to be some curious, misguided policy, despite my frequent protests, to keep any news, particularly bad, from me during this very boring convalescence. I only pray that this reaches you before the court-martial is over, especially as I have also written to your Defending Officer. Being a Scot, I am sometimes a gloomy realist by which, allied to my mature years, I know that it's not always the just who get justice in this world. In case it goes badly for you for reasons I cannot possibly fathom. I have penned what I would modestly term a strong appreciation of your services in the Central India Field Force.

I understand that the accusations against you were laid by Miss Alicia Wentworth. I can only conclude two things: that the poor lassie is still thoroughly unhinged by the ordeal she has been through and also that she has no conception of the gravity of the offence with which the Army must charge you. Or, more to the point, its penalty if found guilty.

I knew all about your former close relations with the Rani through Sir Robert's spy in the palace. However, I clearly saw that this in no way affected your duties, even when we were outside Jhansi city. When I released you to command the assault column to strike for the palace, I had no idea whether your ultimate intention was to help her to escape if you both came face to face. Perhaps you do not know either, to this day, what you would have done if this had happened.

I can see that you are in a most unenviable predicament because it is Alicia Wentworth's story against yours. Neither of you can produce witnesses to the facts of that time at Jhansi and so the whole trial will be coloured with emotions drawing still on those terrible days. Even what I have written can only speak of the period after that which the charge against you covers.

However I know that you are a robust and cheerful laddie and that you will bear through this extraordinary business. I wish I could appear in person before the court but I am still forbidden by the doctors to leave these northern hills. My prayers go for a happy, rightful verdict.

Thank you again for your great services to me when the Field Force marched forward so victoriously, despite some near-run occasions. We were a grand team.

Yours very sincerely,
Hugh Rose

Lalor handed over the letter without comment to Dewhurst and again gazed out into the night whose mild warmth was causing some glow-worms to flit near the verandah. For all the prestige of his name, Sir Hugh Rose was only of some help, as he himself had admitted, if the verdict was guilty and his written statement could stiffen a plea of mitigation.

For some reason Lalor's mind moved swiftly to Hamish Balgarnie's unexplained, agitated behaviour when he had left so precipitately after the court had adjourned that morning. Was that connected with the General's letter to him which he might already have had? What was he up to?

In the court-martial room next morning, watching Kelsey and his members take their seats, Lalor felt an irritable nervousness. Hamish Balgarnie had arrived late and had merely given him a dour, unyielding response to his persistent questioning about the identity of the possible witnesses.

"It's better for the whole defence that you don't know, Martin. It's as simple as that."

"What do you mean?" he had reacted angrily. "I thought I once got a lecture about telling all between us."

"I've come around to your thinking. It pays better not to reveal too much. Martin, trust me. I'm determined to save your life even if you're not."

Balgarnie was outwardly his cool, diffident self but Lalor sensed an inner excitement in the Scot and this made him suspicious and uneasy. Before he could speak again, Kelsey had established himself and Balgarnie rose with alacrity.

"Sir, with your permission, the Defence will now call its next witness."

Kelsey nodded. Hamish Balgarnie called out clearly and loudly to the expectant Coady: "Miss Alicia Wentworth!"

Kelsey, his members and Curtis sat dumb-founded. Fury consumed Lalor. He lunged to his feet and grabbed Balgarnie by his tunic. Tony Dewhurst's restraining arms closed about him but his pent-up rage burst the grip aside. He shook Balgarnie dementedly.

"What the bloody hell are you doing to her?" he muttered almost incoherently. "I told you to leave her alone!"

Dewhurst's arms pinned his own to his side. Balgarnie held his wrists and spoke calmly. "She's a volunteer to say what you don't want her to say, Martin."

Sergeant Coady appeared by them. The big NCO said to Lalor reproachfully: "Sir."

Lalor released Balgarnie and Dewhurst cautiously ceased to

hold him. He stood there for several seconds, breathing deeply.

"Major Lalor," he heard Kelsey say coldly, "it would help the court, and indeed your own case, if you conducted yourself like an officer and not a beer canteen rowdy."

He heard himself mumbling: "I apologise to the court for my behaviour." He sat down. Was he right to give in so abjectly? Did Hamish Balgarnie really know what he was doing?

He did not look up when he heard the door re-open and Alicia Wentworth slowly walk by their table to the witness chair. When he had collected himself, he stared at her. She was deathly white and again dressed in black. She sat tensely, once again ignoring all about her. *Alicia dear, you don't have to do this for me*, he thought agonisingly to himself. *They won't shoot me, not with my past record of service. At least one Irish regiment will mutiny if they do and they know it. Don't humiliate yourself before them.*

"Miss Wentworth," Kelsey said ponderously, "your re-appearance for the defence has rather taken us by surprise. The procedure is somewhat unusual. To say the obvious, I assume you have given this step much thought and that you have been enlisted by the defence of your own volition, under no coercion or duress whatsoever?"

"I am here this morning," she answered faintly, "because I wish to say what you must hear."

"Then I will merely remind you that you are still on your original oath. Defending Officer?"

Hamish Balgarnie cleared his throat. He said to her gently: "Miss Wentworth, I understand that you wish to explain to the Court some vital background to the reason why you laid information against the accused which led to this very grave charge against him."

She sat still and silent, looking at the five officers confronting her along their table. When she spoke, her voice was almost harsh.

"Gentlemen, I do not intend to prolong this matter, both for your sake and my own. I will speak bluntly and to the point."

She paused. The atmosphere in the courtroom was hushed and expectant.

"You should be aware," she went on firmly, "that the underlying reason that Martin Lalor has been accused by me is that I fell in love with him and he not only rejected me, he went into the arms of an Indian woman, the Rani of Jhansi. The affair did not happen while I was there with them but I could see that it was only a matter of time, when I was out of the way."

Lalor saw the incredulous expressions on the faces of the court-martial members. Kelsey's heavy features were a mask of hard blandness.

"A severe case of feminine jealousy and spite, you may well consider." Her voice now began to tremble. She clasped her hands together tightly. "But for me there was far worse to come, almost indescribably. You will recall that I felt that Martin had cruelly deserted me when he allowed me to travel to Saugor alone. I was escorted but he would not accompany me. That journey became a terrible nightmare, one that still keeps recurring and will haunt me forever."

Again she stopped. Hamish Balgarnie crossed swiftly and quietly over to her and held a glass of water to her lips. She drank gratefully. When he had gone back to his chair, she looked at Kelsey tautly.

"You see, the leader of the escort, a cousin of the Rani, soon began trying to seduce me. After the first few nights of being repulsed, he raped me."

A gasp of horror came from the whole court except Lalor and Balgarnie. Lalor admired her numbed courage with all his heart.

Her eyes dropped to the polished floor before her and she continued dully: "And from then on, he raped me every night until he delivered me outside Saugor and abandoned me there."

The faces of Kelsey and his members, of Curtis and Dewhurst, mirrored compassion with which began to mingle an obvious welling anger.

"He had taken me—safely I think the requirement was—to Saugor as he had sworn on the most sacred Hindu oaths to both the Rani and Martin. But he destroyed me, he degraded me, he used me like an animal! I am broken in mind, if not in body as well!"

She broke down, sobbing convulsively, and buried her face in her hands. Dewhurst gripped Lalor's arm rigidly. Kelsey was about to shout to Coady when Hamish Balgarnie quickly stood up, holding forward a restraining hand. Strangely, Kelsey accepted his unspoken plea.

"Miss Wentworth, I know we are bringing back awful memories for you," the Scot said softly. "The sympathy of the court goes out to you totally. But as we discussed, it is probably much better for you to expunge openly now the whole nightmare from you. I think I am right in saying that after your horrific experience on that road to Saugor, you wanted Martin Lalor to suffer too."

Curtis did not object to the leading question. Alicia Wentworth turned her tear-stained face towards Balgarnie. "Yes, I wanted to punish him," she said bitterly, "to hurt him, to bring home to him something of what I had endured!"

"But I think I am also correct to say, from our talk, that you do not want him to be—how shall I put it?—sacrificially killed?"

"Oh no! No!" she cried brokenly, "I never meant that to happen even in my darkest moments! God forgive me that this should appear to be! I just wanted to humiliate him publicly. I had been humiliated, abused, both physically and mentally, even if this had been in secret. Now I am humiliated publicly as well but somehow I don't mind any more. The whole shame and horror is no longer suppressed inside me."

Lalor saw again the grinning, jeering face of Ghulam Muhammad, the mercenary, as he lay in the embattled, smoke-filled courtyard of the burning stables at Jhansi, spitting and choking out the obscene words to taunt him even as death closed rapidly in.

"The witness is very distraught," Kelsey said sharply to Balgarnie. "I do not wish to prejudice your defence case but if you wish to continue at any length, I insist on an adjournment."

"I have only one more question, sir," Balgarnie replied hastily. He paused for effect, then said with deceptive quietness: "Miss Wentworth, what was the name of the leader of your escort to Saugor, the man who raped you?"

"Rao Chaudri," she answered simply.

"That is all, sir."

Curtis got to his feet briefly. "I do not wish to cross-examine this witness, sir."

"You may step down, Miss Wentworth."

She stood up and turned to move quickly towards the door. Lalor glimpsed her pale face before she held her handkerchief to her mouth. The expression in her tearful eyes when she glanced at him as she passed was enigmatic but somehow he felt it acutely. As well as misery, bitter reproach was still there.

Barely had the door closed behind her when he heard Hamish Balgarnie speaking impassionedly. "Members of the Court, I ask you to note that name—Rao Chaudri, cousin of the Rani, an influential personality at her palace, and Miss Wentworth's vile, scheming, ruthless rapist! The defence is now going to introduce evidence that this disgusting creature—who has indeed featured as a seemingly—admired character in prosecution testimony so far, though you did not know his real identity—is now a respectable pensioner of Her Majesty's Government!"

Lalor, once he had cleared his confused mind of Alicia, could see that the Scot was in full spate, with frequent gesture and a voice that alternately throbbed with emotion or ebbed to a subdued but equally effective monotone.

"And why, gentlemen? Because Rao Chaudri, Miss Wentworth's rapist, is the one and same brilliant and efficient agent—I think I correctly quote Sir Robert Murray's own description—or traitor, it all depends how you look at these things—who sent such high grade intelligence from inside besieged Jhansi. This is the man, the type of man, who first sowed the seeds of the accused's possible destruction, stating that the accused and the Rani were lovers. What possible credence, worth, can you give to the machinations of such an intriguer, devious double dealer, vicious person as Rao Chaudri?

"Gentlemen, I will now bring forward evidence to support what I have just alleged. The defence now wishes to call its final witness—one who has also consented to come forward at short notice through this new turn of events—Sir Robert Murray."

"Cheer up, Martin!" Tony Dewhurst cried jubilantly as they rode away from the court-martial through the cantonment to the officers lines. "Hamish has retrieved the whole desperate business against you superbly."

"With a superb bit of irrelevance about Rao Chaudri? All that bastard told Murray was that the Rani and I were lovers. I've admitted that in court myself anyway."

"Ah, but you must have seen how they were knocked sideways, backwards and everywhere by the revelation that our precious spy at Jhansi and poor Alicia's rapist were the one and the same. Legally irrelevant it may have been but I'll wager it's done your cause a mighty lot of good. It's probably saved you."

"I'm only baffled that Curtis didn't pounce on all that. He's gone all subdued since Alicia's real story has come out. As well all of us might, for the love of Mary. But even his closing address lacked conviction. However, he's been fair, though that Irish bit was rather below the belt."

"I'd lay a hundred sovereigns to a pork pie that the first thing old Kelsey did when they retired just now to consider the verdict was to send Rao Chaudri's name to Army Headquarters. The hunt will soon be on for that jackal."

"When Ghulam Muhammad mocked me in his dying words about Rao Chaudri and Alicia, I vowed then there would be a second man in India I would kill personally. The other is Daffadar Karim. Now, rather ironically, I may be summarily despatched by my own comrades while those two swine go free and survive."

"Martin, you're going into a decline, old boy! You were always the incurable optimist, remember? Who kept us going when we were freezing, half-starved and exhausted in the trenches at Sevastopol? Who was the life and soul of the Mess—rivalled only by Daniel O'Regan—in peacetime? Who was the cheerful pillar for Sir Hugh Rose to lean on from Mwow to Gwalior? Martin Lalor, no less!''

"Perhaps I'm getting some sense in my old age.''

"Oh, c'mon Martin, man of little faith! I'm telling you, Hamish has achieved victory for us this morning. I feel like breaking open a bottle of good wine to celebrate now.''

"Tony, there's many a slip betwixt, as Sir Hugh said before Kalpi. Let's steady on.''

They had reached the bungalow where Amin and their syce stood waiting for them. "Yes, I agree in a way,'' Dewhurst said vehemently as he dismounted and handed his reins over, "but we did win there at the end of the day, didn't we?''

Later that day, at teatime when they were sprawled in casual dress in the cane chairs on the verandah, Hamish Balgarnie rode up and joined them. He poured himself a cup of tea and looked at them with a conspiratorial air.

"They've been closeted all afternoon on the verdict,'' he told them. "Tiffin sent in, didn't come out until four. Our ally, Coady, straining hard to listen outside the door, says that Kelsey intervened rarely, letting the others argue it out, until towards the end.''

"What you're really saying is that it's touch and go, isn't it?'' Lalor said. "Well, at least there's a sporting chance which I certainly hadn't thought before.''

Balgarnie regarded him with some circumspection. "Martin, I do believe you'll get off this monstrous charge against you. I'm prepared to hedge my bet a little in that I suspect that they'll bring in a lesser conviction because vengeance is the order of the day and you were just too close, without trying to be facetious, to the arch-villainess, the Rani. Also, to the exasperation of many, you continue to defend her. But with your record, and the Rao Chaudri bombshell, you must get off the main issue.''

"Alicia's admission about the rape will be highly confidential?'' Tony Dewhurst asked concernedly. "I mean, buried in the court-martial papers and not to become scintillating gossip throughout India?''

"Yes, you can rely on that, as I'm sure Martin knows. Even Coady is under pain of death, the secrets of the confessional or some other dire fate. Not even the Sergeants' Mess of the 86th will know.''

"Hamish, what made you go to Alicia?'' Lalor asked quietly.

Balgarnie took the cheroot that Dewhurst offered him, lit it with some deliberation and inhaled with a rather tired satisfaction. He looked at Lalor through the faint haze of blue smoke.

"It was always in the back of my mind to tackle her privately. I had a blinding glimpse of the obvious that she probably had no earthly idea that what she had instigated against you carried the death penalty. But you really triggered off the breakthrough when you gave your evidence. You had great recriminations about letting her go alone to Saugor. It couldn't possibly have been merely that she had walked into another crisis, another mutiny. Your remorse, regret, was too deep and savage for that. No, I said to myself, something terrible happened on that journey to Saugor, something that had almost driven her mad, something that you had got to hear about and which was tormenting you too. When I recalled that she broke down hysterically when she mentioned the Saugor road, I knew I was right. I went to see her yesterday afternoon at Government House and told her about your threatened execution and my suspicions about the Saugor road. Eventually she gave way completely and told me everything."

"But how did you piece together that the Jhansi spy and her rapist were the same fellow?" Lalor asked him. "Alicia obviously named her violator to you yesterday and I'm sure I've mentioned Rao Chaudri to you when describing the general scene at Jhansi but the identity of the Jhansi spy was known only to a handful of people."

"I followed a very long shot. Rao Chaudri suddenly seemed to me to fit the picture. There was only one way to find out. With Alicia's permission, I went on at once to Sir Robert Murray, told him the whole tragic story about her—he was shocked and horrified of course—and he readily admitted that my somewhat desperate shot was right on target."

"What splendid deduction," Dewhurst said admiringly. "How did you ever become a failed law student?"

"I found all those thick law books with small print too hard to read at night when one could be out carousing."

"Hamish," Lalor said earnestly, "I must see Alicia when this is all over, whatever the outcome. As you well know, she has rejected all my requests to see her since Tony and I arrived in Bombay. You've now penetrated her defences, broken down her hostility perhaps, somehow gained her confidence. You must try for me with her."

The Scot contemplated the ash on the glowing end of his cheroot almost sadly and then tipped it off with some finality into an ashtray.

"I'm afraid you're backing a loser there, Martin."

"I don't understand."

"Her last words to me yesterday—and though she was in a

very highly strung state, she meant them—were that while she wanted your forgiveness for what she had done to you in a black, sick period of her life, she didn't want your pity. You must tell him, she said, that we must never meet again."

"But she needs me!" Lalor said, trying to control his exasperation. "For Christ's sake, man, can't you see that? She's all alone in the world. We know each other so well, we've been through the whole tragedy—well, almost—together. She'll go into the most awful melancholia and inward-looking state if she can't lean on somebody like me."

"I think you under-estimate her, Martin. She told me herself that she feels much more at peace with herself now that she has confessed that frightful experience to the court-martial. She's much tougher and self-reliant than you give her credit for."

"I do believe I know the girl somewhat better than you, Hamish!"

"I don't doubt that you do, Martin, in the long run. I'm just recounting what I heard yesterday and when I saw her away at the end of her testimony this morning. Throughout, despite her upset mental condition, she sounded very determined. Let me give you her parting words verbatim. *Tell Martin that it just would not work, whatever he wildly thinks now. He must bury me in a segment of his memory—just like the dead Rani.*"

At 0815 hours next morning, Lalor stood to attention, flanked by Dewhurst, before Kelsey and the four members of the court-martial. Looking on tensely from their tables were Balgarnie and Curtis. Sergeant Coady stood at his door, silent, watchful and durable.

Kelsey cleared his throat loudly. He began reading slowly from a sheet of paper before him on the table.

"Brevet-Major Martin Patrick Lalor, Her Majesty's 86th Regiment of Foot, after due consideration of the evidence lodged for and against you concerning the grievous charge of giving aid and comfort to the enemy, the Court finds you . . ." Kelsey paused and looked up bleakly at Lalor . . . "not guilty."

Lalor heard Hamish Balgarnie gasp and thump his table in quiet elation. Though he had steeled himself with some pragmatism for the verdict of guilty, tension drained away from him in sheer relief.

Kelsey adjusted his reading spectacles and returned his gaze to the paper.

"However, the Court does find you guilty, through the indiscreet and scandalous performance of your duty between July and October 1857 of a lesser offence, conduct unbecoming to an officer."

Kelsey took off his spectacles slowly and laid them down with some deliberation. He looked again at Lalor in his uncompromising way.

"Before the Court retires to consider the sentence to be awarded, is there anything you wish to say?"

So a consolation prize was being given to those who wanted his blood, Lalor thought cynically, both within the court and among the wagging tongues throughout India. He suddenly had a bizarre feeling that he probably owed his salvation to the formidable Brigadier George Kelsey.

"No, sir. I believe enough has been said."

Hamish Balgarnie stood up at once. "But the defence does wish to enter a plea of mitigation written by Major-General Sir Hugh Rose, K.C.B., formerly General Officer Commanding Central India Field Force. I have it here, sir. Do you wish me to read it to the Court?"

"No. The Court will study it during our consultation on the sentence to be passed. Prisoner and escort will now march out."

Again Tony Dewhurst was overjoyed. They had retired to the verandah outside the court-martial room to wait. "Martin old son, we've done it! Hamish, what a leading contender the Scottish Bar has lost! You were magnificent! Wouldn't you agree, Martin?"

Lalor smiled his gratitude to the beaming Balgarnie. He reached out and shook the Scot's hand warmly. "Thank you, Hamish. I'm sure I owe you my life. You tied us all up in knots in there. Only you could have done it."

"Put it all down to a certain feyness and Lowland guile," Balgarnie said lightly, "certainly not to any book learning."

"Conduct unbecoming!" Dewhurst repeated the words mockingly. "Why, they charge fellers with that who've broken up the mess in a wild binge, who've got into debt with cards! I'll wager yet again you'll only be fined—say, a hundred guineas at the most. They won't dare touch your brevet or seniority, seeing you were promoted in the field by our best general in the rebellion, one who is likely to be C-in-C himself one day soon. We really will have a party tonight!"

"And despite that hundred guineas or so," Lalor said seriously to his two companions, "it will be on me. You'll have to get a pink leave pass from the missus, Hamish. When the 86th celebrate, there are no half-measures."

"But you don't appear to be exactly wildly excited about any celebration, Martin," Balgarnie observed wryly. "You should be thankful for big mercies, y'know, laddie."

"I am, I assure you, Hamish, and from the bottom of my heart, too. But I should warn you both that tonight's festivities will be also in the nature of a wake—which should not detract from its enjoyment whatsoever. You see, boys, tomorrow I submit my papers to resign my commission."

Both his friends stared at him in astonishment. Then Dewhurst said, more in disappointment than anger: "What's brought all that on?"

"I want to leave the Army as soon as it's administratively possible. Just that. As soon as the C-in-C puts his dhobi mark on the confirmation of my punishment, I wish to catch the next ship home."

"But you just can't walk away from it all, Martin," Dewhurst said, aghast. "You know you've got the whole regiment behind you and, as a betting man, I'd say the whole Army and three-quarters of India too. The hostile one quarter will be the memsahibs and the bible-bashers. You've got a promising career ahead of you—able to count on the personal chop of Sir Hugh Rose, no less."

"I can hardly serve on in the Army, Tony, famed throughout India as the gallant chap who shared the Rani of Jhansi's bed."

"Martin, do see reason," Hamish Balgarnie broke in, concerned. "You won't stay on here. They'll ship you out as soon as they can. You're an embarrassment to them in more ways than one. They'll post you back home and when the 86th returns early next year, you can quietly rejoin them."

"That's right!" Dewhurst agreed enthusiastically. "Or, knowing what an obstinate character you can be, Martin, if you want to sublimate yourself in more action, I hear that several regiments have been warned to embark for New Zealand where the Maoris are still troublesome. I'm positive you could find some fellow who would exchange with you."

Lalor shook his head, smiling slightly, but he guessed that they could read the pain in his eyes. "No, boys, my mind is made up. Enough is enough. I feel very tired and, frankly, now too hardened in cynicism to be of much further use to the Army. Better to go, if not exactly on the crest of a wave, before one goes under badly. Quite simply, and I do thank you deeply for all your comradeship, I know it's time to go."

A long silence followed. Hamish Balgarnie inhaled deeply on his cheroot until it glowed red. He studied Lalor obliquely through the smoke haze. Tony Dewhurst stubbed his cheroot out savagely and turned in his chair to gaze blankly at the sea two hundred yards away, gently lapping the peninsula where the cantonment lay. Lalor, from where he sat, could see across the cantonment and he absently watched squads of red-coated British infantry marching up and down the parade ground. He could faintly hear the harsh cries of their drill instructors. Probably newly-arrived drafts from home, he speculated vaguely, being acclimatised and toughened up before being sent upcountry to join their regiments. What did India hold for these fresh-faced young soldiers, he wondered idly. How many of them would see England, or indeed Scotland or Wales or Ireland, after ten or even eighteen years when their regiment returned? How many would be claimed by disease in some dreary station or by a bullet or tulwar slash in some petty campaign that everybody would soon forget, commemorated only by a medal or medal bar that the dead would never see? He thought back to when he had landed for the first time at Bombay long ago in 1844.

A subconscious urgency jerked his mind back to the present.

"Hamish, you must do me one last favour."

Balgarnie nodded, his sallow face set watchfully.

"Despite all you have warned me about Alicia, I must see her. Preferably this afternoon or tonight but it must happen soon. Either you arrange this meeting or I earn myself another court-martial by forcing my way into Government House and laying on a dramatic scene."

Dewhurst looked worriedly at Balgarnie who leaned back in his chair, still bland and now almost casual.

"What you ask me to do, Martin, is impossible," the Scot answered bluntly. "And the course of action you prescribe for yourself as an alternative is unnecessary. You're going to be very angry about this. Alicia Wentworth sailed for England on the fast clipper, *Southern Cloud,* which slipped her anchorage at first light this morning. She embarked last night."

Lalor felt the blood drain from his face. He gripped the arms of his own chair and glared tautly at Balgarnie who held up a soothing hand.

"Martin," he said softly, "she swore me to secrecy. If there was to be a betrayal of trust, who was it to be—her or you? You tell me."

Lalor looked across the maidan again at the distant drilling soldiers and tried to smother his anger and disappointment. He said nothing.

"I'm going to get really drunk tonight," Tony Dewhurst said with feeling. "In fact, doubly drunk for both the celebration and the wake."

"I think I might too," Balgarnie said mildly, savouring the last of his cheroot. "And my wee lassie will have to bear with that—

again.''

The door on to the verandah opened and Sergeant Coady appeared. He marched forward to Lalor, halted and saluted.

''Sir,'' he said almost apologetically, ''they're coming back in already.''

''Thank you, sergeant. We'll be right there.''

They stood up, buttoned and tugged down their tunics and placed on their helmets. When they were ready, Lalor regarded his two close companions, who stared back at him glumly, with an affection that he hoped was veiled behind his studied casualness.

''Now we are agreed on at least one thing, aren't we? Whatever the result in there, short of incarceration for Lalor, we are going to celebrate with some dedication tonight. Right, Sergeant Coady, we're ready. Lead on for the honour of the 86th.''

19

Epilogue

Martin Lalor stood on the port side of Her Majesty's Transport *Mysore* and watched his friends being rowed ashore to the jetty by the old Portuguese fort that dominated Bombay harbour. They gave him a last farewell wave which he answered slowly. He could still see their faces turned towards him: Brigadier Harry ffrench-Blake, Hamish Balgarnie, Tony Dewhurst and two surprise arrivals from the north, John Cairns taking his battery through to their new station, Poona, and Joe Morrow to prepare for the 86th's return from Gwalior. Earlier, before he had embarked, he had said goodbye to Coady and several other 86th sergeants, to Amin, and also to Peter Rosario who had suddenly appeared from the kitchens of Government House. That stiff, uncomfortable scene had reminded him painfully of the last social gathering for the small doomed community in Jhansi. Everybody wanted to cheer up the occasion but nobody, including himself, had known how to do it.

In the saloon of the *Mysore* later, however, he and his now-departing erstwhile comrades had enjoyed a convivial afternoon. The court-martial, Manu and Alicia were tactfully never mentioned. He had been mildly amused, indeed quite cheered, when John Cairns told him that he was still looking after Aruna Gupta, or more accurately, the sharp young Gunner had gone on to say, she was now looking after him.

He was remembering the emotional handshakes and final parting words at the gangway that led down to their waiting boat when a voice in cheerful, ringing tones spoke by him.

"Welcome to my old tub, Major!"

A tall naval officer with a ruddy complexion and prominent brown eyes stood near him, burnished telescope under his arm.

"I regret I wasn't here to meet you personally when you came on board but I've been tacking rather heavily against the hospitality of certain merchants. I'm John Topham, by the way."

They shook hands. "Martin Lalor, Captain. I'm grateful to you for the service your stewards gave my farewell gathering."

"No problem, old boy! Curiously enough, I know quite a lot about the Army. I was ashore seven months with the Naval Brigade when we marched to the siege of Delhi. Splendid gunnery—and rather different! The sailors loved it, though they didn't take much to all that bloody dust in their food."

Lalor could hear the chant of the seamen as they laid into the capstan at the bow and the creak and grate of the anchor cable dragging slowly through the hawse pipe. He looked back, as the ship swung slightly with the stirring of the ebb tide, at Malabar Hill where the great houses of the rich merchants stood among trees and shrubbery, to Government House where Alicia had stayed, and, stretching away, Colaba peninsula where the cantonment lay.

"The end of an era for you," John Topham said, following his gaze.

"The end of an era," he repeated absently.

He could feel the *Mysore* now drifting freely with the tide. John Topham threw his half-finished cigar overboard. "I must away now to try to ensure we don't bump anything going out of harbour. We'll see each other at dinner and crack a bottle. Enjoyed Delhi but really don't know how you Army fellers stand that sort of life."

Lalor was alone again. He was unaware of sailors working briskly about and above him. He stood stockstill in his own solitude, watching as the harbour slowly slipped by. He thought back to his many years of service in India, in both peace and war. He recalled ironically that a sergeant's veteran wife once said to him, when he had just landed as a raw young ensign in '44, that in the end you only remember the good times at your last station.

When, sometime later, he turned to face the west, the sinking sun was a thick red rim on the horizon. The *Mysore*, her sails filling out, was dipping into the swell. Somewhere out there on the oceans, between Bombay, Cape Town and Tilbury and four weeks ahead, was the *Southern Cloud* with Alicia aboard.

He stood there for a long while. Before dusk closed in, he looked back to India in the dark, vague shape of the Western Ghats and found himself saying a prayer for Manu. Before he went below, he watched again the Mysore's butting bow and her south-westerly heading but he knew, deep in his heart, that it was highly improbable that he would ever see Alicia again.

Lalor never did have the possibility to pursue his vengeance against Karim and Rao Chaudri. He did learn later, to his satis-faction, from a letter from Tony Dewhurst who had been posted to the staff of the Commander-in-Chief's Headquarters, that his personal vow had been quickly made academic. Daffadar Karim had been captured during Sir Colin Campbell's final clearing operations in Oudh and sentenced to death by being blown away from the guns. From eye-witness accounts, he had marched bravely with other mutineers to the line of guns parked on the parade ground, watched by ranks of British and Indian soldiers. He had scornfully refused a blindfold after he was strapped across the muzzle of a 32-pounder. With a stoic, fatalistic expres-sion, he was summarily shattered into lumps of flying bone and disintegrated flesh and blood and into oblivion forever.

Rao Chaudri's fate was not to be so dramatic but, nonetheless, it was just as final. He was traced to be living in some style in Benares on his spoils from Jhansi and other lost causes, seem-ingly secure in the British patronage that only he knew about, but word suddenly came to him, in the mysterious way of India, that the face of the British had turned blackly against him. He was caught fleeing into Nepal by a Gurkha patrol under a young British officer, Captain Robin Keith. It seems he tried to escape, for he was never brought to custody and trial. The gossip in the cantonments in north India was that he had been thrown over a precipice after being cut many times by kukris.

For once guided, rightly or wrongly, by discretion and his few cautious instincts, Lalor did not try to locate and call on Alicia after he reached England.

Alicia bought a house in the Avon valley outside Bath, away from her relatives in the Midlands. In the highly gossip-charged society of Bath and district, she soon became, and remained, a tantalising, fascinating enigma. Though she took a keen interest in music and the theatre and also certain charities, such as the care of orphaned and handicapped children, she led in the main a strange, aloof and solitary life. It was common knowledge that she had endured the most harrowing experiences during the Great Rebellion in India.

As she grew older, her rather severe beauty seemed to soften and mellow. She did not lack suitors, for she also had money, style, a sharp wit when the mood took her, and a reputation among the gentry as a fearless rider to hounds: as one admirer remarked, she went at every fence and ditch as if she did not care tuppence whether she broke her neck or not. But she frightened or froze the suitors away. She had her own inner world that proved inpenetrable to all hopeful challengers. She never married.

Alicia Wentworth died peacefully by her own hearth at the age of 72 on 17 March 1906. She was found sitting in an armchair by the dying embers of a log fire in her living room almost at midnight, her features composed and her eyes closed as if she had dropped off to sleep. A glass with the remains of a tot of malt whisky was on the table by her. *That was the strange part*, the maid who discovered her always said later, *the whisky. She had been poorly for some time but she hardly ever drank, certainly not whisky. But that night, Florence, she said, it's St Patrick's Day. I shall have a little whisky. Then she seemed to pause, thinking a lot I'd say, and then she said, for him.*

She was buried at Bathampton, in the valley and by the river that she loved so much and where she thought her secret thoughts. A slight stir was caused at her funeral by the attendance of two nuns. When the interment was over and the mourners were dispersing, one of the younger female relatives could bear the mystery and suspense no longer. She ran over to the departing nuns and asked who they were and why they had come. The senior nun smiled at her and the girl was taken back by the uncanny likeness to her dead great aunt: the same clear blue eyes, the austerely beautiful features. The nun said softly with an Irish accent that she was Mother Cecilia, Superior of The Convent, Exeter, and that she was the sister of a long-dead favourite brother who had known Miss Wentworth in India many years ago. *I know he would have wished me to be here*, the elderly nun said with another slow, sad smile before she turned away with her companion.

When he returned to Ireland in early 1859, Martin Lalor stayed only until the spring of the following year. He emigrated to the United States, lured like many others by the Californian goldfields. When the Civil War broke out in 1861, he had only reached the mid West and he went back to enlist in the Union Army. Within a year he was commanding the 88th New York Irish whose ranks contained many Irish ex-soldiers from the British Army. He was killed in action on 13 December 1862 when the Irish Brigade made its bloody assault against the strongly entrenched Confederate positions on Marye's Heights at the Battle of Fredericksburg, Virginia. He was blown to pieces by a high-explosive shell. His body was never found.